IT'S ALL IN HER HEAD

IT'S ALL IN

obsession begins with just one glance

HER HEAD

WYETH DOTY

Wyeth Doty
wyethwrites.com

Meraki Press LLC
11 West Beaver Street
Philipsburg, PA 16866
merakipress.org

ISBN 979-8-9873516-4-2
ISBN eBook 979-8-9873516-5-9

Printed in the United States of America

First Printing, Date of Printing

Endorsements

"Doty's debut novel hooks you with a dynamic setting full of secrets, intrigue and plenty of spooks. But what kept me reading were her layered characters full of struggles, searching for truth. Enrapturing and thrilling, Doty's story is perfect for those who love the combination of high adrenaline and grounding faith."

-Valerie Cotnoir,
author of *Your Home is Here* and *The War Within*

"It's All In Her Head is an accomplished debut. Wyeth Doty weaves together psychological, spiritual, and romantic tensions with the ease of a seasoned storyteller. She pits a likable protagonist against a creepy villain amid the struggles of career and relationships, while giving readers a godly boost. I can't wait to see what she does with her next book!"

-Eric Wilson, NY Times bestselling author of
American Leftovers, Expiration Date, and *The Best of Evil*

"It's All In Her Head, got into my head. When I picked it up, I couldn't put it down. I left like I was in Marnie's shoes and was feeling what she felt. The contrast between a life with Jesus and without is a heavy tone throughout the book. Being in Law Enforcement, this story hit close to home and I'm glad I was able to assist with the making of this book in a small way. If you have any doubt on what God can do, this book is a great testimony to His power, grace and mercy for us. I highly recommend."

-Brody Nolan,
Former Officer with Springfield Police Department

For John.
This story would still be only in my head if it weren't for you.

"Even though I walk through the valley of the shadow of death, I will fear no evil, for you are with me; your rod and your staff, they comfort me."
Psalm 23:4

Contents

One

"HELLO? SOMEONE THERE?"

The dark alley was a shortcut from the main road to Marnie's apartment. It was one of those two story apartment complexes with stairs on the outside. A little cheap, but not terrible. Marnie took the same route every night. Braving the creepy alley was better than walking an extra ten minutes, especially after a long day at work. It took a lot to scare Marnie. As a fan of horror movies and Stephen King novels, she considered herself a tough cookie.

But tonight was different.

Marnie slowed to peer over her shoulder. She heard a noise; the crunch of an old, discarded candy wrapper under foot. The alley was littered with trash and overflowing garbage bins. She had to peel sticky wrappers from the bottoms of her shoes most nights. But this was the first time she ever heard another noise, another person-sounding noise, in the alley.

There was no one in sight.

Marnie returned her gaze to the alley ahead, pulling her headphones from her jacket pocket, and plugging them into her ears. The unease was nothing a little music couldn't solve. Her thumb hovered over the *play* button when another noise from behind reached her. Marnie ripped the headphones out and spun around, hoping the sudden movement would surprise the possible bad guy.

No one.

Get a hold of yourself, Marnie. She started walking again.

The soft glow of the porch lights set in front of each apartment door came into view. She was less than five minutes from safety.

Five minutes still felt too long, so Marnie picked up her pace. She didn't want to run, causing a scene where there was none. But she couldn't deny the loud thump of her elevated heartbeat and the blood rushing to her head. After several steps at a brisk pace, panic overrode her composure. Marnie ran the last few yards and up the stairs to her apartment.

Inside, she locked the door and drew the burgundy curtains closed. Her chest heaved up and down, her lungs begging for a solid breath of air. She inhaled as she sank into the couch in the middle of the living room. Safe at last.

"Alright, no more true crime podcasts for a while," she said aloud.

Marnie's heart rate finally returned to its normal rhythmic drum after looking around her dark apartment from her perch on the couch. It was ridiculous, but she decided to check the entire place for anything out of the ordinary; a stolen item, or worse, an intruder. She pulled herself from the couch when her breath slowed, and moved across the living room to the kitchen, turning on every single light as she went.

It was silly checking for bad guys, childish almost; like a little kid checking the closet and under the bed for monsters. No matter how silly it felt, though, she had to do it. If she wasn't 100% certain that her home was as she left it, she wouldn't be able to sleep at night.

She checked the closets first. Empty. Under the bed. Empty. Behind the shower curtain. Empty. Each place she cleared allowed her to sink into the security that only home brings. After a full search, Marnie went to the kitchen and started a pot of tea. As the water heated, she went into her bedroom to change out of her black slacks and fitted button-down shirt. She threw on a pair of worn sweats and an old t-shirt repping her high school mascot.

Exhaustion from the day snuck up on her in a rush and she

laid back on her bed, closing her eyes. Marnie worked as a therapist for high school students at Golden Meadows Mental Health Facility. She adored her job. Being a therapist for teenagers was fulfilling, but it could be tough on her own mental health. Her teen years were only nine years ago, and they held a whole mess of trauma that she refused to let surface. Working with teens often triggered some of the issues she spent years shoving down. Today was one of those triggering days.

Marnie had seen two of her most difficult clients that day. They both reminded Marnie of parts of herself that she hated, parts she worked hard to change and mold into who she was today. They were teenage girls, wildly different in their issues. One, a junior in high school named Ashley, always pushed Marnie's buttons. Ashley's parents forced her to start therapy because of concerns brought to their attention by a school teacher. Ashley was bullying other students and acting promiscuously in the halls. She all but ignored the warnings from her teacher, and only attended therapy to appease her parents. Getting her to engage was like pulling teeth for Marnie. Every time she came in, Ashley would sit on her phone and only answer Marnie with head nods. Half the time, she wouldn't even look up. Marnie wasn't sure how much more of it she could take.

Marnie was only a year out of grad school, so she met with the Golden Meadows director twice weekly to discuss her cases. The meetings were meant to support Marnie and keep Dr. Carlson, the director, in the loop. She'd expressed concerns about Ashley, but Dr. Carlson wasn't doing anything to change the situation.

"Some clients take a while before they open up. It's our job to be patient and present," Dr. Carlson would repeat every time Marnie brought up Ashley's name.

The second client was Carley, a high school senior from a different school, struggling with anxiety and PTSD after a car accident the previous year. Marnie had been seeing her for a little less than six months. She remembered the first meeting with Carley like it was yesterday.

Carley had come into the office, eyes red and puffy. She slumped on the couch and broke into sobs. It took the entire hour-long session to get her to stop. She came at least four times a week, but lately, it had dropped to two or three. Carley was an incredible student. She played on the varsity soccer team and was known for her confidence. Until the car accident sent her spiraling into an uncontrollable anxiety disorder. Nightmares plagued her, making it impossible for her to get a full night's sleep. The lack of sleep led to more anxiety. It was a vicious cycle, and Marnie had no idea how to help the girl. She hated watching her suffer.

"When will it stop hurting? I hate this," Carley often cried.

Carley was dramatic, like most teenagers. She had the right to be after everything she'd gone through. Helping her work through grief and shame was a slow process. Today was one of the worst they'd had in a while.

Carley was making great progress. Her nightmares subsided, and she returned to soccer practices again. But today, she came in looking like she hadn't slept in days. Scratches covered her forearms. Marnie tried to get to the bottom of it, but Carley was unresponsive. All she could get out of the girl was that the nightmares were back. When Marnie pushed for a description of them , Carley fell into hysterics. She was inconsolable. Marnie settled on trying again the next time they met. Survivors' guilt had Carley in a chokehold, and all Marnie could do was try to loosen its grip.

The kettle screeched, jolting Marnie up from her memories. She went to the kitchen and finished preparing her tea. Tea in one hand and a book in the other, Marnie returned to her spot on the couch and began her nightly wind-down routine. The stress of work and the weird noises in the alley faded into the background.

✦

The subtle hint of coconut shampoo wafted into his nose as Marnie passed him. She was completely unaware of the man who had become obsessed with her in a matter of days. And for now, that was how he wanted it to stay. Cavin stood with his back pressed into the cold dumpster and breathed in the smell. He closed his eyes to relish in the sweet memories associated with the scent, transporting him back through their love story.

A single bump was all it took for Cavin to swoon. Three days ago, Marnie bumped into him on the sidewalk. She breathed an apology without even so much as a glance in his direction. But that didn't matter to him. No, because something clicked inside Cavin's mind and heart. It was as if that single touch lit a spark, and he knew: she was meant for him.

That single bump set off a movie in his mind. He saw them getting married, having children, and growing old together. It didn't matter that he didn't even know her name. It was a simple logistic that would be taken care of later. All that mattered was her and him and the life they were bound to have together. Cavin needed to see her again. So, he began following her. He took note of her daily routine and studied her habits. He even managed to find her home. Every moment of every day, Cavin worked up the courage to approach her. Love bubbled inside his chest, and he knew it was from God. She was the chosen one.

The day after God brought them together, Cavin had waited on the same sidewalk. He had prayed for another run-in and was blessed with one. They hadn't collided that time, though Cavin contemplated staging an accidental "run in" – a "meet cute." Anything to touch her again. It wasn't worth the risk, though. Not yet. He followed her and watched as she went into Golden Meadow Mental Health Facility. She was either crazy or helped those who were. It didn't matter which. She was perfect, with or without mental stability.

Without realizing what he was doing, Cavin followed Marnie into the building. He scanned the waiting room and couldn't find her. That was all the proof he needed to confirm that she wasn't crazy. She must have been a therapist.

"Excuse me, sir? Can I help you?"

The receptionist stared at him with her eyebrows drawn together. He sauntered up to the counter. His cheeks burned red. Busted. It was time to act quickly.

"Uh, yes." He glanced around. "I would like to make an appointment, please."

"No problem. Have you been with us before?"

"Huh?" Cavin's voice came out raspy. He cleared his throat. "No, sorry. I've never been here before."

"Okay well, I'll need you to fill out some forms then. Once you're finished we can go over them and find a therapist that works for you."

Cavin was watching the hallway behind the receptionist's head as she spoke. The Lord worked in his mysteriously magic ways again, and Cavin caught a glimpse of his beloved. She was holding a folder close to her chest and walking into an office. When she closed the door, Cavin saw a golden nameplate drilled into the wooden door.

Marnie Adams, MA.

Marnie, Marnie, Marnie. The name was like honey, dripping from his teeth. He swirled his tongue around, savoring it.

The receptionist set a clipboard in front of Cavin with a thump, and his attention snapped back to her. He was smiling like an idiot. The receptionist looked uncomfortable. And ugly. He didn't care.

"Please have a seat and fill out these forms," she said.

He looked at the forms. There was no way he could deal with all this. He wasn't even sure what kind of story he would give. Definitely not the truth, not yet. He didn't actually need therapy. Cavin had a good head on his shoulders. That much was for certain. Sure, it was hard for him to keep a steady job, but that was because of the idiot bosses he had. His mom had been a little harsh on him growing up, but it wasn't anything he couldn't handle with his level of mental resilience.

"Would you mind if I read up on some of your therapists before doing this? I want to make sure our" – it was an impressive lie – "beliefs align."

"Sure." The receptionist handed him an information pamphlet.

Cavin opened it up and turned to walk out of the building. He didn't bother saying goodbye to the receptionist. She didn't matter.

That was yesterday. Now here he stood in the alley leading to Marnie's apartment. He'd followed her home, making sure she was safe. He was being a gentleman, and she didn't even know it. When she turned around earlier that night, he was sure she saw him. Luckily, he had quick reflexes and was able to hide. He knew if Marnie saw him now, she wouldn't understand what was happening. She needed more time. From what he'd gathered, Marnie wasn't ready for him yet, wasn't ready for the commitment. The last thing he wanted to do was scare her away.

Two

MARNIE WOKE EARLIER THAN USUAL and got ready for the day. She threw her long brown hair into a braid over her shoulder and put on a little bit of mascara. She wasn't the type to care about her looks, preferring to grow her knowledge over her beauty. It came from her mom. Or, rather, the need to be the exact opposite of her mom. Marnie's mom was a gorgeous woman who knew exactly how to enhance her beauty to get what she wanted. And it ruined their family. For a long time, it destroyed Marnie. So much so that she vowed to never do what her mom did, to never care about her looks like her mom did, to never be a home-wrecker like her mom was.

Marnie made a simple breakfast with a large cup of coffee on the side. Having teenage clients meant work didn't start until late afternoon. The mornings before work were her favorite. She sat on the couch, sipping coffee and mentally preparing herself for the day. It was important for her as a therapist to keep her mental health in check. She wouldn't be a very good helper if she couldn't take care of herself.

She crossed her legs into a pretzel and closed her eyes, feeling warmth radiate from the coffee mug in her hand. It was emotional inventory time. Her heart was beating at a steady pace, but it felt quicker than normal. Anxiety bubbled up.

Inhale.

Where was this anxiety coming from? Work was stressful the day before, but it was more than that. There was something deeper.

Exhale.

The steps she heard last night.

Marnie opened her eyes.

Were they really steps? Or was her mind playing tricks on her? Marnie put herself back into that moment and tried to listen again. In her mind, it was clear she definitely heard the sound of shoes on the pavement. She replayed the rest of the day in her head. The day was ordinary, boring even. Scanning the crowds, she couldn't pick out anyone that appeared to be following her to or from work.

What if it had been a client? They had all seemed normal and were long gone by the time she walked home. If one of them had followed her, she would've noticed.

Still, she couldn't shake the feeling that someone - something - followed her.

Marnie laughed out loud. The thought was ridiculous. She was being dramatic, making something out of nothing. There was a fair chance that she let work get the best of her. She was stressed. Carley and her vivid nightmares had bothered her more than she let on. The stress was manifesting in Marnie's mind as some kind of delusion. That had to be it. Carley talked about feeling watched by a faceless man, and Marnie had probably internalized it. Not to mention, that alley was very, very creepy at night. She needed to nip this anxiety in the bud before it affected her work.

Inhale.

I am not my anxiety. I have control over my anxiety.

Exhale.

Marnie chugged the last of her coffee and headed for the door. She was not her anxiety, but there was no denying how freaked out she had gotten the night before. She made plans to meet up with Hannah. The last thing she wanted was to be alone. Even if it was all in her head, Marnie didn't want to risk feeling followed again.

Hannah had been Marnie's best friend since before they could speak. Hannah's mom was the one that convinced Marnie's parents to start going to church. Marnie tried not to hold that against Hannah.

They went to college together. Marnie studied psychology, and Hannah studied early childhood development. She now worked as a kindergarten teacher and got off work at 1 pm every day. They disagreed on beliefs, but still, Hannah was the greatest friend Marnie ever had. She was never afraid to talk straight, even if it hurt Marnie's feelings.

When Marnie opened the front door, there was a large bouquet of roses lying on her welcome mat. She scanned the area around her tiny porch, but not a soul was in sight. She picked up the bouquet and searched for a note but found none. There was something unsettling about such a display without a note. It crossed Marnie's mind that only stalkers and killers leave flowers without notice. But Marnie's love life was dead with no chance of resuscitation, so she pushed that thought away in favor of something sweeter: maybe she had a shy, secret admirer? Inside, she put them in a vase with water and placed them on her living room coffee table, rotating them once to get the best view. She left the house with a smile on her face.

Hannah was sitting at a table at the front of the cafe with two iced Americanos. Marnie saw her through the big window and waved. Hannah stood to give her a hug. "Hey, kid!"

Marnie rolled her eyes dramatically. Hannah was only a few weeks older than her but reveled in the "age gap." "Hi, long time!" They sat down across from each other. "Thanks for this, by the way." Marnie sipped the Americano.

"Yeah, no problem. I got here early, and I know what you like."

"How's it going?" Marnie asked.

"Well, a six-year-old blew boogers into my hand this morning. But other than that, I'm great! How are you? Why the sudden urge to meet?"

"Wow, skipping the small talk, huh?" Marnie laughed.

Hannah gave a coy smile and sipped her coffee, waiting for Marnie to continue.

"Alright, fine." Marnie took a deep breath. "This is going to sound nuts, okay? And I get that, but please, hear me out."

"You're freaking me out, kid," Hannah said.

"I feel stupid for asking, but will you walk me home from work tonight?" She leaned forward, putting her hands together and batting her eyelashes.

Hannah crossed her arms, her eyebrows raised. The reaction

made Marnie feel embarrassed. She prided herself on being self-suffi-
cient, with a solid head on her shoulders. She learned a long time ago
how to take care of herself. It was easy to be brave in the world when
the real danger was inside your home. But a lot had changed since
then, and whether she liked it or not, Marnie had gotten soft.

Hannah sat forward. "What's going on, Mar? Are you okay?"

This was the part where Marnie had to admit she was acting
crazy. There was no way of knowing how Hannah would react, but she
knew she had to say it. "Someone might've followed me home from
work last night."

The concern melted from Hannah's face and was replaced
with a look of mild amusement.

"I'm serious! I took the shortcut through the alley to my building, and I swear, I heard footsteps behind me. They stepped on, like,
a candy wrapper or something. But when I turned around, no one was
there."

Amusement morphed into a full-blown laugh attack from
Hannah. "Honey, you've read one too many horror novels. You don't
need to worry about Joe Goldberg watching through your window."

"It's not funny, Hannah." Marnie bit at a fingernail.

"Is this because I haven't been giving you enough attention?
I'm sorry I've been busy with work and Liam and everything. I promise to spend more time with you. You don't need to make things up
like this."

"I'm not making it up!" Heads turned in the cafe as Marnie
raised her voice. She cleared her throat and spoke quieter. "I'm not
making this up. I'm a therapist; I see a lot of sick people. What if one
of them snapped? I mean, come on, you've heard stories of crazy people turning on their therapists before. Didn't you see that movie with
Jude Law?"

"Okay, first of all, totally different situation. Second, you
don't prescribe medicine like Jude Law did in Side Effects."

"Fine. But what if someone feels extra connected to me or
something and is trying to, I don't know, have a relationship with
me?"

Hannah stifled another laugh. "I'm serious, kid, you gotta stop
reading all those scary books. Pick up a romance once in a while,
geez." Hannah took a sip of her coffee. "If it were one of your clients,
wouldn't there be signs in your sessions? Have you noticed anyone

acting weird?"

Marnie looked at the ceiling, taking inventory of all her clients in her head. None of them exhibited signs of obsession or anger with her. If anything, indifference was the only odd emotion out. "Not exactly…"

"Alright then, see? It sounds like you're over-stressed."

Marnie huffed. "Fine. But will you please walk me today? Only for one day, please?"

Hannah acquiesced, adding "Only cause I love you" to the end. They drank their coffees slowly. Hannah agreed to walk Marnie to work since she was off the rest of the day. They waited out the time talking about Liam, Hannah's new boyfriend, and her job. Marnie wished she could talk about work the way Hannah did, but HIPAA laws made that impossible. As she sat there, listening, her phone buzzed.

I hope you liked the flowers, my flower.

A chill raced down Marnie's spine. There was no phone number. How was that possible? She contemplated telling Hannah but, based on her already unsupportive reactions, decided against it. There was no way this was happening.

❦

It was a delicate process, finding the right time to send the message. Cavin watched Marnie from his spot at the back of the cafe, typing the text, then deleting it only to type it out again.

He finally settled on the perfectly crafted message and hit send. It bounced between cell phone towers and landed in Marnie's lap. He watched for her reaction.

Was that a smile hinting at her lips?

Finding her phone number under the comments section of a Facebook photo was God's gift to Cavin, showing him that he was following a divine plan. Cavin pursed his lips in disdain; he would need to remind Marnie about internet safety. She was too naive. There are bad men in the world who, unlike Cavin, don't have her best interest at heart.

"Excuse me, sir?"

Cavin peeled his eyes away from Marnie for a moment to glare at the barista standing over him.

"I'm sorry, sir. But you have to order something if you want to sit in the cafe." Her voice was hesitant, something Cavin could use against her.

"Are you kidding me?" He kept his voice low but harsh. "Don't you know who I am? I consider myself a regular here; how dare you!"

She looked around, seeking help where she would find none. She looked back at him, wringing her hands together. "I'm sorry, but it's policy. If you aren't going to order something, I have to ask you to leave."

Cavin glanced at Marnie. She and her friend stood up from their table and started out the door. He pushed away from the table and stood inches from the college-aged barista. "I am not going to take this!" He shoulder-checked her and made his way to the door.

Marnie was getting away, and he couldn't let that happen. Cavin sprinted in the direction of Golden Meadow, hoping to catch her before she went into work. He slowed, seeing that she and the little blonde walked
arm-in-arm a few feet ahead.

Cavin cursed under his breath. Who is this chick? And why is Marnie even friends with her? Cavin scoffed. *What a little brat, stealing my beloved away from me.*

With every step, Cavin became more resentful of the woman walking with his future bride. He recalled her words to Marnie in the cafe; she didn't care about her like he did. She would be the first to go when he and Marnie got married.

She's not good enough for you, my love.

They reached Golden Meadow and split ways. Cavin held back, making himself invisible. Marnie went inside, and the other one turned down the road past the facility. He thought about following her, taking out the problem before it got worse. That would mean leaving Marnie, and he wasn't comfortable with that so early in their relationship. He walked across the street to a bookstore with a large window seat. It was the perfect place to wait for Marnie to finish work.

Three

"CARLEY, MS. ADAMS WILL SEE YOU NOW," said the receptionist from her seat at the front desk.

Carley slid through the door that led into a back hallway where all the therapists' offices were. No matter how hard they tried, it still felt so clinical. The walls were beige, a step up from the stark white hospital walls. For some reason, though, it smelled so sterile. Carley hated coming here, but it was the only way to make the nightmares stop.

She stopped in front of a mahogany door and knocked once.

"Come in," a voice from inside called.

She took a deep breath, then pushed the door open.

"Carley, have a seat." Ms. Adams stood behind her desk, grabbing a file. She moved toward the sitting area and motioned for Carley to sit on the brown couch.

At least Ms. Adam's office wasn't as clinical as the rest of the place. She had a large wooden bookshelf that housed more than the typical psychology books. There were fiction books and magazines; she even had some comic books. When Carley first came, she asked about the books.

"I like having my options," Ms. Adams smiled sheepishly.

Carley knew she would like her from that moment forward. And she had. Ms. Adams had a way of making her feel like they were friends, not client and patient. The comfort made it that much easier for her to talk. Carley wasn't crazy. At least, she didn't think she was.

Not yet, anyway. But there was still time.

Carley sat down, her hands fidgeting in her lap. Starting was the worst part. No matter how many sessions she had with Ms. Adams, it was always awkward at the start. Neither knew exactly what to say.

Ms. Adams crossed her legs in the oversized chair across from the matching couch. She watched Carley for a moment, eyes gentle and welcoming. Carley's shoulders relaxed a little bit.

"How're you doing, Carley?" Ms. Adams asked.

Carley shook her head, reluctant to talk. She watched Ms. Adams situate herself, adjusting her notebook to balance on top of her knee.

"Hey, I'm here for you. What's up?" Ms. Adams spoke a little above a whisper. Her brown eyes opened wide, clear. They seemed to talk, too, affirming that Ms. Adams was telling the truth – that she was there for Carley.

That was another reason Carley chose Ms. Adams. She was gentle. Carley needed gentleness. The way things had been since that night, she couldn't handle much anymore. She may not have been crazy, but she was weak. Weak. That word made her want to spit. Was there any worse quality one could possess?
I bet Ms. Adams isn't weak.

"I don't know," Carley choked, on the verge of tears. It was the truth. She didn't know how she was doing. She was suffocating. Every day felt like a battle to survive. She didn't know how to begin talking about it. It'd been a year since the accident, but it was all still too fresh, an insurmountable mountain looming over her. The nightmares wouldn't stop either. No matter how much she talked about them. They kept coming. *He* kept coming.

"Tell me the dream again," Ms. Adams said.

Carley sighed, defeated. "It's always the same. I'm at the party, exactly like that night. Everything is fine, and everyone is having a good time." She closed her eyes. "Then Melissa wants to leave. She was wasted; there was no way I could let her drive. So, I take the keys.

In the dream, I'm sober. But I can remember I wasn't actually sober that night. Not as drunk as Melissa, but still tipsy." Shame gripped her chest, and her hand flew to her brow. She rubbed it, pushing the pain away.

Ms. Adams nodded, giving her permission to continue. Carley was safe.

"We walk outside and." She squeezed her eyes tighter and hid her face with her hands.

"Talking about it will help. Keep going; it's okay." Ms. Adams' voice sounded muffled, far away, as Carley drifted deeper into the memory.

"And he's already there. He's standing by the car. I see him, and I'm scared, but I can't stop walking toward him, toward the car. I know I shouldn't get in the driver's seat, but it's like my brain can't communicate with my body. We get in, and I swear, he somehow materializes in the backseat. I can see him in the rearview mirror. His features are hidden in a shadow. Everything except his eyes." Her voice hitched. She swallowed the sob threatening to burst out. "They're red and glowing. He's laughing at me, telling me we're going to die and that it'll be all my fault." Carley shook her head; it was too much to hold back anymore. She broke down, her body racking with sobs.

She couldn't do it, couldn't relive it. The dream was worse than reality. When it happened in real life, she was inebriated and didn't know what she was doing. In the dream, she knew exactly what she was doing and couldn't stop it from happening.

Carley felt a soft hand land on her back, rubbing it in circles. She took her head out of her hands to see Ms. Adams sitting next to her.

"Carley, I know how hard it is to relive these memories. It's heart- wrenching. But remembering them, talking about them, that's what helps bring healing. When we leave them there, shoved down deep, they fester and grow into this big scary monster that we can't deal with. When you talk about them and face them, they get smaller and much more manageable. You're doing good work here."

Carley's eyes, desperate for truth, scanned her therapist's face. There had to be a shred of hope hidden somewhere. "It doesn't feel like it's getting smaller."

"That's because it's still too early. We won't see results overnight. But one day, you'll look back, and you'll see that it isn't so bad anymore." Ms. Adams put an arm around Carley and squeezed. Then, she went back to her place on the oversized chair. "Can you keep going?"

Carley released a jagged breath, nodding her head. "Next thing I know, the car flipped. I hear the shadow man laughing, saying, 'I told you so,' and stuff like that. I look over at Melissa, and she's bleeding. There's red dripping from her face, and her eyes are open, staring at me. There's no life in them. I try to reach her, but she moves further away. He's pulling her, dragging her by the legs. He takes her from me…and…and he says, 'You're next.' Then, I wake up." She peered past the tears at Ms. Adams, waiting for a response.

"That was great, Carley. Thank you for sharing it with me again." Ms. Adams scribbled something in her notebook, then looked back at Carley. "Let's talk about the shadow man; what do you think he is?"

"What do you mean?"

"Well, is he a man or an angel? A ghost? Do you think he's a part of your own subconscious?"

"He's a demon. The shadow is a demon." It looked like Ms. Adams rolled her eyes, but the movement was so fast Carley couldn't be too sure. Maybe she didn't.

"This feels real to you, doesn't it?"

Carley dropped her eyes to her shaking hands. "He doesn't go away. Even when I'm awake, I can hear him. He's taunting me. At school, when I'm walking or in the bathroom alone, I can hear his laugh. It's like he's there, waiting for me to fall asleep again." She felt ridiculous saying all this. But the way Ms. Adams looked at her, with such understanding. She was the only person Carley could ever admit this to. She was the only one who would believe Carley, even if she didn't think it possible.

Ms. Adams moved back onto the couch with Carley, grabbing her hands. "It sounds like you're scared. We should focus on that right now."

Carley nodded.

"I'm sure you get plenty of homework from school, but I'm gonna give you some, too, if that's okay. Until we meet again, I want you to take some time every night to journal. I want you to write down some truths about yourself and your life. 'I am safe. I am okay. It's not my fault.' Those kinds of things, okay? And then, I want you to repeat them out loud to yourself. After that, I want you to write down some goals for yourself; how you'd like to feel instead of being scared. 'I am healthy and whole. I am strong. I feel happy.' And speak those out loud, too. Do you think you can do that?"

"Yeah, I can do that."

"Anytime you start to feel scared, or the shame from the accident starts creeping back, I want you to repeat these truths over yourself. Along with some deep breaths like I already see you doing sometimes, okay? We gotta work on rewiring your brain a little bit."

"Thank you, Ms. Adams."

"You can call me Marnie, sweetie.." Marnie winked.

"Marnie," Carley said, smiling.

Ms. Adams gave her hands a pat and stood. "What you're feeling is survivor's guilt. It's a monster, but we'll tackle it. Don't worry, okay?"

Carley pressed her lips together. Believing Ms. Adams – Marnie – was easy. "Okay," she said.

"Well, that's it for today." Ms. Adams slapped her thigh, then stood. "I'll see you in a few days. Sound good?"

"Yup." Carley got up. "Thank you again. I'm glad I can talk to you."

Ms. Adams gave her a hug and led her to the door. "You can call me anytime, Carley. I'm here for you."

Carley gave a halfhearted smile and walked out.

❧

Marnie's heart broke for Carley. She could see so much pain in the girl's eyes. It wasn't supposed to be this way. Teenagers were supposed to be full of life. Marnie thought about her own teen years, marked with pain, much like Carley's. She wanted more than anything to take away the girl's pain, to make it all better. But she could only do so much. Hopefully, being a safe place for the girl was enough. She knew she wasn't supposed to have physical contact with clients unless expressly permitted. But Marnie knew Carley needed that comfort, and she wanted to be there for her. Hopefully, it wouldn't come back to bite her.

Marnie returned to her desk to wait for the next patient. Meeting with Carley was draining. Carley struggled with the biggest issues Marnie had ever seen. But today felt different. Her head was fuzzy, a feeling she didn't have twenty minutes ago. Something about Carley's dream felt familiar to her. She couldn't quite put her finger on it. She closed her eyes, trying to collect herself. The next client would be there soon, and she couldn't be in such a haze when they did.

Inhale.

Marnie heard a laugh. It was faint but there nonetheless.

Exhale.

"Marnie."

She looked around. No one was in the room. She shook her head and took a sip of water. Last night's events and Carley's nightmare mixed in her brain, making something out of nothing. Marnie needed to get a hold of herself. Maybe Hannah was right; a vacation would be good.

Marnie started for the door to get her next client. Her vision blurred, and her head filled with static. The room tilted. Marnie stuck an arm out for balance.

The whisper of her name came again, louder this time. Her heartbeat quickened. She couldn't right the room. She tried a few rapid blinks to refocus. Nothing worked.

A knock at the door. "Marnie?"

The room came back into focus. She cleared her throat, smoothed her shirt, and walked to the door. Savannah, the receptionist, was standing there looking pleasant, as always.

"Your next client is here."

"Thank you, send them back." Marnie walked back to her desk and took another swig of water.

After some final touches on her notes, Marnie locked her office door, waved bye to Savannah, and pushed through the double-paneled doors into the night. Hannah was waiting under a street light. The sky was void of stars, the moon a pale blue that offered little light. She was glad she asked Hannah to walk her home, even if Hannah gave her a hard time about it.

"You're such a good friend, Hannah. Seriously, I owe you one," Marnie gushed.

"I know, I'm the best." She added a hair flip for emphasis. "Keep being my unofficial therapist and best friend, and we'll call it even." Hannah linked her arm around Marnie as they started walking.

"Deal. Today has been so weird. I just wanna crawl into bed and forget the world."

When they got to the alley, Marnie's skin chilled. She bit the inside of her cheek. That sickly feeling from the night before struck her again.

Someone was following them.

She brushed her hair behind her ear and tried to sneak a peek behind. Of course, there was no one. Of course. Hannah was with her; there was strength in numbers.

Their silence made the night feel eerie. Marnie considered telling Hannah about all the strange things happening. She still hadn't told her about the flowers, the text, what happened in the office, or that she felt watched now. Based on how she acted at the cafe, Marnie decided against it. She didn't need her best friend thinking she was crazy. She started a conversation about surface-level things, asking Hannah about her day, anything to distract her. She tried to listen, but her mind kept returning to her dizzy spell in the office. The voice was so audible, so real. It scared her. She could almost hear it again.

❧

Cavin waited in the alley. It was better to get there before Marnie. He couldn't mess up again.

He loved this part of his new routine; watching Marnie walk home made him feel so alive. The sway of her hips, the sound of her shoes clanking against concrete. She had no idea what she did to him. Every time he watched her, he could see their future. Walking her home, hand in hand. She would invite him inside; beg him to stay. Cavin couldn't wait for the day.

The alley wasn't his ideal hideout. Restaurant back doors and dumpsters lined either side. Trash littered the ground like sand on a beach. There was a constant smell of rotting food. It took everything within him not to gag when he took his seat behind the green dumpster.

He heard her sweet laugh before he saw her. Cavin leaned deeper into the shadows, blending in with the slime-stained wall of the dumpster. He watched Marnie and her friend walk by. All he wanted was a glimpse of her beautiful face, but it was too dark. He settled for the sound of her voice instead.

"Isn't it a shame you have to hide in the dark? Wouldn't you rather be the one walking her home?"

Cavin jumped. He looked around. He was alone. The voice was a little above a whisper, sinister yet sweet. The tone tickled his ears.

That would be a dream come true.

The voice responded to his thoughts. "Go for it. Make your move on the precious Marnie. Be the man you know she needs."

It's not that easy, Cavin thought. *These kinds of things take time. What if she isn't ready for me?*

"I could help you, teach you some things. I guarantee Marnie will be in your arms and in love with you in no time."

Tempting, but Cavin hesitated. He felt insane. Who was he even talking to? There was a chance this voice was a figment of his imagination. If that were the case, Cavin would have reached an all-time low. Then again, if it was real… what if it was God? Or an angel sent by God. Cavin's prayers had been heard. God was going to help him win Marnie over. How could he say no? He would be nuts not to give in.

"Come on, Cavin. Don't be such a coward. I don't bite. I'm a friend, I promise. Let me help you." The voice growled. "Everyone deserves to get the girl sometimes."

A smile curled the ends of Cavin's lips. The prospect of wowing Marnie was so enticing that his mouth began to water. He was sold.

An icy wave rushed through Cavin's veins making his body spasm. It gathered in his heart and started to burn.

Could something be so cold it burned? Cavin didn't care. It was invigorating.

"Let's get to work," the voice said. It came from inside his own mind like it was a part of him now.

Confidence surged through Cavin. Power. He liked this new friend. He could do anything in the world, and no one would stop him. Cavin stood, following behind Marnie and her friend until they reached the front door.

Until tomorrow, my sweet.

He blew a kiss toward Marnie's front door. He turned back and walked to his car down the street. A new era was beginning. Cavin was no longer the weirdo hiding in the shadows. Now, he was the knight in shining armor. Everything was about to change.

Four

HANNAH WALKED MARNIE TO THE FRONT DOOR, said good-night, and left. Marnie went inside and took a deep breath. She closed her eyes, letting the warmth of the apartment fill her lungs. She made it home unscathed until tomorrow.

The Missouri winter approaching added to her anxiety. It was easier to feel stressed in the cold. The winter breeze had always pricked her skin and put her on edge that much more. But, it all melted away as she got comfortable in her humble home. Marnie was a homebody through and through. She loved her apartment, dingy as it was. It was her safe space – the place she no longer had to act so professionally.

This day called for a special form of decompression: vegging out on the couch for hours watching mindless trashy TV. After changing into comfortable clothes, she moved to the couch, grabbing the remote off the coffee table. Marnie couldn't stop thinking about her session with Carley. Vivid images of Carley's dream played through her mind as if she had been there. It was sudden, like being struck by lightning. How was it possible? Marnie always had a decent imagination, but something about the dream felt so real, so close. Every time she blinked, she could see flashes of it. Then, the dream morphed into something much worse.

A rush of emotions swept over her like waves of ocean water. Emotions she hadn't felt since leaving home clawed at her skin, seeking a place to burrow into her. Terror. It soaked her bones in crimson. Marnie thought of her stepfather, screaming over her while holding a bat. The faded black outline of a shadow stood in the corner of the memory, right behind her abuser. It was the shadow from Carley's dream. This vision wasn't from a resurfacing memory; it was Carley's dream come to life. That was the only explanation. Carley's boogeyman mixed with Marnie's memories, creating a custom-made nightmare.

This is not reality.

Marnie let out a breathless laugh, forcing the fear out. How ridiculous that she had allowed this feeling to get her. She was stronger than this. Smarter than this.

The images faded to gray, and the terror began to subside. Marnie could think again and rationalize the experience.

But Carley's voice rang out in her mind. *"It's suffocating, Ms. Adams. It's like something has its hands wrapped around my neck."*

Marnie inched her hand toward her throat. Her airway tightened. Short gasps of air clawed their way out.

She turned her head, fighting the invisible chokehold.

"I hear his laugh everywhere I go. He's taunting me."

As Carley's voice faded, a vicious laugh filled the dead air. It came from the walls. Marnie stood, her hand still pressed to her neck. She spun around the room, searching for the source. The apartment got darker, though Marnie hadn't touched a light switch. The scarce light cast long shadows across the small living room. They grew by the second, stretching longer and longer – pockets of pitch-black held secrets in the corners.

The terror surged within her stronger than before.

Fear threatened to swallow her whole. She shut her eyes, begging for peace to find her in the darkness.

"You're okay; you're okay." She chanted it aloud as if it could convince her of the truth. "This is nothing. You're safe in your home." She began tapping frantically, ice-cold fingers against her burning skin. Chest. Forehead. Shoulders.

It wasn't working. Her breathing slowed even more, the invisible fingers tightening around her throat. The strange laugh grew in volume. Tears pooled at the base of her closed eyes. Marnie knew panic attacks all too well, a staple in her teen years. But never had she experienced one so severe as this. As she was about to accept her fate, accept this as her end, Marnie heard a gasp escape her lungs, and opened her eyes.

The apartment returned to its bright state. It looked eerily the same like it wasn't just the scene of Marnie's live-in nightmare. Silence shrouded the room. The grip on her neck released. The skin where it had been was warm.

She was alone. She could breathe.

Marnie placed her shaking hand on the wall to steady herself.

"Okay, you're okay. It was all in your head, just a panic attack." Another deep breath. "You're okay."

Marnie went into the kitchen to prepare a simple dinner of chicken and vegetables – anything to take her mind off the incident. The only way to move on was to move forward, to return to the usual. The night ticked by with the mundane tasks of everyday life. She sat at the kitchen island, eating and scrolling through social media. Soon, she forgot the anxiety and fear that had felt so close.

Thoughts of Carley's made-up monster stayed at the back of her mind. In the quiet moments between tasks, Marnie could still make out a faint snicker or a whisper of her name from an unfamiliar voice. She tried to ignore it, and when that became too difficult, she retreated to her bed. Soft sheets and fluffy pillows were the perfect fortress. Sleep was a master at quieting unwanted voices. Marnie tucked herself in, curling in on her side and hugging the spare pillow. She turned out the light that glowed from her nightstand.

The light blinked out. Marnie dragged her eyes around the room; the glow from a streetlamp outside her window cast the room in a pale yellow. She could see every corner, something that gave her peace of mind.

Marnie had finally started to dream when a loud crash startled her awake. Her eyes sprung open, and she forced herself up. Her plush bed was no longer under her body. Instead, it was dewy grass soaking the seat of her sweatpants.

The playground from down the street came into focus as her eyes adjusted. The eerie sting of the metal swings swaying back and forth screamed at her.

How did she get here? Marnie had never been a sleepwalker, even as a child. At least not as far as she knew.

She swept her gaze across the playground, trying to find any signs that this was a dream. Near the jungle gym, the shadow of a man caught her attention. She stood, keeping her eyes locked on the stranger staring at her from across the playground.

"Hello?"

No response. This wasn't exactly the hangout hub for the random adults or drug users. Heck, teenagers didn't even come here when they snuck out. It'd always been a perfectly mundane playground in a perfectly safe neighborhood.

The shadow cocked his head to the side. It was a gesture that could only mean one of two things: Confusion or amusement. The air stilled, and silence rang in the space between them.

Marnie shifted in her stance, rubbing her hands along her bare arms to fight off the crisp night. The silence was unnerving.

"I don't want any trouble," Marnie called out. "I'm just gonna head home."

She turned in the direction of her apartment, keeping her eyes on the figure as long as her neck would allow. The moment her eyes broke from the shadow, a laugh traveled the space between them. Marnie froze. Her skin prickled, and goosebumps ran down her arms and up her neck. It was the same laugh from her office. The same laugh from her apartment that very night. She looked back. The playground was empty; the jungle gym casting stretched shadows in the sand.

He was gone. But that sadistic laugh lingered on the wind, assaulting Marnie's eardrums. She begged her feet to move, but her body was stiff. Her eyes refused to give up their search for the monster. If she knew where he was, she'd have a better chance of avoiding him.

Her search failed, so Marnie turned back to keep walking home. There he was, inches from her face. His skin wasn't solid like that of a human. Rather, it seemed more like a thick fog floating away at the edges. The kind of fog that disoriented anyone unlucky enough to be trapped inside. Everything was shrouded in black except for his eyes. The eyes set deep in his skull burned a bloody red. They bore into Marnie's soul. He could read her, see through her. Marnie trembled.

Warning bells rang out in her mind. She curled her hands into fists at her side. The only way home to safety was around the man who wasn't really a man at all. Marnie wasn't the fittest, but she liked to think of herself as resilient enough to try and fight. She tried to look around him, but those eyes held her gaze. He was a shadow, a fog. Meaning he wasn't solid. If she was brave enough, Marnie could push through him and run straight home. It was her only option. She inhaled, lifting her fists chest high and readying herself to run when a wide smile etched into the shadow's face.

He leaned in close to whisper. "Hello, Marnie."

That was all it took to get Marnie's feet moving. She spun around him, careful not to collide with the animated darkness before her, and bolted for home. Despite all the energy she forced into her legs, she began to slow. It was like trying to run through mud that came up to her knees. Her legs were sluggish. No matter how hard she pushed, they refused to move. Marnie cursed under her breath.

It's a dream.

That was the only logical explanation. A nightmare, to be more precise. That was why the running felt painfully slow.

Marnie closed her eyes and took a calming breath. She could do this. This was her dream. She had the power to make it whatever she wanted.

When she opened her eyes again, her resolve was stronger. She set her sights on the orange glow from her porch and pushed her legs. Her thighs burned from the exertion, but she ignored it. She stole a glimpse over her shoulder to see if the shadow was still there. He was only a few paces behind, lingering like it was a game for him. He didn't need to rush. Somewhere, deep in her heart, Marnie knew he could take her anytime he wanted.

She wasn't one to pray. She hadn't since that night, right before she left home. But at that moment, Marnie uttered a prayer to God or whoever would listen. "Please, just let me wake up."

God was apparently too busy or too indifferent to answer. When Marnie checked behind again, the shadow was there. All he had to do was reach an arm out, and he would have her. A short scream shot out of her mouth without permission as the shadow seized her by the throat, turning her to face him. He lifted her off the ground. Marnie thrashed.

It was impossible. He had a death grip, and her airways were closing. She grabbed onto his wrists. Solid. Even if she'd wanted to, she wouldn't have been able to push through him. During a self-defense class once, she learned that the best way to loosen an attacker's grip is to dig your fingers into the pressure point at the attacker's thumb. Marnie pushed and pushed, but nothing changed.

Her vision was spotty, and it became harder and harder to focus on the task at hand. Her mouth was open, sucking in as much oxygen as it could manage.

"Marnie, Marnie, Marnie." He chided, "Don't worry. We're going to have so much fun together."

He tossed her up, and the moment her body connected with the ground, she shot out of bed. Hyperventilating, Marnie looked around the room, trying to ground herself. Sweat rolled down her forehead and into her eyes. She wiped it away with the back of a shaky hand. The blanket and sheets were in a heap at the foot of the bed. Slowly, everything registered in her mind. She was on her bed, the soft gray sheet under her, her memory foam pillow lying behind her back. Her tall dresser stood across from the bed, holding a vase of flowers and her perfumes on top. The mirror in the corner reflected her frantic image back to her.

She was home. It really was just a nightmare.

Her heartbeat settled back into its normal rhythm. She brought her forearm to her head and laid back on her pillow. After a few moments of calming herself down, Marnie glanced at the alarm clock on her nightstand.

3:45 am.

Sweat made her feel sticky. She reached for the glass of water sitting on her nightstand and took a long drink. Fifteen minutes later and Marnie was sound asleep once again. The rest of the night went by in a quiet darkness. No dreams. No monsters.

Marnie woke early to a shrill ring emanating from her phone. Her eyes burned with exhaustion as she tried to focus them on the caller ID.

"Dr. Carlson" splashed across her screen. Marnie jumped up, grabbed her phone, and cleared her throat before answering.

"Good morning, Dr. Carlson," she said.

"Marnie, I hope I didn't wake you."

"No, not at all! Is everything alright?"

A spontaneous call from the boss is rarely ever a good sign. Marnie sent up a silent prayer to no one in particular, hoping that she wasn't in trouble. She'd only been at Golden Meadow for three years and was still under a sort of probation. Having only a Master's degree made Marnie seem less competent than her PhD'd counterparts. Dr. Carlson had taken a chance hiring her, which meant she was watched more than any other therapist on staff.

"If you're up for it, I'd like to have our weekly meeting this morning. Can you come in early? I'd like to get our talk out of the way before your clients start arriving."

Marnie sighed. A change in meeting times could be nothing. Or, it could be everything.

"That's fine. What time should I be there?"

"Let's say 1 o'clock?"

"Perfect. I'll see you then."

"Make sure to bring your notes from this week's sessions. I want to see those."

"Yes, ma'am. See you soon!" Marnie hung up and ran a hand through her hair. She tossed the phone in the covers and buried her face in her hands. She didn't have the capacity for all this anxiety on top of the nightmares.

Five

BY THE TIME MARNIE HUNG UP with Dr. Carlson and showered, it was only 10 am. For the next few hours, she shuffled between reading psychology studies about dreams and watching Gilmore Girls. Her hands held a slight tremor the entire morning, effects from the nightmare she had. She wanted to understand the dream, to know that there was a logical explanation. But the studies she read were no help. Dreams were such a finicky thing. It seemed like everyone studied them, yet no one truly understood them.

There was no clear reason for Marnie's dream. It was just a dream, and she would have to deal with that. She did her best to forget about it and move on with her day. It was Friday. All she had to do was get through it, and then she would have the whole weekend to recuperate and relax.

And then there it was, tucked in the longing for rest. *Stress*.

The nightmare was most likely a sign of stress.

Like her sense that someone was following her. Or the sounds she heard in the office and at home.

She was under way too much stress.

Maybe talking to Dr. Carlson about it would help.

Marnie left the house at 12 o'clock. The walk to work was

short, usually only twenty minutes, but Marnie refused to be late. That, and she wanted to stop for a coffee on the way.

It was the small things in life. Getting a coffee before work was one of those little perks that made the day that much better. After the night she had, she deserved it.

Marnie stood at the entrance to the alley in front of her apartment. The afternoon sun showered beams of light into the corridor. It was way less threatening during the day. Still, she hesitated to walk through it. The alley felt cursed. Darkness hung in the air that no amount of sunlight could erase. She feared that stepping beyond the threshold would allow the curse to rub off on her.

That wasn't how curses worked – if curses were even real.

But Marnie couldn't shake the feeling.

Man up, Marnie. You're better than this.

She squared her shoulders, standing taller than usual, and took a step into the alley, crossing that threshold. The sunlight faded a little bit. The tall buildings blocked it from permeating all the crevices. It was several degrees colder in the shadowed space. Whether that was her imagination or reality didn't matter much. Little pockets of light lay before her, and it was all Marnie could do to focus on reaching those pockets like a checkpoint in a video game. As long as she made it to each checkpoint, she'd be fine.

Another step forward, and her shoulders slumped. She wrapped her arms across her chest, hugging herself as she walked. The cold pierced through her brown leather jacket.

A few steps further and Marnie swore she felt eyes boring into the back of her head. She pulled her phone out of the back pocket of her black skinny jeans and held it up to her face. She used the reflection to check for someone behind her.

Her furrowed brows and slightly flared nostrils filled the reflection, the green dumpsters against brick buildings in the background.

You're being paranoid. Marnie laughed at herself. This was ridiculous. She was losing it.

The rest of the walk went by without a hitch. Marnie made it to the cafe, ordered her Americano, and was en route to work in no time. Every so often, she could hear someone laughing behind her. She craned her neck to find the source, but there was nothing out of the ordinary. Paranoia was getting the best of her, rubbing her nerves raw.

Marnie walked into the clinic with twenty minutes to spare and nodded at Savannah sitting behind the reception desk. In her office, she gathered everything she needed for the meeting with Dr. Carlson.

Her hands were shaking so bad she almost spilled all the coffee on herself when she lifted it to her mouth.

"Maybe it's time to cool it on the coffee, Ms. Adams."

Marnie whipped around to see Dr. Carlson standing in her doorway. She brushed a few strands of hair out of her face and set the coffee down. Being an anxious mess was not a good look in front of the boss.

"I was just about to come to your office."

Dr. Carlson moved into the room and shut the door behind her. She took a seat in Marnie's chair. Today, Marnie was the patient.

"I thought it'd be nice to meet in here today if you don't mind." Dr. Carlson motioned for Marnie to sit on the couch.

Marnie grabbed the files on her desk and placed them on the coffee table, separating her and Dr. Carlson. The tremor in her hands was noticeable. Marnie held her hands together, hiding it. Dr. Carlson didn't make her nervous. In fact, she was like the mother Marnie never had. Caring, kind, and full of wisdom, a list of skills Marnie's own mother could only dream of having. Dr. Carlson was a saint. Still, these weekly meetings never got any easier. Marnie desperately wanted to please Dr. Carlson, to be the best therapist she could be.

Dr. Carlson's gaze rested on Marnie. She had that special look - the therapist look. She knew how to squint her eyes ever-so-slightly, giving that "it's okay, you can talk to me" look Marnie was still trying to master. It was the kind of look that came from years of experience. By this point, Marnie was sure Dr. Carlson didn't even have to try to do it. It was second nature for her.

Marnie squinted her eyes back, trying to mirror Dr. Carlson's expression and body language. She crossed her legs and leaned back in her seat. She tried to look calm and collected, but the slight quiver in her hand gave away her true feelings.

Dr. Carlson's gaze dropped to Marnie's hands. What Marnie wouldn't have given to read Dr. Carlson's thoughts at that moment.

"Let's talk about this week. How have things been going?"

"Fine. Everything has been going fine." It felt forced leaving her mouth. Marnie readjusted. "I met with Carley on Monday and

Wednesday. She still seems to be struggling with the nightmares. There are some hints of PTSD. Survivor's guilt, too. She's hallucinating a lot, she claims."

"What have you suggested for her to help ease some of the struggles?"

"I recommended she try journaling. Getting her emotions on paper may help her to understand them better and thus work through them. I also recommended she do some daily affirmations. She needs to rewire the neural pathways she created, and the best way to start is by speaking kindly to herself."

Dr. Carlson nodded and wrote something down on her notepad. Marnie stared at the pen moving across the page. Maybe she could decipher the words if she looked close enough. "Any other clients you feel you should mention?"

Marnie sighed. Here we go. "I would like to talk about Ashley Kinney again."

She tried to hide it, but Dr. Carlson rolled her eyes before rubbing them with her thumb and pointer finger. "Ms. Adams–"

Marnie scooted to the edge of the couch, her arms resting on her knees. "Dr. Carlson, please. I think it's a waste of time meeting with her."

Dr. Carlson stood. "I will not be discussing this. You will meet with anyone willing to pay who wants to meet with you. Ms. Kinney's parents are very serious about her attending therapy. It is your job to be her therapist and help her work through the issues she has. End of story."

Marnie dropped her head, defeated. Ashley Kinney was going to be the death of her.

Dr. Carlson turned back once she reached the door. "By the way, you will be getting a new client today. Savannah will bring in his file." She didn't wait for a response.

Marnie flopped back against the couch and stared at the ceiling. That could've gone much better. At least it didn't go worse. She needed to find a way for Dr. Carlson to engage with her about Ashley. There was no way meeting that girl would end well. It was only a matter of time before she tried to end Marnie's career, or worse.

A knock on the door made Marnie jump, accidentally kicking the coffee table. Client files scattered across the floor.

"Come in," she said as she bent to clean them up.

"Sorry to bother you, Ms. Adams. I'm here to give you the new patient file." Savannah walked in and placed the file on Marnie's desk. "You need some help?"

"No, I'm fine." It came out snarkier than she wanted.

"Okay. Well, the new client will be your first today at 3:45 pm."

Today? That was quick. Marnie finished grabbing all the papers from the floor and moved them onto her desk. She opened the new client file; her mood went from bad to worse.

"What is this? He's a grown man." Marnie closed the file and shoved it back to Savannah. "I work with teenagers." Savannah raised her arms away as if it were poisoned. "Savannah, there's been a mistake. This isn't my client." She shoved the file again.

Savannah shook her head. "I'm sorry, Ms. Adams, but he specifically requested you. Dr. Carlson said she was going to tell you about it…"

She had. Dr. Carlson mentioned Savannah bringing in a new client file. And Marnie completely wrote it off because she was too busy throwing a mental hissy fit. She retracted the file. "I'm sorry, Savannah. You're right. Dr. Carlson did mention it. I forgot."

Savannah gave a tight-lipped smile. She was sweet, the type to never say anything mean about anyone. Marnie had connected with the receptionist when she first started. She hated herself for being so rude. It had to be the lack of sleep.

"The rest of your schedule is in there, too," Savannah said.

"Thank you, Savannah. Seriously." Marnie tried to put on her most sincere face.

"Marnie, are you okay? You seem tense."

Marnie pinched the bridge of her nose and closed her eyes. It was Friday. She needed to get through this day, then hello to a weekend of reading and watching copious amounts of TV. "I'm alright. Just a little tired. I didn't sleep well last night. Sorry for snapping at you, Sav."

"It's alright." Savannah gave Marnie a sympathetic head tilt. "Hey, if you wanna get dinner this weekend and talk, I'm free."

"Thanks," Marnie replied.

Savannah gave one last encouraging smile and left the office, closing the door behind her.

Six

GETTING A NEW CLIENT WAS ONE OF THE MOST nerve-wracking things in the world. It was right up there with going to the dentist or getting stopped by the TSA at the airport. Marnie's entire job was talking to people and helping them with their problems. She loved it. But she hated meeting new people. There was an awkwardness that came with the first meeting of a new client. Marnie was never sure how to act or what to expect. She wished she had gotten a little more of a heads up for this new guy, but oh well.

Marnie sat at her desk and opened the new client file: Cavin Grier, age 25, caucasian. There was a headshot paper-clipped to the top of the folder. His green eyes were wide open, and his curly red hair was messy on top of his head. He looked caught off guard. Marnie didn't know why Golden Meadow insisted on having pictures of all the clients. It felt like an invasion of privacy. Judging by the look on Cavin's face, he would agree. Still, he was a handsome enough man. Though a solid eight to ten years older than her other clients, he had an innocence to his face. Marnie didn't care for meeting with adults. That's why she chose to be a therapist for teenagers. But he had insisted, so what was she to do?

Cavin's picture pulled Marnie in. Something about him was

fascinating. Those green eyes beckoned her nearer. She couldn't wait to meet him, to see what he was like. Most of his file was blank. There was no phone number to contact him or any health insurance information. The man was a total mystery.

Marnie set his file aside and pulled out the form that she would fill out during their session. The first session with a new client was the most mundane. They spent most of the time talking about background information and why they decided to attend therapy. It gave Marnie a chance to warm up to the new client to see if they were a good fit for each other. Not that it mattered what Marnie thought. If it had, she would've kicked Ashley to the curb after their very first meeting.

Marnie prepared her office and mind for the day ahead, and ten minutes later, there was a knock at the door. She rose from her oak desk and crossed the room to the door. When she opened it, the green-eyed man stood before her. His auburn hair twisted out around his head as if he didn't own a brush. Dark circles coated his eyelids. There was something very different between the man in the picture and the one standing in Marnie's doorway.
His eyes. In the picture, he had beautiful green eyes that sparkled in the camera's flash. Here, they were much darker, almost gray. The innocence Marnie expected was nowhere to be found. In its place was something dark, something secret.

Marnie brushed a few strands of hair behind her ear and smiled. "Hi! Cavin, right?" She reached out her hand.

"Yeah, that's me." Cavin took Marnie's hand. His icy fingers squeezed it and lingered longer than she was comfortable with. She forced her hand free and shoved it into her jacket pocket, trying to warm it up. "Nice to meet you, Dr. Adams."

Marnie closed the door and walked to her chair across from the couch. "Marnie is fine. I'm not a doctor… yet," she smirked.

Cavin followed. "Marnie," he whispered, nodding his head once.

Cavin looked around the room. He rubbed his palms across his thighs over and over. First sessions with a new therapist are tough, but Cavin's behavior was more in line with someone who'd never been in therapy. Marnie needed to tread lightly and be extra welcoming. She kept her eyes fixed on his face, searching for the man from the picture but coming up empty. Still, something inside of him called to her. In another life, they might have been friends – or more.

Cavin's wandering eyes finally settled on Marnie. He smiled like he knew what she was thinking, then leaned back and brought his arms up behind his head. "So, pretty typical stuff, right? I lay down and tell you about all my mommy issues?"

The change from nervous to calm, almost cocky, was quick. Marnie let out a short laugh. "You don't need to lay down. Unless you want to, that is," she said.

"But I got the mommy issues part right?"

Marnie tilted her head to the left a little bit. This was fun; she should consider seeing adults more often. "You tell me. Do you feel like you need to talk about your mom right away?" She tapped the folder with her pen. "I thought we could use today to get to know each other a little. You know, ask a few questions. That way, we can make sure we're the right fit for each other."

A puff of air followed by a cough escaped Cavin. He held a fist to his mouth and cleared his throat.

Was that a laugh?

"Okay," Cavin said. "But I'm not worried about that."

Marnie laughed again. *What an interesting response*, she thought.

Cavin had a lot of character. Whether that was a good thing or a bad thing, only time would tell. At least it'd been entertaining thus far.

Marnie opened Cavin's file over her lap and skimmed it. Cavin's gaze burned the top of her head. His presence was much stronger than she'd expected, making it difficult to focus. She read the same sentence three, four, and five times before finally giving up and matching his stare. Not once did he take his eyes off her. Marnie shifted in her seat. She crossed her left leg over her right, then switched. Sweat seeped from her forehead, and she wiped it away nonchalantly, hoping Cavin hadn't noticed.

He was perfectly still. If she didn't know any better, Marnie would've thought he was a statue. He wasn't rubbing his thighs anymore. He simply stared. At her.

Marnie looked away first, peeking back down at the file on her lap. She cleared her throat. "Cavin, you seem to have left the history summary blank. Actually, you left a lot of things blank. Can we talk about those?"

He nodded.

"Let's start with history, then," Marnie said. "What was your childhood like? Any siblings?"

"Ah, that." Cavin dropped his eyes to his hands. "Can we talk about something else? I don't think my childhood really matters here. It has nothing to do with why I wanted to start seeing you."

Marnie nodded. "That's fine; we can talk about something else. But sometimes, our past is the key to unlocking the things we struggle most with in our present. We should always look back if we want to move forward."

The corners of Cavin's mouth moved into a grin, and his cheeks flushed. "She's smart," he whispered.

"What was that?" Marnie asked, leaning forward.

"Nothing. But I guess you're right. After all, you're the professional here. So what do you wanna know?"

Cavin still stared down at his hands. He was wringing them together in a constant swirling motion. In the short time they'd been together, Marnie had seen him go from nervous to calm and back to nervous. Something was wrong with this guy. Marnie wanted to pass him on to Dr. Carlson. She would be much more equipped to handle someone like this.

"Let's start with the basics, like a warm-up. Where did you grow up? Do you have any siblings?"

Cavin shifted his body so that he was sitting against the armrest. He turned his head and looked out the window, contemplating. *What was there to think about? It was a pretty straightforward question.*

Marnie took a few notes in the margins of the form.

Volatile emotional state one second, he's cool; next, he's anxious.

He looked back at Marnie, and she crossed her arms over the file, covering the notes. The last thing she needed was to find out just how volatile his emotions were.

"I was born in Kansas City. The Missouri side. And I have a little sister, Stella. We don't really talk anymore." There was a bite in his voice when he said her name.

"Why not?" Marnie asked.

"Stella was the favorite. She got whatever she wanted whenever she wanted it. I didn't like that." Cavin ran his fingers through his hair. "I guess I was the practice run before my parents got the kid they prayed for."

Marnie took more notes: *oldest of two children, strained relationship with parents and sister. Midwest born.*

"What are you writing? Don't write that!" Cavin jumped to his feet, pointing an accusatory finger at Marnie.

Busted. She found the button and pressed it. It turned out Cavin was much more volatile than she hoped.

Marnie closed the file and set it on the ground next to the chair, then held up her hands in surrender. "It's okay, Cavin. I'm only taking a few notes on things I'd like to ask more about. It's nothing to worry about."

Cavin pulled his hand back and ran both hands through his hair several times. "No… No, I don't like it. I don't want you to take notes." He paced back and forth in front of the couch, moving his hands through his hair over and over.

Marnie had set him off, and she froze in her seat. A client had never reacted this way to her note-taking before. Most people thought it was nice of her to write things down; that way she could remember for the next session. She was completely out of her element.

This is why I work with kids.

Marnie willed herself to stand. "Cavin…" She reached out to touch his shoulder.

He pulled away as her hand made contact. "I, uh, I have to go," Cavin said. "Yeah, I forgot about a doctor's appointment I have." He made a beeline for the door and left without looking back. The door slammed, shaking Marnie's master's degree hanging on the wall.

That was weird. What was she supposed to do with this reaction? Did she do something wrong? Marnie sat in her chair and grabbed the file from the floor.

Easily spooked, afraid of the past.

She wanted to talk to Dr. Carlson about him, to beg her to take him on. This was not what Marnie signed up for as a therapist.

Marnie couldn't let one bad session ruin the rest of her day. She went to her desk and checked her schedule. At least it was Friday, which meant Carley. She wanted to know more about Carley's dreams and how she was coping. Marnie was the therapist, but talking to Carley felt like a session for herself as much as for the girl. It was like talking to her teenage self. She was able to say things to Carley she wished someone would've said to her.

Carley's name was missing from the schedule. There had to

be a mistake. It was Friday. Carley always came on Friday.

Marnie called Savannah at the front desk. "Hey Savannah, did Carley Rey leave a message about her session today? I don't see her on my schedule."

"Gimme a sec," Savannah said.

Marnie heard shuffling on the other end, followed by the quick clacking of keys.

"Sorry, Marnie. I don't have any messages from Carley or her parents. She didn't schedule an appointment after her last visit like she normally does either."

Marnie groaned. *Great.* Not only had she dealt with a hyper-sensitive, somewhat scary man, but now her favorite client wasn't coming in. Not that she would ever admit that to anyone.

"Okay, thanks," she said, hanging up.

She opened the top drawer of her desk and grabbed her cell phone. She gave all, well most, of her clients her cell phone number. Many of whom never bothered to use it except Carley. Carley texted Marnie at least once a week. There was a missed call from Hannah, but she would call her back after work. Marnie thumbed through her contacts until she found Carley's name. It rang four times, then went to voicemail.

"You got Carley. Don't leave a message 'cause I won't listen to it, bye-e!" followed by a beep.

Marnie hung up and sent Carley a text.

Hey Carley, everything okay? I noticed you're not on the schedule for today. Just wanted to check in. -Marnie Adams

Marnie stared at the message. She waited and waited for the "read" message to appear. She had to get a hold of Carley. It was important that they talk about Carley's dreams more. Marnie needed to talk about the man Carley claimed to have heard and seen.

She had to know.

What if the man - thing - she saw in her dream was the same one Carley saw in hers? Was that even possible? Marnie had read articles about shared delusions and thought it was crazy. But now, that very well could've been what she was experiencing. She needed more information from Carley.

Had Carley ever described what the man looked like, apart from him being shadowy? Did she know about the red eyes? The sharp teeth? Could she tell what he was wearing?

Marnie checked the message again. Still unread.

She was afraid of the man in her dreams, scared of what he could do to her. She couldn't stop the panic from welling up in her throat and spilling out in short whimpers. Marnie sipped water from the bottle sitting on her desk and stared at her bookshelf.

Count the books, Marnie. Count the books and breathe.

Still, the panic attack came, hitting her like a truck. Her breath hitched in her throat.

Then, her phone chimed. Carley replied.

Thanks, Ms. Adams! I'm doing great, didn't need to talk today. Getting dinner with friends, catch ya later!

Carley was fine.

Carley was fine? How was Carley fine? Or, in her words, *great*? This was the first time since the incident that Carley had seemed so relaxed. The first time she'd hung out with friends again. Marnie set her phone down and leaned back, closing her eyes. Carley was fine. That was a good thing. It meant that therapy was working.

Her next client would be coming at any moment. What had gotten into her? All the panic attacks and nightmares were driving her crazy. And worse than that, it felt like it was only the beginning. Like Marnie was standing on the edge of a cliff, waiting for something to come up behind her and push.

How far would she fall?

Seven

"SUCH AN IDIOT!" Cavin pounded fists into his temples as he stormed down the street back to his car. "Why would you go in there? Therapists bring out the worst in people, you moron. Now Marnie knows you're a screwed-up mess!" People were staring. "You ruined everything!" Another fist to the temple.

An elderly couple watched Cavin walk by, craning their necks to see him as he passed. He didn't care. Let them watch. Let everyone watch. All that mattered was the fact that he'd ruined everything.

"Should've let me talk. I would've been able to spin it in such a way that didn't make us look bad." The voice was gentle. He spoke in a matter-of-fact way, not quite condescending.

"'Us'? What do you mean 'us'? It was my face she saw. My history, she pulled out."

"Yes, us. We're a team now, remember? I've got your back. Didn't you see how chill I made us at first? Or maybe you were too busy staring to notice all my hard work."

The voice had gotten louder since that night in the alleyway. It gave Cavin's confidence a boost when he allowed it. Sure, Cavin was sleeping less, but he had more energy. The voice reminded Cavin of how wonderful and deserving he was of Marnie's affection.

If only he hadn't been such a failure today. First impressions are everything, and Cavin flushed his down the toilet.

"Cavin, Cavin, you need to relax. We can fix this, trust me."

They had spent hours planning how to win Marnie over. Today had been phase one, and Cavin already ruined it, like he ruined everything.

"She hates me," he said.

"She doesn't hate you. She barely knows you." The voice was a comfort usually. It wasn't working this time.

Cavin bit his tongue hard in an attempt to stop himself from crying. The only way to make things worse was to start crying like a wuss. Marnie deserved better than him. She deserved a man, a real man. Not some pathetic low-life like him.

"Did you see the way she looked at you?"

Cavin stopped walking. "What?"

"Come on, man! You didn't see her staring? You mesmerized her with your looks."

Cavin touched his cheek. "She was?" He turned to face the building. The window was empty, the perfect place to stare at his own reflection.

"Totally! She couldn't stop staring at you. You intimidated her."

Cavin turned his head to the right and left. He was pretty good- looking, wasn't he? "You think so?"

The voice chuckled. "I know so, man. She was so nervous around you. She likes you."

Cavin smiled. Maybe it wasn't a total failure. Maybe there was still a chance to come back from this. Not alone, of course. There was no way he could win Marnie alone. He needed the voice in his head. He needed that extra help.

Cavin took one last look in the shop window, then kept walking. He changed courses, turning away from his car and toward Marnie's apartment. He had to see her, maybe even talk to her this time. He could apologize for running out on her like that.

Or maybe he'd wait and watch her walk home like normal.

Yeah, watching her walk home was good. He'd done enough for the day.

Marnie's apartment was only twenty minutes from Golden Meadow. The walk was short and helped Cavin calm down. He cleared his head, letting all the anger melt away.

Everything would be fine. He wasn't alone.

Cavin sat behind the dumpster. The stench of rotten milk and unidentifiable trash burned his eyes. He squeezed his eyes to stop them from watering. It took every ounce of willpower he had not to gag.

Cavin retreated into his mind to escape the smell. There, he could imagine how the body behind the voice looked. Cavin believed him to be an angel. He pictured a tall, handsome man with dark brown hair and blue eyes. The kinda guy that would be in a famous movie. He had a beard because women like bearded men, and he wore a leather jacket and all black. He was a *cool* angel. He was everything Cavin wished he could be. He was exactly the kind of man who would win someone like Marnie over.

Cavin thought about his own looks; Curly red hair and green eyes, a face covered in freckles. He wasn't fat, at least, but he wasn't as muscular as he could be, either.

Push-ups. He'd do push-ups. That would help.

Cavin looked at the man in his mind's eye. He wanted to be him. But he had the next best thing. The man lived inside of him. That was close enough.

"Look, Cavin. Do I think you made the right decision seeing Marnie at her place of work today? No, I don't. But cheer up. I don't think it went all that bad. Like I said, she was checking you out. That's a good sign."

Cavin kicked at a rock. It was weird that there was a rock in his imagination, but he went with it. "What am I supposed to do now?"

"Are you ready to get serious? Are you willing to do whatever it takes to win her over?"

Cavin straightened his posture. "Anything. I'll do anything."

"Good. But it's gonna take some time. You can't expect her to be yours tomorrow. We gotta build up to it, loosen the lady up a little bit." The man moved closer to Cavin and got right in his face. Cavin held his breath. "I don't want you seeing her at work again. Not for a while at least; you're not ready."

Cavin nodded. It was for the best that way, anyways. "When can I talk to her again?"

The man behind the voice walked around, stroking his beard. He paced back and forth for a long time, making Cavin uncomfortable. He'd really screwed the pooch on this one. The man turned toward

Cavin, staring straight through him. Cavin pressed his eyelids shut, waiting for a fist to slam into his face. That was what Mother would do. If Cavin so much as looked at her wrong, Mother would throw an open hand, a fist, sometimes even an elbow at his head.

The blow never came. Cavin eased his eyes open once again to see the man standing in front of him, watching.

"Are you okay?" the man said.

Cavin cleared his throat. "Fine."

"I don't want you talking to her yet. I have a way of helping people loosen up. I'll visit her and make sure she's ready for you." He put his hands on Cavin's shoulders. "In the meantime, I want you to find a way to run into her on the street or at a cafe. Apologize for the way you acted and turn on the charm."

Cavin nodded his head, mulling over the plan. "Run into her at the cafe... I like it."

The man moved to Cavin's side, placing a hand around Cavin's shoulder as he did. "Of course it's a good plan! I'm here for you, my man. Whatever you need. I will help you get the girl."

Regret had a chokehold on many areas of Cavin's life. Inviting the voice to be a part of him was definitely not one of those areas. Cavin opened his eyes to the alley once again, watching, waiting for Marnie to walk by. Any minute now, she'd pass him. The sweet coconut scent would erase the smell of trash and transport him into a world where only they existed – a world of love and joy, and Marnie.

Only Marnie.

Eight

RELIEF.

The day was over. She'd survived.

Apart from Cavin running out in the middle of their first session, the rest of the day had been manageable. Marnie was able to keep her mind focused on the work at hand rather than her anxiety. She kept her composure.

It was all in her head, wasn't it? The nightmare and the voices. The key was keeping herself busy, drowning herself in work. When she focused on that, everything else melted away.

Now, it was a matter of distracting herself outside of work.

Marnie picked up a chicken salad on her way home. It was easier to keep it simple, although cooking would've been a better distraction.

Oh well, she thought, *there's always tomorrow.*

She plopped down on her couch, sitting with her salad balanced between her pretzeled legs. She flipped through Netflix as a pretense as if she was going to choose something other than Gilmore Girls. She gave up and clicked play on Gilmore Girls. That show always managed to help her decompress. In spite of watching it on repeat, the kooky townspeople of Stars Hollow wiggled their way into her heart. Even though they were fictional, they put Marnie at ease.

The night progressed, and Marnie's eyelids were heavy-haden. Her head doubled in size, too, the pressure feeling unbearable. She laid down across the couch. Going to her room was out of the question. Nightmares lived in there.

She stared at the dark threshold into her bedroom. The place that should hold solace, rest, and relaxation looked menacing. Shadows played there. They danced around, laughing at Marnie's childish fear of the dark. They waited beyond the open door to snatch her the second she passed through.

She refused to go. Not tonight. She couldn't.

Marnie crashed on the couch. She pulled the simple forest green throw blanket up to her chin, fluffed the matching couch pillow, and laid down. She basked in the soft glow of the television set that acted as a night light. It was perfectly normal to be a twenty-eight-year-old woman who was afraid of the dark. Right?

Sleep came, devoid of any nightmares. Monsters that live in the dark corners of life can't get to you when the TV is on. Not a single dream played in Marnie's mind. Nothing but a blissful emptiness met her in the REM cycle.

A deafening crash forced Marnie awake. She opened her eyes and sat up, looking around the room. Everything seemed to be in its rightful place. Nothing had fallen.

A scream sliced through the room, and Marnie jerked her eyes to the TV. *The Hills Have Eyes*, quite literally the scariest movie ever, was playing on the TV.

How was that possible?

Marnie had been on Netflix, not cable TV. Changing the channel *in your sleep* from Netflix to cable was impossible.

Marnie scrambled for the remote, finding it shoved between the couch cushions, and turned the TV off without looking. She hated that movie. Marnie prided herself on the ability to watch any movie, scary or not. Movies weren't real, and she could always make that distinction. The one and only exception to that was *The Hills Have Eyes*. She caught fifteen minutes of that movie as a child, and it terrified her beyond rational thought. She hasn't been able to watch it since.

Her cell phone sat on the coffee table before her. Marnie

swapped the remote for her phone and checked the time.

3:45 am.

Hannah's missed call still announced itself across her lock screen. Marnie really needed to call her back; it could've been important. But there was another notification under the missed call: a text message, the number blocked. Marnie's skin prickled.

She unlocked the phone, navigating to her messages.

It was another creepy message from the same sender. The other messages loomed above, taunting Marnie. Her fingers hovered over the keyboard.

She should reply. She should tell the freak to leave her alone, to jump off a cliff.

No, that wasn't smart. This person was unstable. Telling them off could make things worse. But she couldn't just sit around, letting the messages keep coming.

She could play dumb and reply with an innocent, "Who is this?" Would that be too lame? Would they see right through it?

Or would they answer? Tell her who they are, and admit to stalking her.

For all she knew, it was a joke. Prank calls were so early 2000s. Prank texts were all the rage these days.

How many people knew she used coconut shampoo? Hannah did. She'd borrowed it countless times during their sleepovers. Savannah knew, too. Marnie had recommended the brand to her and noticed when she started using it. Any number of her clients could've smelled it on her. It was very potent, after all.

The messages could be from any number of people.

That was the worst part, not knowing who it was from or where they could've gotten her number. That paired with the intense feeling of eyes following her when she walked home. This was all getting to be too much for Marnie.

She was a normal girl. She went to work, grocery shopping, and hung out with friends. She'd never considered herself to be all that pretty. Only a point or two above average, she figured. Heck, it wasn't like the guys were lining up at her door to get a chance with her. So who would want to mess with her like this?

"Pete," she whispered. The bastard had always had it out for her. It wasn't enough that he'd hit her in high school, called her names, and forced her into closets. No, he had to keep attacking, even after she moved out. The sick freak probably still blamed her for ruining his life. How he came to that conclusion, Marnie never understood.

He was the one who chose to sleep with her mom. He chose to leave his wife and kids and move in with her and her mom. He was the one who decided alcohol was the only way to suppress the crushing weight of guilt. The logical jump to blaming Marnie, especially when she was just a kid, was astounding. It was Olympic gold medalist level.

It had to be him.

Fire coursed through her veins. How dare he do this to her after all these years? She left for a reason. She dropped her mom, her friends, and her entire life to get away from him. How dare he drag her back.

Marnie dialed the number she had spent years trying to forget. It was the middle of the night, but she knew they would pick up.

It rang and rang, and with each ring, Marnie's anger boiled closer to the surface.

"Hello?" A groggy voice finally picked up.

Marnie froze.

She hadn't heard her mother's voice in years. What was she doing? This wasn't how she'd wanted to do this. This wasn't the way she'd planned on reuniting with her mom.

But, here she was. She had to act now.

"Hello? Anyone there?" her mom said.

"Can you tell your *husband* to please stop sending me weird messages," Marnie snapped.

"Marnie?"

The anger melted ever-so-slightly. "Hi, mom."

"Oh, Marnie! It's you." Hope oozed from those few words.

She had to hold onto the anger. Conjure up the past.

Don't give in, Marnie. It's all a trick. She's pretending to be nice to get something from you. Stay strong.

"I'm serious, mom. Tell Pete to leave me alone."

"Honey, Pete's gone." She cleared her throat. "I told him to leave. He's been gone a year now."

What was she supposed to say to that?

Silence hung in the air. Marnie searched for words, but none came to her. The silence was so lasting that she thought her mom had hung up. Then, a whimper.

"Baby, I'm so sorry for everything. I'm trying. I really am. I-"

"I gotta go, Mom." Marnie hung up before her mother could protest.

It could still be Pete. But probably not.

No matter how much Marnie begged, morning still came.

At least it was Saturday.

Her mom's voice echoed in her mind. She hated admitting how much she missed her. The old her. The mom from Marnie's childhood was loving and present. She didn't care about the empty shell of a woman who did nothing but lay on the couch and drink beer by the bucket load.

But she sounded good on the phone. Her voice was clear and steady. Maybe she was cleaning up, getting her act together.

She'd kicked Pete out. And it'd been a year. That was the longest Marnie's mom had ever stayed away from him. She had kicked Pete out before – that was nothing new. But it never lasted longer than a month. There was one time it got to a month and a week. Marnie was sure that it would stick. Then, like clockwork, Pete walked through the front door and plopped himself down on the couch.

Marnie ran her fingers through her tangled hair. She couldn't sit at home and think about this all day. She was going through enough: nightmares, hearing things, weird texts, paranoia. She didn't need to add suppressed family trauma to her list of things to worry about.

It was her fault. She never should've called her mom. That was what she got for wanting answers. What she got for thinking it was Pete. He was mean, but he wasn't an idiot. She was stupid to think it had been him texting. Pete always preferred physical pain over psychological.

Back to square one. The mystery texter was still at large.

The good news was Marnie didn't have a single nightmare all night. Aside from the weird TV malfunction and family reunion in the middle of the night, it had been a pleasant night. She slept soundly, dreaming of nothing. And now she had energy to spare.

Marnie decided to take advantage of the extra energy and go for a walk. Perhaps even stop by the coffee shop for a little treat instead of making breakfast and coffee at home. She could go a little "crazy" – take some psychology articles to catch up on reading at the coffee shop.

Marnie missed school. She reminisced about her favorite classes, and the intense discussion and heated debates on abnormal psychology and childhood development. She sighed wistfully. Grad school was the best period of her life. So, Marnie read psychology journals in her free time. She would highlight interesting things and write down the most noteworthy points. It made her feel like she was still in school and helped her be a better therapist.

The dream was to one day go back for a doctorate. The only thing stopping her was the funds to pay for the doctorate. She needed to work at least a few more years to have enough money to commit herself to that. Until then, she had her psych journals and her conversations with Dr. Carlson. That was enough for now.

Marnie changed into yoga pants and a baggy t-shirt. She threw her hair up into a messy bun and grabbed her favorite hoodie. She picked up the freshly printed journals that sat on her kitchen counter and ran out the door.

Today was going to be a great day. Nothing would stop that. She was determined.

The dreaded alley stood before her.

Nothing would ruin today – not even the horrifying alley. It was stupid. She walked through that alley every day, several times a day, for years. And now it was scary? No fair. Not happening.

Marnie took a step forward. The mid-morning sun shot rays of light across the top of the buildings, but at the bottom, it was dark.

In the secluded passageway, Marnie heard it. The voice never went away. She knew that now. It had always been there, taunting her, calling her name. She remembered hearing it yesterday. She heard it between breaths.

"Marnie, I'm watching," it said.

Always calling her name. Always there.

Marnie could hear it – no, him – laughing now.

Fear rushed up in waves. She picked up her pace, trying not to panic while trying to get away at the same time.

Nothing would ruin her day.

Okay, the creepy voice that got louder and louder could ruin her day. But not if she ran fast enough.

"You can't run from me, Marnie. I will always be right behind you." The voice rumbled, low and sinister. Hate dripped from every syllable. Malice edged each word.

He hated Marnie. But why? What did she ever do to deserve this? She wasn't exactly on speaking terms with God, but that didn't mean she was on good terms with evil spirits, either.

Fear solidified in Marnie's gut, and she set her speed to full throttle, running faster than she knew she could. A gust of wind at her back convinced her she was being followed. She looked back once, only to see a shadow growing like black smoke from a forest fire. In the split second that she watched the shadow, a face formed in the middle.

Those eyes. Red like blood. Lips parted in a snarl.

Fear sunk its roots deep into her stomach, and she pushed. Her thighs burned, and her muscles tensed. She couldn't give up now. There was no telling what that monster would do once he caught up to her.

Marnie chanced a glance back again and sent herself falling to the ground, tripping over her own feet. She stuck her arms out with a slight bend in the elbows to cushion the fall and closed her eyes, bracing for impact.

Chest heaving up and down, she kept her eyes closed. The palms of her hands stung, and she could feel tiny pieces of gravel digging into her skin.

This was it. Her clumsiness would actually get her killed. He was coming, and there was no way she could get up and escape before he reached her.

"Whoa, are you okay?"

Nine

THERE WAS A STARK DIFFERENCE IN THIS VOICE compared to the one she was hearing before. This one was gentle. It wasn't very fitting for the present moment, but Marnie embraced the calm presence.

"Can you stand?"

He was still there. She hadn't made him up.

Marnie opened her eyes to see a pair of black and white Converse inches from her face. Her eyes followed the upward curve of the person standing before her: dark wash jeans, a black belt, white t-shirt, and finally, a face. He was tall but not towering. He looked as though he were slouching a little bit like he was ashamed of his height. His brown eyes washed over Marnie with concern. His lingering gaze reminded her that she was still sprawled on all fours on the dirty ground.

Marnie pushed back onto the balls of her feet, then forced herself all the way to a standing position. She rubbed her hands together, loosening the pebbles etched into her palms. They stung a little bit, but not so bad now that a handsome stranger was standing before her.

He was staring at her. Oh God, how long had she been quiet? She had to say something, anything before things got awkward.

"I, uh, there was someone there," Marnie whispered.

The man peered past her into the empty alley. She looked over her shoulder. There was no one. Of course, there was no one because the freaky shadow man lived in her mind.

Duh, Marnie.

"You sure you're okay?" he asked.

"Yeah, I'm fine. That's what I get for not watching where I'm going. Thanks."

"I'm Jason, by the way." He stuck his hand out.

Marnie reached for it. His hand was warm, inviting. It thawed her icy skin.

"Marnie," she said.

"Nice to meet you, Marnie."

Rays of sunshine rained down around them. They were standing at the end of the alley, and Marnie could see the heat of the sun warming her goosebumps. She didn't realize how cold she'd gotten.

Marnie wrapped her arms around herself in a warming hug. "Sorry I crashed into you like that."

"Nah, you didn't crash into me. More like crashed in front of me. I made it out of the whole ordeal completely unscathed." Jason's brown eyes gleamed, and a smirk formed on his lips. "You, on the other hand, will probably have some nice bruises forming the next couple of days."

Marnie released a stiff laugh. "Yeah, my knees are gonna be crying for a few days, I'm sure." She tried to look away, but Jason held her gaze in place.

An awkward silence fell between them. Marnie's cheeks burned red, begging her to break the silence. Jason was so handsome she didn't know what to do with herself. This was one of those surreal moments in life that imitated TV shows and movies. A "meet-cute" moment. Marnie wasn't supposed to have a "meet-cute." Especially not now, not with everything going on.

"Well, thanks for… uh." What exactly had he done except stand there? "Thanks for asking if I was alright." Yeah, good enough.

Marnie brushed past him, then turned to face him again. Seeing this kind stranger against the backdrop of the alley made it appear less menacing. He had a relaxing quality.

It freaked Marnie out.

"Oh, and sorry again," she added, then started walking away.

"Are you busy right now?" Jason called after her.

She stopped, turning to face him. "Not really. What's up?"

Stranger danger is a very real thing. But when that stranger was handsome and nice and seemingly harmless, it was okay to be a little more open to time with them. Besides, everyone is a stranger when you first meet them.

"Well, I was wondering if you'd wanna grab a coffee together? I feel like I should buy you a drink after that nasty fall."

Marnie tried to suppress a smile and failed. She would take any opportunity to turn Jason from stranger to friend. "I'd never turn down free coffee."

Jason's face lit up, and he skipped forward to meet her stride. They walked side by side, keeping time with each other all the way to the cafe. They stayed silent the whole way. What was she supposed to say? Marnie couldn't help but second-guess her decision to grab coffee with him. She would be locked in for at least thirty minutes with a random guy that she knew nothing about. What if he was dull? What if he was crazy?

Then the worst thought popped into her mind: what if he was the one watching her and sending the weird texts?

Marnie brushed a loose strand of hair behind her ear and sneakily looked at Jason. No, it couldn't be him. She didn't know him, but it couldn't be him. She should've been wary, but being with someone was better than being alone. Marnie looked around at the crowded street of downtown Springfield and let out a sigh of relief. It was time to tame her over-active imagination.

In the cafe, Marnie grabbed the exact table she had sat at with Hannah less than a week earlier. It was her favorite spot in the whole cafe. The big window looking out to the street was on her left, and the rest of the cafe was to her right. Being Saturday, the place was full. There were women catching up with friends and parents with toddlers running around. Tucked in the cozy corner was a couple, she could only guess as having their first date, judging by the awkwardness. Life bounced off the walls, and Marnie was grateful to add to the energy.

Jason returned from the counter with two coffees and sat across from her. Marnie thanked him and sipped at the warm drink, stalling as her mind racked for something to say. She knew how to talk to strangers; it came with the job. But as a therapist, Marnie usually had the upper hand in a way. She was the one that people came to; the professional, and confidence oozed out when she was in that scenario.

But, all that flew out the window the second she clocked out.

The silence from the walk overstretched into their cafe time. Marnie stared down at the coffee between her hands, chancing glances at Jason every few seconds. She could wait out the silence. Let time pass so that if he was a dud, she wouldn't have to worry about making conversation for too long. It was another skill she learned as a therapist. Being comfortable with silence was part of the job. Sometimes it was the only way to get a client talking. She wasn't exactly comfortable with this silence, but hey, *fake it 'til you make it*, right?

Jason seemed as comfortable with the silence as Marnie pretended to be. When she managed to sneak a look, he was sitting there, staring out the window or looking at her. It was like they were playing a game of chicken. Who would break first?

Marnie sipped her coffee a little more and mustered the courage to speak. She couldn't take the silence anymore; curiosity ate at her bones. She needed to know more about this man who seemed so chill.

"So, are you from around here? I've been to this cafe pretty much every day for the last three years, and I've never seen you." There, she broke the silence.

Jason stared at his coffee, smiling. Victory sparkled in his eyes, or at least that's what Marnie saw in them. He won the game of chicken.

Jason lifted his eyes to meet Marnie. The sunlight gliding through the large window made his eyes shine a gorgeous amber tint. His eyes matched the color of his hair almost perfectly. And while he wasn't the most handsome man Marnie had ever seen, something about him was very alluring. It had to be the way he carried himself, his smile, and the kindness that radiated off him. If she had ever crossed paths with him in a crowd, Marnie wouldn't have noticed him. But now that she'd met him, she was sure she could pick him out of even the most crowded places.

"I'm not, actually," he said. "I just moved here from Chicago. I needed a change of pace, put in the transfer request at work, and-" he lifted his arms in a 'here I am' motion. "This is where they put me."

"Gosh, I'm sorry this is where you got sent. I'm sure it's not nearly as cool as Chicago," Marnie said.

Jason laughed. "I actually like it here. It's a lot quieter than Chicago, got a good vibe – nice people. Feels like the kinda place you could call home, ya know?"

Marnie watched him, doing the typical therapist nod. The stereotypes were true in some ways. She didn't say, "And how does that make you feel?" as often as people thought, but she still did the nod. It was hard to turn off.

"I guess you're right," she said. "I've been here since grad school, then ended up getting a job and staying. I like it, too. But sometimes I miss home."

"Where're you from?"

"Texas. So as you can imagine, I'm freezing all winter here. But, if I could use your words, the vibe is nice." At least the vibe was nice before a large shadowy man started tormenting her in alleyways.

He laughed again. Marnie liked the sound of his laugh. She wanted to keep making him laugh as much as she could.

"What do you do for work, Marnie?" Jason asked.

"I'm a therapist." She pointed out the window to a building just across the street. "See that big building over there? That's Golden Meadow. I work there." It wasn't the smartest thing to tell a stranger where she worked, but Jason didn't feel so much like a stranger now. "How about you, Jason?"

He rubbed the back of his neck and looked around the room. For the first time since meeting him, Marnie started to worry about who she was spending time with. He took a long swig of coffee, almost reluctant to answer the question.

"You don't have to tell me if it's too personal or something," Marnie added.

"No, it's just that… ah, people get kinda weird around me when I tell them my job. I'd rather that not happen with you yet." He rubbed his neck again. "Let's just say I help people. We'll leave it at that for now, if you don't mind."

Marnie nodded. As much as she wanted to press the topic, she didn't want to scare him away. Jason was cool, the first guy she'd talked to outside of work for who knows how long. How would it look for her if she sent him away, running for the hills?

"Helping people, huh? Well, good enough for now. But my curiosity is gonna kill me." She smirked, hoping it came off mildly flirty and not creepy.

Jason smiled back. It worked.

"Okay, well, is there anything about yourself you *can* tell me?" Marnie asked.

Jason dramatically placed a fist under his chin, scrunched his eyebrows together, and released a long "hmm." Marnie giggled. A total schoolgirl giggle. And it felt good to let it out.

"Let's see. I'm an only child. My favorite color is dark blue. I love pretty much every type of food, but in a totally cliche way, my favorite is pizza. And I am forever stuck in the early 2000s punk rock age of music."

Marnie's eyes lit up. She loved him.

Well, okay, no. Obviously, she didn't *love* him. But the emotions flowing through her veins were very, very strong. Marnie rested her elbow on the table and concealed her smile with an open hand. She couldn't let him know how swoon-worthy he was.

"Your turn," he said.

Marnie sat back in her chair, trying to match his energy. She placed an index finger on her chin and looked up to the ceiling, being as dramatic as he had been.

"I'm also an only child. I love the color maroon. My favorite food is pasta, but pizza is always great. And I watch way too much Gilmore Girls."

"Gilmore? What now?"

Marnie's jaw dropped. She leaned across the table. "Are you serious? You don't know Gilmore Girls?"

Jason's cheeks turned bright red, and Marnie did a little happy dance inside. He wasn't the only one with the power to make the other blush.

"Gilmore Girls is only the best sitcom of the late 90s to early 2000s ever. It's on Netflix. You gotta watch it. I know it's like a 'girl show' or whatever, but it's funny, I promise."

Jason nodded, a large smile plastered to his face. "I'm not a big TV watcher, but I'll give it a shot."

Marnie sat back. The content turned cold, and the hairs on the back of her neck stood up. She rubbed them down, peeking over her shoulder. Was someone watching her?

Ten

CAVIN PERCHED IN HIS USUAL CORNER OF THE CAFE SEET-
HING.

How dare she do this to him?

He didn't plan on visiting Marnie that Saturday, but the voice in his head insisted he go. When he finally arrived, Marnie was standing at the end of the alley talking to some guy. Whoever he was, the man refused to leave her alone. Cavin could tell that Marnie was uncomfortable. She didn't want to talk to him, didn't want to be there. Cavin knew exactly how Marnie felt by looking at her. It was one of the beautiful things about their connection. They didn't need to speak, didn't even need to look at each other. Cavin still knew everything about her. And, as evident by their encounter at her work, Marnie could read Cavin just as easily. It was all the proof he needed to confirm that they were meant for each other.

Their love was written in the stars – a love mandated by God himself.

Yet, now here she was, in a cafe with the jerk. She looked so bored. The man was talking her ear off, holding her captive.

Cavin wanted to do something. He'd followed them from the alley all the way to the cafe, being sure to keep a safe distance. The entire walk took every ounce of self-control he had not to attack the man from behind and rescue Marnie.

He tried to once, but the voice held him back.

"Patience, Cavin. Have some patience."

"He's forcing her to go with him! It's not right. Marnie needs saving." Her shoulders were tense as they walked – his poor, sweet Marnie.

"Do you want to ruin the plan? You have to relax. Everything will work out, trust me."

And so he did. He trusted the voice because there was nothing else to do.

Cavin thought about what would've happened had the strange man not interfered with the day. He would've run into Marnie, rectifying the horrible first meeting they had in her office.

"Marnie, hi! What a surprise, wow. You must have the day off on Saturdays," he would say.

She would smile and push her hair behind her ears. He probably made her nervous. She would be so cute nervous.

Then, he would say something like, "I'm so sorry I ran out of our meeting the other day. I forgot that I double-booked myself. Can I make it up to you and buy you a coffee?"

She would have to say yes. How could she resist his charm or the natural magnetism between them? He could hear her response in his head loud and clear. "Of course, Cavin! I was so looking forward to getting to know you more. Let's grab coffee."

Then, she would link her arm through his, and they'd walk to the cafe together. It would be him sitting with her at the big window, not that freak.

He wasn't even an attractive man. And he was trying way too hard to make Marnie like him. How pathetic. Marnie wasn't interested in guys like that. She wanted a real man, a man like Cavin. Or, at least, the man Cavin was becoming.

Cavin watched Marnie talk to the man she was with. He had to know who this guy was, what his story was. He needed to know how to break him. No one would get between Cavin and Marnie – absolutely no one.

Their words floated across the cafe, though most of them got lost in the murmur of others. Still, he leaned in and listened. He waited for the perfect opportunity to interrupt them. It wouldn't be that weird for a client to approach his therapist in a cafe, right? That was normal. They knew each other. It was polite, even, that he said hello. What if she saw him and he didn't say something? She would think he was rude.

Cavin pushed his seat back, ready to stand.

"No!" the voice in his head replied. "Sit back down and think this through. If you go over there right now, there's no telling what that guy would do. We have to go as unnoticed as possible, Cavin. It's the only way to ensure Marnie's safety."

This was ridiculous. "I should walk up to them and say something! How dare she sit there, entertaining the likes of some loser like him."

"Not. Yet," the voice growled.

A weight fell onto Cavin's shoulders like someone was preventing him from standing. "If you go over there now, as mad as you are, it'll scare Marnie. I know you love her, believe me. I do. But she's very weak and easily spooked. Her mental capacity is pathetic, and she might mistake you for the bad guy. After all, women hardly ever know what's good for them. We need to be smart about this."

The tension in Cavin's jaw eased, and he sat back, relaxed. The voice was right. Cavin had to play this smarter. He couldn't run up and start yelling and throwing stuff. Marnie was too precious; he didn't want to scare her.

"Just because you aren't getting your chance today doesn't mean you won't get your chance ever. Our time is coming. We're playing the long game, remember?"

Cavin brought his chair closer to the table. He hated it, but the voice was right. He'd been a screw-up his whole life, and the last thing he wanted to do was screw things up with Marnie.

He could wait. He *would* wait.

But in the meantime, he needed to find out more about this guy who was so interested in his queen.

Cavin leaned forward, listening, until finally, Marnie said the man's name.

Jason.

He chugged the last of his iced coffee, pulled a hat low over his eyes, and left the cafe.

Cavin drove home in a haze of anger and determination. He didn't have much to go on, only a first name. But it would be enough to find what he was looking for. The voice in his head helped a lot. It seemed to know more than it let on, only filling Cavin in when unavoidable.

Cavin rushed through the front door of his house and went straight to his laptop.

The house he lived in was the same one he grew up in. It was a simple two-bedroom, one-bathroom home at the end of a long dirt road. Mother was not rich, not in the slightest, so this was the only thing she could afford. According to Mother, his dad was a no-good drunk that didn't deserve to know him and his sister. He must have been around when Cavin was young; otherwise, they wouldn't have Stella. Cavin wasn't the smartest guy around, but he knew how babies got made. And Stella was three years younger than him, so Dad had to have been there at least three years.

Cavin sat at the dining room table and navigated to Google. He stared at the search bar, trying to think of how to find this mystery man. All he had to go off of was a first name and a description. It wasn't enough to find someone online.

Cavin had been lucky with Marnie. Her full name was on the brochure from Golden Meadow, and none of her social media pages were private.

"Search Jason Cruz," the voice said.

Cavin dutifully typed it in and hit "enter."

A slew of results popped up in seconds, and Cavin navigated through each one, looking for the right person.

"How'd you know his last name?" Cavin asked aloud.

In the comfort of his own home, it was easier to talk to the voice out loud rather than think things to it. Talking out loud made him feel less crazy.

"He's an old friend," the voice said.

Cavin's hands dropped from the laptop. "Old friend? You mean to tell me you knew that guy, and you didn't say nothin'?"

"I didn't want you to overreact. Yes, I know him. At least, I used to."

"Well, what? Did you live in his head, too? Help him win a lady?"

The voice laughed a low and gurgled sound. "Not exactly. But it's not important. Find what you need to know about him."

Cavin stood up. "No, now wait a minute. Why do I have to

search online for the guy if you know him? Why don't you tell me who he is and what he's all about?"

Jealous. It was shocking, but Cavin was actually jealous. All those ideas of him being special, the first one to have the voice living in his head, were gone. He was just another tool that the voice used to get what it wanted, wasn't he?

"Cavin, please. I knew him a long time ago and I may have said 'friend,' but we weren't actually friends. I wasn't very nice to him. All the helpful information I have I've already given to you. His name, that's all I got."

That had to be enough for now. At least the voice reassured him, he was special. He knew that – the voice knew that. Marnie would soon know.

Cavin sat and continued scrolling.

Geez, this guy was hard to find online. Cavin must've searched through hundreds of social media pages before finding something.

"Gotcha!" he said, clicking on a profile picture that looked exactly like the man in the cafe.

Jason Cruz was going to regret ever pursuing Cavin's woman.

Eleven

MARNIE ARRIVED AT WORK MONDAY MORNING, feeling like herself again. Her cheeks had started to hurt from smiling so much.

"Ms. Adams, look at you! You must've had some weekend to be smiling like that," Savannah said from behind the front desk.

Marnie covered her cheeks with open palms and smiled even wider. "Why yes, Savannah, I did have a wonderful weekend."

"I'm glad! Before you get settled in, I already have your schedule printed and ready for you." Savannah reached for a file across the counter. "Here ya go."

Marnie took the file and did an exaggerated bow. "Thank you," she said.

Savannah laughed at her ridiculous behavior. "My, my, you are in a good mood, aren't you?"

Marnie laughed and went into her office.

Her little run-in with Jason was so refreshing. The rest of the weekend was uneventful in the best way possible. After her coffee and chat with Jason, she couldn't stop thinking about him the rest of the weekend. She had never met someone so genuine. He radiated a level of peace that she only wished she could reach, though it did rub off on her a little bit.

Jason had been sweet enough to walk Marnie home after coffee. She went inside and watched him leave from the living room window. It wasn't until he disappeared from her sight that Marnie realized she'd made a grave mistake.

She didn't get his number. She wanted to see him again and hoped that he felt the same. If he did, he knew exactly where to find her.

Carley was scheduled to come in for a session. Reality crashed back into Marnie's mind. The weekend had been great, but it was time to be serious. Carley canceled on Marnie last week and seemed to be managing on her own. Hopefully, that was still the case, but she still wanted to know more about the shadow that stalked the girl.

It was wrong of her to go into a therapy session with motives different from helping the client. But Marnie was desperate. Whatever the shadow man was, he wasn't only after Carley. He was after her, too. And if talking to Carley helped clear things up, it was exactly what Marnie would do.

The first client of the day was a teenage boy whose older brother committed suicide. He was grieving the loss well at this point. Marnie was sure that in the next few sessions, she would be able to tell his parents that he didn't need to come so often anymore. At first, he blamed himself. He thought it was his constant fighting with his brother that pushed him over the edge. But through weeks and weeks of talking things out, Marnie convinced him that it wasn't his fault.

"We don't make those choices for other people. They make the choice themself. It hurts. I know it hurts like nothing you've ever experienced. But you cannot blame yourself," she'd told him.

Bit by bit, he started believing her.

It was difficult telling patients they didn't need to come as often. Marnie grew fond of her patients. Telling them they could move to less frequent visits was like signing freedom papers. They rarely came back after that. It was a good thing when a patient "graduated." It meant they were adjusting or coping with whatever troubled them. That didn't make the goodbye any easier.

After the session with the teenage boy, Carley was next. Marnie walked the boy to the door and peeked into the waiting room as he left. She could see Carley sitting there, head down. She was picking at her fingernails, blood outlining each of them.

Something's wrong.

Carley's hair was unkempt, and there were stains on her clothes. In all the time that Carley had been coming, she never once looked so disheveled. She was a clean and proper girl, popular – not the type to look anything less than her best, even after the incident.

Marnie waited at the door as Savannah called Carley's name and sent her back.

"Carley? Ms. Adams is ready for you."

Carley walked into the office and sat on the couch, head hung low. She didn't bother to greet Marnie. Didn't even look at her.

Marnie watched her for a moment, deciding what was the best course of action. She took a few deep breaths and eased herself into her chair.

"Hey, Carley. How are you?" Marnie leaned forward, placing her elbows on her knees. Carley had her full attention, and she wanted her to know that.

Carley didn't look up. She continued to stare down and pick at her fingers. Blood oozed from the skin around her right thumb. This was new territory. Marnie fought the urge to run out of the office and grab Dr. Carlson. She wasn't capable of handling this on her own. No way.

But it was her client. If she got Dr. Carlson, all that would do was tell her boss that she couldn't handle the job.

She tried again. "Carley? Are you okay?"

Carley shook her head. It was faint, but there was clear movement. "No," she managed through a strained voice.

Marnie shifted in her seat, uneasy. "What happened? You seemed to be doing great when I texted you last week. You were out with friends; wanna talk about that?"

"That's what he wanted me to think," Carley whispered.

Marnie stared. She wasn't sure what to say. What was a therapist supposed to say when their client talked like this? "He? The shadow?"

"He wanted me to think everything was okay. That… that I was normal again."

"Honey, help me understand what you're talking about. I'm lost."

Carley's eyes still stared at her hands, but her body went rigid. She was stuck, unmoving. It unnerved Marnie, sending goosebumps up her arms.

"He tricked me. I thought he was gone, but he came back. He came back worse than before." Her hands shot up, hiding her face. Carley sobbed into them, her shoulders bouncing up and down.

Marnie moved from her chair, a safe distance from the girl, onto the couch next to Carley. She put her arm around her. It wasn't proper. Therapists weren't supposed to touch their clients unless given explicit permission or request. But desperate times and all that.

"Are you talking about the shadow?" Marnie asked.

Carley's sobs cut off, still echoing in the new silence. She lifted her head out of her hands and looked at Marnie. Her eyes were bloodshot and empty. She was looking through Marnie more than at her.

"He's here," she whispered.

A tremble took over Carley's body. It started in her arms, forcing Marnie to release her hold on the girl's shoulder. Then, it moved through her entire body. The tremble morphed into a violent shake, and Carley fell to the floor between the couch and the coffee table.

"Carley!" Marnie dropped to the ground.

She'd seen people having seizures before and knew what to do. But her brain had melted at Carley's final words. The steps to caring for someone in the middle of a seizure refused to come to Marnie.

"Think, Marnie, think!"

Carley laid on her back, convulsing. Her eyelids stayed open, but her eyeballs turned, the whites shining forward. Marnie hovered over the girl, tapping her cheek with an open palm.

"Come on, Carley, wake up. Please wake up."

On their side... when someone has a seizure, they have to lay on their side. Marnie grabbed Carley's shoulders and coaxed her onto her side. A white foam formed at Carley's parted lips and fell out, dripping down her chin.

"Help!" Marnie called. "Please, someone call 911!"

Savannah crashed through the door. She froze at the entrance and covered her open mouth with both hands. "Oh my!" She turned and ran back to the front desk.

It took five minutes for the paramedics to arrive, by which point Carley's shaking had tamed. A slight tremor ran the length of her body. She remained unresponsive as two paramedics in blue polos hoisted her onto a gurney. Marnie followed them out, holding onto the guardrail.

"Cancel the rest of my appointments," she said to Savannah as they passed through the waiting room. There was no way she was going to send Carley to the hospital alone. Someone needed to be there when her parents arrived, and Marnie wanted it to be her.

Marnie called Mr. and Mrs. Rey from the ambulance. Mrs. Rey was beside herself, unable to speak between sobs. Marnie gave them the name of the hospital and every bit of information she could remember. The only thing she hadn't told them was Carley's statement before the accident. What did she mean by "he's here"?

Carley's tremors finally stopped halfway to the hospital, but she remained asleep. She looked so young on the gurney, with a blanket pulled up to her neck and a breathing mask over her nose and mouth. So innocent, so small. She didn't deserve to go through this. Carley was an excellent student and a perfect kid. She loved her parents and respected them. She got good grades and played on the varsity volleyball team. By all accounts, she was on the path to success.

Until a drunk driving accident claimed the lives of her best friends, leaving her to deal with the damage alone. She tried to move on, tried to process everything. And just when she started getting better, the nightmares and the hallucinations began. That was when she started seeing Marnie. And Marnie loved her. She saw herself in Carley and saw who she wanted to be as a teenager. And saw who she actually was in the post-accident Carley. Marnie wanted nothing more than to help her.

This was not how she thought helping her would look.

Marnie walked into the waiting room, where Carley's parents paced and greeted them.

"They took her back and are running tests. I'm so sorry this happened," Marnie said, hugging Mrs. Rey.

The woman sobbed into her shoulder while Carley's dad continued to pace, staring at the ground. He chewed on a fingernail.

"Mr. Rey, why don't you have a seat?"

He ignored her. Carley's mom let go of Marnie and went to her husband, hugging him around the waist.

"John?" she said. "Let's take a seat, huh? They'll come get us when Carley's ready."

He looked at his wife, his tear-soaked eyes meeting hers, and shook his head. "Our baby... what's gonna happen to our baby?" He broke down.

Marnie watched the heartbreaking scene unfold from her spot in the waiting room. It hurt to see them like this, so she turned away and scanned the room. An old TV was mounted in the corner, playing rerun episodes of *Friends*. There were a few other people in the waiting room. They all sat scattered across the room, giving each other some semblance of privacy. Marnie overheard a gray-haired man on the phone. His daughter had fainted during a ballet performance. Two women wearing far too much makeup sat at the other end, one with her arm around the other. From what Marnie gathered, one of their husbands had a heart attack during a benefit dinner. Each person was so wrapped up in their own sorrows they didn't care about the people surrounding them.

Carley had seemed so distressed. It was like she was teetering on the edge of an unseen abyss when something finally tipped her over. Marnie debated asking Carley's parents about the "he" she kept mentioning today. Would they know anything? Would it even be worth bringing up?

The last thing she wanted to do was add to their distress, so she held her tongue. She would ask Carley if she ever got the chance.

After an hour, a doctor in light blue scrubs spoke with Carley's parents. Marnie wanted to stand, to listen to what he had to say, but it wasn't her place. She stayed seated, waiting for them to invite her into the conversation.

It never happened. Instead, Carley's parents rushed out of the room, following the doctor.

Marnie stopped a nurse walking by. "Excuse me, hi. Could I get an update on Carley Rey?"

"Are you family?" the nurse asked.

"No, I'm her therapist."

The nurse shook her head apologetically. "I'm sorry, I can only give that information to family."

Marnie sat back down, defeated. She wanted to know if Carley was okay – wanted to know what happened. But most of all, she wanted to confirm if the *"he"* was who Marnie thought it was.

Twelve

THE TV DRONED IN THE BACKGROUND while Marnie stared off at nothing in particular. The father of the ballerina left an hour earlier, followed shortly after by the two women.

Marnie was the last one left in the waiting room, and it sucked. She wanted to see Carley and wanted some news, but no one would tell her anything.

As the sound from the television faded, the lights across the entire hospital flickered. A faint laugh floated from down the hall and snapped Marnie out of her stupor. She looked toward the sound, expecting to see a patient wheeling through the hall.

There was no one, nothing.

The laugh died out. In its place, something growled.

The lights dimmed further still. Marnie held her breath, and the voice called out, "Marnie…"

She rose from her seat. Curiosity gnawed at her mind. Could it be Carley calling for her? She walked to the nurses' station only to find it vacant. Marnie followed the voice down the hall. Each room she passed had its door open, revealing disheveled beds void of bodies. Her mind couldn't make the connection that the once bustling hospital now lay empty. Where flashes of warning bells should have been going off, there was silence.

But it was more than silence. There was a deep yearning, a call pushing her deeper into the darkness. It invited her in, offered answers to all her questions. The voice was hypnotic. It spoke her name, beckoning.

Marnie pressed further through the black hallway, her eyes adjusting to the darkness. "Hello?" she called.

The only response was an echo of her voice, throwing the hello back at her. A faint whisper at the back of her mind urged her to stop. Go back to the waiting room. She was acting like one of those girls in a horror movie. It was this exact moment when the crowd would be screaming, "Don't go in there!" at the screen. Still, she pushed on. This was real life, not a movie. There had to be a logical explanation for the dimmed lights and the person calling her. All Marnie needed to do was find the source to prove it.

A tinge of fear made her stomach ache, but she ignored it. She had to know who was calling her, if it was Carley or not. She had to know she wasn't hearing things again.

The hallway ended in a plain white door with a golden plaque bolted in the middle. Marnie reached up and ran her fingers along the metal plaque.

"Marnie Adams," it read.

A chill ran down her spine. She checked behind to see if the hospital was still there or if she was at work. Something wasn't right. A deep, dark silence lay beyond her gaze.

Marnie placed a hesitant hand on the door knob. The metal was cold, making her shiver. She pressed down until there was a clear *click*, then she pushed.

It was a dark room, with little streams of light from street lamps cutting through slits of closed blinds. In the darkness, the room felt abandoned. Shut off from the world, it was a place no one had seemed to visit in a long time. Flecks of dust floated in the light. Marnie felt the wall for a switch. She swatted around until a flick provided bright fluorescent light, driving the darkness back into the corners. Marnie squinted, shielding her eyes with one hand while the other held still on the light switch.

As her eyes adjusted to the abrupt change of light, pieces of the room came into view. It was not abandoned after all. No, in fact, Marnie knew this room well.

It was her office at Golden Meadow.

The bookshelves on the wall, her wooden desk sitting in front of it. The couch where Carley had her seizure hours before sat under the window. The walls were a soft beige that encouraged peace and tranquility.

How was she here?

She looked around, trying to find any sign that this was a dream. Marnie heard somewhere that it was impossible to read in a dream. She went to her desk and scanned the top for something, anything, to read. Her eyes landed on a file sitting behind her schedule.

Every single word was clear. She could read just fine and understand everything written on the page.

It wasn't a dream.

Her mouth felt like it was full of cotton. Her heavy breathing was the only sound in the room. Marnie stared down at Carley's file, reading her notes.

Nightmares, hallucinations, trouble sleeping. Why did it all sound so familiar? Why was Marnie suddenly living in the same mental state as Carley?

A sudden bang startled Marnie, making her knock a cup full of pens to the ground. She looked toward the door, holding her breath.

He's here.

Marnie could feel his presence but couldn't see him. Darkness shrouded the corners of the office; anyone could be hiding there.

She rounded the desk and bolted for the door. Marnie didn't want to stick around and find out if he was actually there.

Marnie pushed down on the door handle, but it refused to budge. She wrapped her shaking fingers around it and jiggled, but still nothing. Marnie pounded her fist against the door. This was a hospital – someone had to be close by.

"Hello? Somebody!" she cried. "Please, help me!" More banging against the door.

"No one can hear you."

Marnie's fist froze in the air mid-bang. It was too late. He was here, and he made himself known.

She dropped her fists to her side and turned around. Standing there behind her desk was a dark figure the shape of a man, but not quite right. Something like smoke outlined his figure as if he weren't solid flesh and bone—the shadow of a man.

"I've been waiting for you, Marnie. You've been ignoring me, and it's very hurtful."

What was she supposed to say to that? She recognized the voice. It was the same one that had been laughing and whispering her name in the background of her mind. It was the voice that never quieted. And she had been ignoring it. She'd filled her days with constant noise, trying to drown it out. But here he stood before her, the owner of the voice. It wasn't as easy to drown him out anymore.

More than his voice was familiar, his form was too. She couldn't quite place her finger on where she'd seen this shadow, this wannabe man. Marnie reached through the deep crevices in her mind until she found it, the memory.

The dream.

He was the man from the nightmare, the one where she was in the park. He had chased her, grabbed her, and disappeared when she woke up.

Marnie spun back to the door and tried the handle again, desperate to get out. She contemplated thrusting her entire body into the door but knew she wasn't strong enough to bust it down. Tears were slipping down her cheeks, leaving stains and blurring her vision.

It's just another dream. It's just another dream.

But was that true? Was it another dream? Everything that her senses processed told her otherwise. The cold steel handle on the door, the musty smell of an abandoned room, the unnatural heat that made her sweat. The five senses didn't usually work in dreams, only in real life.

"You are… so beautiful, Marnie," he whispered. "I'm going to enjoy destroying you."

His breath tickled the nape of her neck, and she shuddered.

How had he gotten from the desk to her without making a single sound?

His hand grazed her hair. She could feel strands lifting and tangling into his grip. A whimper escaped her lips as Marnie pressed her lips together. She had to keep it together, keep it all in. She couldn't show weakness. That would make it worse.

His hand moved onto her shoulder, down her arm, and Marnie closed her eyes. Her muscles tensed. She couldn't hold back anymore. Sobs shook her body.

His hand moved back up her arm, through her hair, and to

the top of her head. The sobs morphed into wails. She was incapable of holding back the terror that overtook her entire body. The screams shoving their way through her mouth made her throat burn. They bounced off the walls, making her ears ring. Marnie pinched her eyelids closed, pushing images of the shadow and evil things from her mind. It didn't work; they persisted. Fear had taken the reins and ran her mind. There was no letting go. It stuck to her like a second layer of skin.

Hands wrapped around Marnie's shoulders and rattled her.

There was another voice, a faint whisper under the screams. She could almost make out the words. It sounded urgent.

"–kay? Can you hear me?"

Everything went quiet.

Marnie's head ached, and her throat burned. She was so thirsty. She tried to swallow the little amount of spit resting in her mouth, but it refused to go down. Bright lights made the inside of her eyelids burn bright red.

Where was she? What happened?

She blinked her eyes open and attempted a look around. The headache forced her to close her eyes again and wait. She took a few deep breaths, building up the courage to try again.

Once she felt capable of handling the drumming on her temples, Marnie squinted, letting details filter in one at a time. Stark-white walls bounced more light than necessary into her face; it was far too bright to be her bedroom. She looked down at the bed she was in. The blanket was scratchy, and her arm poked out the side with tubes protruding from it. An IV. She was in the hospital.

With this new information, she looked around more. Across from her bed hung a whiteboard that said "Nurse on duty: Cathy" with a smiley face next to it. Under nurse Cathy was some sort of chart. According to it and the clock hanging next to it, Marnie was last checked on fifteen minutes earlier.

Marnie tried to remember why she was in the hospital, but a searing headache blocked the memories from coming. She opened her mouth to call out, but the words stuck to her sore throat.

This was all wrong. There had to be some mistake. Last she recalled, she was at work. Carley was her next client and...

Carley. The memories broke through like a dam bursting. Carley's seizure in her office, the ride to the hospital, the who-knows-how-long in the waiting room.

The shadow.

Marnie slid her IV-free hand across the bedsheets.

There has to be a call button somewhere.

Her hand bumped into a remote control. *Bingo.*

She pressed the call button and heard a "ding" from the hallway. Less than a minute later, a thin nurse in pink scrubs opened the door. Her blonde hair sat in a messy bun at the very top of her head. Her brown thick-framed glasses swung on the string around her neck. She was young and beautiful and way too happy to be a nurse.

"Oh! You're awake," she said, grabbing the clipboard at the foot of Marnie's bed.

Marnie winced at the nurse's high-pitched voice. The headache was unforgiving.

"How are you doing? You gave us quite the scare there," the nurse said, scanning the charts and checking boxes.

"What happened?" Marnie rubbed her head with her free hand.

The nurse replaced the clipboard and moved around to Marnie's IV stand, checking the drip now. There must be a specific list of things nurses have to check when they enter a room. Marnie waited for the nurse to stop moving before she asked any more questions; following her around was making Marnie dizzy.

The nurse moved to the bedside monitor to click through various settings. She finished fidgeting with the tech and turned her full attention to Marnie. "We found you in a janitor's closet on the second floor screaming bloody murder. A nurse tried to snap you out of it, but you wouldn't budge." She set a comforting hand on Marnie's shoulder. "That, my dear, is what we call a panic attack. A pretty intense one, I might add."

Marnie rubbed her eyes. That was not what she experienced.

The nurse continued, "After about three minutes of screaming, you started hyperventilating. We brought you into a room and gave you some sedatives."

"I don't remember any of that," Marnie whispered. She pushed against the headache, trying to find the reality of what she experienced.

It had been a dream, at least on some level. But it felt so real.

His touch on her arms, his hands through her hair. How could it not have happened?

She couldn't hold back the tears from falling. Marnie tried to hide them from the nurse, but it was hard to hide something like that stuck in a hospital bed.

"Oh, honey!" The nurse bent over the bed railing and wrapped her arms around Marnie.

Marnie reciprocated the hug, clinging to the nurse's warm body. Warmth. She had been so cold, even though the air had felt so hot. How was any of this happening to her? Was she going insane? Her mind felt fractured. She was losing herself, and she had no idea how to stop it. Heck, she couldn't even pinpoint when or where it started.

The nurse started to loosen her grip, and Marnie clawed at her arms, pleading for the nurse to keep holding on. Marnie felt so alone, so lost. It was as if letting go of the nurse would be like letting go of her final thread on reality. She wasn't ready to lose everything.

"Sweetie, I'm gonna get you some more medicine, okay?" The nurse pried Marnie's hands off her.

Marnie watched the nurse inject something into the IV, and a cold liquid flowed through her veins. She laid her head back on the soft pillow. It felt like a cloud, so airy. She worried her head would fall straight through, but she had no strength to lift it up. Her eyes grew heavy, and the world blurred beyond them. She was dizzy, spinning and spinning, until finally, she fell into a deep sleep.

Thirteen

CAVIN WAS WAITING IN THE ALLEY FOR MARNIE to walk by, tapping his foot to no rhythm in particular. It had been hours, and no sign of her. He checked his phone for the hundredth time. 11:00 pm.

Marnie was late, extremely late. Something Cavin loved about Marnie was how punctual she was until tonight. Had she passed by, and he missed it?

No, that was impossible. Marnie lit up every place she walked into. There was no way he would miss her.

So then, what? Did she take another route home?

Cavin stood. He couldn't sit here, idle, when Marnie was missing. He walked the perimeter of her apartment complex, checking all the different routes leading to Marnie's apartment. There were four, to be exact. She could've sneaked past him.

No, that was still impossible. He had a clear view of her front door from his perch behind the dumpster. He would've seen her there at the door, would've even heard it close, had she gone inside.
She was missing. Something was wrong. Images of Marnie lying unconscious in a ditch or strung up on a tree flashed through Cavin's mind. No one would be able to help her the way he could. He had to do something, but what?

Think, think, th-

"She's not coming home tonight," the voice said.

"What do you mean?" Cavin started pacing. His poor baby, where was she?

"She's having a little sleepover. Don't worry, she's fine."

"Where is she? I'll go to her!" Cavin started like he was going to his car.

"Wait a minute, let's think about this. You have a once-in-a-lifetime opportunity in front of you."

"I do?" Cavin paused.

"Marnie isn't coming home… Come on, Cav, don't you know what that means?"

"It means I won't get to see her tonight," Cavin replied, head hung low.

"Sure." He sounded annoyed. "But it also means that her apartment is empty."

"Empty…" Cavin repeated.

Empty! Now was his chance. He could learn more about his sweet, sweet Marnie.

"Now you've got it," the voice said.

A wide grin planted itself across Cavin's lips. He pulled his hoodie over his head and meandered up the stairs to Marnie's front door. He took a cursory glance around the complex. No one was out. All the windows pointing to Marnie's apartment were dark. If someone was watching, he couldn't see them. The porch light was off, and Cavin wore all black, as he did every time he went to watch Marnie. On the off chance that someone was watching, they wouldn't be able to see him in the dark.

Cavin had experience getting into homes that didn't want him. He rarely needed a key. In fact, this wasn't the first girlfriend's house he'd broken into. His high school girlfriend, Melinda, had gotten mad at him one day and said she didn't want to see him. Of course, she hadn't meant it. Cavin was good at reading the subtext of a woman's words. So, he let himself in through her front door, slipped past her parents' bedroom, and crawled into bed with her. The chick ended up slapping him with a restraining order, claiming she had told him to stay away.

Women.

Cavin was glad Marnie wasn't like that. She loved him, understood him. She would never say one thing and mean another.

Cavin pulled out the bump key he'd carried around since that fateful night with Melinda and gave it a little kiss. His ticket to Marnie's private home. If God didn't want him in her home, why had he given Cavin the knowledge to enter? This was part of his God-given right as Marnie's betrothed.

He slid the key into the deadbolt. Crouching down so that his ear could be close, Cavin listened for the "click" of the rear pin. He inched the key to the left, shoved the palm of his hand into it, and boom.

He was in.

The deadbolt released. Cavin pushed down on the door handle. The front door swung open, and he rushed in so no one would see him lingering. He closed the door, locking it in place once again.

Cavin flicked the living room light switch, illuminating the home. It was beautiful. It was so Marnie. He could see every bit of her personality put on display. There were books and stacks of papers stapled together sitting on the coffee table. Upon closer inspection, Cavin realized they were psychology journals and thriller novels. The room smelt of the lavender candle resting on the kitchen island. From where he stood in the living room, Cavin could take in the majority of the apartment. The large windows stood to his right, while the couch and coffee table were to the left. A TV sat in front of the window, facing the couch.

Cavin moved to the couch, running his fingers along its smooth surface. He imagined Marnie falling asleep watching TV, her head resting on her hand, so peaceful. He would cover her with a blanket and plant a gentle kiss on her forehead.

His body shook with anticipation for the day that became a reality.

Next, he moved to the kitchen. A little island with metal bar stools separated the living room from the kitchen. He rounded the island and opened the refrigerator.

"Marnie, Marnie, Marnie... You are not taking good enough care of yourself," he said aloud.

The fridge was bare. A carton of milk, expired coffee creamer, and some bruised apples were all he could find. When he opened the freezer above, it was completely empty.

That would all change once they got married. Cavin would

make sure Marnie was eating right. He decided a goodie basket of food instead of flowers would be the next gift he left for her.

When he closed the freezer, he noticed a whiteboard stuck to the front.

"Call Hannah back," it read.

He grabbed the dry-erase marker latched to the top, took off the cap, and wrote his own little note on the whiteboard. Marnie would be happy to see it, he was sure. He replaced the marker and made his way into her bedroom.

He pulled out his phone and snapped pictures of everything, from the wooden dresser sitting against the wall to the nightstand on either side of the bed. He paused at the bed – taking special note of the fluffed gray pillows and pristine maroon bedspread. Marnie was the type of girl who made her bed every morning, a reason to love her even more. He crawled onto her bed, shoving his face into the pillows and inhaling deeply. The sweet coconut scent of her shampoo filled his nostrils. The shock sent waves of pleasure through his body. It was intoxicating, a kind of drunkenness Cavin welcomed openly.

A knock at the front door made Cavin jolt. He turned off the bedroom light and dropped to the floor.

"Marnie?" Knock, knock, knock. "Come on, Mar. I saw your light on. Let me in!"

It was the blonde. Cavin recognized her voice. What was she doing here so late at night? How inappropriate showing up at someone's house at this hour. Cavin would need to do something about her for sure.

"Marnie… you haven't called me back in days. You've ignored my texts. I'm worried about you; please let me in."

She was relentless. Cavin pulled the pocket knife from his pocket and slipped under the bed. He didn't want to hurt her, not yet anyway. But he would do whatever was necessary to stay hidden.

She banged on the door a few more times. "Fine, don't let me in. At least call me back! I'll try again tomorrow."

Cavin waited a few minutes, his breath shallow. Once the coast was clear, he crawled out from under the bed. Sweat rolled down his forehead in beads. He couldn't be here anymore. He had to go. He got what he needed, and now he was being overindulgent.

He turned all the lights out and left the apartment, using the bump key to lock the door again. He hadn't been able to see Marnie, but it was still a successful night.

Cavin smiled all the way back to his car. Tomorrow was a new day. He would get to see Marnie then.

Fourteen

MARNIE WOKE TO SUNLIGHT BEAMING through the sheer curtains and a nurse fiddling with her IV. Her headache was gone, thank God, and she started to feel like herself again.

"Good morning, sleepy head." Nurse Cathy was back on duty.

"How long have I been asleep?" Marnie asked, voice groggy.

"About twelve hours. You zonked out."

Marnie sat up in the hospital bed and stretched as best she could with the IV. It had to be late Tuesday, at least.

Late Tuesday.

She missed work! Dr. Carlson had no idea where she was. She was screwed.

Marnie searched the bed, trying to find her phone. She wiggled around the bed rails to open the drawers of the nightstand, but the only thing there was a Bible. Marnie rolled her eyes and closed the drawer. Why were Bibles always found in hospitals and hotel rooms?

"Cathy, where's my phone?"

"Oh!" Nurse Cathy went to a table by the bathroom. On it was a bag that held Marnie's clothes, shoes, and personal effects. The nurse grabbed the phone and brought it to Marnie.

She clicked the lock button on the side, but the screen remained black.

Dead.

She looked up at the nurse, who was about to leave the room. "Uh, do you have a phone charger by any chance?"

"Lemme check for ya," Nurse Cathy said, leaving the room.

Marnie stared at the wall, drumming on her legs. The last thing she wanted to do was disappoint Dr. Carlson. It was unprofessional of her not to reach out and let her boss know she wouldn't be coming to work. Marnie feared the worst, that she would call Dr. Carlson and get fired on the spot.

She closed her eyes, forcing the thought away. That wouldn't happen, right? This was a medical emergency. She had no choice; they had fastened her to the bed with an IV drip.

Nurse Cathy came back into the room. "Here ya are." She handed a black cord to Marnie, who plugged it into the outlet above her bed without hesitation.

"Come on, come on, come on," she pleaded with her phone.

The screen lit up, the empty battery filling with green. Marnie pressed the power button and watched as it came to life.

The flood of notifications made one long vibration in her hand. Messages from Hannah, Savannah, and Dr. Carlson took turns flashing across the screen. They came in rapid succession, and she couldn't open any of them. Marnie's heart raced. Surely she was being canned. If not fired, then in trouble, suspended even.

She tapped the screen impatiently and pushed past the messages from Hannah and Savannah. She still hadn't called Hannah back. That was a problem she would deal with later.

She read the messages from Dr. Carlson and sighed in relief. She wasn't fired, wasn't even put on probation or suspension. According to the messages, Savannah had followed up with the hospital about Carley and found out about Marnie's accident. She passed the information on to Dr. Carlson, who canceled Marnie's sessions. Dr. Carlson was giving Marnie until Thursday off to recover.

Marnie wrote out a quick reply to Dr. Carlson and put all her anxieties away. It was time to face Hannah. She was, without a doubt, furious with Marnie. It would take a lot of apologizing to fix this one. Hannah had called her days ago, and Marnie hadn't responded. Life was too crazy.

She hit the call button and held the phone to her ear, listening to it ring and ring.

"You're alive!" Hannah said, answering the call.

"Hey, Hannah. I'm so sorry I haven't gotten back to you."

"You're sorry? I've been worried sick about you, Mar. I even went to your house last night! Didn't you hear me knocking?"

Crap. Now she had to tell her best friend that she was in the hospital. Hannah would freak even more than she already was. Sometimes she was way too protective for her own good. *Way to go, Marnie.*

"I wasn't home last night," Marnie said, voice shrinking. "I'm kinda in the hospital."

"What? What happened? Are you okay? What hospital? I'll come right now."

"Whoa, slow down. I'm fine. They say I had a very intense panic attack, and passed out. I feel better now; you don't need to come."

"Marnie, are you serious? What is going on with you?"

That was the question, wasn't it? What was going on with her? If only she had the answer. Everything felt so twisted up in her brain; nothing was right. She couldn't even pinpoint where it all began. All she knew was that something was wrong. Be it a chemical misfiring in her mind or someone actually messing with her. She wanted answers more than Hannah did.

"I don't know. Things have been stressful lately." Over the phone was not the way to tell Hannah what she'd experienced. "I think I should be getting out tomorrow morning. They wanna run a blood test and won't get the results til then. Can we meet then? I don't need to be back at work until Thursday."

"Sure, Wednesdays are half-days for my kiddos, so I'll be off around 11 am. I'll call you to find out when you're released. Answer your phone this time!"

"I will, don't worry."

"I love ya, bye." Hannah hung up.

In the chaos, Marnie had completely forgotten about Carley. She wasn't even sure if she was still in the hospital or if the doctors were able to find out what happened to her. She needed to know that Carley was okay.

Marnie pressed the call button on her remote, and a nurse popped in.

"Can I go for a little walk? I'm feeling really cooped up," Marnie said.

"Sure, hon," the nurse replied, untangling Marnie's IV tubes.

The nurse helped Marnie up and hung her IV bag onto an intravenous pole. Marnie stepped into the hallway, pushing the pole with one hand and holding her hospital gown with the other. She wore those scratchy socks with slip-resistant pads on the bottom that all hospitals gave their patients. The one good thing about getting admitted to a hospital was that they always let her keep the socks.

Marnie approached the nurses' station in the middle of the hall, right in front of the elevators. A beautiful young nurse with braided hair was typing away at a keyboard.

"Excuse me," Marnie said.

The nurse didn't look up. She continued typing. Marnie cleared her throat, now second-guessing if she had actually spoken or not.

"Excuse me," she said again.

The nurse paused her typing and drew her eyes slowly up to Marnie. "Yes?"

"Can you tell me if a patient is still here? Her name is Carley Rey."

The nurse looked Marnie up and down and raised one eyebrow. Marnie shifted, pushing her shoulders back and standing taller. She wasn't going to let this woman look down on her because she was a patient.

"I'm sorry, sweetie. I can't give out that kind of information." She resumed her typing.

Marnie leaned over the counter. "No. I know how this looks, but I'm not some random person. I'm Ms. Rey's therapist." Marnie let out a little laugh, trying to seem calm. "I was here waiting for her when I ended up getting admitted myself. It's kinda a funny story."

"Uh-huh, I'm sure it is." Her fingers still clacking at the keys. "The only way I can give you that information is if you can provide your credentials."

Marnie leaned back. "I can do that. I'll be right back."

She shuffled back to her room and fished through the plastic bag for her wallet. She carried her ID badge everywhere she went for this precise reason. She went back to the nurse station and held up her badge, smiling.

The nurse looked at it, huffed, and typed at her computer again. "Carley Rey, room 406."

"Thank you," Marnie said, dipping her head.

There was a large silver '3' hanging between the two elevators. Marnie pressed the "up" arrow and waited. She glanced back at the rude nurse, and when she saw that she wasn't looking, Marnie lifted her middle finger. It was childish, but she was in the hospital after a bad panic attack. She had permission to be a little childish right now.

On the fourth floor, Marnie turned down the left hall. She followed the number plates screwed in next to each room door until she found 406. The door was only opened a crack, and all the lights inside were off.

Marnie tapped the door with a single knuckle. "Carley? You awake? It's me, Marnie." She pushed the door open and crept in.

It was a shared room with two beds separated by a single sheet hanging from the ceiling. The first bed was empty and made, ready for the next patient. Marnie peeked around the sheet to see Carley, her eyes closed. She looked so peaceful, so innocent. It was hard to believe that this precious girl was experiencing so much torment in her mind. It wasn't fair.

Marnie pulled a chair next to Carley's bed and sat. Carley's hand poked out from the covers, and Marnie grabbed it, squeezing once. She felt so much responsibility for Carley like it was her job to fix her. And if she couldn't fix her, Marnie wanted to comfort her. It was the least she could do.

Marnie fell asleep with her head resting on Carley's bed. She woke to Carley stirring.

"Ms. Adams?" Carley said, her voice raspy.

Marnie lifted her head. "Carley, hey. How are you doing?" she asked, rubbing the sleep from her eyes.

Carley scanned Marnie, her forehead scrunching in concern. "You're wearing a hospital gown. What happened?"

"Oh, I…" Marnie searched for the words. How much was too much when sharing private information with a client? "I had some kind of panic attack and passed out. I'm okay. How are you?"

"I was right then." Carley turned to look out the window, tears welling in her eyes. "He was there, and he got you."

Marnie searched Carley's eyes for meaning but couldn't find it. She wished that she didn't understand the girl, that she didn't know what she was talking about. But that wasn't true. She knew exactly what Carley was talking about. And Carley was right. The shadow had gotten her, had burrowed himself deep into her mind. Even at that moment, Marnie could hear him just below the surface. He was calling to her, and he was laughing.

Marnie shook her head. "I thought you were feeling better?"

"I thought so, too," Carley said. "But it was a trick. It's like he wanted me to drop my defenses or something. I was too guarded. He needed me weaker." She paused, cycling through a few deep breaths. "I think it'll all be over soon."

Marnie wasn't sure what to say, so she sat silent. She squeezed Carley's hand, offering the little support she could.

"They say I had a grand mal seizure. And they think it's because of my lack of sleep. I can't sleep. He's there, in my dreams. I'm too scared."

"Carley…" Marnie's voice trailed.

Carley sat up and turned her whole body to face Marnie. She grabbed both of Marnie's hands, holding them firmly in her own. "You have to fight it, Ms. Adams. Don't let him get to you. Fight it as long and as hard as you can. And if you believe in it, I think you should pray."

Marnie nodded along. She wasn't in a position to argue with Carley, not after everything they'd both experienced. But a question started taking shape in her chest. The look in Carley's eyes, her lack of sleep, and now the seizure – all signs were pointing to a psychotic break. Carley was making it sound spiritual in some way, but there had to be a logical explanation.

Marnie broke a hand free from Carley's grip and caressed her hair. Carley leaned back onto the pillow. "They're only dreams, Carley. You're still processing the accident, and it's manifesting in nightmares. You'll be okay, I promise." She hoped the girl believed it, even if she didn't.

There was something more to what Carley was experiencing; it was obvious.

And it scared her.

Marnie was powerless to save her, powerless to save herself. She was losing confidence in her mind and her abilities as a therapist. Something had to be done about all this.

She stroked Carley's head, watching as Carley's eyes drooped, then closed. She fell asleep again. Good, Marnie had done something right. She was feeling tired herself, so she left. Carley couldn't give her the answers she hoped for. She would have to find those on her own.

Fifteen

MARNIE LEFT THE HOSPITAL WEDNESDAY AFTERNOON. She walked out the front door to find Hannah's silver Honda Civic parked along the curb. Hannah stepped out and waved before going around and opening the passenger door.

"I can open my own door," Marnie said, approaching the car.

"Hey, you literally just got out of the hospital. Would you let me try to spoil you?"

Marnie rolled her eyes as she slid in. Hannah shut the door and went back to the driver's side. Marnie closed her eyes, taking a deep breath in and pushing it out. Everything was going to be okay. She would make sure of it.

"You okay? Your head hurt? Do I need to carry you back in?" Hannah said.

Marnie opened her eyes and smiled. "I'm fine. Happy to get some fresh air."

Hannah rolled down the windows, and Marnie appreciated the little gesture.

They grabbed drive-thru cheeseburgers and ate them in the parking lot. Marnie was feeling fine, but she didn't want to be around too many people. If she was honest, she was a little embarrassed about what put her in the hospital. A therapist having such a bad panic attack that a doctor had to sedate her wasn't something to be proud of. Hannah had been kind enough to keep the questions surface-level, even though Marnie knew she was dying to know the details.

She loved Hannah. They were best friends. But sometimes, Marnie hated telling her things. She'd met Hannah at church; only Marnie grew out of all that, and Hannah didn't. She still attended church every Sunday, still read her Bible, and still reminded Marnie that God loved her. She didn't push. She wouldn't, knowing everything Marnie had gone through. But if the opportunity presented itself, Hannah would mention God. She was the only one from Marnie's childhood church that still talked to any of the Adams. Marnie's parents were outcasts, her mom a harlot. But Hannah never held that against her. She stayed in touch with Marnie even after Marnie left home. They both moved to Missouri. Hannah went to a Christian university, taking theology classes alongside her early education. Marnie attended Missouri State for psychology. Through thick and thin, they'd been together. Though, through the years, Marnie learned what not to tell Hannah to avoid her preaching. They managed to have an excellent friendship: the Jesus freak and the jaded atheist.

All the weird hallucinations and voices were sure to send Hannah into Bible mode if Marnie mentioned them. She would find a way to make it spiritual, and that was the last thing Marnie needed. She had enough on her plate; she didn't need spirituality shoved down her throat.

Hannah pulled up to Marnie's apartment. "Want me to come in with you?" she asked.

"Nah, I'm good."

Marnie unbuckled her seatbelt and opened the door, but before she could step out, Hannah grabbed her arm. "Mar, you know I'm here for you, right? If you wanna talk about what happened."

Marnie gave her a reassuring smile. "I know, thank you. I just need some time."

Hannah nodded and released her arm. "Get some rest."

Marnie unlocked the front door. It was nice to be home, even if home hadn't felt all that safe as of late. There was something about being around her stuff that made Marnie comfortable, despite the nightmares. Marnie walked through her front door and flicked on the light. Something was wrong. The smell of rotting eggs permeated the entire living room. Her apartment had never smelt like this before. She moved into the kitchen, looking for the source. She hadn't meant to be away from home for so long; maybe there was rotting food left out. Her eyes scanned the room, but there was nothing out of place, nothing that she could see.

Then, she landed on the whiteboard attached to the fridge. She squinted to read the juvenile-esque handwriting scrawled across it. "When everything is ready, I'll come get you. Then we'll be together forever." The letters were shaky and sloping down. Someone had been in her home and had left a note. Her breathing hitched to keep up with the spike in her adrenaline.

She ran out the front door to catch Hannah before she left. Down the flight of metal and concrete stairs, she waved her arms for Hannah to stop.

Hannah rolled down the window. "What's wrong?"

Panic made Marnie's eyes bulge and her head spin. Why did this have to happen now? Didn't she deserve a break?

"Someone was in my apartment," she said. "Can you call the cops?"

Sixteen

HANNAH WAITED WITH MARNIE FOR THE COPS TO ARRIVE. They sat on the stairs in front of her apartment. She was too afraid to go back in. What if the person was still there, waiting for her? She hadn't gone into the bedroom, hadn't opened any of the closets. There was a chance they were there.

Marnie held Hannah's hand to prevent her own from shaking. It felt like it had been hours since Hannah called the police, yet they still hadn't shown up.

Her leg jiggled up and down, shaking the staircase. Hannah placed her free hand on Marnie's knee to relax her. It didn't help.

"Where are they?" Marnie asked, checking her phone for the time.

"They said they'd be here; relax."

"I can't relax! Someone broke into my house!"

"You don't know that for sure," Hannah whispered.

Marnie dropped her hand and stood. This was insane; her own best friend didn't even believe her. Twenty minutes earlier, Hannah said that she was there for Marnie, but now here she was, not believing her.

"Are you serious?" Marnie said, looking down on Hannah.

Hannah stood. "Come on, Marnie. You've been through a lot, like, mentally the last few days. Don't you think there's a chance you're overreaching?"

Marnie stared. She had to be going crazy because there was no way she heard that right. "What are you trying to say, Hannah? That I'm making this up?"

"I didn't say that," Hannah replied, reaching for Marnie.

Marnie took a step back and glared. "You did. You said that because of my mental state, I'm overreaching."

"I said there's a chance. Not that it's true. I mean, really, what evidence is there?" Hannah sighed. "I just think you might be blowing this out of proportion. Why would anyone break into your house?"

She couldn't stand here and listen to this. Someone had broken into her apartment, her home, and her best friend was saying it wasn't real. What happened to the supportive and loving friend that picked her up from the hospital twenty minutes ago? Marnie was seething. She couldn't look at Hannah for another moment. Marnie turned and stomped back up the stairs to the apartment. She'd take her chances with an intruder over a backstabber; whatever they had planned would probably hurt less.

Hannah followed. "Marnie, please."

"Let's just wait and see what the cops have to say," Marnie said, refusing to look at Hannah. She let the silence engulf them until she saw the flashing lights. Marnie pushed past Hannah without another word and trotted down the stairs. There were two officers dressed in their blue uniforms, stepping out of the squad car.

"Are you the one who called about the break-in?" the taller one asked.

"My friend called, but it's my apartment. This way." Marnie led them up the stairs and into the apartment.

The older, chubbier of the two cops looked around. He inspected the door, bending down to get a good look at the handle before jiggling it. "It doesn't look like there are any signs of a break-in," he said, running one hand along the door jamb.

He carried himself like he was more experienced than the other. Hard lines etched into his face, creating a constant frown, and his hairline was receding. This guy looked like he'd been tired of the job for several years. The name tag clipped to his shirt labeled him as "Marks."

The taller one was younger, with a fresh face and overly gelled hair. He looked excited like he hadn't seen much action. Marnie suspected that he was new to the force. "Gibson" was on his name tag.

Marks pointed down the hallway. "Why don't you take a look around, Gibs?"

Gibson nodded, then disappeared into Marnie's bedroom.

Marks stood in Marnie's living room, his eyes lazily drifting around. She watched as he pulled a small notepad and pen from his breast pocket.

"Alright, ma'am, my name is Officer Marks. Can you tell me what exactly happened?" His pen poised over the open notepad.

Marnie ran shaky fingers through her greasy hair. "Well, I got home a little bit ago, and when I walked in, I smelt something rancid." She took a deep breath. It was still there, the rotten eggs. "Can you smell that?"

Officer Marks inhaled, then frowned. "Can't say that I do."

What? That wasn't possible. The smell was everywhere. Marnie shook her head. "Seriously? It smells so bad."

"Is that the only sign of something amiss?" Officer Marks asked, raising an eyebrow. His pen still hovered over the blank note-pad.

Marnie moved into the kitchen. "Look at this; there was a note left on my fridge." She pointed to it. "I know that doesn't seem like much, but this wasn't here when I left."

Officer Marks ambled over, scanning the room. He got to the fridge and bent down, squinting at the note. "When everything is ready, I'll come get you," he read aloud, then stood straight. "What's that supposed to mean?"

Marnie looked at him, tilted her head. "I don't know, but it wasn't here when I left. Someone broke in and wrote it." She looked at the pen in his hand. He wasn't writing it down – wasn't writing *anything* down.

Please write that down.

Officer Gibson appeared in the kitchen. "Nothing looks out of place," he said. "Is there anything missing?"

Marnie took her first look around, calculating all her belongings and where she'd left them. It was hard to remember after being in the hospital. Her mind felt fuzzy, empty. "I, uh, haven't checked," she said. "But like I said, I smelled something rancid, saw the note, and then waited outside for you guys." Had they expected her to conduct her own investigation? Wasn't it smarter that she'd gone outside, to safety, and called them first?

Both officers took a deep whiff of the air. "I don't smell nothin'," Marks said again. Officer Gibson pressed his lips together and nodded in agreement.

Marnie sniffed. The apartment was back to normal, the smell gone. "We– well, the smell is gone now," Marnie said, head down. "But the note! It's still there."

What is happening?

Officer Gibson moved around the living room, picking up books and putting them back. He moved the curtains to the side and looked at the window, then put them back. It all seemed so… lazy. So half-hearted. Marnie wanted to scream.

She looked at Officer Marks, his notepad *still* open and *still* empty. "Please, I know someone broke in; you have to believe me." Her shoulders shook. "Aren't you gonna write that down?" Her voice was strained.

"Ma'am, I'm sorry, but there is no sign of forced entry, and nothing's been taken." Marks closed in notepad. "Are you sure you didn't write the note and forgot?"

Was this a joke? Was Marnie being punk'd or something? Why didn't anyone believe her?

She crossed her arms and huffed. "I think I'd remember if I wrote something like that. Plus, it's not even in my handwriting!"

"Marnie," Hannah whispered, placing a hand on her shoulder.

"No!" Marnie shrugged her off. "This is ridiculous! Someone broke into my house and left a cryptic note. You need to investigate this!"

"There's nothing to investigate. I'm sorry, ma'am. If something happens for real, you know where to find us." Officer Marks made his way to the door.

"I'm sorry," Officer Gibson whispered, following his partner.

"I can't believe this," Marnie said, storming to her bedroom. She slammed the door and locked it. Anger stung her eyes with tears. She dropped onto her bed and let them roll down her cheeks and onto the pillow below her head.

Marnie had never felt so alone. The police didn't believe her, Hannah didn't believe her, and worst of all, she wasn't sure she believed herself. What if she was wrong? What if no one had actually broken in? It was possible that she had written that note, sure. But it was also very unlikely. Marnie searched her mind for any clue that it was hers, that she had written that note, but there was none.

Although the handwriting was familiar, Marnie felt she had seen it somewhere. That same childish handwriting was somehow recognizable, but she couldn't place it. It didn't matter, anyway. No one cared; why should she?

Marnie cried and cried, letting the tears pull her into exhaustion. She didn't want to think about it, didn't want to remember that her own best friend was against her. The people whose sole job was to protect and serve had refused her. It all made her feel so small, so stupid.

There was a knock at the door. "Marnie? I brought some dinner. Can you come out?"

The tears had dried to her cheeks, leaving little crusty streaks down her face. Marnie got out of bed, pulled a hoodie on, and opened the door. She needed to go to the bathroom, and to get to it, she had to cross the hall. It was the only reason she opened up.

Hannah was standing there, holding a takeout bag. She smiled and lifted it. "Chinese food," she sang.

Marnie dodged her and went into the bathroom, shutting the door.

Her reflection shot back at her, making her shudder. Dark circles formed under her eyes. Her nose was still red, and she could see the pasty streak marks. She was exhausted, not because of some fitful nap but from feeling ignored. She had hoped Hannah would leave, but she was still there. Marnie wanted to ignore her right back, to lock herself in her room and wait Hannah out. But her stomach ached and growled, pleading for sustenance. So, Marnie splashed water on her face and went back out.

Hannah sat at the kitchen island, opening the containers of orange chicken and fried rice. She set dumplings on a plate and poured soy sauce into a small bowl for dipping. It all smelled so delicious, exactly what Marnie needed.

Hannah turned around, her face lighting up. "Hey, there you are. I got all your favorites. I know you must be hungry."

Marnie approached. "Why are you still here, Hannah?"

Hannah put down the empty bag and looked at her hands. "I'm sorry, Mar. I didn't mean to make you feel like I didn't believe you."

Marnie stared at her friend. Guilt pricked her belly, but she chose to hold onto the anger boiling inside her instead. Hannah wasn't getting off the hook that easily.

"You betrayed me. It's bad enough the cops don't believe me, but to have my best friend blame it on my mental health? You can't even begin to know how that feels."

Tears glistened in Hannah's eyes, and the anger in Marnie's stomach eased a little bit. No matter how hard she clung to it, she was weak to her best friend's tears. Hannah wasn't one to cry. In fact, the only time Marnie could recall seeing her cry was when Hannah's father died. She cried for two days straight, refusing food and water. After that two days, she became numb. That was four years earlier and the last time Hannah cried until tonight.

Hannah dabbed the inside corners of her eyes to prevent tears from falling. "Marnie, I don't blame your mental health. It's just... You're so stressed, I know you are. I mean, with everything that's been going on... You don't seem like yourself."

"What does that mean?"

"It wasn't that long ago that you asked me to spend the night with you because you were convinced that someone was following you."

That was it! The person following her and sending those texts was probably the same person who broke in. A stalker! That was exactly it. Marnie had a stalker, and he was getting bolder. How had she not thought of that when the police were here?

"It was the same person," Marnie whispered first to herself, then exclaimed, "The person following me is the same person who broke in. It has to be!"

Hannah shook her head. "That's not-"

"No! Hannah, someone has been following me. I can prove it to you!" She ran into her room.

She still had the text messages, and she needed to show them to Hannah and prove that she wasn't crazy. Once Hannah saw them, she'd believe.

She went back into the kitchen, pulling up the text thread. "Look at this," she said, shoving the phone into Hannah's hand.

"What is this?"

"Texts I've been getting. I don't know who is sending them, but they've been coming since someone left flowers on my doorstep."

Hannah looked at Marnie; her eyebrows pulled together. "Flowers?"

"The day I asked you to spend the night, someone left flowers on my doorstep. I didn't tell you because I didn't think there was anything to it. But that day, I started getting these messages."

"You should've told me. I would've believed you about the break-in!" Hannah gave the phone back. "Marnie, we need to go to the police again."

Marnie slammed the phone down. "No way! They completely blew me off today! I'm not going back to them. It's a waste of time."

"There's more evidence now; they can help," Hannah said.

"No. I shouldn't have even asked you to call them today. They've never cared about people like me."

Marnie couldn't count the number of times she'd called the police on her stepdad, but they never helped. They wouldn't do anything because he didn't hit her – only her mom, and her mom refused to press charges. She couldn't prove that he verbally abused her and that she feared it would turn physical. The police were useless. All they cared about were the rich and the dead. Everyone else was nothing.

"If you get any other messages, or if anything else happens, then you need to promise me that you'll call the cops. Promise me?"

Marnie stuck out her pinky. "I promise." Hannah wrapped her pinky around Marnie's. A little white lie wouldn't hurt her.

Seventeen

HANNAH HAD OFFERED TO SPEND THE NIGHT, but Marnie declined. She needed to be a big girl. Plus, whoever broke in hadn't meant to harm her; otherwise, they would've waited for her to come home. Marnie considered buying a gun to protect herself. If they came back, she would be ready. Then again, maybe a gun wasn't a good idea. Marnie hated guns – hated the thought of even having one. And, if she were caught off guard, it wouldn't help much. She decided against it. Instead, she would need to find a way to get to know Jason better. Then, she could have a large, protective man with her at all times. That would scare away creeps, no problem.

Marnie rose early Thursday morning, excited to get back to work. She didn't like taking time off and didn't like other people handling her clients. She missed them, missed her office, missed Savannah and Dr. Carlson. It would do her a lot of good to return to normal life.

She sat on her couch, drinking her coffee and reading a book. Slow mornings were the best way to prepare for work, to fill her cup before she filled others'. It was difficult not to think about what happened at the hospital.

She couldn't fight the feeling that she was going crazy. The cops and

Hannah disregarding her only amplified it. If she were losing her mind, it would be better to know sooner rather than later. Hannah's words still stung, the way she brushed Marnie off, acting like she was some child afraid of the monster under her bed.

Marnie would prove them wrong. If they thought she was crazy, she'd show them she wasn't. She'd show herself she wasn't. She needed to get a CT scan. It would give her a clear idea of what was going on in her mind. If it came back clear, she would know stress was the primary cause. If it didn't, she would get treatment.

"Oh, Marnie, you're not crazy."

The familiar voice came from everywhere and nowhere all at once, a deep whisper haunting the room. Marnie eased herself off the couch as if sudden movements would make it worse. She tiptoed to the front door, checking the locks. Then, the windows. Locked.

He laughed. Marnie knew why he was laughing. She was pathetic and already his. He'd said as much at the hospital.

Scanning the room, Marnie begged her eyes to find the source. He had to be somewhere, lurking in a dark corner. Always in the darkest corner. But there was nothing, no sign of him anywhere. She was exposed in the living room, an easy target. A glance at her bedroom and she was on the move.

Marnie was about to breach the threshold when a movement from inside the room stopped her cold. She squinted, but it was too dark to see anything.

The bedroom was a no – he was there.

She spun around, forcing her frozen legs to move. Reaching the bathroom, she slammed the door shut and drove the lock home.

Safe.

Footsteps pounded in the narrow hall, getting louder with each step. Marnie backed away, breathing in gasps. So far, home was mostly a safe space. He only visited in her dreams when she was at home. The hospital was the first and only time he'd come to her while she was awake – until now. What opened the door, inviting him from dreamland to reality? Was it something she did?

The footsteps stopped. Marnie crept toward the door. Her fingers were ice cold and clammy as she clutched the doorknob, planting an ear on the door. Marnie held her breath, listening. Maybe she was mistaken; maybe no one was really there. Worry about an intruder still hanging from her shoulders could be forcing her mind to play tricks.

Tap, tap, tap.

Fingers danced on the door. Marnie jumped back, hands flying to her mouth to stifle a cry.

"Marnie, let me in," he said in a sing-song way.

Marnie pressed her hands harder against her mouth and shut her eyes.

He's not real. This is a dream. You fell asleep on the couch, and you're dreaming. She knew it was a lie. She knew this was real; that he was there. And there was nothing she could do about it.

Tears pushed their way through her clenched eyes. She was unable to control the emotions pulsing through her veins, thicker than blood.

"Oh, sweet Marnie. I know you aren't crying in there. Come out. I'll show you there's nothing to fear." Malice dripped off his tongue.

Dropping to her seat, Marnie opened her eyes and watched the door. He could come in whenever he wanted. That much was certain.

He enjoys this. He likes making me feel trapped.

She watched shadows dance along the floor, filtering in from below the bathroom door. He was right there, clear as day. He didn't need to stalk her dreams anymore.

A few more knocks on the door, and Marnie's resolve broke. She hugged her knees to her chest and shoved her head between them. Rocking back and forth, Marnie prayed that he would leave, prayed that he would get bored of waiting, bored of her, and find someone else to torture. What had she done to deserve this? She was a nice person, helpful even. Not a day went by that she didn't put someone else's needs above her own, especially at work. Hadn't she suffered enough as a kid?

Marnie wanted nothing more than to escape reality, escape the life that thrust itself upon her. This wasn't the life she created. This was a nightmare. If God was real, he was cruel. All he wanted to do was play a sick joke on her. It wasn't right. She didn't deserve this.

Time passed, and the air grew silent. Marnie lifted her head from her knees and saw that the shadows were gone. The coast seemed clear. She pushed herself onto her knees and crawled to the door. Bending down, she checked through the crack at the bottom. There was no sign of him, no darkness left.

She stood, unlocking the door and peeking outside.

Empty.

She was alone again. The tightness in her chest eased, and she sucked in a deep, cleansing breath. It was time to book that CT scan; something was wrong.

The clock in her living room read 1 pm. How was that possible? She rushed to the bathroom once more, working quickly. She braided her hair, brushed her teeth, and headed out the door.

Sweat rolled down Marnie's forehead and dripped into her eyes. The stress was too much; she had no clue how she would get through the workday. On her way to work, Marnie called Hannah and asked her to spend the night. She couldn't be alone anymore, not for a while. Hannah hadn't asked any questions. Good, considering how she'd treated Marnie before.

"Can you do me another favor?" Marnie asked. "Could you go to ACE and pick up some window locks and a deadbolt... for my front door."

Hannah was silent for a moment, her breath heavy on the other line. "Marnie..."

"Please, Hannah. Just appease me this once."

Hannah sighed. "Okay."

There was no such thing as being too safe.

They hung up, and Marnie walked at a quick pace, eager to be out of the street and in the safety of her office. The hairs on the back of her neck stood straight up.

Someone was watching her. She could feel their eyes boring into the back of her neck. Was it the shadow or her intruder? Marnie glanced over her shoulder, taking in the empty street. Paranoia peaked after her bathroom incident, rubbing her nerves raw and making her feel more vulnerable than she'd like to admit.

In all honesty, Marnie didn't know what to believe. Had what happened been another panic attack-induced hallucination? Or was the shadow real and actually knocking on her door? Part of her felt insane. Like, lock her up and throw away the key, insane. But the other half felt level-headed. She didn't know how to tell which side of her was telling the truth.

Marnie got to work in record time, clearing the front door and making a beeline to her office. Before she could get there, Dr. Carlson stuck her head out of her office door and called to Marnie.

"Hi, Dr. Carlson. How are you?" Marnie said.

"I'm fine. I'd like to see you for a moment." Without another word, she went back inside.

Marnie inhaled through her nose and exhaled out her mouth, steadying herself. She couldn't act crazy in front of the boss.

Marnie walked into Dr. Carlson's office, closing the door behind her.

Dr. Carlson sat at her desk, looking down at a file. "How are you feeling?" She asked.

"I'm doing much better, thanks." Marnie took a seat on the couch.

Dr. Carlson's office was set up similarly to Marnie's. Marnie's was actually set up to mimic Dr. Carlson's. The large bookshelf built into the wall was filled with colorful books. But, where Marnie had a mix of fiction and non-fiction, Dr. Carlson seemed to only read non-fiction. Dr. Carlson's desk was large and organized, not a pen out of place. Marnie's was messy. It didn't matter how much she tried; the mess took over.

Dr. Carlson finished with the file and moved to her high-back reading chair across from Marnie. She crossed one leg over the other, leaning back – the image of peace. Marnie shifted in her seat, tugged at her shirt and pants, and settled into a mirrored position of Dr. Carlson.

"If you want to talk about why you were in the hospital, I'm here. If you don't, we can focus on your clients," Dr. Carlson said.

Marnie cleared her throat. "It would be more productive to talk about my clients, I think."

"Fair enough. How is Carley?"

How was she supposed to answer that? She hadn't seen Carley since their shared time in the hospital and hadn't heard from her either. She worried about Carley, but then again, she worried about herself more. Carley was probably fine. Marnie had experienced a lot of what Carley complained about, and she was handling it fine. If she could do it, Carley could.

"She's doing fine. She had a seizure during our last session. The doctor said it was due to lack of sleep." Marnie uncrossed her legs and sat forward, elbows resting on her knees. "I have a session with her this afternoon, and can give you better updates then."

Dr. Carlson nodded along, staying quiet.

"There's someone else I'd like to talk about, a new client I had. His name is Cavin Grier. He's a grown man, which is a little out of my comfort zone."

"Okay," Dr. Carlson said. "What's the problem?"

"Well, he ran out in the middle of our first session. He's got some issues that I'm not equipped to handle. Would you mind taking him on instead?"

Now it was Dr. Carlson's turn to lean forward. "Marnie, are you doubting your skills?"

"Not at all! I just don't feel like the right fit for him."

"This is an excellent chance for you to grow as a therapist. I highly doubt you'll be catering to strictly teenagers your whole career. I want you to use this opportunity as a way to grow in your abilities."

Marnie leaned back, resting her head on the couch. That was not what she wanted to hear. She wasn't ready to deal with adults. Teenagers were much simpler, and given everything happening at home, she wanted to keep it simple. It was a wonder she admitted it, but she wanted more clients like Ashley. Clients that didn't care to be there didn't care to talk. Those were the easy ones. Not some grown man who snapped at the smallest thing yet insisted on attending therapy.

She wanted to get out. Talking to Dr. Carlson wasn't helping at all.

Marnie stood. "Well, alright. I better go. I have clients to prepare for. I've got a lot to catch up on from my days off." She went to the door, then turned around. "Dr. Carlson, thank you. For the time off, I mean."

"I am on your team, Marnie. I want to see you succeed."

"I know." Marnie left the office.

Eighteen

MARNIE DROPPED INTO HER CHAIR, huffing. She was angry with Dr. Carlson for shutting her down. Marnie didn't care about professional growth right now. All she cared about was surviving. Having to meet with a seemingly unstable man was no way for her to survive. It was hard enough for her to meet with Carley, but Dr. Carlson didn't care. She was a wonderful therapist and a skilled behavioral analyst. There was a good chance she knew how uncomfortable Marnie felt, yet she chose to ignore it.

Dwelling on the frustration was only going to make the day harder, but Marnie couldn't help it. Maybe it was time for her to find another job, to go somewhere that would respect her and her decisions. That would show Dr. Carlson.

"I'm on your team, Marnie." What a load of crap. Dr. Carlson was on no one's team but her own.

Marnie knew these thoughts weren't her own. They came from somewhere *apart* from her, but she couldn't stop them. She knew she loved Dr. Carlson – even idolized the woman. Yet the anger boiled over and urged her to react. She couldn't turn it off, couldn't stop it. Fighting it didn't feel like an option, so she embraced it.

Her fingers clenched into fists, and she ground her teeth. She would show Dr. Carlson. That woman needed to be taught a lesson. Marnie would refuse to meet with Cavin Grier. She'd ignore Dr. Carlson; what was the worst that could happen?

Well, Marnie could end up jobless.

That wouldn't happen. She was Dr. Carlson's protege; she had job security for life.

Who was she kidding? She was nothing. No one. If Dr. Carlson wanted, she could replace Marnie in an instant.

Marnie shook her head and took a sip of water. What was wrong with her? Stress, that was the problem. It was time to get a grip. Dr. Carlson meant well. She cared about Marnie.

Marnie was only having trouble remembering that.

Carley would be there any minute. Marnie looked around the office, and a chill ran down her spine. It was uncanny how real the hallucination at the hospital felt. She had been in her office – she swore it. Marnie got the urge to check the door, to make sure that she wasn't locked in like she'd been at the hospital. She ran to the door and yanked on the handle. The door flew open, slamming into the wall. The entire waiting room snapped their heads in her direction. Marnie smiled - her cheeks burning red - and closed the door.

"Get it together," she whispered.

She walked back to her desk and sat. "Stop freaking out. You're fine. Fine, fine, fine. It was all a figment of your imagination. You're okay." Closing her eyes, Marnie took several deep breaths. It would all be okay. That was the only thing she could tell herself. It was all she had.

Marnie opened her eyes and double-checked her schedule. Carley would be knocking on the door soon. Marnie's heart sank when she scanned the rest of her day. Cavin Grier was on the appointment list. If she really wanted to ignore Dr. Carlson's wishes and refuse him, she had her chance.

She wouldn't, though. She couldn't. All she could do was grit her teeth and deal with it.

There was a knock. The time for wallowing in her thoughts was over; Marnie had a job to do.

"Come in," she called.

The door opened, and Carley meandered in. Marnie got up and approached her. "You up for a hug?" She asked.

Carley nodded, "Yes," and Marnie wrapped her arms around Carley, pulling her in tight. Carley's arms stayed wrapped around her torso, unmoving.

"I'm so happy you're alright. How have you been feeling since we talked at the hospital?" Marnie let go and walked to her chair.

Carley sat on the couch, not responding.

"Carley? How're you doing?" Marnie asked again.

Carley glanced up at her. "Huh? Oh. I'm fine, I guess."

"Yeah? You wanna tell me what's been going on? Are you back at school?"

The girl nodded.

This was torture. Marnie was not in the mood to be the only one speaking. She'd had it just as hard as Carley had, yet she was here, doing her job. Why couldn't Carley do the same?

"Carley, please."

A tear streaked Carley's cheek, and she wiped it away with the sleeve of her sweater. "Why can't I be free? Why is this happening to me?"

The dam broke, and Carley sobbed. She brought her hands to her face, hiding the tears. Her body heaved, and coughs snuck out between the sobs. Marnie joined her on the couch, placing a soothing hand on her back.

"Shh, Carley. You're safe here."

"That's just it," she managed to get out. Carley inhaled. "I'm not safe anywhere."

"Carley, they are only dreams. All we have to do is work through the trauma, and the dreams will go away."

Carley silenced. Her body stiffened, and she shrugged Marnie off. Carley turned her head, glaring at Marnie.

"You don't get it," she bit.

Marnie leaned back, shocked by the sudden change in behavior. She hadn't done anything to deserve the harsh treatment. And today, of all days, she didn't want to put up with it. "What don't I get?"

"It isn't just a dream. And if you think it is, you're worse off than me."

"What is that supposed to mean?" Marnie stood. She didn't want to be close to Carley anymore. The girl was scaring her.

"He wants me dead, Ms. Adams. He won't stop until my last breath." Carley dropped her head. "I can't keep living like this," she whispered.

Marnie knew. She knew how tough the dreams were, knew how much tougher the hallucinations were. If she could get through to Carley and make her see the real cause, she could help her. Maybe it was time to put Carley on some medications.

Marnie grabbed a notepad off her desk, then went back to her chair. "Carley, I'm going to recommend you to a psychiatrist. I think it's time we consider other forms of treatment."

Carley closed her eyes, her face pinching. "You think I'm crazy."

Marnie scooted to the edge of her seat and reached across the coffee table between them. "No. I do not think you're crazy. You're sleep deprived and traumatized from the accident. Medicine can be helpful for a time until we get you stabilized."

Carley laughed. She threw herself into the couch and laughed. In the course of fifteen minutes, Carley had run through three emotional extremes. Marnie's suspicions were right; the girl was losing it.

"Carley, it's only to get you back on your feet."

The girl laughed more, her voice shrieking. "I'm crazy. You think I'm crazy!"

"Carley, please calm down," Marnie said, trying to keep her voice from panicking.

Carley had never, ever acted like this before. It made Marnie question her abilities – made her question how much she really knew the girl. Telling Carley she wanted to recommend medication no longer seemed like a smart move. Marnie should've kept it between her and Carley's parents.

She added notes about Carley's actions to the girl's file. She would talk to Dr. Carlson. Dr. Carlson would know what to do. Then, she waited for Carley to calm down. She watched, too afraid to speak, as Carley rolled around the couch, crying from laughing so hard.

Finally, she calmed. Carley nodded. "Okay, I'll see the pill pusher." Then she stood, walking out of the office.

Marnie was at a loss. It was the weirdest session she'd ever had with a client, and she didn't know what to do. How did she move forward? Would Carley even want to see her again? It wasn't likely. Marnie worried about her. The medication would help; she had to believe it. Carley could've been too far gone. If only Marnie had noticed sooner – had recommended it sooner. Maybe Carley wouldn't have acted the way she did. If Marnie were a better therapist, Carley would already be better.

A bad morning turned into a bad afternoon, and the day would only get worse. Marnie laid back in her chair, slouching. She didn't want to be here anymore.

A few more clients passed, and Marnie was feeling better. She'd moved past her session with Carley, giving each client all her attention. Those sessions went well. Clients were understanding and talkative. Granted, they didn't have as big of problems as Carley. That was for the best. Marnie didn't want any other clients with problems like Carley. She had enough of her own.

She was between clients when Savannah poked her head in.

"Hey Marnie, can I talk to you for a minute?" she asked.

"Yeah, of course! Come on in."

Savannah walked in, closed the door behind her, and went to the couch. She rubbed her hands together, looking uncomfortable.

Savannah rarely bothered Marnie, especially during business hours. They were casual friends, hanging out sometimes, but usually only saw each other at work. From what Marnie remembered, Savannah was an aspiring therapist. She got her bachelor's degree in psychology and was biding her time earning extra money before enrolling in a master's program. Marnie liked Savannah a lot and thought she would make a great therapist. She was welcoming and kind. Her voice was gentle, she hardly spoke above a whisper, and she only ever had nice things to say about others.

Marnie waited for Savannah to speak. Whatever it was, it had to be bothering her really badly. Savannah looked pale like she was going to throw up at any second.

"Marnie, I hate to say this. I don't usually do this, I..." She wiped sweat from her forehead.

"Whatever it is, Savannah, you can tell me."

"Okay. Here we go." She released a long sigh. "Your next client is here, Cavin Grier. He's been here once before."

"I remember him," Marnie said, hiding the dread in her voice.

"He's, well, something seems a little off about that guy," Savannah whispered. "You know, he ran outta here last time like his house was on fire. The last time he called to set an appointment, he hung up before I could even finish my sentence."

Great. Not only was Marnie hesitant about meeting him, but sweet Savannah was wary of him too. That was encouraging.

"Please be careful talking with him, Marnie. If anything happens, let me know, and I'll call the police." Savannah stood. "That's all. I don't wanna take up any more of your time."

Marnie stood with her. "Thank you for your concern, Savannah. I know he's a little weird, but he's harmless." There was no use in scaring Savannah more.

Inside Golden Meadow was the last place Marnie felt unsafe. Tension was normal, and some clients struggled with very intense issues. It was up to Marnie to help them, even if she felt off her game. She wasn't happy about meeting with Cavin, but she had to give him another chance.

Savannah gave Marnie a hug, one that she relished. Marnie didn't realize how badly she needed a hug.

"I'll send him in," Savannah said, leaving the office.

Nineteen

CAVIN WATCHED FROM THE WAITING ROOM as the receptionist walked out of Marnie's office. She walked to her desk and picked
up a clipboard.

"Cavin Grier? Ms. Adams will see you now," she said.

Cavin smiled. He was finally going to see Marnie again. It had
been days, and his skin itched with excitement. There was no doubt
she missed him as much as he missed her.

He walked through the door to see Marnie standing by her
desk. She looked ravishing. Her hair flowed down her back in a beautiful braid with little curls peeking out the sides. It looked bouncy,
silky. Cavin held back the urge to run his fingers through it. Soon, he
would get his chance soon enough.

She wore dark gray business pants and a white button-down
shirt – the picture of beauty and elegance. Marnie would look good
wearing a potato sack. When she turned to greet him, Cavin straightened his posture. This was his second chance with her, and he couldn't
waste it.

"Hi Cavin. Nice to see you again." Marnie stuck her hand out
for a shake.

Cavin grabbed it. Electricity shot from Marnie's hand through his own, coursing through his body. This was life. He didn't need food or water, all he needed was Marnie's touch, and he could survive. He held onto her hand as long as acceptable, the voice in his head insisting he let go. Reluctantly, he did.

Cavin sat on the couch, bouncing his leg up and down. He didn't mean to, but Marnie's touch was like a drug. Only the effects wore off in an instant. He itched for another hit.

"How's it been going?" Marnie asked.

She was beautiful. She didn't take her eyes off him, and Cavin knew she thought he was handsome, too. Of course, she did – they were meant for each other.

"It's been a pretty long week," Cavin said.

"I hear ya!" Marnie laughed.

Her laugh was angelic. No, that wasn't right. It was more than angelic. Angels were jealous of Marnie's laugh;they wished they could be her.

"Why has it been a long week?"

Shoot. Cavin was too focused on seeing Marnie again that he'd forgotten to come up with a fake problem to discuss. He needed to think of something, anything.

It hit him. This was the perfect opportunity to gauge how infatuated Marnie was with him.

"Well," he said, sitting up straighter. "I've been seeing this girl." His eyes shot up to Marnie, gauging her reaction.

Was that a twitch? He'd upset her, but she was trying to hide it.

"And over the weekend, she sorta disappeared. I sent her messages, but she didn't respond."

Marnie was nodding her head, but Cavin could tell it was eating her alive to hear him talk about another woman. If only he could admit that he was talking about her, then she wouldn't be so upset.

"Did something happen between you two to make her need a break?" Marnie asked.

"I don't think so. Things were going so great. I would walk her home from work every night, leave her flowers, and let her know that she was always on my mind."

Marnie smiled. "It sounds like you've been a great boyfriend."

Cavin was on cloud nine. Marnie called him a great boyfriend; his life was complete. Great boyfriends make great husbands, and that was what he would be for Marnie. Nothing could tear him down from this high.

Marnie continued, "Sometimes, when things are going great, people like to take a step back and assess the relationship. You know, to make sure that it's something they want."

Oh, baby, I know this is what you want. I can see it in your eyes. Marnie was his – hook, line, and sinker.

"And that assessment could be a good thing. It could mean that she is getting ready for the next step. I think you have a keeper on your hands."

"Yeah, I guess I'm just a little worried," Cavin said, playing the part. "I moved too fast with my last girl. I don't want to make the same mistake twice."

Marnie smiled that radiant smile of hers. "I understand that. I think you're being very smart about all this."

Cavin beamed. She was right, he did have a keeper on his hands, and he was being smart. Marnie was looking at him with loving eyes. Cavin was right to book that appointment with Marnie. He'd totally redeemed himself from the last one.

Marnie crossed her legs and leaned back in her chair. She was trying to seduce him, to make him think impure thoughts about her. Cavin was a gentleman, though. He wouldn't give in to such fantasies yet. He leaned back on the couch, spreading both arms over the back of it. If she wanted to try seducing him, he wanted to match her energy. Just because he didn't want to fantasize about that yet, didn't mean he would deny her the opportunity. If it was on her mind already, he couldn't stop her.

"Now, Cavin, what do you think would be a good step for you to take while you're waiting to hear back from her?" Marnie asked.

"I could think about the relationship, too," Cavin said.

That's right, buddy. Play the part.

"Yeah! That is a great idea. You can decide if this is really something you want to pursue. Make sure you're willing to be serious about this girl."

"Oh, trust me. I'm serious about her." He winked.

"Can I give you some homework?" Marnie asked. "This week, I want you to sit down and think about your relationship. Think about the good, the bad, and the ugly. Write in a journal, on your phone, or on a scrap piece of paper how you feel. It doesn't have to be long, only a few sentences or bullet points if you want. Then, write what you're willing to work towards. Is this a person you want to marry? That kinda thing. Sound good?"

"Am I supposed to bring this homework back and show you?"

"No, no. This is for your eyes only. Maybe you could discuss it with the lucky lady. We can talk about how it went for you next time, though."

The homework would be easy. There was nothing bad or ugly about Marnie or his relationship with her. It was all sunshine and rainbows. They were still in the honeymoon phase, and Cavin knew it'd last forever.

The session ended far too soon, and Cavin was reluctant to leave. He lingered at the door, trying to think of anything that would help him talk to Marnie more.

"So, I'll book a session for next week. You're available, right?"

"Check with Savannah, but I'm sure we can meet sometime then."

"Okay, great. Thank you so much, Ms. Adams. I appreciate your help."

"Please, Cavin, call me Marnie."

Cavin's smile took over his entire face. "Right, Marnie," he said, her name lingering on his lips.

"I'll see ya next week," Marnie said, opening the door.

I'll see you sooner than that, Cavin thought.

Twenty

NIGHT HAD GAINED CONTROL when Marnie walked out of Golden Meadow. The orange glow of street lamps lit a path leading into darkness. Marnie knew, with every bone in her body, that something was there. It was hiding in the darkness, waiting for her – waiting to attack.

Hannah stood under one of the streetlights, the glow of her phone reflecting on her face as a hardware store bag dangled from her forearm. Marnie ran up to her, wrapped her arms around her. She inhaled, the smell of Hannah's perfume wafting through her nostrils. Relief washed over her, she really didn't want to be alone.

"Thank you, Hannah," she whispered.

Hannah hugged back. "Of course."

She started to let go, but Marnie squeezed tighter. "A few more seconds." She closed her eyes, letting the security of her friend's arms fill her with courage. She would need all the courage she could get to walk home. She was still hurt by how Hannah reacted to the break-in, but some things were easier to let go of in the face of such strong fear. She needed her friend, even if that meant giving up her pride.

The dark had never bothered Marnie. She learned to get used

to it. After all, she spent most of her teen years hiding in a closet, away from Pete. She had learned to accept the dark – to find solace in it. But now, the dark was where *they* were. Both the shadow that haunted her, and the man that stalked her were there. She could feel eyes on the back of her neck as clearly as she could hear the shadow's voice. Neither of them ever left her.

Finally, she released Hannah from her grip. "Thanks."

Hannah looked at her, worry creasing her forehead. She cocked her head to the side.

"What?" Marnie asked, crossing her arms.

Hannah shook her head. "Nothing. Let's go. It's cold."

Marnie stopped at the entrance to the alley. It was there that everything felt heightened. All her fears and her emotions tripled when she stepped into that alley. He was there. Not the shadow, well, maybe the shadow. But the stalker. It was the alley where she first heard his footsteps. The alley where she was sure he waited for her, even now.

She hooked her elbow around Hannah's and started walking.

"Why do you keep doing that?" Hannah asked when they were halfway through.

"Doing what?"

"Checking over your shoulder. Was there, like, a mugging around here or something?"

Marnie didn't realize she was checking over her shoulder. She'd gotten so used to it that it was second nature now. Where had she gone so wrong in life that it was now subconscious behavior to always look over her shoulder? She thought she'd escaped this when she left home.

"No. I don't know, I thought I heard something," she lied.

Hannah glanced back, and Marnie followed her gaze. There was nothing. Of course, there was nothing. Why would there be any-thing? The only evidence she had that someone was following her were the texts and the flowers from weeks ago. Everything else was pure speculation. Speculation that the police didn't even believe. She needed that CT scan. And maybe a therapist of her own, again.

When they finally reached the apartment, Marnie checked all the windows and doors. She opened every closet, checked under the bed and behind the shower curtain. Safe at last.

Marnie changed into baggy sweats, then plopped on the couch. She rubbed her eyes, fighting off exhaustion. "I don't know what's happening to me. I feel like I'm losing my mind."

Hannah sat next to her, handing her a glass of water. "Talk to me, kid."

"Ever since the hospital, things have felt off. I don't feel like myself anymore."

"Can you please tell me exactly what got you hospitalized?"

Here it was, time to rip off the band-aid. As much as Marnie wanted to avoid triggering Hannah's Christianity in any way, she couldn't keep this from her friend for too long. Marnie knew it would come up again. Eventually, she needed to bite the bullet and share.

"Alright, I'm gonna sound like I've lost my mind now. Just, please don't laugh at me, okay?"

Hannah made an X over her heart. "I'm all ears."

"One of my clients had a seizure mid-session. So, I rode in the ambulance to the hospital with her. I was sitting in the waiting room, waiting to hear from her parents, when things got really weird." Marnie looked down at her hands. She held them together to control the shaking. "The doctors called it a panic attack, but it was more than that. I saw something, Hannah."

"Saw something?" Hannah asked.

Marnie glanced at her friend, then back down. She couldn't bear to keep eye contact; it was all too much. "It was so real. I heard someone call my name. I thought it was my client, so I followed the voice. Then, I was in my office at Golden Meadow. I mean, exactly my office. The papers were even on the desk exactly as I left them."

"Uh-huh…"

She was losing Hannah.

"That isn't even the craziest part. There was this man, or like a man. I'm not entirely sure what he is."

"Marnie, you're freaking me out," Hannah said.

"I'm almost done." She ran trembling fingers through her hair. "He was talking to me, saying all this weird stuff about destroying me. I don't know; it was freaky. Then, he put his hand on my shoulder, and I felt, like, this electric shock. It hurt, and it terrified me. This deep fear paralyzed me, and I started screaming. That's when the nurses came, I guess. Next thing I knew, I was in a hospital bed, hooked up to an IV."

"So, you hallucinated during the panic attack?"

"I guess, but it didn't feel like a hallucination. It felt real. As real as sitting here next to you." Marnie met Hannah's stare. She was sure that she sounded completely whacko. Hannah was going to get her committed for sure. "There's more," she said.

"More?"

"After the hospital, when I came home. I had another… experience. It's the reason I asked you to spend the night."

Hannah watched her, not saying anything.

Marnie continued, "I saw him again. Here. I locked myself in the bathroom, and he knocked on the door. I was so scared, Hannah. I stayed there for two hours."

She watched as Hannah's expression remained completely neutral. There wasn't a single sign of shock or confusion. Nothing on Hannah's face.

"Am I going crazy?" Marnie whispered.

Hannah didn't answer right away. The longer she stayed quiet; the more Marnie was sure she thought it was true – that Marnie was crazy. She was simply looking for the right way to say it.

Marnie couldn't take Hannah's silence anymore. "I'm gonna get tested," she blurted. "Gonna get a CT scan. If there's anything on my brain causing hallucinations, I can find out. Then, I can get medication to help it."

Hannah placed a steady hand on Marnie's leg. She wasn't shaking like Marnie was. Marnie remembered what it was like to be still, to be strong. She longed for those days to return. She hated who she'd become.

"I don't think you're crazy," Hannah said. "I think there's more to all this."

Marnie rolled her eyes. *Here we go*, she thought.

"I know you don't like me talking about religion, but have you considered that this could be a spiritual thing?"

Marnie lifted herself off the couch, throwing her hands into the air. "Hannah, I don't want to get into that right now. You know I love you, and I would never judge you for still believing all that 'Jesus stuff,' but I don't anymore. I need you to respect that."

"I do respect that. But what kind of friend would I be if I didn't tell you what I really think?"

"A supportive one!" Marnie didn't mean to shout, but any talk about church or God made her lose control.

"I think it's real," Hannah said. "I think what you're seeing is a demon."

Marnie laughed. Hannah couldn't be serious. She knew she was seeing things, and she knew how real it felt. But a demon? That stuff was fantasy, made-up. Demons were boogeymen for Christians, a monster that parents scared their children into behaving with.

"I'm serious, Marnie. There are forces of good and forces of evil, light and dark. And they're after you, after everyone. Yours just happens to be extra loud."

"There isn't a demon after my soul." She couldn't help the condescension from slipping out. She walked into the kitchen, placed her glass of water in the sink and reached for a wine glass. If they were going to talk about demons, she was going to need a little help. Hannah was quiet while Marnie poured herself a glass of wine, then went back into the living room.

"Marnie, please listen to me. Good and evil both want you. And from the looks of it, evil is winning."

Marnie covered her mouth to prevent herself from doing a spit-take. It all sounded so cheesy. But more than that, it reminded her of when her parents started attending church. She was nine years old, and at first, it was great. The pastor always talked about good and evil, light and dark, angels and demons. It was pretty convincing until that same pastor ruined her parents' marriage. He was the evil one, not some unseen devil.

"This is real life we're talking about, Hannah. Not some fairy-tale."

"It's more real than you think."

Marnie had to give it to Hannah; that girl held strong to her beliefs.

"Look, I'm not gonna tell you what to believe, okay?" Hannah said, raising her hands in surrender. "I know how all this hits you. And I know what Pastor Pete did."

"Don't." Marnie's glare bore holes into Hannah's skull.

Hannah dropped her hands, her face solemn. "I wouldn't be a good friend if I didn't warn you. That's all I'm saying."

Marnie searched Hannah's eyes. They were sincere, honest. She truly believed all this stuff.

"What happened to you in the hospital – in your own house – is all real. This demon is trying to make you lose your mind. He's trying to scare you."

Marnie swirled her wine glass, watching the red liquid slosh. "What am I supposed to do, then?" She looked at Hannah. "Because if he's trying to scare me or make me feel crazy, it's working. I'm terrified."

Hannah stood and walked to Marnie. She wrapped her arms around her. Marnie looked up, trying to hold back the tears.

"Marnie, God loves you so much. And he wants to help you," Hannah whispered in Marnie's ear.

Marnie pushed her back, hurt stinging her eyes. "If God loves me, where was he when my parents' marriage fell apart? Where was he when Pete moved in and blamed my mom for losing the church? When I had to hide in the closet cause Pete was on a rampage? Huh? Where was he then?"

Compassion etched into the lines around Hannah's eyes. Marnie hated it. She wanted to slap the compassion away. But she knew it wouldn't help.

"I'm going to bed." Marnie set the wine glass on the kitchen counter and went to her room, locking the door.

She checked her phone – plugged in and resting on the nightstand. There was a text message at the top, sender Unknown.

Goodnight beautiful. I'm thinking of you always.

Twenty-One

MARNIE WALKED OUT OF HER BEDROOM, still sleepy from a night of tossing and turning. Her argument with Hannah left her feeling drained. It brought up memories of her childhood that she preferred to keep locked away in the deepest parts of her mind. She'd worked through all that during her college years. That was one of the perks of getting a psychology degree: required counseling. Do first, then teach and all that. Still, the issues managed to pop up every once in a while.

Hannah was sitting at the kitchen counter with a cup of coffee and a book spread open. Marnie's plan was to put last night behind them, to act like nothing had happened.

"Whatcha readin'?" Marnie asked, reaching into the cupboard for a mug.

"I'm reading the Bible," Hannah said. Her voice sounded stiff, hesitant.

"Oh." Marnie poured coffee into her mug until it reached the rim. She sipped at it and sat next to Hannah.

"Our conversation last night reminded me of a story in here. I figured it wouldn't hurt to read it again."

Marnie stayed quiet, focusing on her coffee.

"You know," Hannah continued, "there are actually tons of demon possessions in the Bible."

"I am not demon-possessed," Marnie interjected.

"I know. But a demon is toying with you. Close enough."

Marnie rolled her eyes and took another sip. It was going to be a long morning.

"Anyways, there's this story about a guy who is so tortured by demons that he lives in a graveyard. He ran around naked, cutting himself on rock and screaming. The townspeople chained him up, but he broke out of them. Everyone was terrified of the dude."

"That's horrible. I bet he had undiagnosed schizophrenia or something, and they didn't have the means to take care of him. And you're saying this is how I'm gonna end up?" Marnie scoffed. She thought they would put all this demon talk behind them. Didn't Hannah realize how mad Marnie was last night? It was time to give it a rest.

"That's not what I'm saying! Let me get to the good part."

Marnie gave a tight smile. "Please, continue."

"As I was saying, the townspeople were terrified and didn't know what to do with the guy, right? But then, Jesus came along, and the man saw him. He ran to Jesus, and the demons cried out to him, asking what Jesus wanted."

If Hannah asked, Marnie would deny it, but the story was intriguing. Fictional but intriguing nonetheless.

"Jesus commanded the demons to leave the man, and they obeyed. They ran into a field of pigs, and the pigs ran into the ocean. When the townspeople came to see what was happening, the man was calm, dressed, and acting normal again. Jesus healed him."

"Why are you telling me this story?"

"Don't you see? Jesus saved that man. He sent the demons running. He's the only one who can do that, and he can do it for you."

"Hannah, that was an interesting story. It makes for good fiction. I'll admit that. But that is nothing like what I'm going through. I told you, whatever I'm going through is much more mental." She tapped her temple. "Once I go to the doctor, I'll know for sure. Then, I can see a psychiatrist about medications to curb the hallucinations." Marnie wanted to believe what she was saying, but something about demons rang true to her. The hallucinations and nightmares felt so real; was there a chance they were?

Her logical brain said no. No way. There was a loose connection in her head, and that was it, end of story. But another, deeper part of her believed Hannah, believed that all this was a spiritual battle. And it took every ounce of her resolve to shut that part up.

"Alright. But if you change your mind and want to believe, you know where to find me."

"No offense, Hannah. But I've heard all this Jesus stuff before, and look where it got my family."

That silenced Hannah. She changed the subject to Marnie's relief. Hopefully, that was the end of the religious talks, at least until everything blew over. Regardless of what she believed, Marnie was glad to have Hannah there with her. She was one of the few Christians that practiced what they preached.

Hannah worked much earlier than Marnie, so she left first. She promised to meet Marnie at work again that evening. Even if she thought it was all demons and spirits, Marnie was glad she still agreed to walk her. She felt silly needing a chaperone, but it helped ease the anxiety.

Getting another text last night had been frustrating. Marnie wanted to reply, to tell whoever it was to leave her alone. But she worried about what implications that would bring. If they were following her and had broken into her house, making them mad was the last thing she wanted to do.

Everything Hannah talked about stuck in her mind. Marnie couldn't shake the story about the demon-possessed man. She decided that it wouldn't be the worst idea in the world to read it herself. She could see if any other details pointed to mental illness or something.

Marnie got ready for work and left early. She wanted to stop at a bookstore and buy a Bible. She made a plan: figure out the hallucinations, then uncover the stalker. She knew solving the hallucinations wouldn't get rid of the stalker, but at least it would resolve some of the terror that rested below the surface. At this point, she'd try anything to get rid of the shadow.

She just wouldn't tell Hannah that.

Marnie was lucky enough to have a few cancellations at work, giving her time to go to the hospital. It was awkward walking into the same hospital she stayed at after the panic attack. She caused such a huge scene that all the nurses knew who she was. Humiliation made her cheeks burn. She didn't want the reputation as "the lady who screamed in the janitor's closet." But that was what she got.

She sat in the waiting room, filling out forms for the test. The questions were standard and straightforward. *Do you experience anxiety or depression?* Check. *Have you experienced anything odd lately?* Check. *Are you on medications?* Check. She looked over her checked boxes and added "trouble sleeping" and "hallucinations" at the bottom. Of course, everyone in the hospital already knew. Crawling under a large rock sounded perfect at that moment.

A nurse called her back, checking her height, weight, and blood pressure. Marnie hated going to the doctor. Always had. It felt invasive, like they could see something no one else could. Between this and her previous stay, Marnie spent more time than she ever cared to at the hospital.

The CT scan went smoothly enough; she went into a large machine that scanned her brain. The technician was nice enough. But when Marnie asked her questions, she only replied with, "The doctor will let you know."

That was the worst. Marnie wanted answers now – needed them now. But when all was said and done, all they told her was that the doctor would call with results later.

She sighed as she gathered her coat and bag, glad to be done but anxious to hear the results. How would this affect her career if it turned out that she had something wrong? What would Dr. Carlson say? What if she got fired? How could a sick person help people?

The thought made Marnie's heart skip a beat. She couldn't lose her job; that would be worse than losing her life.

On her way out of the hospital, Marnie saw a familiar face. Butterflies swirled around in her stomach, and her face turned bright shades of pink. Jason was sitting in the waiting room on the first floor, flipping through a magazine. He wore a red and black plaid flannel open over a white t-shirt. His blue jeans were cuffed at the ankles, the logo on his Converse All-Stars showing.

He was stunning. Marnie searched for words but was at a loss. Everything in her mind disappeared as she watched him. Fate had placed him in her path again, and she wouldn't waste it. She straightened her shoulders, brushed her hair behind her ears, and walked up to him.

"Jason, hi," she said, smiling big.

Jason looked up from his magazine. He locked eyes with Marnie, and his face lit up. More butterflies did somersaults in her stomach.

"Marnie, fancy seeing you here," Jason said.

"I came in for a test. What are you doing here?"

"Visiting a friend," he said. "It's good to see you again. I was hoping to run into you at some point."

Hoping to run into me? Be still my beating heart! Marnie placed her hands on her cheeks. They were burning, and she hoped he didn't notice.

"I'm happy to see you too," Marnie said. She tried to think of something else to say, anything to keep talking to him, but nothing came. Her mind was blank. That stupid, gorgeous smile of his wiped her mind of any intelligent thought.

A few seconds of awkward silence stretched between them. Marnie felt the pressure building, the pressure to fill the silence. As a therapist, she knew how to keep from caving. But here, staring Jason in the face, she wouldn't fight it much longer.

Finally, she gave in. "Well, I better get going," she said, pointing a thumb at the entrance.

Jason shot up out of his seat. "Wait. If you aren't busy right now, you wanna grab a bite to eat?"

Thank you, thank you, thank – you whatever supernatural entity is helping.

Marnie nodded. "I could eat."

"Great!" Jason grabbed his coat, draped over his chair, and they left.

Down the street was a little Korean restaurant that Marnie loved. They found a table near the back and sat with their bibimbap bowls. Marnie became obsessed with Korean food when she moved to Springfield for university. She'd spent hours at the restaurant eating and working on homework. One day, she wanted to visit Korea. Until then, she'd settle for the food.

Jason closed his eyes before eating, mumbling under his breath.

Oh no. Not him, too. It was hard enough dealing with Hannah being a Christian; why did the attractive guy have to be one too? What was she supposed to do? She liked Jason; he was cool. She wanted to keep seeing him, but it was a personal rule that she only allowed one Christian in her life. And that spot was filled.

He opened his eyes, smiling. "Sorry, I hope you don't mind that I did that."

Marnie tried to control the look on her face – tried to be pleasant. But based on Jason's apology, she imagined her face was twisted up in a grimace. "I don't mind at all," she said, playing it off.

"Do you believe in God?"

Wow. So it was *that* kind of lunch. Marnie shoved a spoonful of bibimbap in her mouth, stalling for an answer. What was the polite way of saying, "*I believe anyone that trusts an invisible man in the sky that lets humans run around causing pain to one another without doing anything is a complete idiot*"?

"No, not really." That would have to do.

Jason nodded, stuffing his mouth with food. The smile never left his lips. Even when he chewed, it remained. Marnie had never met anyone like that before, so happy. Something had to be wrong with him.

"So, uh, is your friend okay?" Marnie asked, looking for any way to change the subject.

"Yeah, he's alright. A work buddy of mine. He got into a car accident yesterday. I wanted to make sure he was healing right."

"Oh, I'm so sorry. I hope he gets better soon."

"Me too. Is everything okay with you? What test were you getting – if you don't mind me asking?"

Great. Marnie had already lost points insulting his religion; now she also had to explain to him how she was maybe, possibly, kind of, a little bit crazy.

She tucked a strand of hair behind her ear. "It was nothing. I just had to get an MRI. I've been having these weird nightmares… some of them even when I'm awake. So, I wanted to get checked."

Marnie refused to look Jason in the eye. After everything she'd been through the past few weeks, she felt especially vulnerable. Weak.

"Nightmares, huh?" He sounded genuinely interested. Marnie couldn't let that go on.

She waved it off, laughing. "Yeah, but it's nothing. I have an overactive imagination."

"If this is too personal, you don't have to answer. But what exactly are you seeing in these nightmares?"

Marnie chanced a look at him. His eyes were narrow, intense.

They zeroed in on her face. It was almost as if he related, in a way – like he knew what she was going through – like he'd been there before. She wanted to tell him, wanted to know if he'd seen it too. Carley had. Carley was the first to mention the shadow. Maybe they weren't the only ones.

Marnie cleared her throat and dropped her voice as low as it would go. "I see a man. Well, he's sort of a man. He's very shadowy, like, not fully there. And he calls my name, tells me I belong to him. Weird stuff like that."

Jason's hand rested under his chin, and he was nodding along. He sat at the edge of his seat, hanging on her every word. Marnie stared back at him, waiting for his response. He looked like he understood her exactly. Though he must have thought she was a little nuts and was regretting asking her to lunch. Still, she waited. Pushing for a reply would make things worse.

He leaned back, rubbing his chin. "I know you don't believe in God, but I don't think you're dreaming. What if it's actually a spiritual being that's messing with you?"

What Marnie's eyes did was not merely an eye roll. They went so far back in her head that it was more like an eye back-handspring. "Not you too, Jason."

"What'd I do?"

"You and my friend Hannah would get along great – you know that?"

"Hey, I'm just saying. There's more to this world than what we see. And the part that we don't usually see is making itself known to you. I wouldn't ignore it."

"Look, that's great and all, but I gotta go." Marnie pulled a Golden Meadow business card out of her wallet. "This has my cell and work number. I'd love to see you again without having to 'accidentally' run into you. And next time, let's talk about anything else, okay?"

Jason took the card and smiled. How could she resist that smile? It begged her to sit back down, to stay and chat more. She had to fight it, to force her legs out. She couldn't take any more talk of angels and demons.

"I'll call you," Jason said.

Marnie waved and walked out of the restaurant. She hoped he would.

Twenty-Two

MARNIE SLUMPED ON THE COUCH next to Hannah. "Did I tell you?" Marnie said. "Apparently, I'm completely healthy. Not a thing wrong with me." She slid from the couch onto the floor in front of it, leaned her head back, and let out a heavy sigh.

"That's a good thing, isn't it?" Hannah asked.

It was a good thing. She should be happy – relieved. Instead, she felt confused and frustrated. Back to square one, with no answers and no way to solve the nightmares and hallucination problem.

Hannah uncurled herself from the couch and set her book down. She was a saint to stay with Marnie, especially after their fight. Hannah's hands drifted to Marnie's head, playing with her hair, comforting her. It was something she'd always done. Hannah's mom had done it to her as a kid, and she grew up doing it to Marnie. On nights when Marnie would escape to Hannah's, she'd lay her head on Hannah's lap, crying. And Hannah would gently scratch her head until she fell asleep.

"I'm sorry, kid," Hannah said. "I know this probably leaves you with more questions than answers."

Marnie dropped her head into her hands. "I just don't understand what's happening to me." Her head shot up, and she turned to face Hannah. "And don't you dare say spiritual warfare or something like that," she said, pointing a warning finger at her friend.

Hannah pinched her forefinger and thumb together, then ran them across her lips. Sealed. Exactly how Marnie wanted it.

Marnie pulled herself off the ground. "I'm gonna shower." Her shoulders hunched, she dragged her feet to the bathroom. Her goal was to be as dramatic as possible, at least today.

Warm water washed over her, loosening her muscles and opening her pores. Marnie felt the anxiety slipping off her body, whisked away by the cleansing liquid. She hated how disappointed she felt. She was sure there would be a logical explanation for the shadow. Instead, she was left with more questions. Her mind refused to rest. It ran in circles, seeking logic where there was none.

Marnie closed her eyes and let the water fall over her face. She had to stop, had to think about something else.

Jason.

That was a nice thought. Apart from his outlandish beliefs, he was a great guy. Charming, kind, and incredibly handsome. Oh, how she hoped he'd call her. The way they'd parted ways at the Korean restaurant made Marnie cringe.

She was so rude. Why had she been so rude? He was the nicest. He didn't call her crazy, even though he had every right to. And how did she repay him? By metaphorically spitting in his face and high-tailing it out of the restaurant.

He wasn't going to call her back, was he? No way, not after the way she treated him.

A clear bill of health or not, Marnie should be admitted simply for her attitude toward Jason.

The water was no longer sliding down Marnie's skin. It stuck to her, slowly crawling down in thick rolls.

Marnie opened her eyes, looking down at her stomach. Dark red streaks painted her skin where water should be. She ran her fingers across her stomach and lifted them to her face. It smelled like iron, making her jaw tighten at the back.

Blood.

The shower head spurted and shot thick chunks of blood at Marnie. She wanted to scream, but the blood filled her mouth, making her choke.

She spit it out and shoved two fingers against the back of her throat – anything to get rid of the taste.

Her skin felt sticky and warm.

She wanted to run out, but what good would that do? Who could help her?

Marnie sank into the tub, pulling her knees to her chest. The entire shower was red, like some sort of sadistic Jackson Pollock painting.

"Nonono," she whispered, rocking back and forth. But it kept coming, kept spraying her, covering her, filling her mouth and lungs. She felt frozen in place, giving in to defeat.

Her head snapped up.

Turn the water off. Of course! That would stop it. She lunged forward, grasping the dial. Her hand slipped off, and she cursed. She had to stop the water, the blood, whatever it was. She pressed down on the handle, the water trickled, then stopped.

"Thank you," Marnie prayed to no one in particular.

Now all she needed to do was find a way to wash off the blood. It would stain.

Then, it started again. Spurting out of the shower head once again.

She checked the handle. It was still off.

No, no, no, why? How?

"This is your fault, Marnie."

He was back. And why wouldn't he be? Clearly, he was incapable of leaving her alone for long.

"Your precious friend can't help you. And God certainly can't help you," the voice sneered.

Marnie wrapped her arms around her bare skin. She was exposed here, vulnerable. What would he do to her? She folded in on herself, becoming small, becoming nothing.

Fingers crept down her back. They were freezing cold. She shivered, more from fear than the cold. Then she felt a strange warmth wash over her. Emotions surged in her battered heart, and Marnie let the tears roll out, letting them wash away the stains. It was the only clean water she had, might as well put them to use.

She watched as the tears fell onto her red-stained feet, dissolving the red and washing it away.

How long until she stopped crying? Until she no longer felt anything? Tears poured out of her clenched eyes until they ran dry.

She felt the waves of panic and defeat recede and peeked through sore eyes.

Clear water filled the tub. She looked up again. The blood was gone; the water was clear. There was nothing left on the walls, no stains. It wasn't real – another hallucination.

Marnie jumped out of the shower. She wrapped herself in a towel and ran to her bedroom. Her mind was spinning. She hated this house but now knew that no matter where she went, he'd find her. Her heart pounded as he paced, racking her brain for a solution. There had to be something.

The Bible she'd purchased sat on her nightstand, calling out to her. Hannah wouldn't mind hanging out on her own for a while longer. Marnie crept to the door to listen. She could hear Hannah's voice lilting and laughing on the phone, most likely chatting with her new beau. Marnie eyed the Bible with a little trepidation.

Hannah's story of the tortured man played in her mind. It wouldn't hurt to read it, right?

With a fresh hoodie and sweats on, Marnie crawled under the covers and opened the Bible. She searched the index and found countless instances of Jesus coming face to face with demons. Every single time, he won. Marnie didn't remember hearing these stories in church. Vague memories of a loving God were there, somewhere. Mostly they were hidden under the hate Pete spewed from the pulpit, followed by the hate he spewed at her mother. God had seemed so cruel. Jesus seemed narrow-minded. All that was in direct contradiction to what she read now. Jesus was not the mean, narrow-minded man she believed him to be. He was loving and patient. He didn't force people to change; all he did was love them and give them another option.

Marnie devoured the gospel of Luke, drinking in every word as if she were a wanderer in the desert, and this was the only water for miles. The story of a man plagued with leprosy and cast away hit her the hardest. He approached Jesus, saying, "If you're willing, you can heal me." Jesus didn't push the man away; didn't call him unclean. All he said was, "I'm willing." And the man was healed.

Marnie was that man, removed from everything she knew, plagued by nightmares. She felt as unclean as that man. If Jesus was willing to heal him, perhaps he could do the same for her.

The love of Jesus filled her heart. How could she have been so blind? All the hate, the anger, the disgrace fell away bit by bit and was replaced with an everlasting love.

Marnie cried. They weren't tears of fear or hopelessness like moments ago. These were tears of joy and grief. How could she have believed such lies? How did she miss this truth that was right in front of her? She felt heavy and guilty at once. Then a small chiding from within brought her back to the image of Jesus. Love burst forth in her. She knew what was true now, and that was all that mattered. Repentance rushed out of her in waves.

"Marnie? Are you okay?" Hannah was at the door, peeking in.

"I had no idea," Marnie said through sobs. "I was so wrong."

Hannah climbed into Marnie's bed and hugged her. She had been such a jerk to Hannah when all along, Hannah had shown her the same love that Jesus showed. Never once did Hannah force anything onto Marnie; all she'd ever done was present another path. Marnie saw that now.

Marnie cried for hours. Her body was reacting to this new light that had overcome the lies nestled in her mind. It was strange, yet freeing. It was almost like the chemical makeup of her body had changed.

Hannah sat with her, not asking any questions. She comforted Marnie. When the tears subsided, Hannah spoke. "What's this?" She picked up the Bible.

"You were right, Hannah. I'm sorry I never listened."

"Come on, kid. I knew you'd come around."

They talked late into the night about God and life and what Marnie was experiencing. Marnie prayed for Hannah. She prayed for Jason. She prayed for herself. Then, she fell asleep.

Twenty-Three

THE PHONE RANG TWICE. Each time, she let it go to voicemail. Staying awake until the wee hours of the morning with Hannah hadn't been her best idea, but it was what she needed. Marnie's body was exhausted, but her spirit was soaring.

When the buzzing finally stopped, Marnie grabbed her phone from the nightstand. She sprung up.

There were two missed calls from an unsaved number. It could've been Jason. Why she didn't ask for his number in return, she would never know. She shouldn't have rushed out on him so fast.

The little voicemail icon appeared in the notification bar.

Who left voicemails anymore?

Marnie clicked through and listened. Sure enough, it was Jason.

"Hey Marnie, it's Jason. Thought I'd give you a call. I'd love to see you again. I'm thinkin' dinner this time? Whaddya say? Call me back? You have my number now."

Marnie squealed, kicking her legs in a happy dance from a sitting position. She hadn't scared him off completely. All hope was not lost! She still had a chance with Jason. This time, she promised herself not to screw it up.

She started to redial his number, then paused. Would it look desperate to call back right away? If only the butterflies would stop spinning in her stomach, she'd be able to press "call." She settled on sending a text instead.

Hey Jason, sorry I missed your call. Dinner sounds great. Saturday night work for you?

Marnie hit send, then threw her phone across the bed. It had been two years since her last date. Two years too long. She couldn't remember the last time she was interested in a guy. She felt like a schoolgirl again, giddy and excited.

She walked out of her bedroom to find Hannah sitting at the table, reading her Bible.

"I guess I should start doing that, too, huh?" Marnie said.

"Good morning! Yeah, probably a good idea."

Marnie opened her Bible next to Hannah's and stared at it. "I don't even know where to begin."

"What did you read last night?"

"The book called Luke."

Hannah opened her eyes wide. "The whole thing?" Marnie nodded sheepishly. "Dang, Marnie! For someone who was adamant against Christianity, you tore through that book."

Marnie laughed. "I know! I can't believe it myself."

"Well, I recommend sticking with Jesus' stories. Check out the book of John," Hannah said.

She turned to the book of John and read. They sat next to each other, silently reading. It was mind-blowing how different everything sounded compared to Marnie's childhood. She was actually enjoying what she was reading now. After finishing, Marnie's phone buzzed.

Perfect. I'll pick you up at 8.

A date with Jason. Nothing could wipe away the smile plastered onto Marnie's face.

Marnie got ready for work, feeling like a new person. The entire morning passed by without a single hallucination. Her anxiety was nothing more than a speck sitting in the back of her mind.

Things were finally turning around; she could be happy again. This was a turning point in her life.

Marnie left with Hannah, opting to spend the rest of her afternoon at the bookstore before going to work. They walked through the alley without a hitch. Marnie breathed in, fresh air filling her lungs. The smell of garbage couldn't bring her down. She couldn't smell it at all.

"Hey, I wanna thank you for staying with me the past few nights. You didn't have to, and I know it's never easy being away from your home," she said.

Hannah nudged her shoulder. "Anytime, kid. Plus, something wonderful came out of it."

"I don't think you need to stay with me anymore, though. I'm feeling good. I'm not scared or anxious at all. I'll be okay."

Hannah stopped walking, putting her hand on Marnie's shoulder to stop her too. "Marnie, are you sure? What about the texts, the possible break-in?"

Marnie shook her head, smiling. "We don't have anything to worry about. Nothing has happened yet, and maybe the cops were right, and no one broke in. I'm not worried."

"I could stay another night, just in case."

Frustration bubbled up in Marnie's chest. Their roles had switched. Hannah was the skeptical one, telling Marnie she was stressed at first. Why was it so hard for her to let go now?

"Hannah, I'll be fine. I swear."

"Alright." Hannah started walking again. "But if you need me at all, I'm a phone call away!"

Marnie hooked her elbow with Hannah's. "I know, thank you."

❧

Cavin followed Marnie as she and her friend walked through the alley. He stayed far enough back that they wouldn't notice but close enough to listen to their conversation. He was annoyed, frustrated, even. Not at Marnie, never at Marnie. No, it was that friend of hers, a viper. That woman sucked the life out of Marnie, kept her away from him, and ruined everything. Something was off about Marnie, though. He admitted that. There was a stench to her. It singed his nostril hairs and made him want to gag. Gone was the smell of coconut from her hair; instead, it smelled of sulfur.

"She's rotten," the voice said with a shudder. "Rotten to the core. We should ditch her and find a new lady."

Are you insane? Cavin thought. *That is the love of my life you're talking about. You better watch it.*

He felt the voice back off, retreating deeper into his mind. As much as she stunk, Cavin would never trade her in. He loved her. Regardless of the smell, his bones ached for her, down to the marrow.

The pain was unbearable. Cavin missed Marnie. The sound of her voice, the gentle rise and fall of her chest as she sat in the cafe reading. He wanted to watch her, to study her, to be near her. But her pesky little friend kept getting in the way. Why was she staying with Marnie, anyway? Didn't she have her own place? When Cavin and Marnie finally move in together, she wouldn't leech off Marnie anymore.

His ears perked up when Marnie spoke, and a rush of excitement coursed through his veins.

"You don't need to stay with me anymore," she'd said. A shiver tickled Cavin's spine. His lovely Marnie finally had the nerve to kick the annoying chick to the curb.

He planned to visit Marnie that night. With her friend gone, Marnie would be alone in the apartment. One last look at her home to make sure he'd prepared everything correctly. Marnie was a heavy sleeper; he could be in and out before she ever woke up. Letting himself into her apartment would be easier while she was at work, but then he'd miss out on watching her angelic slumber. He'd be an idiot to let an opportunity like that pass him by. Plus, he needed to work today. Buying new furniture for Marnie wasn't cheap, and he needed to be able to provide for his bride.

Cavin had just enough time to follow Marnie out of the alley, before he needed to leave for work. Cavin hated work, hated anything that involved him being so far from Marnie for so long. Though, he was lucky that the packing plant outside of town was willing to hire him under the table as needed. Legality wasn't important, and the less those people knew about Cavin, the better.

Marnie turned her head a little too far to the right, and Cavin ducked behind a dumpster. He held his breath, praying she hadn't caught him.

Oh, how he longed for the days when he didn't need to sneak around anymore. When he could crawl into bed and hold her. His skin itched with anticipation. But it wouldn't be long now. He was preparing a place for her like a proper groom should, and she would love it.

At the edge of the alley, Marnie turned right, and Cavin turned left, back to his car.

Until tonight, my sweet. I'll meet you in your dreams. He blew a kiss at the back of her head, watching it land gently in her hair.

Night fell, and Cavin finished his work at the packing plant. The entire crew was made up of idiots and lowlifes, people he was appalled to spend any length of time with. At least the money was good.

The drive back to Marnie's apartment was an hour. He spent the entire time dreaming up his life with Marnie. He imagined their wedding, a beautiful day in mid-June. Marnie, the bride of a lifetime, in a white lace dress. She'd cry walking down the aisle, mouthing "I love you" at Cavin. He'd cry, too. Real men cried. They would dance to "At Last" by Etta James, and Marnie would cling to him like he was the only important thing in her world. And he was – like she was for him.

Such fantasies made the hour's drive feel like a moment. Before he knew it, Cavin was parking at the Kum & Go and walking to Marnie's. He shoved his hand into his pocket, thumbing the bump key. Lucky for him, Marnie hadn't changed the locks. The deadbolt was still a little broken from his last forced entry, making it easier for him to get in this time.

Cavin eased the door shut behind him. What little light shone through the closed curtains helped him find his way to Marnie's bedroom door.

It was cracked open. He could barely make out the sweet form of Marnie's body, her chest rising and falling in a pattern of deep sleep. She was so peaceful, undisturbed.

He loved her so much. It made his chest burn.

Cavin walked on light feet to the edge of her bed, watching her sleep. She was beautiful. The way her eyes gently rested shut, a look of contentment on her face.

What he wouldn't give to lean down and kiss her right then and there.

He reached a hand to her hair, stroking it. His fingers tickled a few strands; he didn't want to wake her. He knew he shouldn't risk it, but it was impossible to resist. Her hair was silky, that of an angel. The rancid smell was still there but weaker. Or Cavin didn't care. He'd withstand fire to be near her – a little smell was nothing.

I could take her tonight… We could finish preparing the house together.

"Are you crazy?" The voice in his head replied.

It'd been quiet the past few days, not bothering to comment on Cavin's daily activities.

This, though, had stirred him.

Why not? Cavin thought. *She's right here, and she's asleep. I bet I could get her to the car before she woke up.*

"I said no! Are you really that dense?"

The hand that caressed Marnie's hair dropped to his side. He didn't deserve this. After days of silence, the voice got mad at him – the one who was putting in all the actual work? Ridiculous!

"Cavin, buddy. I'm sorry I snapped." The voice went up an octave, sounding sweet. "I need a little more time. She isn't ready yet."

"I'm tired of waiting," Cavin whispered, raising his hand to Marnie's plump cheek.

"A little longer, my friend. Your time is coming."

Marnie rolled over, and Cavin stepped back. It was time to go before she woke and blew the whole thing. Cavin backed out of the room, watching Marnie the whole way.

"Sleep sweet, love. I miss you."

It was only a matter of time.

Twenty-Four

MARNIE STOOD IN FRONT OF HER BATHROOM MIRROR, arranging her curly hair into a twist. The last two days were a dream. Life was finally returning to normal. Work was great, her friendship with Hannah had deepened, and she had a date with Jason. But, more important than all that, the nightmares and hallucinations were gone. Things had leveled out. Marnie could breathe again.

There was only one slight problem, Carley.

She'd canceled her appointments for the rest of the week. Marnie worried, but there was only so much she could do. She called Carley's parents to check in, but they didn't help. All they'd done was assure Marnie that Carley was fine, that she didn't need therapy anymore.

"She's been wonderful, spending time with us, going out with friends. She's even been telling us how much she loves us, isn't that wonderful?"

Still, it didn't seem right. Carley was at her worst the last time Marnie saw her. There was no way she did a full 180 change overnight.

Marnie cautioned Carley's parents, reminding them that healing is a journey and that change doesn't happen overnight like that.

But they refused to listen. They were too excited to "have their little girl back" to care what Marnie had to say.

And what else could she do? It wasn't like she could force Carley to go to therapy. Marnie prayed for Carley, prayed that she was doing better, and prayed that Carley would continue therapy.

But all that was work-related. Marnie didn't have time for work worries; she was getting ready for her date.

Jason hadn't called it a date. But, dinner on a Saturday night between a man and a woman, both single, usually constitutes a date.

Marnie made a mental note to check with Jason on that.

She finished her hair, applied a clear lip gloss that gave her lips an enticing shine, and took a step back to check herself in the mirror. Not bad. She wore a dark purple top with a leather jacket and black skinny jeans. It was edgy, the way she liked it. Marnie had never been the type to wear bright, frilly things. When she dressed up, she preferred to do it in a dark, Vampire Diaries-esque way. Jason had only ever seen her in a T-shirt and jeans. Hopefully, this ensemble didn't scare him off.

Marnie felt pretty.

She hadn't felt that way in a long time. Tonight, the stars aligned, God was good, and she felt pretty.

A honk outside alerted Marnie that her date arrived. She gave herself one more top-to-bottom glance, then whispered a silent prayer.

God, please let Jason think this is a date.

"Wow, you look–"

"Too much?" Marnie blushed.

"Absolutely not." Jason's eyes sparkled, moving up and down. His smile proved that he meant it.

Marnie blushed some more, buckling her seatbelt.

"I was thinking Italian, you like Italian?"

"Pasta and pizza? Sign me up."

"Great," Jason said.

He looked great, too. Jason always looked great. His short brown hair was styled to the side with the faintest amount of hair gel. Marnie took that as a sign that he put in effort for the date-not-date.

"Hey, uh Jason?" Marnie asked. Her voice cracked, and she had to cough to clear it.

"What's up?"

"Is this a date?" She picked at the hem of her shirt, avoiding his gaze.

Jason shot a glance in her direction. Her skin caught fire. Was it too soon to ask? Bringing it up at the restaurant might've been a better idea. At least that way, he couldn't swing the car around and take her back home. Marnie focused on the road; there was a chance for a U-turn coming up. She waited to see if he'd take it.

He passed the intersection.

Whew.

Now it was his turn to clear his throat. "I mean, dinner on a Saturday night… Doesn't that kinda scream 'date'?"

Marnie shifted her entire body to face him, excited. "Yes! Thank you. Okay! I was a little nervous you'd say no."

"And miss my opportunity to say I took Marnie Adams on a date? Not a chance." He winked.

Marnie stared at him, the smile on her face forming without her consent. He was cute. Not only in looks but in personality. Exactly the kind of guy Marnie wanted to be with.

She sat against the seat again, feeling self-conscious for staring so long. "I haven't been on a date in a long time," she said.

"Me either. I haven't dated since moving here."

Unbelievable. A guy like him? He had to be lying.

"Work is stressful, but it keeps me busy. I don't usually like bringing people into it."

"Oh, well, thank you for choosing me," Marnie said with a dramatic eye roll.

"It's not like that! I mean… I don't know what I mean."

Marnie smirked and nudged his shoulder.

Touch was allowed on dates, right?

"I get it," she said. "Relationships have always taken a backseat for me, too. Helping people has been my main priority. Not to mention I didn't grow up with the greatest role models."

They pulled up at a red light; now it was Jason's turn to face her. The glow from the stoplight made him look like a character from a rom-com.

Marnie subtly wiped the side of her lip, checking for drool. All clear.

"I'm the same way," he said before facing forward again.

"Hey! You still haven't told me what you do for work. I'm half-tempted to think it's something illegal."

"Oh yeah?" He raised an eyebrow. "What are your guesses?"

"Hitman is at the top of the list."

Jason laughed. "You answered way too quickly! How long have you had that one saved?"

"Pretty much since the day I met you." Marnie hoped Jason heard the flirty edge to her voice.

"I hate to disappoint, but I'm not a hitman." Was that a little bit of flirting to his voice, too?

They pulled into a parking garage along downtown's main street. The streets were bursting with life; people on dates, families with small children, and singles on the hunt. Each one passed them, radiating with life. It was invigorating. The world seemed brighter tonight. The moon shone clear. Its beams danced with the street lights and neon signs of bars and restaurants, inviting people in.

Jason grabbed Marnie's hand as they walked out. Her heart skipped a couple of beats and threatened to stop altogether.

The hostess led them to a table with a reserved sign. Jason had thought this through, going so far as to reserve a spot. So, this was how it felt for someone to like her? She could get used to this.

They sat, ordered drinks, and stared into each other's eyes.

"Seriously, Jason. What do you do?"

He sat back, rubbing the back of his neck. "You really wanna know?"

"Yeah, I really wanna know!"

"Alright, then I'll tell you." Jason picked up his drink and took a long, slow sip. He made direct eye contact with Marnie as he did it, and she swore she saw him smirk behind the glass.

Marnie rolled her eyes and checked the invisible watch on her wrist. She had no idea Jason was such a tease.

What felt like thirty seconds went by and he finally put the drink down. "I'm a detective with Springfield PD," he said.

"Ooh, a cop," Marnie teased. "Do you have your badge with you right now?"

"I do not," Jason said. "I'll show it to you next time."

"Why didn't you wanna tell me?"

He moved his silverware around, picking up each one and placing it back down. Marnie felt bad about how uncomfortable he seemed. She shouldn't have pushed it. But it wasn't like it was that bad of a job – she didn't understand what was so uncomfortable.

"People get weird around cops; I don't know," his voice trailed off.

Oh yeah, Marnie didn't particularly like cops. After the incident with the break-in, cops weren't on her list of favorite people. She didn't trust them, at least not the ones that came to her apartment. Jason was different, though. He cared about people, cared about her. Next time, she'd call him if there was a break-in.

Marnie reached her hand across, grabbing Jason's. She rubbed the back of his hand with her thumb. His skin felt soft for a guy, another reason to like him.

"Hey, I think it's brave what you do. And if it makes you that uncomfortable, we don't have to talk about it anymore." She gave him her best therapist smile.

The corner of Jason's mouth lifted. "Whaddya wanna talk about then?"

Marnie perked up, straightened her shoulders, and looked him dead in the eye. "I've got something really important to tell you," she said.

"Let me have it," he said.

"I bought a Bible the other day. And I read it. And I sort of, kind of, am a Christian now."

"Get outta town! You read the entire Bible?"

She rolled her eyes. "Not the whole thing, but I did read the entire book of Luke. Pretty good stuff, I gotta admit."

"That's incredible, Marnie. What brought you over?"

"Over?"

"You know," he winked, "to our side."

"Something finally clicked. It's like, all these years, I've had something missing in my heart, something I didn't even know was missing. When I started reading that, I knew." It sounded stupid; she knew that. "I'm not making any sense, am I?" Her cheeks burned.

Jason's smile was the brightest Marnie had ever seen it. He shook his head. "You're making perfect sense." He flipped his hand over, wrapping his fingers around hers. "I am so proud of you; this is amazing."

"I'm on top of the world." Marnie beamed.

Jason's smile faded. He looked serious, and Marnie shrunk back. "Marnie, I don't want to bring you down. But I want to remind you that just because you feel good now doesn't mean that everything is resolved. Have you had any more nightmares or hallucinations?"

Marnie ripped her hand away, crossing her arms. "Are you serious?"

"I only want you to be aware of the reality. Something is still going on. You should know that even more now. There is still something after you."

"Did you not hear me? I said I was better. And for your information, I haven't had a nightmare or hallucination since I became a Christian." She shook her head. How could he do this to her? Why was he trying to ruin this moment? This was a date; they should be celebrating. Instead, Marnie felt the need to defend herself.

"That's great, I'm glad. Now, you gotta stay prayed up, okay? I have a feeling this isn't over." His eyes held hers. They were strong. But Marnie felt a sliver of betrayal; how could he take this away from her?

What did he know? All the butterflies and first-date jitters were gone. The only thing left was frustration. Marnie wanted to run out, to leave him. He was her ride, though, so she was stuck.

"Can we talk about something else?"

Jason pressed his lips into a line, then smiled. "Sure."

When the date was over, Jason drove Marnie home and walked her to the door. After the uncomfortable conversation about her issues, they had a moderately pleasant evening.

They stood at her front door, holding hands.

"I had a great time with you tonight," Jason said. "I'm sorry I upset you."

Marnie leaned forward, bumping into him. "It's alright. I had a great time, too."

Jason leaned in and landed a peck on Marnie's lips. It was quick, so quick that she almost missed it. She would've missed it if not for the shockwave it sent through her body.

A kiss from Jason. The perfect way to end the night. She couldn't hold back the grin as it spread across her face.

A loud noise pulled her out of the moment. It came from the alley. Marnie strained to see, but it was too dark. "You heard that, right?" she asked.

"Yeah." Jason took a step toward the alley, peering into the darkness. "Something must've fallen out of the dumpster. It's probably nothing."

Marnie kept staring, willing her vision to cooperate. Nothing.

"I better get going," Jason said, stepping back close to her. He planted another kiss, this one longer. He winked as he pulled away.

"Goodnight," Marnie whispered, watching him trot down her stairs.

Once inside, she pressed her back into the front door, letting all the emotions wash over her. Marnie was able to swoon at full volume now that she was alone. She squealed, squeaked, and danced around. Her night with Jason was amazing; it was everything she could've ever asked for.

This was more proof that life was on its way up for her.

Twenty-Five

CARLEY SAT ON THE EDGE OF HER BED, her feet dangling over the edge. She stared down at the floor. Her soccer jersey crumbled in a heap.

She wouldn't need that anymore.

Shadows danced along the wall, fueled by the low candle-light. After a year of being afraid of the shadows, she'd started to accept them. She'd be joining them soon, becoming a shadow herself. She already was, in a way. A shadow of her past self, that girl dead and gone.

The doctors called it manic, but she knew it wasn't that. It was death. The biggest part of her died with Madison in the car accident.

That night played like a horror movie in her mind, over and over and over. It never turned off. She tried to fast forward through the bad parts, but they always ended up slowing down, forcing her to savor them.

"I saved you, Carley. You're mine."

That was what he said to her that night. The car flipped on its head – Madison bleeding out next to her.

If only she'd worn a seatbelt, she would've survived too.

Carley cried, screamed for help, and begged someone to save

them.

He was the only one who showed up. Carley watched as his fingers wrapped around her wrist. Her mind played with her that night, making her think he was a real person. Solid like the rest of them.

If only she'd known then what she knew now, she would've spit in his face. She would've kicked and screamed. No, she would've never screamed in the first place.

If she could go back, she'd stay silent. She'd let the life drain out of her and join Madison on the other side.

"I'm coming, Maddie. Sorry I'm so late," Carley whispered.

It wouldn't be long now. Carley had made all the arrangements. She made sure her parents knew how much she loved them.

She didn't mean to hurt them. She did love them, after all. But she was out of options; life left her in the dark. It was time she embraced it completely.

Carley couldn't remember exactly when she knew.

He told her to do it. She knew that much.

He made it sound so enticing, so freeing. He made it sound like it was the only way.

And it was.

She saw that now.

She tried fighting him. All it got her was more hurt.

She tried ignoring him. He didn't like that.

The only thing she hadn't tried was joining him. Maybe now he'd stop digging into her head and planting weeds.

Carley stood from her bed. She was prolonging the inevitable.

"It's like going to sleep." That was what the blog said – nothing to be afraid of.

Carley opened her bedroom door and listened carefully. She could hear the TV downstairs, her dad coughing. Her parents watched TV for two hours every night before bed. There was time.

Carley slipped through the door and tiptoed to her parents' room. Mom kept Carley's pills from the doctor. She was worried Carley would accidentally take too many. They would do the trick. Mom had dealt her two pills earlier that week because of the nightmares. They worked like a charm.

She searched the cabinet under their bathroom sink for the little orange bottle. It sat tucked away behind a bottle of St. Ives body wash, the smell of her mom. She opened the body wash, breathing in every last essence. Closing her eyes, she held onto the scent. She wanted to take it with her.

At the top of the staircase, Carley called down to her parents. "I'm going to sleep; love you guys."

"Love you, honey," her dad said.

"Goodnight, baby. Sleep well," Mom said.

In her room, Carley sat on the edge of the bed, her legs dangling over. She stared at the pills in her hand. She opened her mouth and dumped them in, followed by a long swig of water.

Carley laid back on her pillow and closed her eyes.

You win, shadow.

She turned onto her side and fell asleep finally at rest.

Twenty-Six

THE MOST TERRIFYING CALL PULLED MARNIE OUT OF BED.

"I need to see you now." Dr. Carlson's voice was deep, serious.

Marnie left the apartment in a hurry, her heart racing to get there first. Whatever prompted the meeting was bound to be bad. Marnie ran her mind through the past few weeks, trying to find any reason for Dr. Carlson to call the meeting. She'd been doing her job, hadn't been late, and hadn't complained. Even when she tried to get Dr. Carlson to take on Cavin, she was professional. In fact, she was glad Dr. Carlson made her keep him. He wasn't so bad, after all.

Marnie barreled through the entrance of Golden Meadow, startling Savannah.

"Sorry," Marnie mouthed as she approached Dr. Carlson's door.

Marnie knocked twice, heard "come in" from the other side, and inched the door open. Dr. Carlson was sitting at her desk, straight back with her hands interlaced in front of her. She was leaning forward a little, pulling her eyebrows together in a look of sincere concern. Marnie didn't notice the two people sitting with their backs to her until

Dr. Carlson addressed them.

"Good morning," Marnie said.

The guests turned around. It was Mr. and Mrs. Rey – Carley's parents. Sweat beaded on Marnie's forehead, and she wiped it with the back of her hand. Something was wrong; she could feel it in her bones. There were only ever a handful of reasons for parents of a client to be sitting in the director's office. Either Marnie had done something horribly wrong, or Carley had.

"Ms. Adams, please take a seat." Dr. Carlson gestured to a third chair in line with the Reys.

Marnie dropped her head and eased into the seat, taking a deep breath. She was ready for whatever came her way.

"Thank you for rushing down here."

"Dr. Carlson, is everything alright?" Marnie asked.

Mrs. Rey hitched, releasing a short sob, then held a crumpled tissue to her nose and mouth. Marnie watched the woman. Why wasn't Carley here? She was the client. She should be involved in any decisions made regarding her care.

"Ms. Adams…" Dr. Carlson started.

"Where's Carley?" Marnie blurted out. She tried to ignore the sinking in her stomach, the warning bells alerting her that there was a very specific reason Carley wasn't there.

"Ms. Adams, please. That is what we want to talk about." Dr. Carlson sounded sad.

When had Dr. Carlson ever sounded sad before? Never. Not since Marnie had known her. Marnie couldn't look away from Mrs. Rey. She stared as the woman blotted the tissue under her eyes, then reached for another.

No one was answering her question. They all stared at different places in the room, refusing to make eye contact. Dr. Carlson looked at Marnie; she could feel her eyes burning against her skin. Mr. Rey kept his eyes down at his lap, his hands shaking . And Mrs. Rey had her eyes closed, the tissue glued to her face.

Finally, Dr. Carlson broke the silence. "Marnie, I'm so sorry."

Marnie met Dr. Carlson's stare. She never used her first name in front of other people. The alarm bells sounded louder.

"Carley is gone," Dr. Carlson said.

What did that mean? Why wasn't anyone speaking clearly? They were all avoiding something, leaving Marnie in the dark. She hated it, hated feeling lost. "Gone? Where?"

Mrs. Rey cried louder. Mr. Rey placed a hand on his wife's back. It didn't help.

"Carley committed suicide over the weekend. Mrs. Rey found her."

The room spun, flipping all of them upside down. Marnie was grateful to be sitting. Dr. Carlson was lying – she had to be. Carley wouldn't do that; she wouldn't take her own life. Not when they were so close to a breakthrough. Marnie sucked air into her burning lungs. She hadn't realized that she was holding her breath. Tears warmed her cheek; she didn't bother wiping them away. Everything felt distant. The tears, the room, and the beat of her own heart felt far away.

"No," she whispered.

Mr. Rey stood. He loomed over Marnie, pointing a finger in her face with one hand, forming a fist with the other. "This is your fault!" he yelled. "You were supposed to be helping her! And now our baby is gone!"

Bile rose in her throat, and Marnie covered her mouth to stop it from coming out. She was already responsible for the death of this man's daughter. She didn't want to throw up on him too. Problem was, he was right. Carley had been her responsibility, and she'd failed.

"I didn't…" Marnie shook her head. Her words got stuck behind the vomit, and she retched. She pushed past Mr. Rey and collapsed at the trash can next to Dr. Carlson's desk. It kept coming out, her stomach betraying her. When it finally stopped, Marnie clutched the trash can and cried, sobbed, and screamed. This wasn't fair. Carley couldn't be gone. She was getting better.

A hand rested on Marnie's shoulder, and she saw Dr. Carlson holding a bottle of water out. She took it and sipped. Regaining control, Marnie returned to her seat.

"I don't understand," she said.

"She took sleeping pills. I found the bottle on her nightstand." Mrs. Rey took a deep breath. "It was empty."

"Were there any indications, Ms. Adams? Did Carley say anything?" Dr. Carlson was the only one in the room not entirely blaming Marnie.

Marnie shook her head. "She was getting better."

A long silence fell, interrupted only by the soft sobs of Mrs. Rey.

"We thought so, too," Carley's dad said. He dropped his head and joined his wife in crying.

There wasn't much else to say. Nothing would fix it. Marnie couldn't bring Carley back, no matter what she said. Carley's parents left at the prompting of Dr. Carlson. She promised them that she would be in touch and saw them out. Marnie stayed fixed in her seat, silent tears falling, soaking her shirt.

Dr. Carlson sat next to her and placed a hand on her knee. "Marnie," she said. "I know this is tough. Trust me, I've been there. When I first started out, I had a client pass away, too. It's hard."

Marnie closed her eyes. She didn't want to hear this. It didn't matter what Dr. Carlson had been through; didn't matter that she understood. Because truthfully, she didn't understand. No one knew the relationship Marnie had with Carley. No one could ever understand their connection. Carley was the only person in the world who knew the shadow – the only one who could relate to Marnie, even if Marnie never told her. They were going to beat him together, overcome their fear together. Survive together. *Weren't they?*

Now, Marnie was alone.

"I need you to take some time off. Two weeks." Dr. Carlson's voice was kind, almost gentle. "You have to mourn Carley. You have to rest. The board and I will discuss your future with the company." The words stuck in Marnie's heart like a dagger.

"My future with the company?" Marnie asked.

"Marnie, I think you're an incredible therapist. You do amazing work. But something like this can't go unnoticed."

It made sense. She killed a client; she needed to be punished. Firing would be the easy way out.

"Go home," Dr. Carlson said, releasing her grip on Marnie's knee. "I'm going to take over your clients. Get some rest."

Marnie nodded. She couldn't focus, couldn't see Dr. Carlson. Her words were whispers, floating around the room before registering in Marnie's mind.

Going home was a good idea.

She stood and walked out the door.

"Marnie," Savannah called.

She ignored her, walking out the front door.

Shame covered her in a blanket, acting as a comfort and a reprimand for what happened. She deserved it. Marnie decided from that moment forward; she would not accept anything but shame. This was hers to bear, her way of taking responsibility for Carley's death. If she had pushed harder for Carley to return or pressed her parents when they said she was fine, then Carley would still be alive. But no, Marnie had been too wrapped up in her own problems to care about Carley's. That was what it came down to in the end, she knew she should've said something, but she didn't because she didn't care enough. And that had cost someone their life.

She wasn't cut out to be a therapist anymore. At one point, she had been a good one. Now, all she cared about was herself. Her stupid nightmares, her stupid stalker, and her stupid faith. What did any of that matter anymore? Jesus wasn't going to forgive a murderer like her.

Speaking of God, where was he now? Why did he let Carley die? He could've stopped it, could've pushed Marnie to do more. Why didn't he?

She didn't apologize to Mr. and Mrs. Reys. Even after the fact, Marnie was selfishly focusing on herself more than Carley's parents. They were the ones who lost a child, and she hadn't even mustered a lousy apology.

Walking into her apartment, the first thing Marnie did was call Mrs. Rey. She had to apologize. She couldn't leave things the way they were at the office.

"Hello?" Mrs. Rey sounded exhausted. Her voice was hoarse like she'd aged ten years in the past twenty-four hours.

"Mrs. Rey, it's Marnie Adams from Golden Meadow. I need to tell you how sorry I am. If I would've known, I…" Her voice cracked. She couldn't finish.

"Did she make any indication? Did she say anything to you?" Mrs. Rey pleaded.

"No, I'm so sorry. I thought she was getting better. She was getting better."

They cried together on the phone, their souls connecting through sorrow. Marnie knew that Mrs. Rey hadn't forgiven her, but a door to reconciliation opened. Marnie wasn't going to forgive herself, either.

"I'd like to come to the funeral if that's okay," Marnie said.

"Of course, you can come. Carley would want you there."

A chance to say goodbye, a chance to apologize to Carley in

person – that was all Marnie wanted.

"I'll email you the details," Mrs. Rey said before hanging up.

Marnie dropped her phone onto the couch and sank to the floor. She left the lights off, a small stream of sunlight peeking through the closed blinds. Marnie brought her knees to her chest, hugging them. She cried. She cursed at herself. When she closed her eyes, she pictured Carley's lifeless body lying on her bed. She imagined Mrs. Rey trying to wake her to no avail. The beautiful, happy, and hopeful Carley was gone. She would never walk down the aisle, never go to college. She would never be free from the shadow's grip.

When Marnie finally fell asleep, she dreamt of the shadow dragging Carley into darkness, away from life forever.

Twenty-Seven

HER TIME OFF WORK CRAWLED BY in a blur of ignored phone calls and reruns of Gilmore Girls. Marnie left her house only once – a task that felt too big at the time – to get groceries.

She lay under a fuzzy blanket, staring at the TV screen. Marnie preferred the shallow companionship of Lorelai and Rory over real-life friends. This was one-sided, she wasn't expected to do anything but watch. If she answered Hannah's phone calls, she would have to respond. Responding would mean telling Hannah what happened. Marnie wasn't ready to talk about it.

Jason called, too. He left messages expressing his concern, but Marnie refused to engage. She didn't want him to know how terrible she was, how selfish and evil she was. Most of all, Marnie didn't want anyone's pity. She didn't deserve it.

Marnie watched Rory sitting in her Yale dorm room doing homework. All she could think about was how perfect it would be to live in a fake world. Nothing devastating ever happened in Stars Hollow. No one died. It was nothing like the real world. In the real world, clients died, people blamed other people, and monsters stalked. The real world was a nightmare.

A week had passed, and the pain of Carley's death refused to ease. Marnie begged God to let her go to lessen the grief. He didn't answer. He was probably too busy answering the prayers of good Christians. And why shouldn't he? Why should he answer the prayers of a murderer by proxy? Marnie didn't deserve God.

The Gilmore Girls episode ended, and it was time for Marnie to peel herself off the couch.

It was the day of Carley's funeral – time to say goodbye, forever.

Marnie dreaded this day. She didn't want to go, didn't want to face her mistakes. But she needed to. She needed to tell Carley that she was sorry.

She stared at her open closet, looking for appropriate funeral attire. Sweats were off-limits, though that was all she'd worn the past week. Marnie pulled out a black dress that tied around the waist. It was simple, clean, and exactly what was expected of a funeral attendee.

She promised to burn the dress after the funeral. Wearing it again would be impossible.

Marnie kept her face clear; makeup would get in the way of crying. When she'd finished getting dressed, Marnie stood in front of her mirror.

Funny, she thought. The last time she'd stared at herself in the mirror was before her date with Jason. How quickly life changes.

"You can do this for Carley," she said, swatting away the tears that slipped out.

Even with her newfound faith, Marnie hadn't stepped foot in a church for at least a decade. The sting was still there. She loved God, although his silence was pushing her closer toward apathy each day. It was church people she didn't care for. They were the ones that caused pain.

Walking through the large oak doors felt surreal. The sanctuary was crowded with grieving family and friends. Soft murmurs and muted sniffles drifted atop the instrumental music playing in the background. The air was heavy and damp. Marnie felt it weigh her shoulders down. A blown-up picture of Carley stood over the bouquets. Her eyes sparkled, and her mouth was open in a wide, carefree smile. She looked so young and full of life. How could someone like that be capable of taking their own life? Had things really been that bad?

Marnie contemplated going to the front and giving her condolences to Carley's parents, but the thought of talking to them again stopped her. When she'd last seen them, the accusation in their eyes wounded her. This time, it was sure to strike her down for good. She opted for a seat in the second to last row. She sat on the edge, easier to make a clean getaway if necessary.

Marnie watched Carley's parents hug person after person. Both their noses were bright red, a sign of near-constant crying. They had more wrinkles even since last week. Mr. Rey was hunched over; gone was the confident man Marnie had met when Carley first came to Golden Meadow. He reached out a hand for Mrs. Rey, who shrunk away from it. A loss like this was sure to drive a wedge between them. Parents should never outlive a child. Marnie's heart broke further, something that didn't seem possible considering how much it'd already shattered.

Being in this church on a beautiful Saturday afternoon to mourn the loss of a teenager was not right. Carley should've been alive. She and her parents should've been spending the weekend at a park or shopping. On a normal Saturday, Marnie imagined Carley would be daydreaming about a cute boy or meeting up with friends. Everything was so backward. She had entered the Twilight Zone.

The reality struck Marnie harder seeing Carley's friends and family gathered in the front, an open casket between them. The reality was that Carley was dead. She wasn't going to have another weekend. No more talking to friends, shopping, or graduation.

All because of a monster that forced her into the arms of death – the same monster that was after Marnie.

What would happen to her?

A woman sat in front of the piano on the stage and started playing. A choir joined her, and all the attendees stood to sing an old hymn. Voices swelled in the familiar tune of "I'll Fly Away," and Marnie tried to hold back a shiver. The song felt morbid, eliciting images of ghosts and ghouls floating in the sky. She wanted to stand, too, but the power in her legs was completely wiped out.

Two questions lingered in Marnie's mind: Was Carley in heaven? Did she blame Marnie for her death? Marnie prayed for God to open the heavens and give her an answer to the questions. She glanced up at the ceiling expectantly. Nothing happened. For the first question, Marnie didn't care about the answer unless it was "yes." For the second, she knew it was a yes. She blamed herself, and Carley's parents blamed her. It was a given that Carley would blame her, too.

The minister took the stage, inviting everyone to sit. He talked about suffering and death and how Jesus knows it all.

"You know what the shortest verse in the Bible is?" he said. "It's two simple words: Jesus wept."

It was cliché and not at all comforting. Why should she care that Jesus wept? That didn't ease her sorrow, and it sure as hell didn't bring Carley back.

The minister ended his message with a call to salvation, inviting those listening to accept Jesus into their heart. Marnie wanted to scoff, to shout, "Don't do it! It's a scam!" But she knew that wouldn't go over well with Carley's family, and she'd already done enough damage for them. It was true, though. She felt like God had scammed her, tricked her into believing in him. Now she sat here, dealing with an endless stream of pain and guilt, begging him to take it away. And what did he do? Nothing. Absolutely nothing. He sat in the sky and watched. Marnie had half a mind to go back to not believing in him altogether.

It was too late for that, though. She already drank the Kool-aid. She'd settle for being angry at him; it was better than being angry at only herself.

Carley's mom spoke next. She shared memories of Carley's childhood while a slideshow of pictures played behind her head. She talked about Carley's obsession with horses and how she was so sure that she'd grow up to be a horseback rider. As Carley got older, she was embarrassed by that. Her mom talked about how Carley was getting ready for prom. They were supposed to go shopping the next week to pick out a dress. Mrs. Rey was still going to take that shopping trip.

This was too heavy. Marnie couldn't carry it anymore. Every bone in her body screamed at her, telling her to leave. She was at the back; she could dip out without anyone noticing. But her mind held her still. She needed to stay for Carley. She needed to tell her how sorry she was.

One by one, different friends and family members shared memories of Carley or read poems they thought fit the circumstance. And with each one, Marnie felt the pressure of guilt sit heavier on her chest until it was the weight of an elephant. She was going to pass out.

❧

Cavin snuck into the church while a redheaded high schooler cried from the stage. He'd stood outside for twenty minutes, debating on entering. The place gave him the heebie-jeebies. Something about the atmosphere rubbed his nerves raw, but he had to be with Marnie. If she was at a funeral, she was feeling very sad and vulnerable. Cavin wanted to comfort her in any way that he could.

Marnie sat near the back. He recognized the back of her head. The brown curls cascaded down her back like a waterfall. It was the most beautiful back of a head he'd ever seen. Scanning the crowd confirmed that.

The seat directly behind Marnie was empty. Cavin slipped into it and sent up a prayer of thanks to God.

Cavin had sat outside Marnie's apartment for days, waiting for her to leave for work. She never did. According to the voice, she was put on leave. The voice always knew things about Marnie. Cavin didn't know how, but he didn't care. He was happy to have the inside information.

When she'd finally left that morning, Cavin had to follow. He had no idea she'd head to a church. A small sacrifice he had to make for his love.

"At this time, if anyone else wants to share a memory of Carley, feel free to come up," someone announced.

Marnie turned her head, and Cavin caught a glimpse of her glowing bare skin. Her cheeks were splotched red – from crying, no doubt. She wasn't wearing any makeup, not even on her eyes. Marnie's natural beauty surpassed that of a supermodel. Cavin made a mental note to tell Marnie never to wear makeup again. It only ruined her skin. Cavin watched the subtle jerks of Marnie's shoulders. She was crying, and it took everything within himself not to wrap her in his arms. He reached his hand out, letting his fingers tangle with a few strands of her hair. She must've felt it because her hand reached back and smoothed the pieces. Cavin let his hand linger inches from Marnie's. He wanted to touch her, but then she'd know he was there. She couldn't know, not yet.

Attendees all around rose to their feet, including Marnie. A fat man in a black button-down shirt closed his eyes and started praying. The service was nearly over, and Cavin hadn't heard a single word.

He snuck out the back before anyone would notice him. He had some more work to do preparing their home.

Twenty-Eight

ALL EYES WERE ON MARNIE AS PEOPLE EXITED THE CHURCH.

They knew. Carley's death was all her fault, and the whole church knew it. Carley's parents probably told everyone by now that she was Carley's therapist, and how she failed the girl.

There was no way Marnie was going to the burial site, not with everyone glaring at her. She walked home. Fear threatened her sanity. The shadow's voice was back, louder than ever. He taunted her as she walked, speaking words she already knew.

"It's your fault she's dead," he said. "If only you'd done your job."

Marnie pressed her palms to her ears, but his voice persisted. She couldn't drown him out. He'd gone silent for a while, and Marnie was sure it was over. Why had he come back? God was supposed to be protecting her. Why were the demons louder?

When Marnie got home, she ran through the house and checked every possible hiding place. If someone broke in again, she'd know about it.

She sat on the couch, pulling her knees to her chest. Her eyes bounced around the room, seeing monsters in every corner. The paranoia that another hallucination would pop up at any moment kept her on edge – her nerves frayed.

"God, please. Do something, anything. Make this stop," she prayed.

There was a knock on the front door.

Marnie slid off the couch and looked through the peephole. Hannah, with a bag of food in one hand and an iced coffee in the other, stood on her porch.

"Thank you, Lord," Marnie sighed.

Marnie opened the door and let Hannah in. As she was about to close it again, something in the alley caught her eye. A man was standing on the side, and it looked like he was staring straight at her. Marnie stepped onto the porch, staring back at him. Recognition sparked. She knew that man but couldn't quite place how or from where. He was far enough away that details were hard to catch, but something about his posture was familiar.

He took a step back, disappearing into the shadows. Marnie's heart jolted.

It was the man from the texts. The man who left her flowers. The man who broke in.

He was waiting, watching.

Marnie slammed the door, locking both the deadbolt and the handle lock.

How long had he been out there? How often did he watch her?

She was spiraling; she could feel it. But what else was she supposed to do? The hallucinations and nightmares and Carley's death distracted her from the most substantial threat of all. She was the target of someone's obsession, and just because he'd been quiet for a while didn't mean he wasn't still there.

She knew that now.

"Marnie, you okay?" Hannah asked, placing a hand on her shoulder.

Marnie jumped, shooing Hannah away. She ran to the window and closed the curtains, then inched the corner open and peeked through. The alley was in clear view, but it was empty. At least, that was how it looked.

He was still out there, though. She sensed him.

"Marnie, what is going on?"

Marnie let the curtain fall. She turned around and faced Hannah. Marnie ran sweaty palms through tangled hair and shook her head.

"Hey," Hannah grabbed Marnie by the arm and pulled her to the couch. "Let's talk."

Where was she supposed to start? So much had gone wrong since they last hung out. Marnie's entire life had crumbled to dust in mere days, and she wasn't sure if she could put it back together.

Hannah's eyes burned holes into Marnie's skin. She had to tell her – to come right out and say it one thing at a time.

Marnie opened her mouth to speak, but instead of words, sobs came out. Hannah tried to hold her, but Marnie broke out. She stood and started pacing. She didn't want comfort; she didn't deserve it. The shadow was right; she deserved to be stuck in his torturous grip forever. She wrapped her arms around herself and kept pacing. She checked the window, paced, then checked again.

He was still out there.

"Marnie, you need to calm down and tell me what's going on."

Marnie stilled, staring at Hannah. Tears pooled in the corner of her eyes, and she blinked to get rid of them. She'd never be able to get the words out if she kept crying. "I'm on suspension from work," she said. "Have been for a week." The pacing started up again. "One of my clients, a girl named Carley, I -" Marnie took a deep breath. "I killed her."

Hannah shot off the couch. "You what?"

"Well, she died – killed herself. But it's my fault! I should've seen the signs, should've stopped her."

Hannah reached for Marnie, holding her still. "First of all, please never say you killed someone again unless it's actually you pulling the trigger or wielding the knife." She pulled Marnie in, wrapping her in a hug. "I'm so sorry, kid. That's horrible."

Marnie finally gave in and rested her head on Hannah's shoulder. She was exhausted. "I went to the funeral this morning."

"This isn't your fault, Mar," Hannah said, rubbing her back.

"It is, though. It's all my fault. I was her therapist. I was supposed to do more. I was supposed to make her better. I should've seen this coming." Marnie lifted her head from Hannah and slid to the ground, her back propped against the couch. Hannah sat next to her. Her presence was enough to calm Marnie, even a little. "There are certain steps you're supposed to take as a therapist when someone expresses suicidal ideation," Marnie said. "You're supposed to address it right then and there. Carley hinted at it; I know she did. I wrote it off. I thought it was teenage angst. Now she's gone."

They sat on the floor for a long time. Hannah stayed quiet. She was good at leaving space for others to grieve. Marnie did her best not to break apart.

"He's back," Marnie whispered. "He's back, and he's after me. They're both back, actually. It won't be long now."

Hannah was whispering something. Marnie looked at her. Hannah's eyes were closed. She was praying. Good. Marnie needed all the prayer she could get – Lord knew she wasn't praying for herself anymore. Hopefully, he'd listen to Hannah.

Hannah lifted her head. Compassion filled her eyes as she looked at Marnie. "Have you thought about seeing someone? You know, to talk about all this?"

Marnie laughed. "A shrink for a shrink? No, I haven't thought about it."

"Everyone needs someone to talk to. This is serious stuff, and there's only so much I can do, Marnie."

"I don't know," Marnie said. "I'll think about it."

Marnie tossed and turned for hours. Every time she closed her eyes, she saw Carley sitting in her office. She spent countless days with Carley, talking about her trauma and the car accident. Marnie played over her actions and picked apart every response to Carley. There were so many things she'd done wrong, so many things she should've said differently. She was a horrible therapist, especially in the last few months.

How had she let herself be so selfish? Marnie's one goal had always been to help others. Lately, it was like she only cared about helping herself.

Exhaustion finally settled in, and Marnie fell asleep.

She opened her eyes to see a vast desert. The moon cast a heavy gray over the sand, the light catching on little twigs and dry plants that rose like bones clawing out of graves. Tiny granules of sand dug into Marnie's forearm. They felt like thousands of needles prickling her skin.

Marnie scanned the horizon. The air made her throat dry. She knew it was a dream, but it felt different. It was more real than the last dream, the one at the playground.

His presence was heavy; she could feel him there. Marnie stood and let her eyes adjust to the darkness. She wanted to find him. Knowing where he hid was better than waiting for him to pop out, but the silent part of her hoped she didn't find him.

Something dark and distorted moved in the corner of her eye. She turned to catch it, but there was nothing. A low groan emanated from behind. She turned, and the sound moved with her. It stayed barely out of sight.

He was playing tricks. He loved tricks.

Something slithered across Marnie's bare feet. She jumped, kicking it away. When she looked down, there was nothing there.

Panic was a mild scream echoing inside her mind. Creatures crept and crawled all around, whispering in her ears, never showing themselves.

She ran.

It was no use. Her legs moved in slow motion, like running underwater. No matter how hard she pressed, they wouldn't go faster. She looked over her shoulder and was met with the empty desert.

It wasn't really empty, though, was it? He was there with all his little minions messing with her mind, tickling her skin.

The moon lit her path and nothing else. An inky blackness lay before her.

I'm running toward him.

She pushed the thought away and kept pressing forward.

The sand cut into her feet like broken glass. She wanted to scream out in pain but was afraid it would announce her position to whatever lurked around – or worse – to him.

Marnie slammed into a wall and fell back, her buttocks stinging.

It wasn't a wall. It was him in his full form.

A creature, nothing like a man, stood before her. Stark red eyes set into a pitch-black face. Two long, jagged horns rose from the top of his head – she hadn't seen those before. A long cloak, as black as the fur beneath, trailed out behind him, flowing softly in the slight breeze.

Marnie squinted, but no other details came in. He looked different, stronger. But it was still him.

At first, it appeared that he was holding a stick in his right hand. A closer look revealed a long silver sword, stained red.

Marnie held her breath and scooted backward, trying to get as far away as possible before he noticed. He wasn't looking at her, more like through her.

Scooting was too slow. Marnie eased onto her knees, then pushed up onto her feet. She stood still for a moment. One hand reached forward in surrender.

He didn't move.

She took a step back, landing on her toes.

Another hesitant step back.

He charged. Marnie turned and ran back the way she came. Her thighs tensed under the pressure, threatening to blow. She had to get away, find a place to hide. She searched the desert as she ran. It was too dark. At this rate, he was going to catch her.

What is he going to do to me?

Marnie's foot caught on a rock and sent her flying through the air. She landed hard on a patch of dry grass. Immediately upon impact, Marnie started crawling. The ache of the fall didn't matter; all that mattered was staying far away from him.

Survival. That was most important.

A sharp pain sliced through her mind, and she screamed. She was no longer crawling forward but being dragged. She grasped for sand, and it slipped through her fingers. She tried to hold onto the grass, but it came loose. Her shirt rode up, exposing her stomach to the earth. The rough ground rubbed it raw.

She looked back. He'd sunk his claws into her right calf, leaving deep gashes like rivers flowing. It burned. The idea of cutting off her leg sounded better than continuing in this pain. Marnie tried to kick her legs, but it only made him tighten his grip.

Past the monster, Marnie saw a cave.

He was taking her home.

Oh, God, please.

Marnie flailed, one leg coming free. She kicked at his arms, slamming the heel of her left foot into his hand. Nothing was working; he was too strong.

He turned her over and pinned her down with his foot. More claws were stabbing into her thigh now.

He stood above her, his hot breath tickling the pores on Marnie's face. He lifted his sword.

Marnie closed her eyes. *I'm going to die. Jesus, forgive me. Let me come to you.*

He plunged his sword into her stomach. Marnie coughed, blood spitting from her mouth. There was no point in screaming any-more – no one would hear anyway.

He lifted his sword again and sunk it deep into her stomach once more. The pain was deafening. There was nothing else in the world. Pain was all that was left.

Another stab into her gut and Marnie's will to hold on loos-ened. Her eyes slipped closed; the pain was fading.

Marnie jolted, gasping for breath. She ran panicked fingers across her stomach. No wounds. No blood. She looked around, taking in the sights as quickly as her mind could register them.

She saw her room, her dresser, her bed. Blankets all tossed in a heap on the ground.

Her leg stung. Marnie looked down.

Blood soaked through the sheets and covered her right leg. She screamed, the pain surging back to life.

❧

Hannah crashed through the door, staring at Marnie with wide eyes. Marnie met her stare, still screaming.

Hannah met the paramedics outside and led them in. Marnie had finally passed out. From pain or blood loss, Hannah didn't know.

She rode in the back of the ambulance with Marnie. The para-medics assured her that Marnie would be okay. There was so much blood; it didn't seem possible.

"A few stitches will get her all settled," they'd said.

"Why did she pass out? She looks so pale," Hannah replied.

Shock. That's what they'd said. But it seemed like more.

Terror. Marnie looked terrified.

"It won't be long now." Surely she didn't mean… Did she do this to herself? Was she trying to follow Carley?

Hannah held Marnie's limp hand in her own. Why wasn't the ambulance going faster?

They were almost there now. Hannah stared down at her friend, so tortured and alone. If only she could do more to help.

Marnie's eyes snapped open. She tried to sit up, and a para-
medic held her down. She looked at Hannah. The terror was gone,
replaced with confusion.

"Call Jason, please?" Marnie went limp again.

Twenty-Nine

TWO DAYS. They'd forced Marnie to stay in the hospital for two days. They put her on suicide watch because people didn't just wake up with huge gashes on their legs.

They believed Marnie had self-inflicted wounds. The theory was backed up by Hannah, who claimed Marnie wasn't acting "like herself." It was a load of crap. With everything going on, Hannah knew Marnie was stressed. Marnie would never, ever harm herself.

Who would listen to the girl who acted strange and blamed herself for someone else's suicide? How could they explain away large gashes unless they were self-inflicted? Marnie huffed under their suspicion. She knew no one would believe her.

Marnie met with the on-site psychologist and convinced him she was well enough to go home. Not that she wanted to go home. Home wasn't exactly a safe space anymore. Still, it was better than the sterile environment of the hospital. And at least at home, she could wear her own pajamas.

Jason picked Marnie up in front of the hospital. He'd been wonderful the last two days. He came to see her the night she was admitted. He and Hannah stayed all night, talking to Marnie and each other. Although she was annoyed that Hannah even suspected, let alone reasoned, Marnie's injury as self-harm, she resigned. It was nice having her two favorite people there to support her. Hannah had talked with the psychologist, too, and finally backed off. Though she threatened Marnie with hourly calls to make sure she didn't do anything stupid.

It took nearly an hour of cajoling on Jason's part to get Hannah to let him take Marnie home. He promised to watch her. As if she needed babysitting.

They were a lot alike, Hannah and Jason. It should've freaked Marnie out more than it did. It proved that she had good taste in friends and significant others.

Jason kept one hand on the steering wheel and one hand laced with Marnie's. The butterflies fluttered in her stomach at full force.

"How are you feeling?" Jason asked.

Marnie looked out the window at the stores passing by. People talked on the phone and shopped. What monsters stalked their dreams? Were they the same as hers?

Jason squeezed her hand, pulling her back.

"Huh? Oh. I'm fine, I guess."

"Wanna talk about it again?"

Marnie shook her head. "I've talked enough. I want life to go back to normal." The cut on her calf itched.

They pulled up to her apartment. Jason held Marnie by the waist, helping her up the stairs. She couldn't bend her leg without worrying about busting the stitches. At that moment, it was a good thing. Having Jason's arm around her made all the uncomfortable pain totally worth it.

"Alright, this is where I leave you," Jason said at the top of the stairs. "You sure you'll be alright?"

"I'll be fine," Marnie lied. "I'm gonna sleep." Another lie. This was getting to be a bad habit.

Jason hesitated, his eyes searching her face. The past two days had been filled with looks exactly like that one. No one trusted her to be alone. She swore she didn't do it, swore it was someone else who left those cuts. Her words meant nothing to them.

There was love in their eyes, of course. Care, even. But trust? None.

"I promise, Jason. Nothing is going to happen."

Cavin watched Marnie step out of the car. Jason's car. The white Nissan pulled all the way up to the staircase, and Jason had his grimy hands on Marnie's back.

Marnie was wearing plaid pajama pants and a tank top. It was fifty degrees out; she was probably freezing. Jason didn't care enough to give her a jacket. What a jerk. That was exactly why he wasn't fit for a girl like Marnie. He wasn't fit for anyone. Once things settled with Marnie, Cavin would make sure to take care of Jason for good.

Marnie limped up the stairs; the sight broke Cavin's heart. "What happened to her?" Cavin said, keeping his voice low.

"I wouldn't worry about it," the voice replied. "Just the results of a little fun. She's nearly ready for you now, buddy."

His fists clenched. "You did that to her?"

"She's quite the screamer; you're a lucky man. I bet she'll yell real loud for you."

Cavin's fist flew into the metal dumpster. The sound ricocheted off the walls. He bent down, hiding. It was loud. Marnie might've heard it.

"Don't you dare touch her again; she's mine." Cavin's jaw clenched. "We had a deal."

"Hey, man. I'm sticking to our deal. I promised to help you get the girl, no matter the cost. This is part of the process."

Cavin forgot he was talking to the voice as he watched Jason's hand slide down Marnie's back and land on her waist. He bent over, sure that puke was about to spew from his mouth. What was keeping him from running up those stairs and pounding Jason's face into a bloody pulp?

Marnie. He didn't want to scare her like that.

Cavin looked back. They were standing at her front door. Marnie shifted, trying to get out of Jason's sleazy grasp. Women had to deal with so many creeps; it was a wonder she kept her cool all this time. Marnie was too sweet, though. She'd never purposely offend someone. That was what she was doing with Jason; she was being polite.

Wait. What is she doing?

Marnie took a step closer to Jason.

Marnie, no. Back up, you're too close.

She lifted onto her tiptoes, her head inching toward Jason's.

Stop it, stop it! Cavin's mind screamed.

Her hand was on Jason's cheek, caressing lightly. Then, Cavin's nightmare played before him. Marnie pressed her lips to Jason's. The smacking sound reverberated through the air and slapped Cavin in the face. Jason pulled at her hips like a starving lion, ready to devour its prey.

Disgusting. This time, Cavin bent down, and chunks of vomit spewed to the ground. He placed his hands on his knees to steady himself, then wiped the remnants from his mouth with his jacket sleeve.

The cheating little whore. She'd pay for this.

Cavin pressed off his knees and stood tall. He stomped forward. Marnie was coming with him now.

The man in his head pulled him back. "Whoa, buddy. I wouldn't do that. If you storm in now, you'll ruin everything we've prepared for. You don't want him to see you, not yet."

Cavin froze. His eyes flamed.

They were still kissing.

He couldn't watch this anymore. He ran back to his car at the gas station. It was time to change things up. Marnie didn't deserve the warm home he'd prepared for her. She needed to be punished.

In his car, Cavin pulled out his phone and sent her a text.

You messed up this time, Marnie. Say goodbye to your little boyfriend.

Thirty

CAVIN THREW THE DOOR OPEN. It slammed into the wall, leaving a dent in its wake. Rage pulsed through his veins, turning his vision red. Standing in the living room, Cavin looked around at all his hard work. He'd spent weeks preparing his home for Marnie, making it beautiful like she was.

It was all tainted now. Ruined by her infidelity.

Didn't promises mean anything anymore? How could she betray him like this? She'd ripped his heart out and stomped it into the ground.

Cavin wouldn't do that to her, not physically. He loved her. Still, she needed to be punished. Cavin shook his head. Go figure. This was the first time Cavin ever saw one of his girls as "the one," and she had to go and ruin it. The first time he'd ever gone the extra mile to prepare a home for her, but she was just like all the others. Cavin thought Marnie was better than Julie, better than Stacy. As it turned out, all women are unfaithful and need to be punished.

Following the pounding of his heart, Cavin ripped the living room to shreds. He pulled the maroon curtains from the window, rod and all, and ripped the fabric. They lay in a heap at his feet. He pressed the sole of his right boot into the heap and ground it, the mud from his shoe staining it. He spat on it. His anger was justified.

The couch sat across from the large window, just like at Marnie's place. It was almost an exact replica of hers. He'd forgotten the exact brand, so he improvised.

A waste of time now.

Cavin opened his pocket knife, sliding his index finger along the blade. He plunged it into the couch, ripping, shredding, and stabbing it over and over again. In his mind, he pictured Jason. He saw his chest cavity snapping open under the weight of his knife, leaving his heart unprotected.

His chest heaved. Cavin stared at the damage done to the sofa. Gone were the opportunities for couch cuddles and warm kisses while watching TV. Marnie would have to earn her way back to a couch.

Cavin blew through the kitchen like a tornado, smashing plates and bowls as he went. He pulled out the custom "Mr." and "Mrs." mugs he'd ordered from Etsy. They shook in his trembling hands. The movie of his and Marnie's life played in his mind. Marnie sat on the counter, sipping coffee from her mug, gazing at Cavin as he cooked breakfast. The memory sizzled and burned up, replaced with the replay of her locking lips with that monster.

Marnie had destroyed their future of happiness. They would still have a future; he wasn't going to give up on her. Commitment took work – he understood that. It would be a long time before there was happiness, though. He'd make sure of that. *Love had to be harsh sometimes.*

Those words slammed into Cavin's temple, snapping his head sideways. A bible dropped from the blow into his hands. He stared at it, disbelieving.

"Worthless!"

Cavin looked up to see his mother standing across the room. Spittle spewed from her mouth, her face red with fury.

Cavin fell into the memory of her as the lines of reality blurred around him. He threw his hands up, still clutching the Good Book. "Mother, please," he said.

"A worthless, good-for-nothin' bastard! That's what you are!" she screamed. Her voice hit an octave that could shatter glass. "It's your fault your daddy left! He couldn't stand the thought of being your father."

Cavin's mother got like this every time she drank, which was practically every night. Except for Sundays. Sundays were for the Lord.

A vodka bottle came flying next, whizzing past Cavin's head. He jumped to the side, dodging. Mother had gone into a frenzy this time after finding a picture of Cavin's father under his pillow. Keeping the picture reminded Cavin of the good days; it kept him alive.

"Keep still, boy!" His mother yelled. "The Good Book says to obey your mother."

She charged at him, then, wrapping her slender fingers around his arm and digging her nails into his skin. He obeyed, as he always did. She led him to the basement, opened the door, and shoved him through. Cavin stumbled down the stairs. He looked up at Mother, shrouded in light.

"I'm sorry," he said softly.

"I love you, Cavin. But love has to be harsh sometimes." She slammed the door, leaving him in darkness.

Cavin shivered, pushing the memory away. He'd teach Marnie a lesson. Someone had to, and it looked like Cavin was the only one who loved her enough to do it. Cavin stalked down the hallway towards the most sacred room in the whole house. Photos of their wedding, their honeymoon, and their children lined the walls leading to the bedroom. Cavin stopped, staring at each one. He spent hours photoshopping them, he had to get them just right. They made such a beautiful couple, a lovely family. It was a true shame Marnie had gone and defiled their love. Cavin's heart broke further; he didn't know there was more to break. The grief began to snuff out his anger, making him feel weak.

He slammed his fist into each picture, shattering the frame and leaving behind drops of blood – a physical representation of the pain in his chest.

Frozen at the closed door of their bedroom, Cavin heard the sound.

The voice in his head was laughing.

He enjoyed this; he liked watching Cavin's dreams burn with his home.

The laughter should've made him turn his anger to the voice; instead, it fueled him. It reminded him who the real culprit was – Jason and his once sweet Marnie.

Cavin opened the door. The room was shrouded in darkness.

He felt for the light switch, igniting the room in color.

More pictures lined the walls. This room was special; he worked extra hard preparing it for her. It was an exact copy of Marnie's bedroom. He hadn't forgotten to get the brands of the furniture in here.

Cavin pictured their first time together, their bodies tangled in the sheets. He'd be gentle with her; she was the type to enjoy tender love over aggression. They'd cuddle afterward, fingers intertwined above their heads.

Marnie would whisper, "I love you, Cavin."

"I love you, too," he'd say.

That was the last straw. All of his hope; all of his expectations were shattered. He should rip down the pictures, cut the blanket in half and tear out the stuffing in the pillows.

He stood, frozen in place. He didn't want to lose his one true love – the one God himself sent to him. Cavin thought hard. There was still a chance. They could still have the love they were meant to have. He would find a way to make Marnie come back to him. But how? The pain of losing everything and the hope of true love mixed noxiously inside him, and he felt sick, torn.

A scream ripped from his throat, gutting him. As he let the uncontrollable sobs finally come, Cavin sank to the floor, rocking back and forth.

He couldn't destroy their room, not yet, not when the possibility of their future was still there.

Cavin cried. The anger faded, and he cried.

Thirty-One

MARNIE'S TWO-WEEK SABBATICAL WAS OVER. She'd dreamed of this day since getting out of the hospital. A near-death experience, dream or real, has a way of changing your outlook on life.

Carley's death still ached; the pain would never go away. But it was a little more bearable now. Her confidence, however, was shot. DOA. No resuscitation was necessary. She failed at protecting Carley; how could she possibly help her other clients? She cringed at the thought.

Her phone rang, Jason's name flashing across the screen.

"Hey there," she answered as a smile slowly bloomed.

"It's your first day back; hope you aren't nervous."

"Me? Nervous? No way, I'm cool as a cucumber, baby."

Jason's laugh vibrated the speaker on her phone.

It wasn't that funny.

"Now I know you're nervous. No one says 'cool as a cucumber' anymore," he teased.

She rolled her eyes and hoped he'd hear it, even if he couldn't see it.

"Babe, you're gonna do great. Don't worry. What happened with Carley..."

"We're on cutesy nicknames now?" Marnie cut him off.

That laugh, oh Lord, that laugh.

"I'd say yes, *baaabe*," drawing out the last word for emphasis.

Goosebumps covered her arms, and those all-too-familiar butterflies returned to her stomach. Her smile blossomed, replacing the worrisome grimace she had earlier.

"Alright, well, I'm here. I'll call you later?"

"I'm praying for you today," he said. With Jason's encouragement, she could fly.

Marnie walked through the front doors of Golden Meadow. Savannah met her at the door, a coffee cup with "Marnie" and a heart written on the side.

"Welcome back," Savannah said, wrapping Marnie in a bear hug. "I've missed you so much!"

Marnie placed her hands on Savannah's back and laughed. "Wow, what a great welcoming committee. I've missed you, too."

Savannah released. "I'm serious, Marnie. Things haven't been the same since you've been gone. The whole office has felt bleak. You light it up."

Marnie's cheeks turned bright red. She needed to escape; all these compliments in a row were not good for her head.

"Thank you," she said. "Is Dr. Carlson in her office? I wanna talk to her before getting started."

"Yup, she's expecting you." Savannah returned to her desk.

Marnie walked to Dr. Carlson's door and knocked.

Dr. Carlson opened the door. "Marnie, it's nice to have you back. Let's go to your office," she said, crossing the threshold and closing her office door once again.

Marnie's office was dark. It looked exactly how it had in the hallucination at the hospital. For a split second, she worried she was back there. How could she be certain that this was real life? The shadows permeating the corners seemed darker, alive almost. She waited for the shadow to step forward to remind her of his never-ending presence.

"Aren't you going to turn on the light?" Dr. Carlson asked.

"Oh." Marnie snapped out of it and flipped on the light.

Her cozy office came into view; the shadows chased away. The large sofa and adjacent chair were still fluffy and inviting. Nothing had changed since her last time in the office; what a relief. Familiarity bred comfort; comfort bred security. Marnie was secure here, safe.

Work was the only place she *hadn't* experienced a hallucination. Only the voices. Always the voices.

Dr. Carlson sat in Marnie's chair. "Let's talk about your time off," she said.

Marnie rolled her eyes at the power move. That was Marnie's chair; she wanted to be the one sitting in it.

She sat on the couch. "What'd you like to know?"

"How was it?"

Marnie rubbed her calf. The cuts were healing, but they still throbbed at times. It was a reminder of what was to come. "It was fine. I rested a lot."

Dr. Carlson had her fist under her chin and was nodding. Didn't she believe Marnie? Could she see through her?

"How have my clients been?"

"They've been fine. Everyone missed you, as I'm sure you did them."

Marnie stood and shuffled over to her desk. "Yes, well. I have a lot of preparation to do; could we talk later?"

Dr. Carlson didn't move. Therapists are often the most difficult people to deal with, especially when they know you as well as Dr. Carlson knew Marnie. Marnie wanted to hide. She didn't want to talk about her time off. Frankly, her time off sucked. Carley's funeral had been traumatic and a slap in the face at the destruction Marnie had caused. Then, there was her terrifying nightmares that may or may not have been real, which led to her time on suicide watch.

Yeah, let's talk about my time off. I'll tell you all about how I was considered a suicide risk; sounds great.

"Marnie?" Dr. Carlson pulled her from her thoughts.

Marnie turned her head toward Dr. Carlson.

"Sit down. We need to talk."

Letting out a loud sigh, Marnie sat back down on the couch. She didn't have time for this, and she definitely didn't want to make time for it. All she wanted was to lose herself in work, to forget everything else, and to focus all her attention on her clients. They needed her.

Carley had needed her.

She wasn't going to let anyone else down.

"How was the funeral?" Dr. Carlson's voice was gentle, like she was talking to a hurt kitten.

"It was lovely. They paid tribute to Carley very well." Marnie refused to say more.

"Wanna talk about it honestly or do you want to keep avoiding my questions?"

Dang, she was good.

Marnie leaned forward, resting her elbows on her knees. "Dr. Carlson, I've had a rough two weeks. The only thing that got me through was knowing that I'd be coming back to work and helping my clients again. It's a kind of penance for what happened to Carley. I'm not going to let any other clients down."

"It isn't your fault she died." *So matter of fact.*

"She was my responsibility," Marnie said, equally matter of fact.

"Yes, she was. But her decision was her own. You can't let it define you."

Marnie stood again. "Dr. Carlson, please? Can't we talk about this later?"

Finally, she stood. "Alright, I will see you at the end of the day." She paused at the door, turning back to Marnie. "I have faith in you. Let's move past this."

Marnie gave her a curt smile and dipped her head. She wanted more than anything to move past this and for life to go back to normal. It was time for her to get everyone to believe she was capable once again.

Dr. Carlson left, and Marnie went back to her desk. She looked over her schedule, scanning the names and double-checking the notes. Not much had changed with each client, according to Dr. Carlson's notes. That was good; less for Marnie to prepare for. It was a light day, too. Only three clients. She'd get to go home early, back to laying on the couch and watching mind-numbing TV.

One small hitch, she had to meet with Ashley. Luck had been on Marnie's side the past few weeks. Ashley and her family had been on vacation. They got back the previous week while Marnie was on leave. She'd had several blissful weeks of no attitude. Now all that was gone.

Before Ashley, Marnie met with a new boy. He was a freshman

in high school struggling to adjust. He was popular in Junior High. But when his family moved to Missouri and he changed schools, things were different. He joined the school year late, making him an outcast among his peers. He was a nice kid; he didn't deserve the neglect.

He knocked on the door. Marnie whispered a quick prayer, "Jesus, please help me get through today." Then, she answered.

The session flew by without a hitch. Marnie was back and better than ever. This was going to be fine, she was going to be fine.

Ashley burst through the door without so much as a knock. Marnie startled, dropping Ashley's file on the floor.

This was not a good start to the session.

Marnie sent up another silent prayer to God, tacking on a "please listen to me this time" at the end for good measure. She needed all the help she could get with this one.

Ashley went straight to the couch, her eyes glued to the cell phone in her hand. She had checked out before they'd even started.

"Hi, Ashley," Marnie said, dropping into her seat.

"Hey."

Marnie waited to see if the girl would come up for air, add something to her greeting. She didn't. She kept staring at the screen, her thumbs moving across at the speed of light.

What could she have possibly been doing that was so important? She acted like if she looked away, the phone would disintegrate.

Marnie shoved down the annoyance bubbling up. Now was not the time to cause a scene.

Be cool, Marnie. It's fine.

A full minute of silence passed by before Marnie spoke. "How about we set the phone down for today, huh?"

Ashley ignored her, continuing to scroll.

"Ashley, come on. Let's talk about your weekend. You do anything fun?"

The girl looked up and rolled her eyes. She scoffed, then went back to her phone. Marnie's pulse quickened. How much more of this insolent behavior could she take? The dismissiveness was getting to her, building up after so many sessions of the same thing.

"Ashley, I'm serious. Put the phone away, and let's talk." Marnie deepened her voice, trying to sound as serious as possible.

Ashley dropped the phone beside her, crossing one leg over

the other. "You wanna talk? Alright, let's talk." She leaned forward, flipping her long blonde hair over her shoulder. The pretentious brat thought she was so much better than Marnie. Girls like that deserved a slap every now and then.

Marnie kept a relaxed posture. She couldn't show any reaction to Ashley; it would only provoke her further. Marnie tilted her head to listen and smiled, inviting the girl to keep going.

"I don't know how many times I have to say this, but the only reason I come is because my mom forces me. If I didn't, she'd stop paying my phone bill. So let's just pretend we talked. That way, you get paid, and I get left alone. Deal?" The look on her face sent a chill down Marnie's spine.

This girl was evil. She didn't care about anyone or anything unless it served her purpose. Marnie wanted to crack her so bad, but how? What could she say to get Ashley talking more?

Bingo.

"You have a boyfriend? Wanna talk about him?" Marnie asked. High school girls loved talking about their boyfriends.

"I was hoping you'd get the message and leave me alone. Guess we gotta do things the hard way." Ashley sat back, spreading her arms across the back of the couch. She acted like she owned the world. "I know what you did. I know one of your other clients killed herself. Do you really think I'm gonna talk to you after that happened? So I end up like her? No thanks."

Marnie blinked. "What did you just say?"

"You heard me. Everyone knows you were that girl's therapist, and look where that got her. So you're gonna let me sit here and look at my phone." She picked her phone up and waved it in the air before holding it in front of her face. "Be glad you're still getting paid for the hour."

No. That was it. This little brat crossed a line. All Marnie had ever done was be nice to her and try to get to know her. Clearly, it wasn't enough. Someone needed to teach the girl a lesson in manners.

Marnie shot up and crossed to Ashley. She ripped the phone from her hands and chucked it out the window behind the couch.

"Hey!" Ashley leaned over the back, staring out the window. "What the hell was that?" she yelled.

Marnie hovered over her, pointing. "You listen here, you little brat. I am here to *help* you because you have issues that Mommy and

Daddy are not equipped to deal with. You are an entitled, insufferable little snake who deserves to be shipped off to boarding school rather than sitting in my office. I have tried for months to be patient with you. I have been kind and completely understanding, yet you continue to be the rudest, most obnoxious *child* I have ever met." Marnie took a breath. "You are beyond saving."

Ashley snapped her jaw shut and stood, forcing Marnie to take a step back. Her eyes were blazing; her mouth curled on one end.

Oh no. What did I just do?

Marnie faltered. She'd made a huge mistake, and by the look on Ashley's face, she was about to pay for it.

"You have no idea what you've done," Ashley said. "I am not the one with issues; that's obviously you. I hope you enjoyed being a therapist because you're done! First, you get a girl to literally kill herself. Now you're standing here, verbally abusing another client and destroying my private property."

A rebuttal refused to form in Marnie's mind. She shoved Ashley. "Get out of my face!"

Crap. Why did I do that? Crapcrapcrap.

If Marnie wasn't worried about losing her job before, she was now. Ashley had gotten under her skin so deep Marnie wasn't even sorry for the things she'd done. Marnie was only sorry that she was about to be caught and most likely fired. Time to kiss this career good-bye.

Marnie stepped back until her legs ran into her chair, and she fell to her seat. She watched as Ashley held her breath and shook. Tears welled in her eyes, and she bolted for the door, putting on a show. Outside, Marnie could hear her shouting and crying. Dr. Carlson's calm voice responded, but Marnie couldn't make out the words.

Ashley was good. Believable.

Marnie dropped her head into her hands. That was single-handedly the dumbest thing she could ever do; so much for proving to everyone that she was capable. Clearly, she wasn't. Better to know now than twenty years down the road.

Marnie heard footsteps stop at the door. A cough. She peeked over the side of her chair at Dr. Carlson, standing with her arms crossed over her chest. She shut the door without saying a word. Marnie lifted her head high.

Be strong.

"You wanna tell me what just happened?"

Marnie looked toward her desk. She couldn't – wouldn't – look at Dr. Carlson. Not now. Her mentor, the woman she aspired to be, was standing over her and expecting a logical answer. Marnie had none. There was no excuse; nothing she said would change what happened with Ashley – or with Carley.

"Well?"

"I threw her phone out the window." Marnie forced herself to meet Dr. Carlson's eyes. "I have no excuse. I just… lost it."

Dr. Carlson shook her head and sat on the couch. "Marnie, I like you. I think you've been a wonderful asset to this team. Not to mention how much you've helped so many young people."

It was coming. This was the "you're great, but we can't have an unstable therapist working for us" talk. Marnie was getting fired. She held her breath.

"But," Dr. Carlson continued. "Too much has happened lately. I no longer trust that you can do your job."

If there was ever a time to let the shame win, it was now. Life was over. Everything Marnie had spent years building was down the toilet. What was she going to do now? Counseling was all she'd ever wanted. Oh, no. She'd acted like Pete. The man she'd vowed to never let into her life again had morphed her mind. She yelled like Pete yelled, shoved like he shoved.

Lord, forgive me.

"Pack your belongings by the end of the day. I'll have Savannah call your clients and let them know."

Dr. Carlson got up to leave, and Marnie stood to see her out. When they reached the door, Dr. Carlson wrapped her arms around Marnie. Tears shoved their way past Marnie's closed eyes, spilling down her cheeks.

Dr. Carlson released. Compassion shone on her face. "Marnie, please get some help."

Marnie nodded, wiping away her tears.

But who could help her now?

Thirty-Two

AN ABSOLUTE DISASTER.

There was no other way to describe the events that unfolded. And the worst part of it was Marnie deserved it. She deserved to be fired. Everything she built in that office, at that company, blew away in a moment of bad decisions.

If only she felt bad about it.

Instead, she felt relieved. All that pent-up anger exploded exquisitely onto Ashley, a deserving victim. Marnie wanted to feel bad, believe it or not. But she couldn't bring herself to. Call it self-sabotaging for what happened to Carley. Call it running away in fear. Call it whatever you want, she did it, and she wasn't upset.

The only upsetting thing was how Dr. Carlson looked at her. Those pity eyes, pleading with Marnie to get help.

She had never seen such disappointment and worry in a person's eyes before. That right there had the power to break her in two.

Marnie cleared out her office. All her personal items fit into one medium-sized cardboard box. Excluding her books, of course. Those she would have to return for later.

She took the pictures of her and Hannah off her desk and stuffed them into the side of the box. Then, grabbed the cup full of pens and dumped them in.

Why do I have so many pens?

In all the years she'd worked at Golden Meadow, she only went through four pens at most. No amount of work warranted having so many pens.

I just lost my job. Am I really worried about the number of pens I have?

She hoisted the box onto one hip, her arm wrapped around the top to hold it in place. Marnie took one last look at her office. It hurt to say goodbye. She flicked the light off and closed the door.

She caught another pity stare, this time from Savannah, as Marnie handed the receptionist her keys.

"Call me, okay? We'll get together," Savannah said.

Why didn't Marnie believe her? Promising to make plans was something people did without committing to follow through. Marnie's heart sank; she was never going to see Savannah again, was she?

Marnie walked through the crowded street, heading back to her apartment. It hadn't fully set in yet that she wouldn't return to work. It probably wouldn't for a few days.

Oh no. What was she going to tell Hannah? Hannah already assumed Marnie was losing her mind, this was one more thing to prove it. How would she react? Marnie knew she needed to call and tell her everything. It was kind of embarrassing, though, getting fired for throwing a tantrum at a client ten years younger than her.

Who was she? Where'd the old, mature Marnie gone?

Her thoughts came to a crashing halt as she ran into something hard. The box in her arms bounced off a man's shoulder and landed on the ground, spilling its contents.

"What a klutz, I'm so sorry!" Marnie said, crouching to pick up her things.

The man bent down and helped her gather everything. "Don't worry about it. I wasn't watching where I was going."

Marnie looked at him. She'd recognized that hair and those eyes anywhere. "Cavin?" Marnie said.

He glanced up. "Marnie? Wow, what a surprise!"

She grabbed the box and stood. Cavin held one of her books in his hand, and he set it on top of the box.

"I was actually on my way to see you, but Golden Meadow called and said our session got canceled." He looked at the box. "Is everything alright?"

She'd been so worried about telling Hannah that Marnie never considered what it'd be like to run into a former client. She teetered, unsure how much information was too much. "Oh, um. I don't work there anymore." Marnie picked at a hole in the corner of the box.

"You're kidding?" Cavin said, covering his mouth. "Did you quit?"

"More like fired," Marnie laughed.

"Oh my gosh. That's terrible." Cavin reached his hand out and placed it on her shoulder. He squeezed once, then let it sit there. Marnie shrugged it off; the gesture was a little too close for comfort.

Cavin cleared his throat and ran his fingers through his messy red hair. "Well, listen, can I buy you a coffee? You look like you could use one."

Marnie hesitated. The lingering shoulder touch already made her uncomfortable. It'd also be highly inappropriate to meet a client outside of the office. Then again, she didn't work there anymore, so technically, Cavin wasn't her client. Plus, she could use a cup of coffee.

"You know what? Why not? I'd love a coffee," Marnie said.

Cavin took the box from her hands, and they walked to the coffee shop together. Whether Marnie worked in the area or not, she planned on visiting that cafe as often as possible. It was still her favorite.

Marnie grabbed a table while Cavin ordered drinks.

Finally, one on one time with Marnie.

He was still mad at her, of course. That betrayal wasn't going to be forgiven so easily. But he couldn't deny the quickening of his heartbeat at seeing her. The best part was he hadn't lied to her. He really was on his way to their appointment. Though, the run-in wasn't as authentic as it seemed. He knew exactly where he was walking. He'd meant for the chance encounter.

And from the look on Marnie's face, she was pleased to see him.

Cavin ordered two Americanos, well aware of Marnie's go-to drink, then rushed back to the table. When he returned, Marnie's face lit up in excitement.

The battle between his anger with her and his enduring love made his head hurt. He wasn't sure how to act or which emotion to give in to.

For now, he chose love.

"Thank you," Marnie said as she took the drink from his hand. Their fingers brushed together, and a tingle of excitement ran the length of his spine.

She was a sneaky one, his Marnie. Stealing little touches wherever she could get them. Cavin would make sure to give her as many opportunities as possible.

He took a drink of his Americano, sucking from the straw while keeping eye contact with Marnie. He gave his best seductive look, sure to make her swoon. "So, what happened?" he asked.

Marnie stared out the window. Cavin could see the disappointment on her face. Something had happened. Poor Marnie, God was punishing her for her infidelity in more ways than one. Maybe now she'd learn her lesson.

When she looked back at him, Cavin felt bad for the harsher punishments that were to come. "It's nothing. We hit some procedural differences, the director and I." Marnie sipped her coffee. Why did she have to be so sexy? "It's for the best. Now I can move forward in my career."

Cavin was a wonderful listener. He sat patiently, completely focused on Marnie. She wasn't used to this kind of attention. Marnie had trained herself to be the listener; it was nice to be the talker for once with someone other than Hannah.

"That's right. I'm sure there's something far greater than that job right around the corner. You're a great therapist; you'll be fine," Cavin said.

Marnie smiled. She'd had hesitations about getting coffee with Cavin, but it was turning out to be a great time. Cavin was a nice guy, and if Jason weren't in the picture, she'd probably be attracted to him.

Oh, Jason. Another person she had to tell about her job. What was he going to think? They had only been going out for a short time.

What a catch she was. Hospitalized twice, labeled a suicide risk, and now fired. Jason could do better.

Marnie snapped out of it. She couldn't think about Jason right now. It was rude to be so distracted. She turned all her attention back to Cavin. "Anyway, how are you doing?" she asked.

"I'm alright," he said. "You remember that girlfriend I told you about? She cheated on me. I haven't confronted her about it yet. I'm not sure what to do."

"What? How could she do that to you? I'm so sorry, Cavin." Marnie reached across the table, resting her hand on his arm. "You deserve someone who is wholly committed to you."

Cavin stared down at her hand, then placed his on top. He rubbed his thumb along the back of her hand. It was too much. Marnie pulled away.

That was crossing a line, and by the look on his face, Marnie was sure she'd given him the wrong impression.

She rubbed her neck and looked around the room, trying to think of an excuse to leave. "I'm sorry, I better get going. Gotta start job hunting if I wanna keep paying rent," she laughed.

"Oh, yeah. No problem!" Cavin said. "Do you want me to walk you home?"

The idea of an ex-client walking her home did not sit well in Marnie's stomach.

Hadn't Savannah warned her about Cavin? What was it she said?

"I'm okay," Marnie said, standing.

Cavin stood, too. He grabbed the box. "Are you sure? The box is pretty heavy. I can carry it for you."

"I got it." Marnie tried to pull it from his hands, but he held it tight. "Seriously," she pulled harder, "I got it."

Cavin released, and Marnie stumbled back. Strange how quickly he'd gone from cool to creepy.

"It was nice seeing you, Cavin. Take care." Marnie made a dash for the door.

She walked around the neighborhood for twenty minutes before heading home. She wanted to be positive that Cavin wasn't following her. His sudden change in behavior scared her, the insistence on walking her home. What was all that about?

Meeting with a client outside of work, she added it to the list of mistakes from that day.

While she was still a long way off, Marnie saw something at her doorstep. Red lines of something indistinguishable stuck to the front door, and she picked up her pace.

She took the stairs two at a time, panting when she reached the top. Marnie's arms went limp, dropping the box. SLUT was written in red paint diagonally across her door. It dripped down, creating the illusion that the words were written in blood, oozing from the wood beneath.

Who would do such a thing?

A bouquet of dead flowers laid across the welcome mat. Flies swarmed the flowers, and maggots crawled all around. She jumped back, letting out a squeal.

Her first instinct was to call the police. Then she remembered how well that went the last time. They hadn't even bothered to take her statement; what could they possibly do now? She could hear their voices, claiming it to be a prank from some neighborhood kids. Marnie would have to take care of it herself.

She stepped over the flowers and bugs and went inside. Grabbing cleaning supplies, Marnie marched outside and scrubbed at the letters. She was almost too tired for paranoia but still caught herself glancing over her shoulder. It was a habit, more than anything.

Thirty-Three

CAVIN WAITED A FEW MINUTES, then followed Marnie home. She was sneaky, trying to mix up her route to throw him off. He wasn't so easily tricked. Once he'd caught on that she was going out of her way to confuse him, Cavin changed course and went to the alley. She'd have to walk by eventually; he'd catch her then.

Except she didn't walk by. She took one of the other entrances to the complex, leaving Cavin alone. If it weren't for her scream, he would've missed her. He relished the sound.

There was a strange battle happening in Cavin's mind. On the one hand, he was head over heels in love with Marnie and was ecstatic to have spent time with her. Their run-in was another sign from God that things could be mended. On the other hand, he was still upset by the way she kissed Jason at her front door, and how she paraded him around town. It was obscene, almost like she wanted to hurt Cavin.

That was why he had to punish her. He didn't want to; punishment was difficult and painful. It was necessary, though. It didn't mean he loved her any less. In fact, he argued it meant he loved her more.

It reminded him of something his mother used to say. "Cavvy, baby, sometimes I gotta punish you for mistakes. It's how you learn and do better in the future." Followed by a whack to the head.

Back then, he hated his mom for it. But now, he saw how right she was. He'd do his best to punish Marnie like his mother did for him. He'd do it better, though. He would be gentle with Marnie, unlike Mother.

Cavin watched Marnie scrub at his message on her door. Served her right. She needed to understand how her behavior affected those around her - frolicking around with men, kissing them out in the open – despicable. Now she knew, and hopefully, she would change her behavior.

Cavin sent her a message.

I'm sorry it had to be this way, love. Someone had to say it. Be better, Marnie. I love you.

Cavin beamed, satisfied with the work he'd done. A beautiful day of love and lessons, and it was only the beginning – the beginning of forever.

Thirty-Four

MARNIE THREW HER PHONE ACROSS THE ROOM. She wanted to cry and scream and run away from everything. The more she tried to ignore the incessant messages, the more they dug under her skin. Whoever this monster was, he was getting bolder; coming to her home, leaving messages on her door in broad daylight.

Wait. He was there in broad daylight. That meant someone might've seen him.

Marnie dropped the rag into the bucket of cleaning solution on the living room floor, not caring that some splashed onto the carpet. She flew out the front door and bounded down the stairs. She banged on her downstairs neighbor's door.

"Hello?" she yelled, banging more. "Anyone home?"

"What do you want?" someone called through the door.

"Hi, my name is Marnie. I live upstairs. I wanted to ask you a few questions."

There was a pause. So much for being neighborly.

"Please? It'll only take a moment."

She heard the chainlink clink before the door cracked open. An elderly man in sweatpants and a stained sweater peered out at her. "What?" he said.

"Hi. Someone vandalized my front door. I was wondering if you happened to see anyone suspicious around here today?"

The old man glared at her looking her up and down. "I didn't see anybody." He slammed the door.

Three more neighbors were either not home or chose to ignore her. She was glad to know she could rely on her neighbors in an emergency.

Marnie went back inside, standing with her back against the locked door. She looked over the living room. It seemed too big, empty, and dark. She couldn't stand being alone any longer.

Who should she call? Hannah or Jason? Hannah had dealt with so much of Marnie's issues already. Marnie felt bad calling her yet again. But Jason was, well, Jason. He was nice and encouraging, and of course, she loved spending time with him. It was far too embarrassing for her to admit she'd lost her job, especially after how much he'd cheered her on that morning.

She flipped between the two phone numbers, weighing the pros and cons of each. Hannah, a wonderful friend. Or Jason, cute and equally as wonderful.

She made her decision, pressed call, and paced back and forth with each ring.

"Come on, come on," she whispered.

"Marnie? Everything okay?"

"Hey, everything's fine. Are you free right now?"

A pause. "Aren't you supposed to be working?"

Marnie sighed. "I'll explain when you get here. Can you come?"

"I'll be there in twenty minutes. With pizza."

Be still my beating heart.

Twenty minutes was nothing. She could handle twenty minutes on her own.

Marnie checked the door, making sure it was locked. Twice.

A knock at the door made Marnie nearly jump out of her skin. She was far too easily spooked these days. It was annoying.

Marnie checked the peephole, unable to hold back her smile. She swung the door open. "You came!"

"And as promised, I brought pizza." Jason held up a large plastic bag.

She moved aside and let him into the living room. She glanced past his head at the kitchen counter; it was a mess. There were empty cups, a bowl of half-eaten cereal, and papers everywhere. The sink had dirty dishes piled high. Her eyes bulged out of her head. She then made the grave mistake and looked around the living room. The throw blanket, usually folded and draped across the couch, was lying in a heap on the floor. The coffee table had loose sheets of paper sprawled about.

What had she done inviting him over? She had twenty minutes to clean up but instead sat frozen on the couch, another mistake tacked onto her list for today.

Marnie gasped. The bathroom! When was the last time she'd cleaned the bathroom? It didn't matter. She knew for a fact that there were dirty clothes and an ungodly amount of loose hair sprinkled around the bathroom.

She laughed weakly. "Sorry about the mess. I shoulda cleaned when I knew you were coming." Marnie moved to the counter, clearing trash and dishes. "You can set the pizza here. I'm, uh, gonna go wash my hands." Marnie sprinted to the bathroom.

She frantically wiped the counter with toilet paper, a difficult feat considering it disintegrated at the smallest drop of water. Then, she scooped up the dirty clothes and crossed the hall to her bedroom, throwing them inside. She was positive Jason wouldn't be going in there.

When she came back out, Jason was sitting at the kitchen island with two plates and two cups. He smiled, patting the chair next to his.

"How'd you manage to get pizza so fast? It usually takes like thirty minutes." Marnie poured Pepsi into each cup. "You called at the perfect moment. I was actually waiting for a pizza already. Lucky thing I ordered enough for two."

Marnie gawked at the three large pizza boxes stacked on the counter. "Two? This is enough for five, easy!"

Jason laughed, rubbing his stomach. "Trust me, I can eat."

Marnie shoved a bite of pepperoni pizza into her mouth. Jason was staring at her, a mischievous grin on his face. "What?" she said.

"You cleaned the bathroom a little bit, didn't you?"

She choked on the bite. Busted. "How'd you know?"

He shrugged. "I would've done the same thing if you were

coming to my place."

That made her feel better about her obsessive need to make the apartment presentable. Jason didn't care about that, it seemed. She was lucky.

They ate pizza, both of them focused on the TV in the living room. Marnie forgot to turn it off when he knocked, so Gilmore Girls continued to play in the background. Jason was surprisingly into it. His eyes never left the screen. He even laughed a little. Marnie swooned. She didn't think there was a single man in the world who'd willingly watch that show.

Then again, he was likely just being polite.

They'd spent little time together since the kiss, keeping most of their conversations to calls and texts. Jason was a busy guy, catching bad guys and all that. They were both new to this whole dating thing, she knew it'd take time for them to feel comfortable together.

After eating, Marnie made a pot of coffee, and they moved to the couch. She turned the TV off, and they sat in awkward silence. She could feel Jason's eyes on her but couldn't make herself return the gaze. Marnie wasn't used to having guys in her apartment. In fact, Jason was the first. She didn't know the proper etiquette for having someone of the opposite gender over.
Why had she invited him in the first place?

Oh, right, because she was getting more scared each day.

If she told Jason, maybe he could help with the texts. Being a detective, she imagined he had access to cool technology that could trace phone numbers.

But that would mean she'd have to tell him about the texts. And the flowers. And the *sweet* message left on her door that afternoon. That was a lot to spring on a guy.

How serious were the messages anyways? It's not like the person had directly threatened her. Well, maybe they'd threatened her a little. But they hadn't acted on it yet. That was a good sign, wasn't it? All this back and forth was bringing on a migraine. She couldn't think about it right now, not when Jason was sitting inches from her.

It was best to keep it to herself for now.

The scar on her calf tingled. She reached down to itch it. Sleep was terrifying from that night forward. There hadn't been any more nightmares, but the threat lingered in the air. It was heavy; she could feel the shadow's presence just out of reach.

Finally, Jason broke the silence.

"Now, don't get me wrong, I love a good pizza night. And I'd never pass up an opportunity to hang out with you, but what's going on? Aren't you supposed to be at work?"

Here goes nothing.

"Here's the thing," Marnie said. "I sorta got fired today." She wrung her hands together, her palms sweaty.

"Is it because of your hospital stay? Cause, legally, I don't think they can do that." He was so quick to defend her. Marnie's heart swelled.

"That's not why. I don't even think they know about that." The words refused to come up. Telling Jason the reason had to be the hardest thing she'd done since Carley passed. What would he think of her? "I acted inappropriately during a session with a client. She was being… a brat, honestly. And I threw her phone out the window." Marnie plunged her face into the couch cushion the second the words escaped. Her body stiffened, ready for Jason to yell or leave or laugh; whatever it was, she'd resigned herself to shame.

"Did she deserve it?"

Marnie's head shot up. Jason was watching her, that same mischievous look on his face. "She did. She's been horrible for months. It felt good to finally let out all that frustration."

"It wasn't the smartest way to handle things, but you've been struggling lately. I won't hold it against you."

She dropped her head into the cushion again. "You've been struggling lately" sounded like code for "you're mentally unstable, but it's not your fault."

Jason touched her back. "Maybe this is a good thing," he said.

"Howcoulditpossbbegoodthin?" she spoke into the cushion.

"What?" Jason said.

Marnie lifted her head, resting her chin on her arm. "I said, how could it possibly be a good thing?"

"You're going through a lot. Losing Carley knocked you down hard." Jason grabbed her hand. "Sometimes, taking a step back and changing paths is exactly what we need to heal and grow. Your time at Golden Meadow was amazing, I'm sure. But maybe God has other plans for you now."

"You make it sound so easy," Marnie mumbled.

"Oh, no. It's not gonna be easy. Change is never easy. But it is going to be worth it," Jason said. "One way or another, it'll be worth it."

Marnie released his hand and leaned across the space between them. She embraced Jason. He was perfect; he knew exactly the right words to say. She never wanted to let go.

"Why is all this happening to me?" Marnie said, resting her head on Jason's shoulder.

Jason rubbed soothing circles on Marnie's back. She felt the gentle rise and fall of his chest.

"I mean, why are these 'spiritual forces' after me? Who am I that they would attack me?" Marnie huffed. "I've never played with an Ouija board or conjured spirits… I'm just a normal person."

"You didn't have to do anything to provoke them," Jason said. "Evil doesn't need a reason."

"I want it to stop." Marnie squeezed Jason tighter. "I thought now that I followed Jesus, all this bad stuff would go away."

Jason pulled away, holding Marnie out by the shoulders. His face was calm and caring. "Jesus never promised an easy life, Marnie. In fact, he often promised the exact opposite."

"So, what am I supposed to do, then?"

"Well," Jason said, "prayer, for one thing, is a great tool against the enemies of God. It can be a good comforter, too."

Marnie pressed her lips into a tight smile and looked down. "I guess I should do more of that."

Jason laughed, pulling Marnie into a hug again.

God, please let Jason be right.

Thirty-Five

"TODAY IS THE DAY," Cavin said, stuffing rope and duct tape into a duffle bag. He hummed as he worked. Nothing could ruin his good mood. He was finally going to rescue Marnie from Jason and Hannah and the horrible life she'd lived without him. He'd be her hero, her knight in shining armor.

Cavin finished packing the bag, then went to change. He stared at his closet, hands on his hips, debating what to wear. He wanted to go unnoticed, so dark colors were a must. But he also wanted to be well dressed for Marnie. What good was a knight in shining armor if he didn't look his best?

He pulled out a dark red shirt and a black zip-up hoodie. He wore black jeans and black vans, ready to dissolve into the night. Cavin stared at himself in the mirror, a grin etched onto his face.

It wasn't originally part of his plan to take Marnie tonight. In fact, he'd planned on waiting another week or so. God apparently had other plans. After their coffee date, Cavin could see the longing in Marnie's eyes. She wanted to escape, needed to escape. Marnie losing her job was the best thing to happen to Cavin, and he needed to act fast before she tried to find another one. Now, no one would miss her. She wouldn't have to call in sick to work. It was perfect.

"Marnie, I'm here to help you," he said to the mirror. "No, that sounds stupid." Cavin shook his head, faced away from the mirror, and took a deep breath. He turned back. "My love, I came to rescue you," he said. "You don't have to hide behind your job or your friends any longer. We can be together, and it will be beautiful."

Yes, that was perfect.

❧

The afternoon with Jason left Marnie on a high. His tenderness and encouragement were a sweet balm on her blistered soul. The more time she spent with him, the more she knew that he was exactly the kind of person she wanted in her life.

The moment Marnie shut the door behind him, she started cleaning. Never again would he catch her with a dirty house.

She started in the bedroom, transferring the dirty laundry from the floor to the laundry basket and then to the washer in the kitchen closet.

She made her bed, dusted the nightstands and dresser, and straightened the curtains. Without a break, Marnie moved to the kitchen. She scrubbed the countertops with two different solutions before going over them with a dry paper towel. Her mind buzzed, thinking of her job and Ashley and, *oh God, what's gonna happen to my career?* She shoved them aside, focusing on the task at hand. Marnie sprinkled a cleaner over the stove and in the sink. She paced the kitchen while it soaked.

Anxiety bubbled in her chest. She took everything out of the overhead cabinets, wiped them down, then rearranged the cups and plates in new spots. Nothing like a little reorganizing to clear your thoughts.

Once enough time had passed, Marnie scrubbed at the stove. She bent low over the stovetop, getting her face close enough to the surface that she could see every tiny detail, every stain, every single crumb. Satisfied, she repeated the process on the sink.

Marnie swept like a tornado through the whole house, leaving it sparkling rather than destroyed. By the time she'd finished, not a single spec of dust remained on any surface. Still, her heart jumped.

The walls were closing in. No amount of cleaning would push them back to normal. She had to get out.

Marnie grabbed her coat from the hall closet and marched outside.

A little fresh air was all she needed.

❧

Another gift from God Almighty himself – Marnie left the house. Where she was going, Cavin didn't know. He'd follow anyway.

Marnie had been a hermit lately, hardly leaving her home unless absolutely necessary. Cavin planned on simply using his bump key and nabbing her while she slept. Granted, that would be quite difficult. Too many eyes around; anyone could be watching from any window.

Grabbing her while she was in transit? Much easier.

Cavin followed as Marnie weaved through the crowded sidewalk. She'd never gone this way before. Where could she be going?

It was like the heavens opened, and light from the Lord shone down on Cavin. Marnie walked through a gate into the local park shrouded in trees, with no people in sight. It was the perfect time, far too late for parents to be out with their children.

It was the perfect place. Cavin's muscles tensed, and a tingle shot up from his toes. Marnie would be his very soon; he could just about taste her lips on his.

❧

Marnie had only ever passed this park. It was as good a day as any to explore it. White ash and river birch trees stood tall on either side of the path, their leaves various shades of yellow, red, and some green still holding onto summer.

A slight breeze lifted Marnie's hair around her face, the crisp air bringing vitality to her lungs. She inhaled, letting it permeate her insides. Refreshing. Cleansing.

Why had she never been here before? The park was gorgeous. The way the trees hugged close together made the space feel private, like her own little hideaway.

Marnie let the fresh air clear her head and ease her anxiety. She meandered along the path and prayed.

"God, I don't know what I'm supposed to do next. I thought

213

being a therapist was my life's calling, but now I'm unsure. If Ashley wanted to, and I'm sure she does, she could ruin my career. No one will ever hire me again." Marnie's breathing hitched. "You have to have a plan for all this. Why else would you let me go through it? Please, God. Help me."

Jason came to her mind. His smile, the way he selflessly cares for others. Would she have even noticed him if it weren't for everything going on? Along that same vein of thought, would she have ever come to Jesus if not for the things going on? Suddenly, Marnie remembered all the good that came out of the experiences she'd been having.

Of course, that didn't lessen the bad. There were still the nightmares and the shadow. And Carley. She'd never be able to move on from what happened to Carley.

>

Marnie was walking slowly, taking her time. She didn't seem worried or alert. Perfect.

Cavin stayed behind her, taking in every detail. Her hips moved rhythmically with each step; all he wanted was to run up, place his hands on her hips, and sway with her to the music only they could hear. She was an excellent dancer. Cavin could tell by the fluidity in her movement. She was impossibly sexy.

Cavin sped up a little bit, unwilling to wait any longer. Now was the time. No one was around, he could lead her back to the car, and they'd disappear before anyone even entered the park.

>

Heavy footfalls rose above the rustling trees. Marnie glanced behind.

Someone was there. A man. He was following her.

She turned her head more to get a better look. The man veered to the left, following another path.

Get it together, Marnie. Just focus on the beautiful walk.

She faced forward, dropping her shoulders and rolling her head, easing the tension. She was fine, and this was a public place. No one would risk doing something dramatic in a public place, right? Marnie looked around. The park was empty. No witnesses. It was just her and the man.

The closeness of the trees felt more suffocating than relaxing. They hid the sky, hid any natural light.

When did it get so dark?

Marnie looked at the lamp posts lining the walkway; they hadn't turned on yet. Why not? Why was it so dark?

More footsteps from behind, but when she turned, there was no one. Marnie's mind raced. What if it was the man from the texts? The man who called her a slut.

The man from the alley. She'd seen him. He was real, not a figment of her imagination. And he was here now, ready to do who-knows-what to her.

Marnie froze. The quickest way home was back the way she came. She turned around and took two steps before stopping again.

Back the way she came meant going toward the man, giving him an even better opportunity of attacking her.

Marnie clutched the keys from her pocket, pulling them out and placing one between each of her fingers in a fist. She wasn't going down without a fight.

She kept walking further from home. She had to complete the circle of the park and fast. Going backward was not an option. She jogged, the adrenaline pumping through her body, making her head spin.

Crap. She'd seen him and now was on high alert. Cavin jogged with her, keeping a short distance between them. He would sprint once she reached the corner; that way, he had less ground to cover back to his car.

A dog barked behind him. Cavin turned to see a man in basketball shorts and a hoodie walking with a golden retriever on a leash. Cavin slowed down, letting the man pass. The man watched Marnie, then turned back and looked at Cavin. Cavin stared up at the trees, his hands in his pocket.

Come on, buddy. Move along.

But he refused. The man stayed planted between Marnie and Cavin. He'd seen Cavin's face. He could give a description to the police.

Cavin cursed under his breath when he saw Marnie cut through the gate and sprint. She was going to make it back home.

The man and the dog started jogging, and Cavin quickened his pace to catch up. As he passed the man, he spat. His saliva landed on the guy's shoe.

"What the heck, man?" he said.

Cavin ignored him, heading to his car.

Thirty-Six

MARNIE SLAMMED THE DOOR SHUT, locking it. She leaned against it, panting. That was close, too close. He was closing in and getting even bolder than she'd thought.

How did he know she was walking in the park? How often did he follow her? What was he planning to do once he got her?

Marnie paced, rubbing a line into the carpet. This was far worse than she'd expected. Her life was in actual danger, not just her mind.

She turned the TV on, letting a Lifetime movie play in the background. She took a sip of water, sat down, then immediately stood again. Marnie checked the lock on her front door, then, for good measure, stuck a chair against the door handle.

This was insane. It was 8:30 pm, pitch black outside, and her mind was as dark. She couldn't be alone, couldn't let her mind wander like it was.

Marnie called Hannah; she would know what to do.

"Hannah, can we get dinner?"

"Dude… It's almost nine o'clock. Dinner was like two hours ago."

Marnie sighed. "I'm paying," she said.

There was silence on the other end. Marnie heard papers shuffling. She'd probably caught Hannah in the middle of grading. Being a kindergarten teacher meant "grading" was putting smiley face stickers on papers with the alphabet written on them.

I could be a teacher…

"Alright, fine. Where?" Hannah said.

"Denny's? The one on Campbell. Nine o'clock?"

Since a psycho was stalking her when she walked, Marnie opted for an Uber to meet Hannah.

She made it to the restaurant right at nine. Hannah stood in front of the entrance, staring down at her phone.

"Hannah!" Marnie called, getting out of the car and thanking the driver.

Hannah looked up and smiled, putting her phone in her purse. "There you are," she said. "I've been waiting for like ten minutes."

"Didn't we agree on nine?"

Hannah rolled her eyes. "Yeah, but you're, like, early to everything. I figured it was more like 8:45."

Marnie punched her in the shoulder, and Hannah grabbed it, contorting her face dramatically. "I'm starving," Marnie said.

They sat in a booth away from the windows. If the stalker was out there, Marnie didn't want to know. She wanted to spend an hour with her friend brainstorming, not looking over her shoulder. This dinner was two-fold. She wanted to talk to Hannah about the park and the obscene message across her door, but she also still needed to tell her that she'd lost her job.

Boy, Marnie, you're living the life, aren't you?

Marnie stared down at the menu, tapping the table with four fingers.

"Ahem."

Marnie looked up. Hannah was staring directly at her; her forehead wrinkled all too familiarly. Marnie had seen that wrinkly forehead a lot over the past several months. It seemed like that was the only way Hannah looked at her anymore.

"Why are you looking at me like that?" she said.

Hannah cleared her throat, intentionally relaxing her forehead. "Like what?"

"You're giving me pity eyes."

"Sorry, I didn't mean to give you pity eyes." Her forehead

crinkled again. "Are you okay? Have you had thoughts… again?"

Marnie cocked her head. "Thoughts?"

"You know," Hannah said, her eyes shifting down and back up. "Thoughts about hurting yourself again."

"Are you serious?" Marnie folded her arms and slammed herself against the booth seat.

It was just like Hannah to bring that up again. Low blow. Marnie wasn't sure if it'd be worth talking to her now, not if all she saw was her sick friend.

"Look, I'm worried about you, kid. You really scared me that night."

Marnie leaned across the table, resting on her elbows. "Hannah, I swear those weren't self-inflicted. They were scratches from some monster! Geez, why can't you believe me?" It was like the entire world was against her in one way or another. Either people didn't believe her, or they were after her. Crawling under a rock for the rest of her life sounded like the only way out.

"It's a little far-fetched, that's all," Hannah whispered.

"Hannah, you believe in spiritual warfare. You're the one who taught it to me, right?"

Hannah nodded.

"Okay, so don't you believe it could've been a spiritual attack manifesting in a physical form?" Marnie's voice was low, serious.

"I guess."

"Please, trust me. I'm not trying to harm myself." Marnie tried to sound as sincere as possible, concentrating her eyes on Hannah's face.

"I trust you," Hannah said. "But I still want you to talk to Dr. Carlson. Maybe Golden Meadow can pay for you to get some therapy. They do that, right? I mean, therapists need upkeep and all."

Marnie slumped her shoulders. "About that," she said.

The waiter walked up to their table with a pot of coffee.

Oh, sweet interruptions, thank you.

When he left, Hannah resumed the conversation. "You were saying?"

Marnie played with her silverware to avoid looking at Hannah. "I, uh, don't work at Golden Meadow anymore." She laid her head against the table, speaking to the floor. "I got fired." She looked back up to see Hannah blinking rapidly.

She finally did it. After a lifetime of friendship, Marnie finally caused Hannah to short-circuit.

"Please say something," Marnie said.

"I… I don't know what to say." Hannah shook her head. "How did this happen? Is it because of Carley?"

"No, it has nothing to do with Carley. I kinda lost my cool during a session and threw my client's phone out the window." No matter how many people she told, their reactions were always the same, shock. Marnie waved her hand, trying to make it sound like it wasn't a big deal. By the look on Hannah's face, the attempt was in vain.

Hannah's pitiful eyes returned. Why wouldn't they? She was listening to her best friend admit to temporarily losing her mind, something that before this year had only happened once since they met.

Marnie explained the whole situation, realizing it was not helping her case. Hannah was still convinced that Marnie had tried to hurt herself, throw in anger issues, and things were not looking good.

"I'm sorry, Marnie. But maybe this is a good thing, you know? Now you have a chance to move forward, to properly grieve Carley. You've been getting a little–" Hannah coughed. "Stressed lately."

"Batty, you mean." Marnie raised an eyebrow. "It's okay. I know I've been acting a little crazy." At least Hannah wasn't being judgemental.

Hannah had every right to tell Marnie that her actions were wrong. They were. She knew it; Dr. Carlson knew it. Heck, even Ashley knew it, and that girl wouldn't know "wrong" if it bit her in the butt. Instead, Hannah listened and encouraged. She was a good friend. A skeptical friend when it came to some things, but still good.

"Oh!" Hannah perked up. "I just heard about an opening at the high school in my district. They're looking for a guidance counselor. I could refer you to them! It's not exactly the same as Golden Meadow, but you'd still be working with teenagers."

"In your district? It's a little far, isn't it?" Hannah lived forty-five minutes out of town, whereas Marnie lived in the heart of downtown. Hannah's school district was just as far, in Branson.

Then again, it could be a chance for Marnie to move. Then her stalker wouldn't know where she was. "You know, that sounds great. I could use a change of scenery. Maybe I'll even move out there."

Hannah bounced in her seat. "This is so great. I'll send an

email to the high school principal. Do you think you'd be able to get a recommendation letter from Dr. Carlson?"

Yikes. The thought of reaching out to Dr. Carlson again scared Marnie. Asking her for a recommendation was even scarier. "I can try," Marnie said.

The close call in the park never came up. Marnie's worries subsided after talking to Hannah, and she forgot about the incident. Plus, if she got the job in Branson, she'd move. Problem solved. No need to rope Hannah into it all. She'd thrown enough at her friend.

Marnie had Hannah drop her off in the apartment complex's parking lot. A few other units separated the lot from her apartment. It was better than the alley; the sidewalk between the buildings was well-lit. Still, worry covered her in a blanket. The light's radius was small, and darkness lay beyond. Marnie strained her eyes, but she could only see a few feet in front of her at a time. She wrapped her arms around her chest, hugging herself, and kept pressing forward.

Almost home.

The hair on the back of her neck stood. Marnie felt him, the shadow, close behind. She walked quicker, ignoring him, praying he'd go away.

"Speeding up won't help. You can't outrun me, Marnie." His voice was poisonous, dripping with death.

Marnie didn't look back. She refused to engage. She prayed under her breath. God had control; he wouldn't let her die.

The air around her thickened, the ring of light getting smaller and smaller. He was closing in. She was almost home, almost safe.

Was she, though? How safe was home? He'd been in there, too. He could get her anywhere. She couldn't take it anymore. Marnie stopped and swung around. "Why are you doing this to me?"

"Because you're weak. An easy target," he growled. "And because I can." His voice swirled around her; Marnie spun with it.

She ran the rest of the way home, chased by his laugh. This was torture. How much longer did she have to endure?

Marnie was spent. She dropped to her knees, crying. "Why are you letting this happen?" Marnie cried out to God. "I gave in to you! I decided to follow you. Aren't you supposed to keep me safe?" She folded forward, her head pressing into the carpet. "I thought you were all-powerful, and that you'd be with me no matter what." Tears streamed down her face. The words rose to a shout; Marnie lifted her face to the ceiling. "Where are you, God? Why aren't you doing anything to help me? I'm drowning here, and I can't take it anymore!" The words choked her. Marnie pulled herself into a hug. "I can't take it anymore," she whispered.

Exhaustion overtook her until she fell asleep there on the living room floor.

Thirty-Seven

THE SUN SHONE THROUGH MARNIE'S closed eyelids in brilliant shades of red. Surely the light would blind her if she dared to look. Marnie shaded her eyes with a shaky hand and blinked. She was lying on a bed of soft grass, surrounded by tall sunflowers.

This place was familiar. It felt like home.

Peace washed over her. The darkness couldn't get her here. No darkness was allowed; the shadow was not welcome. She was free to feel calm and didn't have to hide or check over her shoulder. She could simply be.

A sweet, melodic laugh rose in the breeze, tickling Marnie's eardrums. It was starkly different from the sadistic sound she was used to. It sounded like a familiar melody, a song her heart knew well.

Marnie followed the laughter to its source. A girl sat under a large weeping willow, its branches and leaves swaying gently. The girl's head was turned upward, her mouth open in a joyous grin. Recognition hit Marnie, and she sprinted to her.

Carley turned to face her, arms wide. They embraced. Weeks of grief streamed from Marnie, leaving in waves of relief.

"I can't believe you're here," Marnie said.

Carley squeezed. "I've been waiting to talk to you for so

long."

The Carley in this place was a direct contrast to the one who often sat in Marnie's office. Here, Carley's face was bright, almost glowing. Her eyes sparkled, and a smile was fixed on her face. She was full of life and love, and laughter.

"I'm sorry for the way I left. I know it wasn't the smartest decision. I couldn't think of anything else to do." She held Marnie at arm's length and hung her head.

Marnie placed a hand under Carley's chin, lifting her face. Guilt crept into Marnie's heart, and she felt the weight of her mistakes pulling her down. "I'm sorry I couldn't save you. If I had done my job right, you'd still be alive."

"Save me?" Carley laughed. She lifted her clear, bright eyes to Marnie's. There was so much peace in those eyes, so much contentment. "Marnie, it was never your job to save me. Your job was to listen and bring comfort, which is exactly what you did!"

Marnie let her go. She looked out at the fields, the sunflowers gazing at the sun, drinking in the life it offered. "No." She shook her head. "I should've been more aware of what you were saying. I should've taken you more seriously."

Carley grabbed Marnie's shoulders and spun her around. "Marnie, there is only one person in the universe who could save me. And he did. You don't need to worry anymore."

Tears pooled in Marnie's eyes; she blinked them away. There was one question she wanted to ask. It was the one thing she wanted from Carley – the reason she attended the funeral. Marnie bowed her head. "Do you forgive me?"

"Forgive you?" Sweet giggles bubbled out of Carley's throat. "Marnie, I never blamed you!"

Marnie let go, letting the tears roll. She fell into Carley, crying onto her shoulder. Carley held her for a long time, patting her back. The horrible weight that Marnie had carried lifted; she felt light again. She hadn't truly realized how heavy her body had been, how much she'd let her failure rewrite the makeup of her body. Hearing Carley release her from the guilt was like a soothing balm slathered onto burns. It was cooling, relaxing. Freeing.

They sat in the shade of the willow tree and talked for hours. Carley spoke of things Marnie only imagined. Eternity was beautiful, and Carley got to live in it.

A twinge of jealousy sat in Marnie's heart. She wanted to join her, to be with Carley and with God forever. She wanted to escape the shadow and her stalker. It wasn't her time, though. That much she knew.

The sun set on the horizon.

Carley held tight to Marnie's hand. She inhaled deeply, letting her shoulders scrunch up, then droop down with her exhale. "It's time for me to go and for you to wake up," Carley said.

"I don't want to leave," Marnie said. "I'm not ready to go back." She squeezed Carley's hand.

"God heard you, Marnie. He's with you. You're not alone."

Marnie closed her eyes. "If he heard me, why is he making me go through all this?"

Carley touched Marnie's cheek, her palm warm against Marnie's skin. "He's not making you," she said. "People have free will and make decisions sometimes that hurt others. Someone has set their sights on you, Marnie, and they aren't letting go. It just so happens that he has help 'on the other side' so to speak."

"Lucky me," Marnie murmured.

"It will all be over soon. You need to stay strong and have faith; you're almost there. Remember that even though you walk through the valley of the shadow of death, the Lord is with you; he comforts you."

They stood together. Marnie wrapped her arms around Carley once more. Letting go now was harder than the first time.

"I'm truly happy now. Please don't be sad for me."

Marnie smiled and waved goodbye. She closed her eyes and took a strong breath, letting the fresh evening air fill her lungs one last time. The carpet tickled her face, as Marnie opened her eyes in her living room.

"Thank you, God," she whispered, then headed to her bedroom.

Thirty-Eight

CARLEY WAS OKAY.

Marnie had seen her, and she was okay. She was happy and healthy and in the greatest place in the universe. There was nothing more Marnie needed to do for the girl, nothing she could do that would even come close to what Carley was experiencing now.

Marnie's heart soared. She felt forgiven, set free. She didn't need to worry or feel guilty anymore. It was a dream, so there was a chance that none of it was real. There was a chance that it was all her mind playing tricks to make her feel better because she couldn't take the guilt anymore. But something about the dream felt different. In a way, it felt like the nightmare that left her with a gash in her calf. It was so real, more real than the world around her. Marnie was confident that what she'd experienced with Carley was the truth.

She got out of bed and made coffee. Marnie hopped into the chair at the kitchen counter and cracked open her Bible. It was an embarrassingly long time since she last opened it. In all honesty, she had been angry at God. Things were getting worse, and it seemed like he didn't care. She didn't want to read his words if he didn't care about her.

Until last night. That dream. It changed everything.

Something Carley said in the dream stuck with Marnie. It played in her mind since she woke up.

"Even though you walk through the valley of the shadow of death, the Lord is with you; he comforts you."

Marnie typed it into Google, it sounded like something that would be in the Bible, but she wasn't sure. She saw a Bible verse, sure enough, at the top of the search results.

Psalm twenty-three, verse four. It read almost exactly what Carley said, but more.

"I will fear no evil," Marnie read aloud.

The shadow man she'd dealt with was pure evil. She didn't need to fear him; God was with her. He would comfort her. Confidence in Christ was all she needed to stay strong.

Marnie sat tall, pressing her shoulders back. She closed her eyes and repeated the phrase. "Even though I walk through the valley of the shadow of death, I will fear no evil." A deep breath. "I will fear no evil."

Marnie opened her eyes. She walked into her living room. "You hear that, shadow? I'm not going to fear you anymore! Bring on whatever you've got 'cause I don't care anymore!"

Ha, take that!

She went back to the counter and read from John as she did before. Time passed by in a blink. Her stomach growled, pulling her out of the story. When she checked her phone, it was close to three o'clock.

Marnie made herself leftovers from Denny's and got comfortable on the couch. She watched a movie, a comedy to be exact, and laughed. *Actually laughed.* When was the last time she'd done that? Security was so sweet, security in Christ even sweeter. Marnie wasn't worried about the future, she wasn't worried about the shadow.

Hannah would be happy to hear all this. When the movie ended, Marnie called Hannah.

"What's up? Are you okay?" Hannah answered.

"I'm great," Marnie said. "I wanted to see if you could go on a walk with me tonight."

"Darn, I'd love to, Mar, but I'm going on a date with Liam. I'm curling my hair as we speak."

"Oh, Liam!" Marnie said, followed by an onslaught of kissy noises.

Hannah laughed. "Would you stop that? Let's get lunch tomorrow; how's that?"

"Alright, I'll see you tomorrow," Marnie said. "Have fun with Liam."

Okay, Hannah was a bust.

Marnie scrolled through her contacts, pretending like she wasn't already sure Jason was the next person she'd call. Her thumb hovered over his name, nerves making it twitch. Why was she so nervous to call him? Was it clingy to call him so soon after they'd hung out? All things considered, they just saw each other. And they weren't a couple, not officially. So, it was weird to call. At least, that was what she told herself.

Then again, she loved talking to Jason. He was the best. And she wanted to spend as much time as humanly possible with him. Plus, he wasn't the type to get annoyed with her calling. He was sweet.

Whatever. It was silly to overthink everything. It was Jason; they had a great time together. He shouldn't be opposed to hearing from her.

Marnie pressed "call" and held the phone to her ear. It rang and rang and rang. With each ring, Marnie's confidence dropped.

He wasn't answering on purpose. He must have seen her name on his screen and silenced the ringer.

Or he was busy on another date.

No, that wouldn't happen. He liked her. He'd kissed her; that proved it.

"Hello?"

Marnie jumped. "Jason! Hi, what's up?"

"Nothing much." Marnie heard voices shouting in the background. "What's up with you?"

"I'm sorry, are you busy?" Marnie asked.

Doors slammed, echoing through the phone. "A little. I'm at work right now."

Marnie slapped her forehead. *Dummy. He has a job.* "Oh my gosh, right. I'm so sorry to bother you!"

Jason chuckled. "Not a bother! You didn't know."

"Well, I'll let you go. I'm gonna go crawl under a rock now," Marnie said, cheeks turning red.

"You think you'll be able to come out from under that rock for dinner tomorrow night?"

Marnie's blush deepened. "I'll have to double-check my schedule, but I think I can manage that."

"Excellent," Jason said. "I'll pick you up at eight."

Marnie tossed her phone onto the couch and did a little spin. Another date with Jason – life couldn't get any better than that. Life was taking a turn for the better; she felt it in the air. Between the prospect of a new job and a budding relationship with Jason, things were looking up. God hadn't abandoned her.

Being trapped inside all day was getting to her. Marnie needed fresh air and a little exercise. Hannah couldn't go for a walk, and Jason was working. That wasn't going to stop her, though.

"I will fear no evil," Marnie declared as she grabbed her coat. She was perfectly capable of walking alone.

She grabbed a can of pepper spray, too, just in case.

The cool breeze kissed Marnie's cheeks, and she smiled. Trees swayed gently in the wind, and a chorus of rustling leaves played like the soundtrack to her life.

There were a few more people in the park tonight, giving Marnie an extra layer of confidence. After getting spooked a few nights ago, she'd decided to come out earlier when there were more people. A mother pushed her little boy in a stroller, and a couple walked hand-in-hand. Fall brought out the best in people. Something about the weather cooling off put everyone in a better mood.

There was no fear. And if it came back, Marnie didn't care. She wasn't going to let it hold her back anymore. God showed her the answer to her prayer last night, and she believed him. Trusted him. Nothing was going to–

Determined footsteps stomped behind her.

Her joy was cut short, replaced with panic.

Not again.

She kept walking, refusing to look back. It was her mind playing tricks; had to be. Self-sabotage was a real thing, and she was doing that to herself. Too many good things were happening, and deep down, a part of her still felt guilty for what happened to Carley. And about Ashley. That's all it was.

"Marnie," someone said.

She froze. That voice – she knew that voice – had talked to him many times.

"Finally," he said, getting closer. "It's time."

She spun around. "Cavin?"

He was wearing a dark hoodie, standing six paces away. Light glinted off the knife in his hand.

"Such a nice evening for a walk, isn't it?" Cavin said. "Shall we walk together?" He took a step closer, lifting the knife.

Marnie stared at it. Her eyes refused to take in anything else. The knife. What was he planning to do with the knife?

Cavin followed her stare and turned the knife in his hand. "Don't worry, Marnie. I'm not going to use this. So long as you come quietly, okay?"

"Cavin, please." Marnie staggered back. "You don't want to do this," she whispered.

Cavin took another step forward. "I think it's time we stop playing this little game."

She looked around, eyes searching for someone to help. The park was empty. What happened to the couple walking? Or the mother pushing her child?

She was all alone.

"What game?" Dizziness swallowed her. Marnie locked her knees to keep from falling.

"No!" Cavin yelled, waving the knife. He stepped forward again. "We're done with the games, Marnie. You have to stop doing this. Making me think you love me one moment, then pretending you don't know what I'm talking about the next." He pressed his thumb into his temple. "That kinda thing makes a man crazy."

Marnie reached into her pocket, grasping for the pepper spray. Her shaking fingers refused to grip the cylinder. "Let's talk about it, huh? Why don't we find a bench, and we can talk."

Cavin shook his head violently, his hair swinging around. "I'm done talking. You and I belong together, Marnie." This is a step forward. "You just don't know it yet, I guess."

He lunged. Marnie yelped and jumped to the side. "Cavin, please. Let's talk about this."

He huffed, his chest rising and falling clearly through his hoodie. "Honey, we can talk at home." Cavin grabbed Marnie's wrist.

She tried to yank free, but his grip was too strong. Her other hand, still shoved in her pocket, finally tightened around the pepper spray. She pulled it free and pressed down, sending the liquid directly into Cavin's eyes.

He dropped her wrist, rubbing his hands into his eyes and letting out a painful howl. "Why are you fighting me on this?"

Marnie flinched. Her mind was sluggish, refusing to form any other plans. Her leg muscles tensed, and she ran. She didn't look back, her vision tunneling onto the path ahead. Her only focus was getting home. Hiding would work, too. But her legs kept going, kept pushing.

Cavin was close behind her; she heard his heavy breathing as he closed the distance. Images of what he'd do if he caught her flashed across her mind – the knife slicing into her stomach. Or worse, he'd take her somewhere.

Home. He mentioned home, didn't he?

Marnie veered left. If she could throw him off track, she'd get away. He was too close, though. The sudden change in direction didn't slow him down.

Her breath was hot, leaving her mouth in thick jolts. Free, she had to get free. She heard his growl low and deep. A sinister laugh bounced around her. Was that Cavin?

The orange glow from her front porch light caught her eyes. Marnie zeroed in on the light. Safety was within reach.

She bounded up the steps, taking them two at a time. A rough hand wrapped around her ankle, jerking her back. Marnie slipped, and her chin slammed into the concrete steps, dazing her. She clawed up blindly, searching for anything to hold on to. His pull was strong, dragging her down.

"It didn't have to be like this." His voice was distant, muddled by the ache in her chin. Another rough pull, and Marnie lost her grip, her head hitting the concrete step once again.

Please, God. I'm afraid.

The world went dark.

Thirty-Nine

A RUSHING OF WIND SWIRLED AROUND HER, sweeping her legs out and making her fall to the ground. His laughter was back, louder than before.

He won.

Somehow, Marnie knew deep down that this was the shadow's plan all along. Cavin was always meant to take her.

"Marnie, I told you I'd get you. Now, I'm going to destroy you," the disembodied voice taunted her.

She screamed a blood-curdling sound. Her throat shredded as she unleashed the noise. It was no use. Who would hear her? Who would save her?

The darkness was closing in. *He* was closing in. Marnie tried to resist as it closed around her; her vision tunneled as her eyes fell heavy, and the world faded away.

Marnie's eyes fluttered open. She looked around, her breath shallow.

It was dark, and she couldn't stretch her legs out completely. Marnie tried to sit up, but her head hit something metal.

The area lit up in red. A tire iron sat next to her.

She was in the trunk of a car.

Think, come on. Think. This can't be happening.

Marnie wracked her brain, trying to remember everything she learned in self-defense. That class was years ago; the memory was choppy.

There was something about the brake lights, something. *What?*

The adrenaline shooting through her system made Marnie's head throb, jumbling her thoughts. She shook, punching the trunk door with her arms. "Let me out of here!" she screamed, her voice shrill.

The brake lights lit up the space again.

That's it!

Marnie shimmied her body, navigating her legs to the opening of the trunk. Once there, she kicked her heel into the brake light.

It didn't budge.

Her stomach tumbled, nausea rising. Marnie closed her eyes and focused on her breathing.

Inhale, 1...2...3... Exhale, 1...2...3...

She opened her eyes again, kicking the brake light again. On the third kick, it fell out, clanking along the street.

"Yes!" Marnie whispered.

She scooted back around and looked out the opening. A dark road passed by, with no other cars in sight. Her eyes scanned the road, looking for any indication of where she was, any sign that she could remember to tell the police. It was empty – nothing but grass, a wooden fence, and the endless two-lane road.

"You're stuck with me forever," the shadow said. "I'm never letting you go."

He was here, in the trunk. Marnie jerked her head around. Darkness enveloped the trunk. She blinked rapidly, then squeezed her eyes shut for several long seconds. When she opened them, it was still pitch black. Her eyes wouldn't adjust. It was impossible to adjust to this darkness.

"I'm honestly shocked, Marnie. I didn't think you were stupid enough not to notice a psycho among your own patients."

Marnie's chest tightened, and she shivered. He was right. How had she not noticed Cavin? He seemed so normal, so kind – a little creepy at the cafe, but he didn't seem unhinged.

It'd been him all along. The text messages, the flowers. He

was standing in the alley. He followed her that first night in the park.

How long had he planned this? What was his end goal?

Marnie buried her face in her hands, she let the tears come. "I don't want to die," she cried.

❧

Cavin drove the long road back to his house. AC/DC blared through the speakers. Marnie's screams were faint above the music. Things hadn't gone the way he hoped, but he had Marnie. That was enough. And they were going to be together forever.

He was taking Marnie to the home he prepared for her.

Just as Jesus prepares a home for his followers, I've prepared one for my love. We are both saviors.

It wasn't spectacular. By all accounts, their home was plain. But once Marnie learned her lesson, they would fill the halls with love and laughter. Marnie could earn the home back with good behavior and repentance.

It wouldn't take too long.

When that day finally came, he and Marnie would marry, and she'd come out of the basement to fill his home with a happily ever after.

Cavin tapped the steering wheel to the beat, bobbing his head along.

What a joyous day! Everything he had been working towards was finally within his reach.

The house laid back behind trees at the edge of town. It held a lot of horrible memories, being the house Cavin grew up in. Oh boy, if Mother saw him now! She'd blow a gasket.

Cavin was going to rewrite all those bad memories now.

He pulled into the driveway, the headlights shining across the garage. In the future, he'd pull in the same way, and his children would run up to the car yelling, "Daddy's home!" He'd jump out, scoop them into his arms, and give them kisses. Marnie would be in the kitchen, prepping supper the way a good wife does, and he'd plant a fat kiss on her lips.

Dreams of the future were almost too much to bear. His heart was going to burst with anticipation.

Cavin killed the engine and stepped out. There hadn't been

any noise from the trunk for the last three miles; Marnie must've fallen asleep. She had taken a pretty hefty tumble. It was good for her to sleep it off. He pulled her out of the trunk, careful not to wake her.

She lay in his arms like a bride, and they crossed the threshold of their home at the beginning of their forever.

"My sweet Marnie," he whispered close to her face. "I wish I could take you to our bedroom right now. But you've been a very naughty girl, so I'm gonna put you in the basement for a little while until you've learned to behave." He kissed her forehead.

Cavin carried her through the living room and into the kitchen. The basement door was open. He walked down the stairs and laid Marnie on the ground, a thin blanket draped over her chest.

Back upstairs, Cavin locked the basement door. He blew a kiss, then went to the bedroom. He slept soundly, knowing his beloved had finally come home.

❧

The ground was cold and hard. Marnie's shoulders ached, and her chin throbbed. She moaned, touching her chin, then winced. Her eyes adjusted slightly to the darkness.

Where was she?

Marnie lifted herself off the floor, her body screaming with every micro-movement.

She didn't get away. He got her. Looking out the tail light was useless; there were no other cars and no landmarks. She didn't have even the slightest clue where he'd brought her.

The room was damp, the musty smell stinging her nostrils. She breathed in short, quick inhales, afraid of what spores she could be breathing in. Marnie walked to one side and ran her hand along the wall. She pulled it away, wet. The water seemed to move in a constant stream down the wall. A leak somewhere.

It's an old house.

Marnie wanted to drink in every possible detail; anything could be a clue in the right hands. If – No, *when* – she got out, she would need to be able to give as much information as possible. Luckily, she already knew her captor quite well.

The room was a concrete box: four walls, all equal in height and width – her very own cage.

There was a staircase set against one of the walls. Marnie rushed to it and started climbing. Halfway up, she stepped on a nail. She cursed, lifting her foot and stroking the spot.

The psycho took her shoes. Her mind was so fuzzy from everything she hadn't realized until then.

What kind of monster takes a person's shoes? Wasn't it enough he had her trapped down here?

Marnie hopped the rest of the way up and shook the door handle. It wouldn't budge.

She rammed her shoulder into the door, but still nothing. For an old house, the door was sturdy.

"Hello?" she called, banging a fist on the door. "Cavin? Let me out!"

She banged until her fist bled, exhaustion slowing her muscles.

He wasn't coming. What exactly was his plan? Let her stew in panic? Wear her down?

Marnie went back down the steps. How had she missed the signs? The way he looked at her, Savannah's warning. It all made sense now. He acted so nice, but there were moments, weren't there? Moments when the truth slipped through his mask. He held onto her box so tightly, refusing to let go, insisting on walking her home. He said her name in long drawls, savoring it. Sometimes, she caught his gaze. He looked like he wanted to swallow her whole. She should've known.

She missed the warning signs with Carley, and that got her killed. She missed the warning signs with Cavin, and now her life was on the line.

It's settled. You are not meant to be a therapist, Mar.

Goosebumps tickled her skin, and she rubbed her arms. She laid down, resting her head on the old pillow. Dust puffed up, causing her to cough. She wrapped her shivering body in the tattered blanket.

If they were meant to be, why was Cavin treating her this way? Would he ever let her out?

Her head was still throbbing. Marnie turned onto her side. Her stomach churned; she was afraid of vomiting. One more horrid smell she'd have to deal with down here.

This can't be happening.

It was a dream. Had to be! If she closed her eyes and went

back to sleep, she'd wake up in her bed. Her nightmares had been realistic lately. This was one of those - just a nightmare.

Forty

THERE WAS NO REAL WAY TO TELL how much time had passed. Down here, it was always dark. Always night.

Marnie woke from her dreamless sleep, still in the basement. Still trapped. Moisture stuck to her skin like an extra layer of clothes. She tried to wipe it away to get clean. It wouldn't budge. Her damp skin reeked of sweat and blood, two scents she never thought she'd smell together.

What I wouldn't give for a shower.

Something stirred in the corner. Marnie strained her eyes but couldn't make it out. The shadows too thick to see any shapes.

"H-hello?" Her voice shook. "Cavin? Is that you?"

Marnie stood, scanning the room. She looked up the stairs; the door was closed. That didn't mean Cavin wasn't here; he could've slipped in while she slept. Could've been watching her sleep. He'd do something like that, surely.

Marnie wrapped her clammy hands around her stomach. What if he tried to touch her? Had he touched her when she was sleeping?

Oh God, please.

Marnie backed up until she collided with one of the walls; the leaking water soaked her shirt. It made her already cold skin tingle with goosebumps. Her mind was playing tricks. Things moved out of the corner of her eyes, like her dream of the desert.

Someone dragged their nails across the walls, a high pitch squeal ringing around the room. It reverberated off the walls, attacking Marnie from all sides. She clutched her stomach, fighting nausea spurred on by terror.

"Cavin, I've had enough. Please, you're scaring me."

A low, growling laugh.

No. Not him.

The growl moved around the room, digging deep into Marnie's bones. Tears crawled down her cheeks; she couldn't stop them. She'd become familiar with the creature in the dark.

The demon.

"I know who you are," Marnie said. She raised her voice, trying to sound brave, but the tremor gave her away.

He pulled himself from the wall, the shadow of a man becoming clear. Red eyes glowed from the head and a faint impression where the mouth should be curled at the corners.

He licked his lips. "Do you?"

"Yes." Her voice cracked. "Yes. You're a demon, and you have no power here."

"Demon," he hissed, relishing in the title. "You don't even know what that means."

"I know it means you lose. In the end, nothing you do matters." Marnie dropped her arms to her side, her hands squeezing into fists. Anger drowned out the fear that usually possessed her. She was fed up, tired of succumbing to his mind games.

I will fear no evil.

Now, in this pit. In the shadow of death, the words held a stronger power. She wasn't afraid of him.

"You lost the moment you turned your back on the Creator," Marnie whispered.

The shadow shifted; his shoulders twitched. She struck a chord.

Good.

He moved, too quick for her to see, and knocked Marnie to the ground. She landed hard on her tailbone, hearing a crack.

"From where I'm standing," he said, "it looks like you're the one that lost."

He was right. From this angle, she was the loser. Cavin had taken her, trapped her in this hole, and didn't even bother to talk to her. Her hope of freedom was shot to pieces. This was her life now.

She cried, allowing the weight of her predicament to anchor her to the floor. She wanted to wallow, at least for a minute. Then she'd go back to being strong, to standing up to the shadow. But for a moment, she'd wallow and cry.

God, please. Be with me. Comfort me.

The tears fell, wet droplets soaking through her jeans. Marnie flicked a finger across her cheeks, grateful for the darkness around her. She didn't want to give the shadow the satisfaction of seeing her sorrow.

"Get up," he growled.

Marnie shifted from her butt to her knees and brought her hands together. A posture of surrender. Not to the shadow, but to the only one who could save her. To the Almighty, the one in control. Her defender.

"I said *get up*." His voice dropped another octave; it was forceful. Marnie ignored him.

"You said you'd never leave me," Marnie whispered.

"Who are you talking to? Get up."

Marnie shook her head. "I believe you."

The shadow stomped his foot. The ground shook. "Now, Marnie."

"I believe." Marnie opened her eyes. She turned her head, facing the shadow. One side of her mouth curved, giving him a smirk.

Oh, this is going to be good.

"Get up!" His voice shook the room.

His anger was satisfying to Marnie. She struck a nerve. He wasn't the powerful being he was pretending to be. She saw that now.

Marnie locked her eyes on the empty void of his face. "Do whatever you want to me," she said. "You will never own me."

He laughed like he had a secret – like he knew something she didn't. Marnie's resolve stuttered; she second-guessed her strength. He seemed so angry.

"Marnie, Marnie. I wouldn't worry about what I'll do to you." The door at the top of the stairs creaked, opening. "You should worry about what he's going to do." More laughter, uncontrollable this time.

Marnie looked at the door. It creaked open, light poured into the basement. The silhouette of a tall man stood in the middle. Cavin was here.

Marnie sat back, crawling backward. She needed to get far away, far from him.

"Good, you're awake."

Forty-One

HANNAH TAPPED HER FOOT. Marnie was late. Fifteen minutes late, an unheard-of amount. Marnie was never late for anything. She checked her watch; another minute ticked by.

Hannah pulled out her phone, calling Marnie. It went straight to voicemail.

"The heck?" She called again.

Voicemail again.

Given all the insane things happening to Marnie, Hannah decided to cut her a little slack – five more minutes. If Marnie didn't show up in five minutes, she'd go to her apartment. Fair's fair.

She tapped her foot more, hands on her hips. Droves of people came in and out of the restaurant, wafting the sweet smell of pasta and pizza. Marnie was a jerk for making her wait this long. The hangry was setting in, and Hannah started practicing her scolding for when Marnie did show up.

Ten minutes passed. She'd been generous, giving an extra five. Still no sign of Marnie. This was getting to be very strange.

Hannah walked to her car, dialing Marnie again. This time, when it went to voicemail, she left a message. "Dude, where are you? We were supposed to meet like thirty minutes ago. I'm starving. Either show up or call me back."

She sat in the driver's seat, staring at her phone. One more call wouldn't hurt. The voicemail message played. By this time, Hannah had it memorized down to the inflection of Marnie's voice. "Alright, I'm officially pissed at you. I'm coming over, and you better have a good explanation!" She hung up and threw her phone into the passenger seat. Marnie was going to get an earful.

She peeled out of the parking lot and sped down the road toward Marnie's apartment. Anger was highest on her emotional scale, but worry was climbing the ranks, threatening anger's spot. Marnie was worried about someone breaking into her apartment before and following her at one point. What if it was all true? Until now, Hannah had written it off as paranoia. There was no evidence of a break-in, and she never saw anyone when she walked Marnie home. But what if that was the point? What if the guy was that good?

Hannah pressed her foot harder on the gas pedal. She sent up prayers as she raced to Marnie's.

She swung her Toyota into the parking lot of Marnie's apartment complex, and jumped out before turning the car off. She turned back, yanked the keys from the ignition and locked the door. Running down the sidewalk to Marnie's unit, she could see the blinds closed.

Weird.

It was mid-afternoon; Marnie liked to keep her blinds open when the sun was up. She loved natural lighting.

Hannah ran up the stairs and knocked. "Marnie? You in there?" She put her ear to the door.

Nothing.

Hannah stuck her spare key into the door, letting herself in. The living room was dark, but by all accounts, it looked normal. Nothing was disheveled or out of place. It looked exactly the same as the last time she'd been over.

When was that, again? Last week?

"Marnie?" she called, walking around the apartment.

She checked the bathroom behind the shower curtain. Empty. Marnie's bedroom was empty, too. The bed was made, and the curtains drawn shut. The room emanated an eerie vibe like something bad happened. Hannah couldn't quite put her finger on it.

This was getting spooky. Hannah didn't like it.

Hannah dialed Marnie's number again. 50th time's a charm.

It went, of course, straight to voicemail.

"Where are ya, kid?" Hannah dropped to the couch. She sat on something hard and – shifting over she pulled it out from under her. Marnie's phone. Powered off. She pressed the power button, but nothing happened. Dead.

Her pulse quickened, pumping against her throat. Hannah swallowed hard. Wherever Marnie was, she was without a phone. Not good, not good at all.

Hannah gripped Marnie's phone and ran out of the apartment, sprinting to her car. Marnie was missing, and she had to do something.

Hannah bounced from place to place, looking for Marnie. If there was even the smallest chance that Marnie went somewhere and simply forgot her phone, Hannah would find her. She hit all Marnie's usual spots. The coffee shop, nothing. The bookstore, nothing. Denny's, nothing. Dread overcame her. Hannah was at the end of her rope; the only left to do was go to the police.

Maybe now there'd be enough evidence of something wrong.

Hannah had never been to a police station before. She prided herself on the fact. But here she stood, staring up at the brick two-story building before her, ready to report her best friend missing.

"Deep breaths. I can do this," she whispered before launching herself up the steps.

The glass door opened inward to a large room. On the left, chairs sat in neat rows. The waiting room. To the right, a long table with dividers. And directly in the middle, the front desk. A nice-looking woman with large wireframe glasses sat behind what Hannah assumed was a bulletproof window. The lady didn't look like a cop.

She looked up and met Hannah's stare. "Can I help you, miss?" she asked with a polite smile.

Hannah approached, gripping the counter with both hands. "Hi, are you a cop?"

The woman giggled. "No, but maybe I can help you."

"Ehh," Hannah said, looking past the woman. "I really think I should be talking to a cop. This is serious."

"Alright, tell me what it is, and I'll grab an officer for you."

"My best friend, Marnie Adams, she's missing. I went to her house, but she wasn't there. Her phone was on the couch, dead. I don't think she's been home in a while."

The woman shuffled through a filing cabinet under her desk,

clipped a stack of papers to a clipboard, and passed it through a small window. "Please fill out these forms to the best of your ability. And before you go, please sign in with your name and phone number." The woman indicated a sign-in sheet in front of Hannah.

She signed in, then sat in the waiting area with the clipboard. They asked for a physical description of Marnie, including any identifying features. Hannah kicked herself for not studying her friend more. Did Marnie have tattoos? Were her ears pierced?

Note to self, take a good long look at Marnie the next time you see her.

She also filled in information about herself. Age, name, phone number, and address. Why they needed so much information on her – who knew? Whatever helped them find Marnie quickest.

She took the completed forms to the front desk.

"Thank you, dear. I will pass these to an officer, and they'll contact you via phone for more information."

Hannah raised her eyebrows. "That's it? Didn't you hear me? My friend is missing. She's gone. Poof. I need to find her."

"I understand that." The woman nodded her head. "But there is a system we must follow. An officer will be in touch today; don't you worry."

"Unbelievable," Hannah mumbled. "Can I talk to someone now?" she asked.

Behind the woman, a man in a blue uniform walked by. "Him!" Hannah pointed. "He looks free. Can I talk to him?"

The receptionist's pleasant demeanor started to slip away; her smile turned serious. "Ma'am, I'm going to have to ask you to step outside. You are causing a scene."

Hannah rolled her eyes. "Oh, come on, lady!"

"Someone will call you," the receptionist said matter-of-factly.

Hannah let out a huff, then turned on her heels and stormed outside. There was no way she'd be leaving that police station. Not until someone listened to her about Marnie. She plopped down on the front steps, resting her chin in her hands.

She did what the receptionist asked and went outside. Right outside was where she planned to stay.

Hannah looked up at the sound of footsteps. Two uniformed officers were walking by, staring at her. Blood pumped in her ears, and

245

she shot up.

"You morons!" she yelled, pointing in their faces. "This is all your fault!"

Officers Marks and Gibson each took a step back. "Ma'am?" Officer Marks said.

"If you would've just believed her, none of this would be happening!" Hannah was spiraling. She knew it; they knew it. She couldn't control it. "My best friend is *missing* because you didn't take her seriously!"

Recognition clicked in Officer Gibson's eyes. He stepped forward, placing a hand on Hannah's shoulder. "What happened?" His eyes were serious, boring into hers.

Hannah couldn't stop the tears, so she swiped at them as they fell. "Someone took her. I know it."

Officer Marks scoffed. "I'm sure there is a perfectly reasonable explanation." He moved past Hannah toward the front door. "Come on, Gibs."

Officer Gibson released Hannah's shoulder and shrugged. "I hope you find your friend," he said.

Nothing. Just like last time, they did nothing. Hannah plopped back down, covering her face. She did a mix of crying and praying, back and forth.

Please, God, keep Marnie safe until I find her.

Forty-five minutes passed, and the growling in Hannah's stomach was loud. It rumbled as officers walking in and out of the building turned their heads; hands poised on their holsters.

"Sorry," Hannah shrugged.

After another ten minutes, her phone rang. She didn't recognize the number, but it could be Marnie.

"Marnie? That you?" she answered.

"Hello, is this Hannah Trystan? My name is Officer Noles. I see your missing person's report. Is there a good time I can meet with you?"

Hannah shot up. "I'm at the station; can we talk now?"

"Oh, uh, yes. That's fine. I will meet you in the lobby."

Hannah rushed through the doors. The receptionist stood, with a stern questioning look on her face. Behind her, Hannah saw the officer she'd pointed to before. He looked only a few inches taller than her, with a sturdy build. The man's muscles were bulging out of his uniform. Hannah pitied any criminal that messed with him.

He walked up to the receptionist and placed a hand on her shoulder. She smiled at him, then sat down before shooting a glare at Hannah. Hannah did the mature thing and stuck her tongue out.

Officer Noles walked through the door to the right and approached her. "Hi, Ms. Trystan?" He stuck out his hand.

Hannah took it and shook. It was firm, strong. She could feel the calluses rubbing against her smooth palm. She looked him up and down, suspiciously at first. But suspicion slowly gave way to appraisal.

You have a boyfriend, Hannah. Cool it.

He cleared his throat. "Yes, hi. I'm Hannah. Thank you for meeting with me."

Officer Noles hooked his thumbs on his utility belt, like Batman.

"If you don't mind, Ms. Trystan. We can talk in a private room; would you be okay with that?"

Hannah nodded. "Yeah, yeah, totally."

He led her back through the door, past the receptionist, and into a small room. It had a large window on one wall.

A one-way mirror for the bad guys.

And a large table in the middle, with two chairs on either side.

"Please, have a seat," Officer Noles said, gesturing across from him.

Hannah sat down and looked around the room. "I'm not in trouble, right? I mean, I'm just trying to find my friend."

"No, you're not in trouble." He interlaced his hands on the table. "I need to ask you a few questions about your friend," he glanced at the paper in front of him, "Marnie Adams."

"Okay." Hannah kept her hands in her lap, wringing them together.

Officer Noles poised his pen. "How old is Ms. Adams?"

"Twenty-eight."

He wrote it down. Hannah watched the pen scribbling.

"And can you tell me the last time you saw her?"

Hannah looked up, searching her memory. "I haven't seen her in a few days, but I talked to her yesterday afternoon on the phone. We made plans to get lunch today."

He didn't look up, just kept writing. "What was she doing

when you talked to her?”

“Nothing. She wanted me to go on a walk with her, but I couldn’t. So we decided to meet for lunch today.”

“What time was that, Ms. Trystan?”

“Please, call me Hannah. It was late afternoon. Maybe around five o’clock.”

“Okay. What kind of lifestyle does Ms. Adams live? Does she take any drugs, drink, anything like that?”

“What?” Hannah’s voice cracked. “No. She doesn’t do anything like that.”

“Any history of mental illness in Ms. Adams or her family?”

Hannah touched her mouth, picking at the dry skin on her lips. If she answered truthfully, he’d write Marnie off as a flight risk or something. He wouldn’t take looking for her seriously.

Then again, how sure was Hannah that Marnie hadn’t disappeared on her own? Gone somewhere of her own volition.

“Ms. Trystan?” Officer Noles said.

Hannah looked at him and dropped her hand. “Hannah,” She said again, mild annoyance piquing, “sort of… Marnie was recently hospitalized for a… situation.”

“What kind of situation was that?”

“Uh, I was spending the night and heard her screaming. When I went into her room, her bedsheets were covered in blood, and there were three huge gashes on her calf. She stayed in the hospital for a few days, suicide watch.”

“I see. And is the address and phone number you have in this form correct?” He pointed to the form in front of him.

“Yes, sir.”

“Thank you, I will try calling Ms. Adams and see if I can’t get a hold of her.”

“You won’t. I have her phone.”

He cocked his eyebrow. “Oh? And why do you have her phone?”

“Well, when she didn’t show up for lunch, and she wasn’t answering, I went to her apartment. I have a key. When I went in, the blinds were all shut, the lights were off, and her phone was on the couch, drained of battery.” Hannah touched the pocket of her jeans, debating on pulling it out. Depending on how this interview went, she’d decide if she wanted to give it to them or not.

Officer Noles eyed her carefully. "Alright then." He stood. "Ms. Trystan, Hannah. I will enter this information in our nationwide database. I promise you we will be looking for Ms. Adams. In the meantime, please go home. If she shows up, let us know." He passed her a card with his name and a number on it. "Now that's my personal cell. If you need anything else, call."

He led Hannah back out to the waiting area. She paced, not ready to leave yet. There had to be more that could be done. The way Officer Noles sounded made Hannah feel like he wasn't going to be taking it seriously.

A detective! She needed to talk to a detective. They'd be able to help her more than a plain ole' officer.

The front door opened, and a man in plain clothes strode through the room. He went straight to the front desk. Ms. Stickler-for-the-rules was all smiles.

Wait. I know him.

Hannah approached the man from behind. "Jason?"

He turned. "Hey! Hannah, right? What are you doing here?"

"I could ask you the same thing."

Jason smiled, covering it with his hand. "I'm a detective. I work here."

Hannah hopped, clapping once. "Yes! I need your help." She grabbed Jason's arm. "Marnie is missing. We were supposed to get lunch, but she didn't show up. I went to her house, and it was empty, her phone was there too. I don't know where she is."

Jason's eyes widened. "No, that's not right. I was on my way to pick her up. We have a date tonight."

"Well, I can tell ya right now, buddy. She's not there."

Jason broke out of Hannah's grasp, rubbing his eyes. "Did you- did you file a missing persons report?"

"Yeah, but these bozos won't help me." She shot a begrudging glare at the receptionist.

"Hey!" the receptionist snapped.

Jason's eyes wandered the room. Sweat glistened on his forehead. "Alright, come on." He marched toward the front door.

Hannah jogged, pushing her short legs to keep up with him.

Forty-Two

MARNIE FLINCHED WITH EVERY ONE of Cavin's footfalls on the stairs. The sound felt amplified, ringing in her ears.

God, please don't let him touch me, she prayed.

His eyes never left her. Even in the dark, she knew. She could feel them. His stare flared her skin; made her sweat.

He wandered around the room. It was as if he relished in the moment, relished in Marnie's fear. She tried to back up further, then remembered she was already against the wall. Marnie drew her knees into her chest. If she could make herself as small as possible, maybe he'd go away.

Cavin stopped inches from her, crouched down, and placed a hand on her cheek. "My dear, I've been waiting for this moment my entire life."

Marnie pulled her face away, shrinking from his touch. Her skin crawled with a thousand invisible mites, transmitted from his hand to her face. She resisted the urge to swat at them.

They're in your head.

Marnie turned her attention to the light coming from the top of the stairs. The door was open. If she could get past him, knock him out somehow, she could escape and find help. He had to have neighbors.

There was bound to be someone nearby.

Cavin gripped her chin, focusing her back on his face. Marnie winced. He was inches from her. She could feel his hot breath, stale, wafting through her nose. Bile rose in her throat; she swallowed it down.

"Why are you doing this?" she asked.

"Marnie, you insult me." He let go. "I know this isn't the best setup, but it's only temporary." Cavin leaned back on his heels and crossed his arms. "You need to learn your lesson before we can be together – truly together."

There was a simple explanation for this. Marnie knew that, but her head was spinning way too much for her to think of it. She pressed against her temples but failed to come up with a reasonable scenario where this would be okay. Her psychologist brain definitely took a hit.

"What am I being punished for?"

Cavin leaned forward again, pressing his hand to her cheek. She tried to pull away, but he reached his other hand behind her head, keeping her still. Marnie's bottom lip trembled. She bit down on it.

"Honey, you must be in so much pain." He stroked her cheek. "If only you hadn't run from me, you wouldn't be in this kind of pain," he tsked. "I did ask nicely, you know." Cavin winked. His voice was sweet, but the words cut like a knife.

Marnie wanted to spit in his face. To take her chance and run for the door. But he was right; she was in a lot of pain. She wouldn't be able to make it far. She'd buy her time and gain back her strength. Then, when he least expected, she'd make her move.

"You should get some rest," Cavin said, standing. "We can talk more later."

"Wait!" Marnie grabbed his arm. She needed to know why she was here, what his plan was. She had to gain his trust. Maybe then he'd take her upstairs. Somehow, she needed to apologize for whatever she'd done. "I wanna talk now. Can't we talk now?"

Cavin kissed her forehead. Marnie's skin crawled. "I'll be back in a while with some food, we can talk then." He left her sitting there with her back against the wall.

At the top of the stairs, Cavin turned around. Marnie couldn't see his face. The light behind wrapped around him, making him seem more sinister. "Get some rest, my love." He closed the door.

She was alone again, enclosed in darkness. Panic seeped through her pores, pulling her from her seat. She stood, pacing the room. She counted how many steps it took from one wall to the next. Fifteen. All she had were fifteen steps in any direction. But the walking helped; it built her strength. The more she moved, the more her headache subsided.

She tried to count the seconds passing by, but time didn't matter down here. There was no time. No night or day. Just darkness, a never-ending sea of darkness.

When she finally wore herself out, Marnie laid down under the tattered blanket. Moisture from the air clung to it, making it stick to her skin. She shifted, trying to get comfortable – something that would never happen here.

The ground was rough and scratchy. It reminded her of Cavin's chapped lips, pressing into her forehead. She heaved. Sooner or later, something was going to come out of her.

Marnie closed her eyes and ran her fingers through her matted hair.

This was all so messed up. She failed herself like she failed Carley. Though, maybe death was easier than this. At least Carley was at peace now.

Hannah told her to call the police again. If she had, would things have turned out differently? Would they have taken her seriously? Maybe then she'd be on a date with Jason right now instead of lying in a cage. Oh, Jason. She almost forgot about the date. Her heart ached; would she ever see him again?

I'm going to die down here.

The thought scared her. She felt the familiar tension in her chest and gave over to it. There was no Cavin, no shadow; she was alone with her thoughts and feelings. She cried until her eyes burned – until sleep dragged her down.

The sweet aroma of teriyaki chicken and french fries pulled Marnie from her sleep. When she opened her eyes, Cavin was sitting there cross-legged with a brown paper bag in front of him. He smiled, beaming with pride. A lamp stood behind him.

Precious light.

"Good morning, sleepy head," Cavin said. "I brought your favorite, chicken and fries. I'm sure you're starving."

How long had it been since she ate? Her stomach screamed. She sat up, reaching for the bag. She hesitated, looking at Cavin. He nodded once, and she snatched it to her chest. She ripped the bag open, grabbed a handful of fries, and shoved them in her mouth.

Sweet Lord.

Marnie double-fisted fries until the little cardboard container was empty. She pulled out the box of teriyaki chicken. Cavin handed her a fork. She paused, coming up for air. The glow of the lamp allowed Marnie to see more details of the basement.

It was exactly as she imagined, old and damp. A short dresser with two drawers sat in the furthest corner. Surprising. Marnie thought she'd walked around the whole room. Close to the dresser was a white bucket that had black spots around the bottom. A roll of toilet paper was next to it.

If Cavin expected her to do her business in that, then he had another thing coming.

Marnie's gaze fell back to her food. She stabbed a piece of chicken, shoved it into her mouth.

"You slept for so long," Cavin said. "I almost thought you were dead." He spat the words out, following them with a laugh.

Was this all just some sick joke to him?

"What time is it?" Marnie asked, her mouth full.

"Time doesn't matter. We have all the time in the world."

Marnie took another bite. She chewed slowly, putting together a plan. Cavin seemed convinced that they were in love. She could use that against him, gain his trust again.

She held the box out to him. "Want a bite?"

Cavin pushed the box back to her. "No, sweetie. I already ate. This is all for you."

"I'm supposed to be meeting someone, you know. They'll wonder where I am."

Cavin's smile dropped. His eyes narrowed. "Who? Hannah or Jason?"

A chill ran down her spine. He knew her friends. He knew Jason. He'd been watching her – of course he knew them. It all started to make sense. If Cavin saw her with Jason, he knew she was dating someone. She betrayed him, in his mind, by showing love to Jason. Marnie needed to win back his trust somehow. She needed to convince him that there was a chance at a happy ending for them.

"Hannah," she said slowly, wiping her mouth. "I broke up with Jason."

"Hannah isn't the best influence, either. I don't want you seeing her anymore."

Marnie cleared her throat, then spoke, raising her voice an octave. "She's my best friend. She's very supportive. I bet she'd love you."

Cavin's shoulders dropped, releasing tension. "Really? You think so?"

"Of course. Especially if you take good care of me; Hannah only wants what's best for me. That's why she hated Jason. He wasn't good for me."

"No," Cavin said. "He wasn't good for you. He can't love you the way I do."

It's working.

"I didn't mean to hurt you, Cavin. I'm sorry."

Cavin snatched the box of chicken from Marnie's hand, standing. "Sorry is just a word, Marnie. There are consequences for your actions. That's why you're down here. It'll give you a chance to think about what you've done and how you can fix it."

Marnie shifted to her knees, holding her hands up in a prayer pose. "Please, Cavin. Let me come upstairs. I'll be good, I promise. I won't hurt you again." She rubbed her hands together. "Please?"

Cavin stared down at her, frozen. Marnie could see a battle going on behind his eyes. She was almost there, almost convinced him.

He shook his head. "No. It's only a few more days; then we can talk about the future."

Marnie slumped. *So close.*

"I'll leave the light for you, okay? It's the best I can do."

"Thank you," Marnie whispered.

"I'll be back later." Cavin disappeared behind the door.

Marnie bit her nails, looking around the room. There had to be something she could use to get out. Maybe she could pry the door open somehow.

She rushed to the dresser, pulling open the top drawer. Nothing but papers and letters were inside. That wouldn't help. She closed it, pulling open the bottom drawer. A pen and stamps. Nothing else.

A pen! Marnie threw a glance over her shoulder. The coast

was clear. She grabbed the pen and shoved it into the waistband of her pants.

Forty-Three

CAVIN'S BODY WAS HEAVY AS HE PACED. He walked to the basement door, placing a shaky hand on the doorknob. Marnie seemed genuinely sorry for what she'd done; she deserved a little lenience. He loved her, after all. It couldn't be all punishment.

He pulled his hand away. No. She said sorry, but sorry wasn't enough. Her actions need to show how truly sorry she is. Plus, she didn't say what she was sorry for. She was just paying him lip service. If he gave in to her now, his mother would be right. He couldn't let that happen.

Cavin walked away from the door, picking at the dry skin on his lips.

"Be patient," the voice said. His friend, Cavin's only friend. The one who'd been with him from the beginning. What would he do without the man living in his mind, this absolute God-send of a friend?

He sauntered down the hall, entering the bedroom he prepared for Marnie. Cavin ripped the blankets off the bed. They'd gotten wrinkled. He made the bed again, sweeping his hands along the surface to smooth it.

"She seems really sorry, though. I think it's safe to bring her up," Cavin said.

The voice snarled. "No! Not yet. She's sneaky; she will trick you, then run away. You have to assert your dominance over her; then she'll be controllable."

Cavin dusted the nightstands and dresser, moving sporadically. "I don't know... We love each other; it's supposed to be a partnership, not dominance."

"Cav, would I steer you wrong? No, of course not. So trust me! If she doesn't know who's boss, she'll try to escape." The man in his head metaphorically patted Cavin's back. "You don't want that, do you?"

He didn't want that. He wanted to be with Marnie forever. Cavin vacuumed the room, then went into the living room to rest on the couch. From his spot, he could see the basement door.

What was Marnie doing down there at this very moment? Was she sleeping? Pacing? Or worse, was she crying?

Cavin shot up and approached the door. "I should check on her."

"You were just down there. Give her some time to stew, to really embrace her new environment. If you keep checking on her, she'll think you care too much. She'll see you're weak and think she can manipulate you."

He picked at his lip some more. It started bleeding. Cavin sucked his bottom lip, tasting the metallic liquid spill into his mouth. The voice was right; she needed to be alone longer. Mother did that to him, and it worked. She'd lock him in the closet and leave him there for a few days. Mother always said it hurt her to punish her baby that way but that it was necessary. This was the same. He hated punishing Marnie, but it was necessary. He needed a moment of quiet darkness too.

Cavin walked into the hall, stopped at the door in the middle, and opened it. The empty closet stared back at him. Tick marks for how many days he'd spent there as a child were etched into the wooden planks. Cavin crawled in, sat in the corner, and closed the door. The darkness surrounded him, wrapping him in a familiar blanket. He closed his eyes and took deep breaths.

Yes, everything was going to be fine. He needed to clear his head and trust the process.

Mother would be so proud.

A bad thought entered his mind. Stella never had to sit in the closet.

It was bad. The kind of thing that Mother would punish him for. He had to respect his sister, to love her. She was special. Still, Cavin hated Stella for not having to sit in the closet. For moving on, going to college, and getting married. She never bothered to check on him, never even called. Heck, Stella couldn't even spare a text message for her big brother.

But none of that mattered now that he had Marnie. She was his family and all he needed.

Forty-Four

FALLING.

Marnie swung her head back and forth but couldn't see anything. All she knew was that she was falling deeper and deeper into a pit.

Voices drifted in and out of the wind passing her by. Some she recognized, others not so much. Still, she continued to fall.

She landed hard on her back, bouncing once, then slamming down again. She sucked in a breath, recovering from the wind being knocked out.

"You get back here, Diane!"

Marnie swung her head toward the sound. Pete.

She looked around the room. Posters of heavy metal bands were taped to every wall. A white vanity sat across from where she was on a matching twin bed, the sheets black. Blood isn't as noticeable on black sheets.

How'd she get here? Was it all a dream? The past decade just a lie, a fantasy in her head while she slept?

A fist slammed into the wall outside her bedroom. Pete was on a rampage again. Best to stay hidden.

Marnie jumped up and lunged for the door. She pressed the lock. If Pete couldn't get her mom, he'd come for her. That was what he did. He blamed everyone else for his problems. He never took responsibility. Marnie would forever regret the day she and her parents walked into that church. The day Pete and her mom locked eyes. Her life was ruined from that day forward.

She missed her dad. He was gentle and funny. Hilarious. Marnie couldn't count the number of times her dad had made her laugh so hard she shot soda from her nose. It was like his whole purpose in life was to make her laugh, and he was good at it.

When was the last time she'd laughed?

Pete wasn't funny, even in a good mood. He'd try, but he never made her laugh. Not for real. She laughed anyway, though. Pretending was easier than making him mad.

"Diane! I'm gonna count to three, and you better open this door!"

He never really needed a reason to be mad.

"One…"

Mama being a seductress who ruined his life was enough for years of anger.

"Two…"

Marnie cupped her hands over her ears. She hated this part. Hated her life.

"Three!"

More banging. Mama wasn't coming out. Not today.

Loud footsteps got closer and closer to her room. Marnie screwed her eyes tight. See no evil, hear no evil.

Pete kicked the door, making her flinch. "Marnie! Get out here." He jiggled the handle and cursed. "What'd I say about locking this door? No locked doors in my house!"

It's not your house, Pete.

If she said that out loud, he'd break it down and beat her with it.

"No!" Diane called. She came out.

Mama was good like that. If Pete ever came for Marnie, she'd sacrifice herself. So why did Marnie blame her so much? Probably 'cause she was the one who let him into their lives. She fell for him. Now they were stuck.

Marnie pressed her hands into her ears harder. The sound of a fist connecting with flesh made her sick. She didn't bother praying. God never listened anyway. After all, Pete was one of God's shepherds.

"Marnie." His voice was right there, right against the door. "Why don't you come out here and join me and your mother? A little family time." The way he said "family time" sent a shiver down her back. He pounded on the door.

Marnie shot up, hyperventilating. The orange glow cast long shadows all around. Her eyes searched the room, Pete got in.

No. That was a dream, a memory.

She looked up; the door was open. Cavin was standing at the top of the stairs.

"Hope I didn't scare you," he said.

❧

Cavin walked down the stairs, a slow sway in his step. Marnie met him at the bottom but faltered, falling back down.

The lamplight shone on her darkened face as Cavin reached out for her. He held a paper plate stacked high with food. Marnie's eyes moved from the food to his face; she licked her lips.

It's working; she wants me.

"Good morning," Cavin said.

"Morning." Marnie perked up, watching him move, watching the plate. "Is that for me?" She placed both hands on her stomach.

Cavin smiled, holding the plate out. "I made you pancakes."

Marnie took the plate, scarfing down the food. Cavin loved watching her eat. Of course, it wasn't very ladylike, but could he blame her? He felt a little bad. It'd been a few hours since he'd last seen her. She looked weak – tired. The cut on her chin was caked in dried blood. As she sat cross-legged on the ground, Cavin saw a large hole on the bottom of her foot.

"What happened to your foot?" he asked.

Marnie swallowed. He could see the muscles in her throat struggling to move up and down. "I stepped on a nail."

My angel, no.

He stood. Determined. Cavin ran up the stairs, being sure to lock the door behind him. He went into the bathroom and grabbed the First-Aid kit from the medicine cabinet. He wasn't going to let his bride suffer.

Back in the basement, Marnie was done eating. She sat with

her head drooping low. When Cavin approached again, she sat straight.

"Let me see your foot," he said, sitting next to her.

Marnie silently complied.

I'll show her how much I care for her.

He cleaned her wound with alcohol. Marnie winced.

"Shh, it's okay. We gotta clean this, or it'll get infected."

When Cavin looked up at her, Marnie was biting her bottom lip.

She's so beautiful, so sexy. And all mine.

He finished with her foot, wrapping it in an ACE Bandage. Now, it was time to address her chin. The scrape she got trying to run away from him. He wouldn't hold that against her, though.

Cavin cupped her chin in his hand, inspecting the scrape. It wasn't too bad. She wouldn't need stitches, thank God. He didn't know how to give stitches.

"Can I clean this cut too?" Cavin asked.

Marnie nodded her head once. Her eyes were wide, worried. Cavin didn't want her to be afraid. He would show her how gentle and loving he could be.

"Hold still." He cleaned the cut and put a bandaid on it.

Cavin paused when he finished, holding Marnie's gaze. Her eyes twinkled in the dim light. She looked exhausted. He was worried about her and wanted nothing more than to bring her upstairs. But it wasn't time. She would try to escape, the shadow said so, and so far, he had never been wrong. He just had to trust the process. He could tell that a battle was going on inside Marnie's head. Part of her wanted him. He saw the way she looked at him, the desire in her eyes. But her posture said otherwise. She was stiff, rigid when he touched her. It's just because she's sore, not because of his touch, he assured himself. They loved each other. They were meant to be. Right?

Which side of her would win? Cavin prayed it was love. That love would win.

"Honey, you look exhausted. Are you not sleeping?"

"It's hard to sleep with the smell..." Marnie looked toward the white bucket. It was full, putrid. "You think you could clean it out for me? Or, if you want, I can clean it out. If you let me upstairs."

Cavin got up and walked to the bucket. He looked inside, covering his mouth and nose. His shoulders hunched forward. Who knew something so beautiful could make something so nasty? Now was his chance to show her again how much he loved her.

Cavin lifted the bucket, still pinching his nose, and went straight to the stairs.

I'll show her what a gentleman I am, cleaning her mess.

Cavin cleaned the bucket with bleach, then carried it back down.

Marnie smiled and thanked him, music to his ears. Her body language wasn't so guarded now.

It's working.

❧

Marnie stood to meet Cavin. She watched as he returned the bucket to its place, then faced her. She threw her arms around his neck, thanking him again.

Cavin stood still for a moment before slowly reaching his arms around her waist. His calloused hands were sharp – scratchy even through her clothes. They were a stark contrast to Jason's smooth, strong hands. She missed Jason with every bone in her body. The only way she managed to hold onto Cavin was by thinking of seeing Jason again. She had to survive if she wanted a future with him.

Marnie pulled away slightly, keeping her arms laced around his neck. She stared up at him, trying to imagine Jason's face on his. If Cavin wanted a loving girlfriend, Marnie would pretend. She needed to put on the show of a lifetime. Marnie lifted onto her toes, inching her face closer to his. She closed her eyes and took a deep breath, holding it in. She pressed her lips onto his for a second, then pulled back. Cavin's eyes were wide, his lips parted.

"Was that okay?" Marnie asked, raising an eyebrow.

Cavin dropped his arms from her waist. He didn't respond, didn't even look at her. He started at his feet.

"Cavin?" Worry wrinkled Marnie's forehead. "I thought this was what you wanted. You want me to love you, right? I do."

"That's not right," Cavin whispered.

"What?"

His hand flew up and smashed into the side of his head. He pulled it back; smashed it in again. "Shut up!"

Marnie backed away. She clenched her fists, tightened her muscles. If he turned those swings on her, she'd be ready to block.

263

"No! No! No!" Cavin bolted up the stairs and slammed the door.

Marnie could hear him speaking; his voice muffled through the walls. He was angry. At who, she didn't know. Who was he talking to? From the inflection of his voice, he was getting a response. Was he on the phone? Did someone else know she was here?

Marnie paced, listening to Cavin but not quite understanding the words.

❧

"She's lying! Can't you see that?" the voice said.

"No! She loves me! Didn't *you* see that kiss?"

He'd finally heard the words he craved. Finally felt Marnie's lips on his own. Finally, finally. It was all falling into place.

And then the voice. He had to go and ruin it all. He kept talking and talking, making it impossible for Cavin to focus on Marnie.

"She's good. I'll give her that," the voice said. "The little slut knows how to work a room."

"Would you shut up for one minute!" Cavin grabbed a coffee mug from the kitchen counter and hurled it at the wall. "I'm tired of your constant talking in my ear! Let me think!"

"You're an idiot if you can't see what she's doing."

Cavin rubbed his temples. "You don't know her like I do."

"Know her? Buddy, I'm the one who brought her to you. You wouldn't have her if it weren't for me."

Cavin shook his head. "She loves me."

The voice laughed, the sound booming in Cavin's head, bouncing off the walls. "Loves you? Loves you? I'm sorry, but you really do have a screw loose somewhere if you think she could possibly love you. She wants out, man! Wants you to let your guard down so she can run out of here."

He couldn't think clearly, not with all the noise. Cavin went to the closet and shut himself in. She couldn't be lying. That kiss was real; the hug was real. Marnie loves him. He felt it in her touch.

"Cav, have I ever lied to you?"

"No…"

"Alright then! I'm gonna say this one more time; maybe then it'll get through your thick skull. She is lying. She doesn't love you."

He dropped his voice. "No one will ever love you."

What? "Why are you acting like this? I thought you were my friend. You're being cruel."

"I am your friend. Marnie is a conniving little brat, and she's going to hurt you." The voice quieted, giving Cavin space to think.

She wouldn't do that. Would she?

"Cav, buddy, I think you know what you gotta do."

Cavin shook his head, biting his nails down to the skin. "No."

"Yes. You need to get the truth out of her. Beat the truth out of her."

"I can't."

"Don't be a little punk. Just do it. Then you'll know I'm telling the truth."

Cavin wanted to fight it, deny it. He wanted to run back into Marnie's arms and cover her in sloppy kisses until their bodies collided in a masterpiece of love. But there was a gnawing in his mind, telling him the voice was right. He needed some time to think.

Cavin slid against the wall, down to the floor. He placed his head between his knees. He needed to think.

Forty-Five

IT FELT LIKE HOURS HAD GONE BY. The yelling upstairs ceased, and Marnie was left in utter silence. Even the shadows' endless taunt was gone.

She was alone, completely.

Cavin's sudden anger scared her. It could turn on her. She'd moved too quickly; it wasn't real enough. He wasn't buying it. She knew that the moment he ran upstairs.

Marnie waited. He'd be back. And she'd have to put her game face back on, convince him of her love.

As if on cue, the door opened. No light shined through this time. Instead, Marnie only saw Cavin's silhouette saunter down the stairs.

"You're back," Marnie said, straining her voice to sound relieved. The tremble of her shoulders gave away the truth.

"Marnie, you wouldn't lie to me, right?" His eyes were dark, serious.

"No, of course not." Marnie's voice cracked. "I would never lie to you."

He tilted his head to the right, his eyes narrowing. Marnie wished she could read minds. She wished she knew what he was thinking and exactly what she could say to make him believe her.

"If you lie to me, I have to punish you. It's only fair."

Marnie stepped up, closing the distance between them. She stroked his cheek, smiling. She came in closer, pressing her body against his in a warm embrace. Cavin wrapped his arms around her, holding tight. She looked up, past his shoulder. The door was open. His guard was down. She could make it; she had the energy now.

Marnie wrapped her leg around Cavin's and pulled it forward. Cavin's knees buckled, and he dropped. She shoved him as he fell, throwing him completely off balance. He landed hard with a thump. Marnie fumbled for the pen in her waistband. She wrapped her fingers around it tightly.

"I'm sorry, God." She lifted it, then brought it down hard on Cavin's thigh.

Cavin wailed, clutching around the pen that stuck straight up from his leg. Marnie wasted no time running for the stairs. She bounded up, two at a time. It was dark, but she practiced going up those stairs a thousand times. She could do it in her sleep.

Bursting through the door, Marnie took a quick glance around. She was in the kitchen. Through a window, Marnie saw the dark blue sky. Stars shone brightly. There was no door but an entrance to the living room. Through it, she saw the front door. Marnie turned right.

Cavin grunted. She heard him climbing the steps. How? The pen should've slowed him down more.

There wasn't time to think about it. She ran for the door, tripping once but catching herself on the couch. She yanked on the handle. It didn't budge.

"Come on, come on," she cried.

The lock. Marnie flipped it, and the door gave in. She was free, the fresh air pumping through her lungs.

No time to glance behind – he was coming; she didn't need to know how close. All she needed to do was run. Run as fast as she could on weak legs.

Down the long, country driveway, Marnie sprinted to the edge of Cavin's property.

Right or left?

She paused for a second. This decision seemed important. If she chose the wrong way, that would be the end.

Left. She turned sharp and kept running. As she turned, she

caught a glimpse of Cavin limping behind. He was gaining on her.

The gravel road scraped her feet, but she didn't care. She had to keep going, keeping pushing forward. There was bound to be another house up ahead.

"Help me!" Marnie screamed. "Anyone, please! Help!"

There were no other houses, no cars. Nothing. But she kept screaming.

"Marnie!" Cavin roared, his voice rising above her own.

He wasn't afraid to yell. He wasn't afraid of someone else hearing. Marnie whimpered and begged her legs to move faster. Pumping her arms, she soared ahead.

Gotta exercise more.

Something latched onto her hair. She screamed and fell back. Her butt crashed on the ground; another scream came involuntarily.

Cavin dragged her by the hair. She wrapped her hands around his, trying to loosen his grip. She could feel strands of hair ripping free from her scalp.

"No!" She screamed, flailing her legs.

"You have been a naughty girl, Marnie. You're only making things worse for yourself."

His grip was iron-clad. There was no breaking free. She missed her chance. There wouldn't be a second.

Marnie was used to the throbbing in her head now. In fact, it was a welcome distraction from her failed escape. She moaned, reaching up to touch the bald spot on the back of her head. The cuts on the bottom of her feet bled, leaving red footprints everywhere she walked.

Trying to run was definitely in the top ten list of dumb things she's done. Right up there with throwing Ashley's phone out the window and dying her hair platinum blonde in high school.

She opened her eyes, praying Cavin would be gone but knowing he'd still be there. She could hear him breathing, the rhythmic in and out. How was he so calm? He'd dragged her back. Now, he wasn't going to leave. He couldn't trust her. Now he knew the truth.

Chances of escaping again were slim to none. She would die down here. Or be trapped forever. It was better than being upstairs, forced to be Cavin's bride. Now that he knew, she didn't have to pretend. She didn't have to remind herself that he was her captor anymore, either. That was crystal clear now.

"Cavin," Marnie said. "I'm sorry I ran. I was scared – am scared."

His eyes were closed. He sat cross-legged next to her, a white cloth wrapped around his thigh. There was a patch of blood seeping through, still bleeding. Had he heard her? Was it possible he was sleeping? No way. Not in that position.

Marnie pushed herself onto her elbows. "Cavin?" she raised her voice an octave, sounding sweet. Innocent. She didn't have to act in love anymore, but treating him like a human being would garner her better chances at freedom. She shifted closer to him, touching his knee.

Cavin's eyes shot open, and he grabbed Marnie's wrist.

"Cavin, that's too tight. It hurts." Marnie twisted her arm to break his hold, or at the very least loosen his grip.

He squeezed harder. His own arm started shaking. Cavin pushed himself off the ground, wincing. He pulled Marnie along with him and held her wrist above his head, his face inches from hers. She stood on her toes, stepping constantly to keep her balance. Marnie's stomach twisted. She sensed something was coming.

"You lied." Cavin spat the words in jagged pieces. "I trusted you, and you lied to me!" His words held more than anger. There was pain behind them.

As a therapist, she'd worked with many patients and learned that people often asked for love in the worst ways possible. She knew she shouldn't feel bad for him, but that little voice in her head reminded her that behind his poor choices was a wounded inner child. Still, she grappled with her own need to survive. Guilt would take a back seat on this round.

"I didn't lie. I just got scared. Please, Cavin. You can't keep me down here. I'll go crazy." Her breath was quick. "It's dark down here," she whispered. "That's what scares me." it was another lie. The dark didn't scare her. The shadow didn't even scare her. It was his unpredictability that scared her. She was trying to play to his humanity; make him pity her. Marnie stood there, watching the broken man that took her, pleading.

It worked at first. The lines in Cavin's face softened. Then, like a switch, it changed. Anger burned bright through his eyes. His lips turned up in a snarl. "No!" he yelled, throwing Marnie's arm down. "You said you loved me, but you don't! You love Jason, don't you?

Or are you some slut who goes around kissing men? Huh, Marnie? Is that the kind of woman you are?" He was stepping closer, forcing her back until she bumped into the wall. Moisture from the wall soaked her shirt.

Marnie shook her head, rubbing her wrist where he'd held her. Her eyes were wide, pleading. She could feel the little bugs running across her skin again. She opened her mouth to speak, but a blow from Cavin's fist into her stomach knocked them out. She gasped hard and doubled over. Cavin lifted her by the shoulders so that she was standing straight, then slammed his fist into her gut once more. Marnie's legs gave out, and she buckled. Cavin caught her wrist before she could fall. He stared at her, and Marnie swore she could see fire in his eyes. Hatred. He let go, shoving her into the wall.

Marnie hit the floor and immediately puked; her stomach was sore and spasming from the repeated blows. "Cavin, it's not like -" He kicked her, toppling her onto her side. She coughed her breaths in hitches. She couldn't catch it.

"You ungrateful, lying, cheating, horrible woman!" He crouched down to meet her gaze. "Don't you see I'm trying to take care of you? Give you a better life?"

Tears crowded her vision. Her body shook violently. Marnie tried to think of something to say, anything. But there was nothing. The pain clouded her mind; she could barely think.

"I should throw you out. Leave you in the dumpster like the trash you are." He grabbed another handful of her hair and lifted her up.

Marnie groaned and wept. Any plan to appeal to Cavin's humanity would fail. He'd lost his humanity, given in to something far darker and far stronger than himself. It was hopeless. She was going to die here, at the hands of this man.

"Cavin," Marnie gasped for breath. "I-" She lost the strength to speak. Too broken and in too much pain. Crying even seemed like too much effort.

"You did a bad thing, Marnie. You need to be taught a lesson." He let go of her hair, grabbing her arm.

The circulation in her arm slowed. Marnie felt it tingle. She wrapped her other hand around his, trying to wedge her fingers under his grasp.

"I tried to be gentle – tried to be nice. I loved you, Marnie. But you just can't seem to learn your lesson." Cavin slapped her across the face and let her fall.

Marnie's cheek burned almost as much as her knees ached from the crash. It was becoming harder for her to focus. Cavin was getting blurry. There were two of him.

"Mother always said I was stubborn as a bull. She said being gentle wouldn't work on me." Cavin sat down next to Marnie. He patted her head, and she winced. Soft sobs wracked her body. "I guess you and I are a lot alike. It makes sense." He stood, unplugging the lamp and carrying it up the steps with him. "It's almost over, sweetie. I promise."

He was gone, finally gone. Marnie curled into a ball, rubbing raw hands over her battered body. Her head was numb, her body heavy - a bag of broken bones. The cool concrete acted as an ice pack; she rolled onto her stomach. Death would be better than this.

Marnie longed for relief. She longed to be free. He'd done it, broke her. The pain was unbearable; she couldn't stop the shaking.

Jesus, take me home. Let me die.

Marnie prayed. It was the only thing left.

Sleep came quickly, her body already halfway there, the pain knocking her out.

Forty-Six

JASON HAD TOLD HANNAH TO GO HOME, told her to wait for his call.

It'd been two days. Still no call.

She couldn't take it anymore. The longer she waited, the longer Marnie was stuck wherever she was with whatever monster took her.

The morning of the second day, sitting at home was no longer an option. Hannah got into her car and drove to Marnie's apartment. If she returned, Hannah would be the first to know.

That was where she was now, where she'd been for the entire day.

She pulled Marnie's phone from her pocket and plugged it in to charge. It was the right decision to keep it; that cop wasn't going to help. At least this way, Hannah could get more answers. It was wrong to go through someone's phone without permission, an invasion of privacy. But desperate times called for desperate measures. She'd apologize to Marnie about it later.

Hannah sat on Marnie's couch, her legs tucked under her and the TV on in the background. She scrolled through Marnie's pictures. Nothing. Literally, nothing. Marnie took pictures of books and the sky and sometimes a coffee. That was it.

Looking through Marnie's pictures was one thing… reading her text messages was entirely different – a whole other level of invasion. Hannah clicked the messages icon. Her palms started sweating; the phone slipped. She wiped her hands on her sweatpants and tried again.

There were the usual messages from Hannah and Jason, mostly. But then, Hannah came across a string of texts from an unknown number. She clicked on it and scrolled up. There were endless texts, creepy ones at that. Marnie never replied; still, they came.

Two months' worth of messages. Why hadn't Marnie said anything?

Hannah's heartbeat quickened. This had to be a clue to where Marnie was - screw waiting for Jason's call.

Hannah called him.

"Detective Cruz," he answered.

"Dude, I turned on Marnie's phone, and I know it's not good to go through someone's phone, but I found something that I think you should see."

"Where are you?"

Hannah hesitated. Marnie's apartment wasn't technically a crime scene yet, so why did she feel guilty about being there? "I'm at Marnie's."

Jason's disappointment was palpable in the silence. "I'll be there in ten." He hung up.

While she waited, Hannah took screenshots of all the messages and sent them to herself as backup of the evidence. This was all too wacky. She couldn't believe Marnie kept this from her.

Well, actually. It wasn't all that surprising. She hadn't been the most supportive friend. When Marnie was sure someone broke in, Hannah's skepticism had her siding with the cops. When Marnie was worried someone was following her, Hannah appeased her but didn't believe it. Meanwhile, Marnie had been right all along. A sinking settled in Hannah's stomach. What if this was her fault, all because she didn't believe her?

From now on, Hannah made a promise before God that she'd believe Marnie no matter what. If she ever got to see her again.

Jason barged through the door.

Hannah jumped. "Thanks for knocking," she said.

Jason looked serious, his eyebrows pulled together and his mouth in a straight line. "This is a potential crime scene. Now your DNA is on everything. This could really screw up the investigation."

Hannah threw her arms up. "Well, excuse me, but I didn't know there even was an investigation happening. You said you'd call, and you didn't."

"I've been a little busy," Jason said, hands on his hips. "I've been looking into Marnie's habits. There's nothing there to indicate that she's a flight risk."

"I coulda told you that," Hannah mumbled.

Jason rolled his eyes. "What was it you wanted to show me?"

"Right!" Hannah snatched Marnie's phone off the couch. "I was going through her texts and came across this weird message thread. Look." She passed the phone to Jason. "Some unknown number has been sending her creepy messages for like two months. Don't you think this could mean something?"

Jason scrolled. His eyes went wide, and his thumb stopped moving. Hannah followed his gaze to one message.

Say goodbye to your little boyfriend.

"Are you the 'little boyfriend'?" Hannah asked.

Jason shrugged. "I wouldn't doubt it."

"What are you gonna do?"

Jason's grip tightened around the phone; his knuckles turned white. "I'm taking this to the station to see if I can find the sender."

Hannah grabbed her purse off the coffee table. "I'm coming, too."

"Fine. Let's go."

They ran into the station, and Jason shoved through the door into the offices without looking back. Hannah was left in the waiting room, pacing back and forth.

He shouldn't have left her out there. She was an asset to the team. Without her, Jason would've never found out about the messages! How dare he.

She approached the receptionist. It was a different person from before, a younger guy now. Hannah smiled, turning on the charm.

"Can I help you?" He looked her up and down.

"Hi, my name is Hannah. I came with Detective Cruz, but he seems to have left me out here. Could I go back to his office? I'm helping him with a case."

"I don't think I ca–" Before the receptionist could finish, Jason came back out.

He walked past Hannah straight to the door. She watched him go, her jaw slack.

Jason stopped at the door and turned to her. "You coming or not?"

Hannah snapped her mouth closed and chased after him. "Where are we going?"

"A man named Cavin Grier purchased the phone with a credit card. He has a rap sheet. A history of stalking ex-girlfriends and breaking and entering. We didn't find an address, but he paid Golden Meadow with the same credit card." He jumped into the driver's seat of his pickup truck. "We're gonna go talk to them; maybe they can give us more info."

Hannah climbed into the passenger seat. Before she could buckle her seatbelt, Jason peeled out of the parking lot. Hannah clutched the safety bar above the door so hard her fingers ached.

Jason rubbed his eyes with one hand, the other at the top of the steering wheel. The truck swerved.

"Jason! Road!" Hannah yelled.

He opened his eyes, correcting his course. "Sorry. Headache."

"Yeah, well, I'd like to live long enough to find my best friend; thank-you-very-much."

He was quiet, staring absently out the windshield. "I can't believe she's missing. And this sicko might be responsible." His grip tightened on the steering wheel. "When I find that son of a–"

"Jason." Hannah reached across the seat, squeezing his shoulder. "You're gonna catch him and put him in jail. That's where he belongs. Don't do anything hasty."

Jason nodded once.

They pulled into Golden Meadow. Through the front doors, the waiting room was empty due to a lull in visits. Savannah sat at the desk, looking at a computer and typing. Hannah recognized her from the few times they'd hung out with Marnie. She was a nice lady, very easygoing.

Savannah looked up as they approached. Her smile was genuine, bright. "Can I help you?" She looked at Hannah, squinting before recognition shined on her face. "Hey, I know you! You're a friend of

Marnie's."

Hannah gave a curt smile. "Hi, yeah."

Savannah's eyes traveled between Hannah and Jason. "What can I do for you?"

"We're looking for some information on a possible client. His name is Cavin Grier," Jason said.

"I'm sorry, I can't give that information out."

Jason opened his jacket, revealing his badge. "It's for a case. Is there anything you can tell us?"

Savannah's face darkened. "Is this about Marnie?"

"Why would you think that?" Hannah asked.

Savannah rubbed her chin. "Well, Cavin was one of her clients. He kinda gave me the creeps. Real aggressive dude."

"Do you have his address?"

Savannah turned back to the computer, typing. "Ah, here it is." The printer roared to life, and she grabbed the paper from it, passing it to Jason. "This is the one we have on file. I hope it helps."

Yes!

"Thank you so much." Jason turned back for the door.

Hannah waved at Savannah, smiling again.

"If you need anything else!" Savannah called after them.

In the truck again, Jason's eyes were set dead ahead. His jaw was clenched. Hannah could see all the small details; the muscles tightened together. Cavin Grier was in for a tough ride.

"Alright, what's the plan? Are we going straight there? Busting down the door?" Hannah hopped in her seat. This was the most action she ever imagined getting. Kindergarten teachers didn't get out much.

"We're going back to the station. I'm going back out, and you're waiting there."

She slumped. "No fair! I'm coming with you. She's my best friend."

"No way. I will not endanger a civilian. You'll wait at the station, and when I get her, I'll tell you."

Hannah folded her arms. "Fine," she huffed.

Forty-Seven

PEACE LIKE A RIVER.

Marnie heard the rushing of water first. Streams running across rocks, splashed along the edges. The sound sent waves of peace over her like a soothing balm. It filled every crack and covered every bruise. The aches faded away.

Her hands swept across the plush grass. The smell of flowers and freshly cut grass filled her nostrils.

She kept her eyes sealed tight. Opening them would kill the fantasy; ruin the illusion. If she opened them, she'd see the basement again. She'd return to the hell she was stuck in, counting down the minutes until Cavin came back for round two.

No. She wouldn't let this moment slip away.

Wind pushed all around, begging her to sit up. Just like opening her eyes, Marnie feared that moving at all would snap her back into reality. She took a deep breath, drinking in every scent and sound she could.

Is this heaven?

Cavin might've kicked too hard, sending her to God earlier than expected.

Let it be true.

She'd much rather be in paradise with her savior than in Cavin's makeshift prison.

"Open your eyes, Marnie. It's okay." The voice was fresh honey, dripping down and covering the space between here and hope. It was familiar. Safe. This had to be heaven.

Marnie let her eyes flutter open, blinking to adjust to the light. The sun. It warmed her icy skin and thawed her frozen muscles. Sunlight gleamed through thick trees to her left, a river lying beyond them. To her right, a field of wild daisies, bright and beautiful, danced across the grass. Everything pulsed with life. Marnie was home. She knew it.

A giggle. "I've been waiting for you."

Marnie pushed up onto her elbows and followed the voice. It was bright, too bright to make out a face. But before her stood a woman, long brown hair flowing in wild waves past her shoulders. She wore a bright blue dress with daisies printed on it, matching the background. She was beautiful. Marnie knew that without even seeing her face.

"Am I dead?" Marnie asked.

The woman laughed. Marnie knew that laugh. She hadn't heard it in years, not since her father left.

"Mom?"

The woman crouched down; her face came into view. Marnie stared at her mother. The sweet wrinkles set into her kind face, her hazel eyes shining. Her mother smiled, a smile Marnie didn't know was possible.

"Mom," Marnie cried.

She didn't realize how much she missed her mom. When Cavin's fists were beating into her, all she could see was her mom. And Pete. And the way her mother accepted the beating to spare her.

She made a mistake cutting off her mom. She didn't understand the sacrifice. Not until now.

"Hi baby," Diane said.

Her strong arms wrapped Marnie like a blanket. They were warm and inviting. Marnie melted into them, burying her face in her mother's chest.

Marnie knew it was a dream. It had to be. But it didn't matter. She let it take over her senses, let herself believe it was real. She wanted to stay here forever. There was nothing but sorrow waiting for her in real life. Here, there was light and hope and a love so deep it'd take a lifetime to explore.

Diane released her, holding Marnie out at arm's length. She smiled, her skin glowing in the sun. "Now that you're here, we have a lot to talk about." Diane grabbed Marnie's hand and raised her up. "Let's take a walk."

Diane led Marnie down a dirt path that paralleled the river. The rushing water was a sweet lullaby, grounding Marnie in the dream. She could wake up at any moment. Cavin could come back and shake her, pulling her away.

She didn't care. Where her body was no longer mattered. All that mattered was here and now. She was safe here. Cavin could do whatever he wanted to her body, but as long as she slept, he couldn't touch her mind.

"Are you okay?" Diane asked, touching her fingers to the bruise on Marnie's cheek. "He hit you pretty hard."

"I'm okay." Marnie's voice strained. "The physical pain doesn't hurt as bad as the mental. I'm scared, Mom."

"What are you scared of, honey?"

"The dark." Marnie looked up at the bright sun. Darkness didn't exist in a place like this. "Cavin took my lamp. He left me in the dark."

"And what's in the dark?" Her mother's question was pointed, like she knew the answer.

"He's there. The shadow. It was so easy to stand up to him at first. But now… I'm too weak."

They were silent, letting Marnie's fear have the space it deserved. Every emotion is valid in its own way, and in that moment, Marnie's fear was real and present. It needed to be accepted. Her mother didn't call her silly or childish for being afraid of the dark. She accepted it. She didn't belittle the fear; rather, she let Marnie get used to it. It was the only way to walk through it.

"Marnie, he can only hurt you if you let him. His power ends when you stop allowing it." Her voice was soft, loving. It lacked condescension. "Just as you've allowed Jesus into your life and heart, Cavin has allowed the shadow into his."

"What?" Were they working together? Of course! Why else would the shadow have been there? Marnie thought the shadow had been following her this whole time.

"The shadow is tainting Cavin's mind, bleeding hatred and violence into it. Cavin may not even know what he's doing."

"Look at me, Mom!" Marnie spread her arms wide. "Don't you see these bruises? How could he not know what he's doing?"

Diane's eyes were full of compassion. "You're right. Cavin is the one who hit you, and a part of him carries that aggression. But the shadow amplified it, lit a match, and dropped it in a line of gasoline that led straight to Cavin's mind. You can put out the fire."

"How?"

"Forgiveness. Compassion. Jesus. Sharing love with Cavin. Not the surface-level love from your own strength, the deeper love. The love of a man willing to give up his life for the very people that beat him – even killed him. The love that covers a multitude of sins. That's how." Diane held Marnie's hands. "You can dispel the darkness, kill the flames and light a new fire in Cavin. A fire of love."

Marnie dropped her head. "I can't do this, Mom. I'm not brave enough. I can't fight back."

"Honey, it's not about fighting back. It's about forgiving."

"I don't want to forgive him. Not after everything he's taken from me."

Diane ran her hand over Marnie's hair. "The enemy comes to steal, kill, and destroy. But Jesus came to bring you abundant life. Cavin has taken your freedom on earth, sure. But you are free here." She lifted a finger, pointing to Marnie's heart. "He can't take the life you have inside of you. No one can."

Marnie couldn't hold back the tears; she let them roll. Marnie fell into her mother's arms, holding tight.

"Hold onto that truth, my precious daughter. No matter how scared you are or how bleak your situation seems. Hold on and trust that the one who holds you will carry you free."

"Though I walk," Marnie whispered. "Through the valley of the shadow of death."

"I will fear no evil," Diane finished.

She felt herself slipping away, felt consciousness sneaking back in. Marnie held onto her mother, screwing her eyes tightly closed. It was ending too fast. She wasn't ready to leave, wasn't ready to let go.

Her mother evaporated from her arms. The air turned cold. Marnie opened her eyes; the darkness returned.

Forty-Eight

MARNIE WIPED AT HER WET CHEEKS. She took a deep breath, doing her best to remember the conversation with her mother.

Oh, mama.

If Marnie got out of this alive, she wanted to call her mom. To reconnect and rebuild. Forgive.

Everything her mother said seeped into her bones, strengthening them. She held fast to the truth, that though she was in the shadow of death, she would fear no evil.

The silence in the inky black room was deafening. Marnie longed to return to the riverbank, to the flowers and the warm sun. Here in this room, the world stood still. She was hidden away, removed. Marnie felt like she was in limbo, waiting for Cavin to return or the shadow to speak. Half her heart prayed one of them would; the other half prayed they wouldn't.

My spirit is willing, my flesh weak.

Nothing happened for several minutes, and Marnie's muscles relaxed. She had some time. Her body ached, and she was still exhausted, but she knew if she didn't stay alert, strong, it would be the end of her. She wasn't ready for that. Death was not the answer, not anymore.

"Lord, please be here. Fill this room and strengthen me," Marnie prayed.

"It's useless." The shadow said, appearing out of the darkness. "You're going to die down here."

Marnie jolted at first but rolled her eyes. Compassion for Cavin did not translate to love for the monster that plagued him. A power rolled through Marnie. She pushed her shoulders back and sat up tall.

Let him come.

Marnie hadn't felt this confident in months. She remembered the day she became afraid. That first night when she walked through the alley, and knew someone was watching. There were two people watching, a man and his monster. That was the day she'd lost her power. The day the shadow started winning.

Not anymore.

Marnie faced the darkest part of the room. The place the shadow hid. "Shut up," she said.

His laughing ceased, replaced with a snort. "How dare you talk to me like that. I hold your life in my hands." He stepped forward, detaching himself from the darkness of the wall. "You should be quivering at my feet."

Now it was Marnie's turn to laugh. The sound ricocheted off the walls, traveling around the room. The atmosphere began to shift. Marnie felt it, energized by it. The shadow felt it, too; his demeanor changed, and he shrunk back a step.

Fear was falling from Marnie like the shedding of skin. She felt fresh, renewed.

"Cavin is coming." His voice was shaky, anxious. The words spilled out in a mess. "He listens to me and will do whatever I say. You stupid girl, you're going to regret laughing at me."

"I'm done being scared of you. Scared of Cavin."

"I've destroyed your life. I said it before, and I'll say it again, you're mine, Marnie." He hissed the last three words.

"No." Marnie stood her ground, tall and in control. "I know whose I am, and I am not yours. You killed Carley, destroyed my career, and tried to steal my peace. But no more. I will not let you have my life. I believe in the one who came to give life. He is the one I belong to."

The room got brighter. Light bounced off the wall from behind her head. It took her a moment to realize that it didn't come from her. Marnie froze. Fear threatened to climb up and attach itself to her skin once again. She fought it off, turning to the sound of footsteps falling on the wooden stairs.

Cavin was back.

His hair was matted to his forehead; the once bouncy curls were limp. Dark circles bled out from under his eyes, and his skin looked three shades too pale. The darkness was draining him, killing him.

Marnie's heart broke for the man before her. He was nothing like the man she'd met at Golden Meadow. She remembered his intake photo, how kind and boyish his eyes were. When he came for their first session, his eyes had appeared darker, more haunted. Now she knew why. He'd been influenced then, too. But now it'd grown, his body couldn't handle it anymore, and this *parasite* was killing him.

"Cavin," Marnie breathed.

"Looks like you're feeling better." His voice was harsh, raspy.

There was no time. Marnie needed to let him know the truth now. He was going to die like this, to be lost forever.

She stepped forward, reaching an arm out to him. "Cavin, you are so loved. I want you to know that."

He grimaced. Paused.

Marnie pushed on. "There is a love so deep and so real. It's calling you, Cavin." She stepped closer to him. "It's the kind of love that pulled a king from his throne for you."

"Shut up!" the shadow yelled from behind.

Marnie pressed further. "Jesus loves you, Cavin. He loves you more than I ever could. And nothing you do will ever change that."

"She's lying again, Cav! Don't listen to her! You fell for her tricks once before, don't be a fool again." Marnie whirled around, realizing then that the shadow was speaking to them both. He really was real, not just to her but to others too. Could Cavin hear him, though? She couldn't believe how naive she was this whole time. It wasn't all in her head after all.

Cavin stood eerily still. He didn't respond to either of them. Didn't even look at them. He stared straight, as if he saw something beyond all of them. Something that confused him. His face twisted in pain, and Marnie reached him. She placed a hand on his shoulder and shook him.

His eyes focused on her. "You keep lying to me, Marnie.

Won't you stop? Haven't you had enough?"

She dropped her arm; held it tightly to her side. "I'm not lying this time. I admit I lied before. I tried to trick you. I won't do that again. I may not love you, but Jesus does."

The shadow released a guttural scream. Marnie and Cavin both flinched. "Leave him alone!"

Cavin flinched too. Marnie pulled in a quick breath. "You can hear him?" she asked Cavin.

He nodded once.

If Cavin could hear the shadow, that meant he knew what was happening. He knew she was making the shadow angry. It was working. "Cavin, there is freedom. You don't need to listen to him anymore." She shoved a finger accusingly in the direction of the shadow. "He is nothing. He is weak. He doesn't care about you! As soon as you're no longer useful to him, he'll chew you up and spit you out."

Cavin brought both fists to his head, grinding them into his temples.

"Cavin, buddy. Don't believe this little whore. I'm your friend, your pal. You know me."

"No, no, no!" Cavin shouted. "I've had enough!" His hands shot out, grabbing Marnie. He shook her violently, Marnie's head ricocheting.

She felt dazed; the room blurred.

"Why won't you stop lying?" Cavin threw her to the ground, kicking her. "I'm tired of having to teach you so many lessons." Another blow to the stomach. Marnie curled in, lifting her arms to cover her face.

An unspeakable peace covered her. If she died, she would be ready. She could handle it.

"Freeze!"

The blows to Marnie stopped. She peeked through her hands. Flashlight beams danced around the room. The room swarmed with people in motion; she couldn't register what was happening. Voices blurred together in the commotion. Marnie heard a strong voice over Cavin's grunts.

"Cavin Grier, put your hands up!"

"Jason?" Hope filled her belly.

Jason was here. All was not lost.

Forty-Nine

MARNIE SAT UP, grunting from the sharp pain in her side. Blood dripped from her arms like sweat. She watched as Jason cuffed Cavin, then passed him off to another officer. A blanket was suddenly around Marnie's shoulders as if appearing from thin air. She clutched the edges, pulling it tightly around her. It was thick and warm and dry. A stark comparison to the tattered thing Cavin gave her.

Jason rushed to her, wrapping her in his arms and helping her to her feet. "Are you okay?"

Marnie was still, her arms loose at her sides. She rested her head on Jason's shoulder. "You found me," she whispered.

"I'll always find you," Jason replied, tightening his arms around her.

Marnie looked over Jason's shoulder. Cavin had his head turned around, staring at her. Pain etched into his face, his cheeks wet.

He's crying.

Marnie's compassion and disgust were at war within her. In an ideal world, Cavin would have come to grips with his trauma and overcome the shadow's manipulation, but he didn't. She tried not to internalize it as her fault for not doing enough to save him – some habits were hard to break. But like Carley, maybe Cavin wasn't hers to save.

Jason cupped her face in his hands. He was a wonderful sight, an angel sent from heaven. Marnie smiled, a big toothy grin. Her knight in shining armor.

"Let's go, okay?"

Marnie placed her hands over his. She closed her eyes, not wanting to give up this moment. Freedom. That's what it was. She felt completely, utterly free. "Okay," she said.

Jason took her hand and led her upstairs. Uniformed officers and forensics with cameras flooded the basement. Halfway up the stairs, Marnie took one last look at the basement. What would've happened if Jason hadn't shown up? By the way things were going, Cavin had decided to listen to the shadow over her. He was going to kill her.

"Jason?" Marnie asked. "How long was I gone?"

His face was downcast, disappointed. In himself or her, Marnie didn't know. "Three days. I'm sorry, Marnie."

Three days. It felt like years. She'd been a naive twenty-eight-year-old who'd just lost her job and fell out of touch with herself when she entered the basement. Looking around now, as disturbing as her experience was, Marnie felt a reserve of strength swell within her. This basement changed her. She was walking away knowing exactly who she was, with a renewed confidence in her faith. She knew how to move forward now, starting with a call to her mom.

They reached the top of the stairs and were standing in the kitchen. It was daytime now. When she tried to escape, it had been night, and she didn't care about the details. Now, Marnie let them flood her senses. Sunlight filtered through cracks in the windows. It was beautiful. She missed the sun.

The kitchen was old. Paint chipped and peeled from the walls. Piles of dirty dishes and trash littered the countertops and the sink. A cockroach scuttled across the stovetop.

Jason pulled her into the living room. The couch was small, with cigarette burns dotting the cushions. Stains in the carpet told Marnie this house hadn't been cleaned in Lord knows how long. She covered her nose. The smell was worse than the basement, oddly familiar, like rotten eggs.

Jason dropped his eyes to Marnie's face. His eyebrows pulled together. She was the beaten and bruised one, but he looked like he'd been gut punched. Jason reached a hesitant hand to her face. Marnie flinched. Jason would never hurt her; she knew that. Still…

He recoiled at her reaction. Marnie grabbed his hand and placed it on her cheek. It stung, but the warmth of his hand outweighed the pain.

Jason swiped his thumb across her cheek. "We're gonna get you out of here soon, I promise. But first, there's something I think you might want to see." He took a deep breath. "We searched the house before going to the basement. I found a room at the back… I wouldn't normally do this, but I want you to see it. Maybe it'll help you process some of this." Jason dropped his hand from her cheek and grabbed her hand. "This might be hard to see."

Marnie shivered, pulling the blanket closer, then nodded. She followed Jason down the narrow hall. They passed two closed doors. The walls were bare. Where normal families hung pictures, Cavin's had done nothing. The whole house seemed devoid of any personal touches.

Jason stopped at the end of the hall. He moved to the side, and Marnie stood facing a closed door. She took a deep breath.

"Whenever you're ready," Jason said.

Marnie grasped the door handle, turned it, and pressed forward. Goosebumps pricked her arms. The room was an exact replica of her bedroom at home. The bed frame, the sheets – even the nightstands were identical. She was right; he had broken in. Nausea washed over her. *He was in my house.*

Along every wall hung pictures of Marnie, pictures of her and Cavin superimposed onto a bride and groom. There were photoshopped ones, ones of her walking, and at her at work. She felt violated. This went far beyond what she imagined. Cavin was sick, and Marnie hoped he would find the help he needed.

Marnie's heart skipped, and her pulse quickened. "Can I go now?" Her eyes pleaded with Jason.

Jason nodded once, placed an arm around her, and walked her out.

They stepped outside, and Marnie inhaled the fresh air. The first breath of fresh air in days. What a glorious feeling.

An ambulance was waiting for her. She scanned the sea of police, paramedics, and other authorized personnel. Cavin was gone; they'd taken him away faster than she could get out.

It was over. Really over.

Jason helped her into the ambulance; the steep step up made her wince. He climbed in and rode with her to the hospital.

As they pulled away, Marnie watched the house fade through the back window. Her captor was arrested. Her prison was destroyed.

She looked at Jason. "I could really use a cup of coffee right now."

Fifty

MARNIE BEGGED TO BE RELEASED. She was trapped in Cavin's basement for three days, then five more days strapped to a hospital bag by IV. Her bones ached and screamed to be free. She wanted to be home. Not the apartment. A new home. She'd already let the landlord know she was moving out.

Hannah spent every day by her side, and when Marnie asked, Hannah packed up all her stuff. Though they went to college together, they never had the opportunity to be roommates. It was going to be like a second chance. Luckily, Hannah had a spare room in her apartment, and all her things were waiting for her there.

Marnie was poked, prodded, and stuck under every X-ray machine known to man. A psychologist stopped by her room every day at noon to talk about what happened. The meetings would continue long after she got released from the hospital.

A knock at the door pulled Marnie from her thoughts. She looked over as the door opened. Jason walked in, wearing a brown leather jacket and dark-wash jeans.

Those pesky butterflies returned to her stomach, and the heart monitor machine beeped faster. Marnie blushed.

Way to call me out.

"How ya feeling?" Jason asked, pulling a chair next to her bed.

"Can't complain. Though I really, really wanna go home."

Jason looked at the door, then back at Marnie. He leaned forward, whispering. "A little birdie told me you'll be getting out real soon."

Marnie perked up. *Finally.*

"What brings you here?" She asked.

Jason sat back and interlaced his fingers. "I wanna talk to you about something – ask you something."

That sounded serious. Marnie started to sweat. Was this the relationship talk they'd been putting off?

"Okay?"

"I wanna talk about the dreams you had. I've been keeping something from you."

Marnie stared at him. He refused to look up at her. Jason, keeping something from her? Impossible. He'd always been so open.

"What is it?" Her voice strained.

Jason was quiet for a moment, his head down and his eyes closed. "Okay," he whispered, then looked up at her. "I've had dreams, too. The shadow. I've encountered him before."

Marnie opened her eyes wide. Had she heard him wrong? "Why didn't you say anything before? What are you talking about?"

"It's kinda a long story," Jason said. "And to be honest, I wasn't sure you'd believe me before now."

Marnie lifted her arms dramatically behind her head, leaned back, and crossed her ankles. "I've got nowhere else to be."

Jason let out a short laugh. "Back in Texas, I was a uniform cop. I breezed through the police academy and had a good reputation on the force from the get-go. I'm embarrassed to say, but I thought I was hot stuff. It made me a little lax when it came to procedures. I was reckless."

Marnie watched him, staying quiet. She didn't want to interrupt. This was the first thing Jason had told her about his past. Their relationship really was moving to the next level.

"One night, my partner and I got a call from a rough neighborhood. There had been a lot of gang activity there, prostitution, drug use. You name it. Scary place. The call was about a domestic disturbance." He took a deep breath, rubbing the back of his neck. "When we got there, we could hear shouting inside the house. We couldn't tell how many people were there, but being the hotshot that I was, I didn't care. I thought my partner and I could handle it." He paused, looking over Marnie's face.

Marnie reached her hand out to him. "It's okay, keep going."

Jason licked his lips. "Long story short, it got out of hand. My partner was shot. He died on scene." Jason covered his face.

"Jason, I'm so sorry," Marnie said.

"I was a mess. If I'd just called for backup, he'd still be here." He lifted his face, his eyes red and puffy. "After that, I started having vivid nightmares. This shadow of a man would follow me in my dreams, telling me that I was useless and a murderer. After a while, I believed him."

"Oh my gosh." She didn't know what to say. What was she supposed to say?

"I wanted to end my life, wanted to make it stop. But then, something incredible happened. I found myself stumbling into a church. It was empty, except for one man sitting in a pew, praying. I sat behind him, and for the first time in my life I started praying, too. I don't know what came over me, but I broke down sobbing. The man turned around and prayed for me. He held me in his arms while I wept. It doesn't sound very manly, but I don't care. It's what happened."

Marnie nodded along, completely immersed in Jason's story.

"That man and I met several times a week for a few months. We prayed together and studied the Bible. He taught me about God. I learned to forgive myself."

"Did you still have nightmares?"

"For a while, but slowly they went away. I stopped giving them power."

Marnie had done the same in the basement. She stopped giving the shadow power. His ever-looming presence lifted when she left the house. Come to think of it, she hadn't felt him at all since then.

"Why are you telling me this, Jason?"

He held her hand and met her eyes. His were clear, welcoming. "I just want you to know that you aren't alone. I am here with you through all this and every day after. I don't know if the fight is over; it's probably not. But I'm gonna stand by your side and hold your hand. We're in this together now; you don't have to fight alone."

Marnie smiled at him, beaming with pride.

I picked a good one.

"I know you might be afraid of people not believing you. You don't have to be afraid with me. I'll always believe you, I promise."

Those words. They were the words she'd been searching for. The trust and belief she craved since the beginning. Marnie leaned forward, ignoring the tug of her IV, and hugged Jason.

"Thank you," she whispered.

They spoke a while longer, then the pain pills kicked in, and Marnie got drowsy. Jason kissed her forehead and left.

Marnie stared out the window, watching the stars twinkle in the sky. It was beautiful; she could almost see heaven. She drifted to sleep and dreamt of nothing. Pure, beautiful, nothing.

Epilogue

4 months later

HIGH SCHOOLERS IN BACKPACKS SPED through the halls, racing to their next classes. Marnie stood to the side, watching them go. It was her first day on the job. She couldn't stop the trembling in her arms, the quick pulse thumping in her neck, nor the wide smile plastered to her face.

I hope they like me.

Hannah was a saint for putting in a good word. Her therapist, too. Without them, she'd still be unemployed. But now, she was the new guidance counselor at Branson High. A fresh start away from the city. Away from that apartment.

Living with Hannah was a dream. They stayed up late, talking about everything serious and silly. They danced and sang and blasted music through the entire apartment. They had movie nights, took turns cooking, and shared clothes. Marnie was living her best life.

Jason was pretty great, too. They'd officially taken their relationship from "casual" to "serious" in two seconds flat. Marnie couldn't be happier.

Now, here she stood, holding a list of students in her hands and watching them pass by. She'd heard rumors that Ashley, her former client, transferred to Branson High. Marnie prayed she wouldn't run into her. Not again.

Something strange caught Marnie's attention. When her eyes focused, it stole her breath. A girl with short hair and square glasses clutched books to her chest. She kept her head down, focused on the ground. The girl wasn't the problem, though. It was what followed her.

The shadow.

He sauntered close behind, hanging onto the girl's backpack. Marnie held her breath. She pressed herself into the wall, clutching the list of students in front of her. The tremble in her arms turned into a violent shake.

As they passed, the shadow looked toward Marnie. His red eyes glowed brighter. The gaping hole where his mouth should be turned up in a smile. He lifted his hand to wave at Marnie. The scar on her calf burned; itched. Marnie reached down, scratching it.

It isn't over.

Acknowledgments

I want to be honest. I've not finished the book yet as I'm writing this. In fact, I'm about halfway through the second draft. Here's to hoping future me finishes it off with a bang.

I never thought I'd get here. My dream of writing a book has been nothing but that for a long time. Now, that dream is a reality, and it wouldn't have happened without a whole slew of people who cheered me on and held me up along the process.

First, a massive thank you to my publisher, Meraki Press. Katie is a rockstar among rockstars. What started as an email on a whim turned into one of my most cherished friendships. Her critiques and ideas helped turn this story into the best it could be. Not to mention she made a killer cover design. I'm forever indebted to you, and immensely proud to not only have you on my team, but to be on your team as well. I see many more books in our future!

Next, to my cousin Brody, a police officer for the Springfield PD: I tried to keep everything in the story as accurate as possible. Any artistic changes were made to help the story. Still, your extensive knowledge helped take my story from fantasy to reality. Thank you for responding to my messages with highly detailed answers.

A huge thank you to author Erin Phillips for her vast knowledge about marketing and publishing. I believe this book will end up in many hands because of the things I learned from Erin. She is also the one responsible for my book blurb. To all my readers, go read Erin's books. You won't be disappointed.

To my mom and dad, you fostered imagination in me from a very young age and always encouraged me to shoot for the stars. I wouldn't be who I am without you.

To my husband, John: words cannot describe the joy I feel to be married to such an incredible man. From the day I said, "I wanna write a book." You have been my biggest cheerleader. You bought the writing program for my computer and turned my dream into a reality. You listened as I cried, plotted, and screamed with excitement. Your input and love has been invaluable to this process. I don't care what anyone else says; I am the luckiest woman alive. John, thank you for supporting my dream. Thank you for loving me even when I talk about murder and stalking and all the sketchy stuff a thriller writer talks about. Thank you for holding me accountable to this story and every story after.

Finally, the biggest thanks goes to my Creator, without whom I have no story. My imagination is only mine because He gave it to me. I pray my words bring hope to anyone who reads them. I owe my life to Jesus Christ, my good and faithful savior.

Author's Note

Stalking is a very scary and very serious crime. According to SPARC (Stalking Prevention Awareness and Resource Center), 1 in 3 women and 1 in 6 men are stalked at one point in their lifetime. Often, those stalking cases take a violent turn. I want to give a few tips from the SPARC website on how to keep yourself safe.

1. Trust your instincts. If you think someone is following you, do not shove that feeling aside. Do not let anyone downplay it or convince you it's not as serious as it is. Seek help as soon as you feel like you're in danger.

2. Call the police. I know in my story, Marnie is hesitant and avoids calling the police. That is just for the dramatization! PLEASE do not follow in Marnie's footsteps if you think you are being stalked. Call the police or your local domestic violence hotline.

3. Keep a record. Save everything. No matter how small it seems, it could help save your life. Grab at any evidence you can.

4. Get connected with a local victim service provider. These services can help you explore your options and find a way to keep you safe.

It can be a scary place out there in the world. We have to stay as alert as possible. I don't mean to scare anyone, but the reality is that stories like Marnie's are very common and often end in a much more deadly way. If you or someone you love is experiencing stalking victimization, please don't stay silent. Get help.

Author's Bio

Growing up as a pastor's daughter, Wyeth Doty often found herself balancing between "too Christian" for her school friends, and "not Christian enough" for her church friends. Her love of both Jesus and thriller/horror books played a major role in that balance. Now as an adult, she prides herself on that identity, putting it on display in her debut novel It's All in Her Head.

When she isn't writing, Wyeth enjoys reading thrillers, watching movies with her husband, and wandering the streets of Seoul, South Korea where she currently lives.

Learn More about her writings at www.wyethwrites.com

www.ingramcontent.com/pod-product-compliance
Lightning Source LLC
Chambersburg PA
CBHW061218310726
48971CB00007B/1867